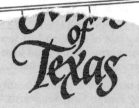

of

Texas

From Ruth Langan

Diamond, Pearl, Jade, Ruby and now Malachite

Malachite Jewel burned with hatred
for his stolen past...

Millie Potter burned with the fear of an
uncertain future...

Together their passion would ignite
the town of Hanging Tree, Texas

Dear Reader,

With over forty books to her name, from medieval novels to Westerns, Ruth Langan has made a name for herself in the world of women's romance fiction. We are thrilled to have this *USA Today* bestseller return with *Malachite,* the fifth and final book in her popular THE JEWELS OF TEXAS series. This stirring tale of the long-lost Jewel brother, Malachite, pits him against family and love—until a gentle widow and mother captures his wild heart.

Blackmailed into marriage to a silent beauty with angel's eyes, the charming Earl of Graydon learns the power of unspeakable love in *Beguiled,* an emotional Regency by Susan Spencer Paul, who is also known for her mainstream historicals under the name Mary Spencer.

My Lady's Desire by Claire Delacroix is the dynamic sequel to her May 1997 release, *Enchanted,* which earned her a 4¹/₂★ review in *Romantic Times.* In this story, a powerful blade for hire agrees to marry an exiled noblewoman to reclaim a lost estate, and together they find an unexpected passion. And don't miss Liz Ireland's adorably funny Western, *Prim and Improper,* about a prim young spinster who falls for a very improper cattle rancher who she believes is in love with her sister.

What a terrific lineup we have for you this month! Whatever your tastes in reading, you'll be sure to find a romantic journey back to the past between the covers of a Harlequin Historical®.

Sincerely,

Tracy Farrell
Senior Editor

Please address questions and book requests to:
Silhouette Reader Service
U.S.: 3010 Walden Ave., P.O. Box 1325, Buffalo, NY 14269
Canadian: P.O. Box 609, Fort Erie, Ont. L2A 5X3

Ruth Langan

Malachite

Harlequin Books

TORONTO • NEW YORK • LONDON
AMSTERDAM • PARIS • SYDNEY • HAMBURG
STOCKHOLM • ATHENS • TOKYO • MILAN
MADRID • WARSAW • BUDAPEST • AUCKLAND

ISBN 0-373-29007-1

MALACHITE

Copyright © 1998 by Ruth Ryan Langan

This edition published by arrangement with Harlequin Books S.A.

® and ™ are trademarks of the publisher. Trademarks indicated with ® are registered in the United States Patent and Trademark Office, the Canadian Trade Marks Office and in other countries.

Printed in U.S.A.

RUTH LANGAN

traces her ancestry to Scotland and Ireland. It is no surprise, then, that she feels a kinship with the characters in her historical novels.

Married to her childhood sweetheart, she has raised five children and lives in Michigan, the state where she was born and raised.

To Patrick Jacob Langan
The newest jewel in our family crown
And to his proud parents, Pat and Randi

And of course, to Tom
Patriarch of the dynasty
And love of my life

Prologue

Indian Territory, 1844

"Weather's changing. There's snow coming. I can feel it." Onyx Jewel tossed aside the furs and placed a log on the dying embers. Almost at once the flame licked along the dry bark and burst into flame.

From the nest of furs the young Comanche woman watched as he strode to the entrance of the tepee.

"You are restless, Warrior with Heart of Eagle." His name rolled easily from her tongue. A name this white man had earned when he'd leaped into a fray between the lone chief of the Comanche and a group of brutal buffalo hunters. Had it not been for Onyx Jewel's courage, the leader of the Comanche would have surely been killed, for the buffalo hunters had the advantage of rifles.

But though he'd saved the life of their leader, Two Deer, it had not come without a price. Onyx had teetered on the brink of death for days. It was only because of the loving care of the chief's sister that he survived.

"Yeah, I'm restless." Onyx peered at the land, still shrouded in darkness. "I've been away from my herd for too long. By now they've probably scattered over half of Texas."

"Let them run free. What need have you of cattle? You are one of the People now," she said with a lazy smile. Lifting the edge of the blanket, she coaxed, "Come lie with me, and I will make you forget the land you left and the work you once did."

He turned and shot her a wicked smile. "That's what you've been doing now for months. Making me forget everything. Look at me." As he spoke he touched a hand to the soft cowhide leggings that molded his hips. "I look more like a Comanche than a Texas rancher. Pretty soon my hair will be long enough to braid."

She tossed aside the furs and strode naked toward him. Just seeing the sway of her hips, the jut of her high, firm breasts had his throat going dry.

She slipped into his arms with the ease of a woman in love. Against his throat she whispered, "Why can you not forget about that other life? You are one of us now."

Oh, how easy it would be to forget everything except the press of that lithe, young body against his. Hadn't he managed to put aside his obligations, his hopes, his dreams for too long now?

He framed her face with his hands and stared down into those dark, liquid eyes, seeing himself reflected there. He combed his fingers through her hair, loving the feel of it against his flesh. "I love you, Evening Star. You're the first woman to ever claim my heart. Did you know that?"

When she said nothing, he lowered his head to press soft kisses over her eyes, her cheeks, the corner of her mouth.

"You've taught me so much about life and love. And women," he added with a smile. "Out here in this Texas wilderness, that's the last thing I expected to learn. But it's time to get back to my own people. I want you to come with me. As my woman. My wife."

Even as she experienced the jolt of pleasure at his words, she felt the tip of a blade pierce her heart. Felt the pain, sharp and swift. For in that moment she knew. Knew, as she had feared from the beginning, that the love she carried in

her heart for this brave warrior would not be enough to hold
him here.

"I cannot go. I cannot leave the People."

"Of course you can. If you love me." He lifted her chin
and forced her to meet his narrowed gaze. "Do you love me,
Evening Star?"

"More than my own life."

"It's settled then." He wrapped his arms around her, kiss-
ing her with a fervor that rocked her. "I give you my word.
When you are my wife, there will never be another woman.
You're all the woman I'll ever need."

They tumbled onto the furs. And even as she gave herself
up to the wild sweep of passion, she knew it would be the
last time. The last time she would hold him. The last time
she would savor his touch, his smell, his loving caress.

For she was Evening Star, sister to the chief of the Comanche. Her life, her future were here with the People. As
was the future of the child she carried. A child that must be
kept a secret from this hot-blooded warrior. For to reveal
such a thing would be to tie him to her against his will. A
bond that might, in time, cause his love to sour and turn to
resentment. And that she could never bear.

Despite her youth she was wise enough to know that a
man like Warrior with Heart of Eagle must be free. To follow
his heart. To return, unfettered, to his own people. Just as
she must remain here with hers.

But as their kisses deepened and their sighs whispered on
the wind, she found herself wondering what would become
of the child of their two cultures.

The shaman, the healer and wise elder of their people, had
already told her it would be a son. A proud, headstrong warrior like his father.

Where would this child belong? With the mother who nurtured him? Or with the father, who would be a stranger to
his own son?

Her gods were powerful. She would ask them to be her
son's guide on the long and difficult journey of his life.

Chapter One

Texas, 1871

He'd been in the saddle for five days, stopping only long enough to catch a few hours of sleep and change horses. The journey, from an isolated ranch in Montana to the Texas hill country, had already cost him two good horses. He'd been forced to leave the first behind in Wyoming, the second in Colorado. Still, with any luck, he should reach his destination before morning.

He slid from the back of his mount and knelt in the snow to drink from an icy stream. Running a hand over his heavily bearded chin, he waited impatiently until his horse finished drinking. Then he pulled himself into the saddle and was on his way once more.

He was driven by a sense of urgency. The message had been brief. *Evening Star is ill.* But he knew that his mother would never have permitted those four words to be sent unless the illness was grave.

He urged his mount up a hill, then into the waters of yet another ice-clogged creek. And prayed that he'd be in time to make peace with the mother whose heart he had broken so many years ago, when he had left his home and people, turning his back on their way of life for good.

* * *

The Comanche had taken refuge for the winter in a small, heavily forested area of Texas. To the occasional rancher or cowboy, their tepees were indistinguishable from the trees.

As his horse's hooves churned up the snowflakes, the word spread quickly through the encampment. Son of the Eagle had returned.

By the time he entered his mother's tepee, a crowd had gathered, though everyone remained at a respectful distance.

A young woman, seated beside the bed, looked up in surprise before quietly taking her leave.

At once he dropped to his knees and took his mother's hands in his. How small they seemed. How cold.

"I knew you would come, Son of the Eagle." Her voice was little more than a whisper. Even that small effort seemed too much.

"How could I not? I need to mend this thing between us, Mother. I should not have stayed away so long. I should have…"

She roused herself enough to place a finger to his lips to silence him. "There is no time to dwell on past mistakes. Yours or mine. Let us learn from them and move on. I realize now that a son has every right to know his father. But I refused to reveal his name to you, because I did not want to lose you to him. And in so doing, I lost you anyway. But now, before I leave this place, I must put things right between us."

Even as he exulted at her admission, he felt the razor edge of fear slice his heart. "You aren't leaving, Mother. You're still young. You have a long life ahead of you."

She shook her head. "The spirits call to me. And I have not the strength, nor the will, to refuse."

He wanted to argue, but he could see for himself the ravages of illness. He could feel the throbbing at his temples. Could hear the way his breath left his lungs. After all these years apart, he hadn't expected to feel such pain at losing his mother. "Will you tell me now of my father?"

"That is why I sent for you. And why I resisted the call of the spirits. For I knew in my heart that you would come."

In short bursts, her breathing labored, she retold the legend of the courage of his father and the battle with the buffalo hunters. "Our people called him Warrior with Heart of Eagle. That is why I named you Son of the Eagle. But you had another name. Your white man's name."

"Malachite." His eyes narrowed at the hated name. The others in the village had ridiculed him for it. When he'd left to work in the white man's world, he'd taken the name Mal. Mal Eagle.

"Malachite." His mother's eyes softened, as did her voice. "I named you for your green eyes. So like his."

Another thing that had caused him endless ridicule among the People. A Comanche with green eyes could never be a leader. He would always be known as a half-breed. Son of the Texan.

"Your father gave me this." She removed a narrow strip of rawhide, on which was affixed a glowing green jewel. "The malachite is a stone that gives vision, my son. Strength. Power. That was why he gave it to me. And why I gave you the name. His name. For he was a legend among his own people, and among mine. And you are his son. You are so like him. With your own dreams. Your own goals. Go to him. Not with shame, but with pride. With love. And tell him that Evening Star carried him in her heart all the days of her life."

His voice deepened with simmering anger. "If he loved you, why did he leave you?"

"He had to return to his own people. To follow his dreams. And they were fine, big dreams. About carving out a life for himself where no other whites had been. About building a bridge between our two worlds."

"A bridge," he said in a choked voice. "I see no bridge between our two worlds. I see only an endless chasm."

She squeezed his hand, wishing there were some way to ease the restlessness that had plagued him, driven him from the time he was a young brave. "Know this, my son. Know this and be proud. Your father did not wish to abandon me. He asked me to go with him, to be his woman. It was I who chose not to leave. I was sister to Two Deer, chief of the Comanche. Among the People, I was respected. Among your father's people, I feared I would be reviled."

He detested the note of censure that crept into his voice. But it couldn't be helped. These were the things he'd waited a lifetime to say. The questions he needed to ask. And now, despite her weakness and infirmity, knowing his words would hurt her, he spoke them anyway. "What you're really saying is you didn't love him enough."

She took a deep breath, fighting the pain that kept building, building, drawing her toward the inexorable end. "I loved him as much as I could love any man. More than my own life."

"But not enough to live with him."

"Not enough to live with him." She was surprised by the sudden rush of tears. She'd thought there were none left, for the pain all these years had been too deep for tears. "I did not have his courage. Or yours." She waited while he wiped her tears with his thumbs. "When I follow the spirits, you will finally be free. Free to walk your own path in life, without regret, without guilt. Choose well, my son. I sense that you will follow the trail carved by your father. I ask only that you forgive me for waiting so long to tell you all these things. As I hope your father will forgive me."

For long moments she lay so still, so pale he had to touch a hand to her throat to assure himself she was alive. The pulse was so feeble and thready he knew her time had come.

Yet she managed to open her eyes for one last look at her beloved son. He was the image of the man she'd loved. The image she'd carried in her heart for a lifetime.

"Go to him, Malachite. Go to your father. And proclaim yourself proudly as the son of Onyx Jewel."

At last he had a name. Jewel. The name of the man who had fathered him, then left him. Onyx Jewel.

Now, finally, he had a focus for all the years of rage and anger and bitterness. All the years of loneliness and hunger and desperation. Wasn't that one of the reasons why he'd left his childhood home and struck out on his own? Not only because he felt like an outcast among the People. But because he had been searching, looking into the eyes of every white man he'd met, wondering if he would recognize his own father in them.

His mother proclaimed him the son of Onyx Jewel. But he knew what the white man, Onyx Jewel, would call him.

Bastard.

"Señora Potter. What are you doing?" Carmelita Alvarez, housekeeper at the Jewel ranch for the past twenty years, looked up from the fresh bread she was slicing.

Across the room Millie Potter was slipping an apron over her head. "I thought I'd give you a hand."

Carmelita dried her hands as she charged across the kitchen. "You are a guest."

"But that's quite a crowd in the other room, and I'm used to serving crowds in my boardinghouse."

"It has been a long time since I have been able to fuss like this," the housekeeper said with a smile. She took hold of Millie's elbow, steering her to the door. "Besides, there are handsome men in the other room." She opened the door and motioned toward Byron Conner, the handsome young banker of Hanging Tree. "Go. Smile. Flirt. Let me worry about the food."

"You sound just like Ruby," Millie whispered. "She made me this beautiful gown and insisted that I come here tonight. But I feel so—" she made a gesture with her hands "—useless, just standing around. I'm not used to being idle."

"Go now. Enjoy." Carmelita took back the apron, gave her a shove and firmly closed the kitchen door.

Ruby, who had been snuggling close to her new husband,

Marshal Quent Regan, disengaged herself long enough to whisper, "Millie, what were you doing in the kitchen?"

Millie shrugged. "Just swapping recipes with Carmelita."

"Well, stay out here. We didn't invite you here to hide out in the kitchen and think about food."

"But I can't help it. In my business, I'm always thinking about food. What to cook. How many I'll be cooking for. How to use what's left over."

Ruby nodded toward the handsome young banker, Byron Conner, who stood to one side talking to Adam Winter, Cal McCabe and her husband, Quent, who had just joined them. "Save those thoughts for another time, *chérie*. You're supposed to be over there, making big calf eyes at our eligible bachelor. That's why we insisted on bringing you out to the ranch today."

"Oh, Ruby." Millie's cheeks turned a becoming shade of pink.

"At least talk to him," Ruby whispered.

"I don't have anything to talk about."

"Then let him do the talking. You just stand there and look pretty and listen." Ruby linked her arm with Millie's and dragged her close.

Jade passed among them with a tray of stemmed glasses and decanters of whiskey and wine. The Oriental beauty was wearing a floor-length sheath of green silk with black frog fasteners and a sleeveless coat of the same fabric to hide her growing middle.

"Will you have some elderberry wine, Millie?" she asked.

"Thank you." Millie sipped and watched admiringly as Jade moved on.

"I don't believe I've ever seen anyone as graceful as your sister," she said to Ruby.

"*Oui*. She seems completely unaffected by the fact that the widow Purdy says she is carrying twins."

"Mrs. Purdy's never been wrong," Millie said with a smile. "So I think, if I were you, I'd be sewing two infant layettes."

Ruby shook her head, sending auburn curls dancing. "The way our family is growing, I could spend all my time just keeping us in clothes. In the past year I have made over a dozen gowns just for my sisters alone."

"None of them as pretty as this." Millie smoothed her hands down the softly gathered skirt of her brand-new russet velvet gown, which Ruby had forced on her. "It's far too fine for me. I'll be in debt to you forever, Ruby."

"Nonsense. I told you it was a gift."

"It's far too expensive a gift. I never should have accepted it."

"If it will make you feel better, you can pay me back by allowing Quent and me to take some of our meals at your boardinghouse."

"Fair enough. I'll expect you to start coming around at least once a week," Millie said.

The two walked up to Pearl, who was holding baby Amber and engaged in quiet conversation with Jade's husband, Reverend Dan Simpson, just as Diamond also joined the group. Despite the fact that this was a special occasion, she was dressed in her usual buckskins and boots. "Oh, Dan, that was such a beautiful service. I got all teary-eyed thinking about how much Pa would have loved it."

Out of the corner of her eye she saw her infant son pull himself up at the edge of a table and reach for a glass of his father's whiskey. In one smooth motion she snatched him up and handed him off to Adam. "Keep an eye on little Onyx or Carmelita will have his hide."

"The way she dotes on him? Not a chance." Adam grinned and held the baby easily in the crook of his arm while he continued a conversation with the others.

The Jewel family had gathered at the big ranch to celebrate the christening of Amber, Pearl and Cal's baby daughter.

"Wasn't she an angel through the service?" Pearl's pride in her infant was so sweet and so obvious the others merely smiled. For this special occasion the new mother wore a pale pink gown. Her long blond hair had been pulled back with mother-of-pearl combs, framing a delicate face.

"Not when Reverend Dan dunked her in that water," little Daniel said. He and his brother, Gil, who had been adopted by Pearl and Cal, hovered around the baby like mother hens, touching her, staring at her as though they still couldn't believe she was real.

"I thought Daniel was going to have a fit right in front of the whole congregation when she started squalling," Gil said with a laugh.

"You were none too pleased yourself," Cal teased.

Everyone laughed, while Gil, fifteen and as tall as the men, blushed.

Pearl took pity on her two sons. "Would one of you like to hold her for a while?"

"I will," Gil shouted.

"I will," Daniel echoed at the same moment.

"Gil first," Pearl said gently. "And then Daniel. But bring her to me when she gets fitful."

The two boys crossed to a sofa pulled in front of the fireplace and settled down side by side to coax smiles from the cooing infant.

"Did you hear about one of Lem White's ranch hands?" Cal's tone lowered so the children wouldn't hear. "Got it in his head to chase that devil mustang. They found him dead up on Widow's Peak."

There was a long silence. The festivities had chilled by degrees.

"That horse is a devil." Byron Conner glanced around the group, studying the grim faces. "As long as he runs free, there will be more deaths. And more ranches failing. And heaven knows what other bad luck will come our way."

"That's crazy," Diamond said.

"Is it?" Byron drained his glass. "How many wranglers does that make who have died chasing that devil?"

He saw heads nodding and added, "And how do you explain little Jimmy Burgess? One minute he's playing in the school yard. He spots that black stallion on a hillside, and the next minute he's dead."

"Doc Prentice said he was born with a weakness in his heart. Doc thinks all that talk about the mustang being a devil scared poor little Jimmy to death."

"Maybe," Byron said. "And maybe that stallion really is a devil, with a devil's powers."

Millie Potter shivered. "Really. All this talk is just so...terrifying." She colored slightly as she saw Byron turn to study her.

Carmelita entered, wiping her hands on her apron. "Supper is ready. And I have made so much, I hope you are all hungry."

"We're starving for some of your hot spices," Cal said, grateful for the interruption. It was well-known that Pearl, though she'd adjusted to her husband's love of spicy food, still preferred bland meals that reminded her of the way her proper Boston mother used to cook.

Diamond and Adam, holding little Ony, led the way to the big formal dining room, which was rarely used. Usually when this big, raucous family came together, they preferred the scarred table and rough-hewn chairs of the kitchen.

Behind them walked Pearl and Cal McCabe, trailed by Daniel and Gil, holding baby Amber.

Jade and Dan Simpson held hands and were followed by Ruby and Quent Regan, who still behaved like newlyweds, whispering and touching.

Byron Conner gallantly offered his arm, and Millie had no choice but to accept.

At the table Byron held her chair. The women sat on one side, the men on the other, with Gil and Daniel at one end and little Ony at the other.

As Carmelita bustled in and out carrying trays of steaming food, Millie said, "I've never seen your housekeeper so happy."

"*Oui.*" Ruby giggled. "I think for a while she was feeling very left out because we had all moved on to homes of our own. But now, with children, and more on the way, she realizes that we have not really left. Heaven knows she will be needed for a very long time. This big ranch house of Papa's is still the heart of our family. We could never completely abandon it. Or Carmelita.''

When they had filled their plates, they all caught hands around the table. And as Dan led them in prayer, Diamond happened to glance up at the tintype of her father and mother hanging above the breakfront.

For a moment she felt a sharp tug at her heart. "Oh, Pa," she whispered. "How you must love seeing all your children together at last."

Cookie stepped out of the bunkhouse and paused to hold a match to the pipe clenched between his teeth. He sucked until the tobacco caught, then blew out a rich cloud of smoke.

From the big ranch house came the sounds of muted voices and laughter. He walked to the corral and leaned against the rail, smiling in the fading light of early evening. It was good to see so much life in the Jewel ranch again. He shook his head in wonder. Who'd have believed that he'd live to see another generation of Jewels? How Onyx would have loved all this.

He idly rubbed his sore leg, knowing by the pain that a storm was brewing over the mountains. He hated to admit that his leg pained him more each year, and that sooner or later he'd have to give up what he loved most in life—cooking for the cowboys, especially taking the chuck wagon out on the trails. He'd always told Onyx he wanted to die with his boots on and the sweet smell of grub roasting on the fire.

What fine adventures he'd had with Onyx through the years. He missed that man every day.

At a sound he swiveled his head, peering into the gathering darkness. Looming out of the shadows was a horseman.

Cookie felt a shiver along his spine and realized he'd been careless. His rifle was back in the bunkhouse.

He heaved away from the railing and managed to take one

step before he was stopped cold by a voice that whispered across his nerves. It wasn't just the deep timbre. Or the ring of authority. It was the voice itself. As familiar as yesterday.

"I was told this was the Jewel ranch."

Cookie swallowed and gave a barely perceptible nod of his head. The horseman nudged his mount closer. Just then the clouds parted, and in the moonlight he was clearly visible.

"I'm here to see Onyx Jewel."

Cookie found himself looking at a ghost from the past. Staring in openmouthed surprise at the face of a man he'd met and befriended almost thirty years earlier. But that was impossible.

"What in tarnation...? Who...?" His mouth opened. The pipe dropped and fell, unnoticed, to the ground. For the space of several seconds he couldn't find his voice. Then, turning on his heel, he sprinted in an uneven gait, covering the distance from the corral to the ranch house in a matter of minutes. And all the while he was shouting at the top of his lungs, though the words were coming so hard and fast they were completely unintelligible.

It was Pearl who heard him first. Perhaps it was because she was a new mother and her ears were attuned to the slightest sound from baby Amber. But just as she lifted her head, Adam and Cal pushed back from the table, their hands automatically going to the guns at their hips.

Marshal Quent Regan was the first one at the door, gun in hand, when Cookie pushed his way inside.

"You aren't going to believe this," the old man shouted.

By now everyone had left the table and gathered around the doorway.

Struggling to catch his breath, Cookie pointed outside.

Everyone turned to study the horseman. He slid from the saddle and strode up the steps. Even in the darkness it was plain that he was tall and lean, and walked with a measured, purposeful gait. As he approached, he studied those gathered in the light of the lanterns, searching the face of every man.

His tone was rough with impatience. "I'm here to see Onyx Jewel."

As he drew close enough to be caught in the light spilling from the room, he heard the women suck in their breath. One of them, holding a little boy to her heart, actually let out a cry.

"Sweet heaven, it's..." Diamond turned and buried her face against the shoulder of the man beside her.

That caused the others to react in like manner. Pearl lowered her head and began to weep. Cal stood beside her, awkwardly patting her shoulder while he stared at the ghostly specter. Jade, with both hands pressed to her swollen middle, had to be supported by her husband. Ruby clutched Quent's hand and began babbling in a mixture of French and Cajun. A pitcher of cream slipped from Carmelita's fingers and crashed on the floor, but she took no notice as she lifted her apron to her eyes and began to chant and pray aloud in Spanish.

Seeing the confusion, Millie Potter gathered her courage and stepped forward. After all, these were her friends. And this was an extraordinary situation. One she wouldn't believe, if she hadn't witnessed it with her own eyes.

"I...hope you'll forgive our reaction. We don't usually treat strangers like this. But you've given us quite a shock. You see, you're the image of Onyx Jewel."

Malachite rounded on her. At some other time he might have remembered his manners and removed his hat. Or offered polite conversation. But the painful death of his mother, the long miles in the saddle and the years of anger had taken their toll and brought him near the boiling point. He wanted nothing now but to see this ugly, hated thing through to its conclusion.

"I need no reminder of how I look. I've paid the price of Onyx Jewel's legacy for a lifetime. Now all I want is to see him. Man to man. Call him out here and tell him that his bastard son—'' he spat the hated name ''—Malachite Jewel, is here.''

That set up another round of wailing. Millie watched helplessly as Diamond, sobbing against Adam's shoulder, was helped to a chair. Cal handed the baby to Gil, then scooped Pearl up in his arms and carried her toward the fire. Dan insisted that Jade recline on the sofa. And Ruby, white and shaken, was led inside by Quent. Carmelita stood rooted to the spot, tears streaming down her cheeks as she recited a litany of Spanish prayers.

None of them seemed capable of getting beyond their emotions to offer a word of welcome or to acknowledge that they were, indeed, family. They were all too stunned by his uncanny resemblance to Onyx Jewel.

Squaring her shoulders, Millie said, ''Malachite…won't you come inside? We were just having supper. Perhaps you'll join us.''

Malachite's anger grew. These people were making no sense. Were they all touched in the head? ''I have no time for food, woman.''

''Coffee, then,'' she said, feeling completely helpless.

Cookie hadn't moved. The banker, Byron Conner, was staring around at the chaos with a look of utter disbelief. Because he was a newcomer to this part of the country, he had no idea what was going on. He knew only that this stranger's arrival had brought the fine celebration to an abrupt end.

''Why are you wasting my time?'' Malachite said through clenched teeth. ''Are you afraid to summon Onyx Jewel?'' He took a menacing step inside, glancing around the sumptuous room.

Millie backed up, then lifted her chin. She wasn't about to let this stranger intimidate her, no matter what he called himself or how much he looked like the man he'd come seeking. ''Afraid?'' she demanded. ''Why would we be afraid?''

Malachite couldn't keep the fire, the heat from his tone.

"Because you know Onyx Jewel will be embarrassed at having to acknowledge a bastard."

"That does it." Millie's eyes shot sparks, and her chin jutted as she put her hands on her hips. "Look around you. Are you blind? Can't you see what you've done?"

"I've disturbed your evening. But don't expect an apology. After all, Onyx Jewel disturbed more than my evening. He disturbed my whole life and that of my mother. Now call him, woman, or I'll shout down this house and everyone in it."

Millie's anger spilled over, and she didn't bother to hide it. This rude, crude man had spoiled little Amber's celebration and had sent the entire Jewel family into a state of shock. It was all this talk about Diablo, the devil horse. It had everybody in Hanging Tree spooked.

"Go ahead, then," she taunted. "Shout down the entire house. But that won't bring back Onyx Jewel. Unless you know how to raise a man from the grave."

She saw Malachite flinch. Saw the way his eyes narrowed, as though he'd taken a blow to the midsection. She could almost feel sorry for him. Almost, but not quite. After all, he lacked even the most basic manners.

For long moments Malachite stood ramrod straight, absorbing the pain the only way he knew how. Stoically. Unwilling to let the enemy see a weakness.

He had come so far. Endured so much. And all because he'd needed to look into his father's eyes, just once, and confront him with the fact of his existence. And his abandonment.

And now his quest was over. But he'd been denied the prize. He would never have the satisfaction of seeing his father's face. Of hearing his voice. Of unleashing this lifetime of frustration.

When at last he spoke, his voice was controlled, revealing none of the emotion that churned in his gut. "Tell me where you have buried him. I intend to visit his grave. And then I'll leave his land and bother him, and you, no more."

Chapter Two

It was Diamond who managed to pull herself together first. Getting to her feet, she muttered, "I don't know what's wrong with me lately. Ever since little Ony was born, I get all weak and weepy. Like a damned silly female."

"Maybe that's because you are a female." Adam smiled gently as he kissed her cheek. "But you're not a silly one. You're just sensitive."

"We all know I'm about as sensitive as a mule." She drew away and crossed the room to stand beside Millie, facing the stranger. But the closer she got to him, the harder her heart started pounding. She couldn't help it. Just looking at this man was like looking at her father.

She forced herself to stick out her hand and offer a proper welcome. "Sorry for the way I acted. My name's Diamond. I'm Onyx Jewel's daughter. And these other three—" she indicated Pearl, Jade and Ruby as she introduced them "—are my sisters."

Sisters. The word shook him to the core. He hadn't expected this. Wasn't ready to accept it. He'd come for confrontation. To expel the demons that had festered for a lifetime. He'd come hoping for a knock-down-drag-out fight that would leave him bruised and bloody and somehow cleansed. He'd wanted to look a beast in the eye and then conquer it.

Instead, he was meeting sisters. Half sisters, he corrected, determined to hate them as much as he hated their father.

He accepted her handshake, then nodded a stiff acknowledgement to the others.

"I don't know why I should be surprised by this," Diamond said with a shaky little laugh. "I always figured Pa'd have a few more surprises up his sleeve."

She felt suddenly awkward. This man was watching her with her father's eyes. But he hadn't said a word. And there was no way to tell by looking at him what he was thinking. He gave nothing away.

To ease the situation she said, "This is my husband, Adam Winter. He and I live on the adjoining ranch."

The two men shook hands.

Pearl regained her senses in time to say, "And this is my husband, Cal McCabe."

As the two men shook hands, Pearl added, "Cal is the foreman of Daddy's ranch. We live in Daddy's old cabin, across Poison Creek, where I've set up a schoolroom to teach the town's children."

Daddy. The word grated. He'd never had anyone to answer to that name.

"And this is my husband," Jade said, forcing herself to show the proper respect. "The Reverend Dan Simpson."

Again there was a formal handshake and a cool appraisal. Malachite studied the man, who looked too tough, too trailwise to be a man of God. He had little use for such men. The ones he'd met preached one thing while they did another.

"And this is my husband, Marshal Quent Regan." Ruby linked her arm through Quent's as they crossed the room. "We live in the town of Hanging Tree, above my dress shop."

Malachite shook the marshal's hand in stiff, sullen silence. He'd dealt with enough lawmen in his time to want nothing more to do with them.

Diamond turned. "This is our housekeeper, Carmelita Alvarez. She's been keeping house for me since I was a baby."

Carmelita lowered the towel, damp with her tears, and offered a trembling hand.

"You are the image of your father. I thought, when I first saw you, that it was Señor Jewel, back from the grave."

Malachite merely stared at her in cool silence.

"This is our banker, Byron Conner." Diamond spoke quickly to cover the fact that Carmelita was crying again. "And this is Millie Potter, who owns the boardinghouse in Hanging Tree."

Malachite shook Byron's hand, then turned to the flame-haired woman in the fashionable gown. The heat in his eyes had begun to cool. But when his hand engulfed hers, he felt heat of another kind.

He studied this woman who had remained calm while the others had panicked. Now he understood. She wasn't directly affected by this. She was not a Jewel. Not one of Onyx Jewel's daughters. Though he didn't know why, he found himself oddly relieved to know that.

At the touch of him Millie felt a strange tingling that shook her to the core. When she finally managed to withdraw her hand, she stood very still. There was such strength in this stranger. Such anger seething in those eyes. And such control. He was nearly rigid with control.

"About your desire to see Pa's grave." Diamond was making a valiant effort to ease some of his tension. "It's a far piece from the ranch. And since it's so late, I think we should wait until morning. If you'd like, you can stay here. I know Carmelita'd be happy to have someone to fuss over. She'll be here anyway, cleaning. And she's a fine cook. You could have Pa's old room. It's right upstairs, and you'd..."

"No." Malachite didn't bother to hide his disapproval. His response was abrupt and firm.

"But you're welcome to..."

"I want nothing of Onyx Jewel's. Not his home. Not his bed. Now that I know he has joined the spirits, I want nothing more than to see his burial place before I leave Texas. Since you feel it's too late, I'll honor your request and wait until morning.''

Diamond swallowed. His words were blunt enough. He'd made himself abundantly clear. "All right. Tomorrow morning will be fine. We can meet here, if you'd like. Or in town.''

Malachite considered carefully before saying, "It will be better to meet here. I expect my reception in your town would be even less enthusiastic than my reception here.''

"What is that supposed to mean?'' Millie drew herself up stiffly. The nerve of the man, demeaning these people. Demeaning her town.

He heard the note of disapproval in her tone and flung his words like a gauntlet. If he couldn't have the satisfaction of a physical fight, he would settle for a verbal war. "Let me make myself clear. I may be Onyx Jewel's son, but I didn't come here to be embraced by him. Only a fool would expect such a thing. I came here to be acknowledged. Nothing more. But I could hardly expect to be welcomed into his town. You see, my father—'' he spit the name with obvious distaste "—may have been a Texan. But my mother was a Comanche.''

He saw the slight lift of an eyebrow, the wary look that came into her eyes. He wasn't surprised. It was the typical reaction when people were confronted by that fact. He knew what people called him behind his back. Half-breed was one of the kinder terms.

As he turned away Millie called, "Wait. Where will you spend the night?

"It's cold and it's late,'' she added, hoping to explain her outburst. "If you'd like, you can take a room at my boardinghouse.''

He paused, then turned. She caught a glimpse of a fleeting smile, before it was wiped from his lips. "I've slept in the cold many times. For a Comanche, it's as elemental as breathing.''

He walked out the door, crossed the porch and pulled himself onto the back of his horse. And then he was gone. Swallowed up in the darkness.

And the others were left to speculate about this strange, angry man who had come, unbidden, into their lives.

"I intend to sit down with Diamond and her sisters in the next few days." Byron Conner's voice was muted in the darkness as he sat beside Millie, guiding the team. "They're going to need some advice."

"About what?" Still shaken by the encounter with Malachite Jewel, Millie looked up at the sky and watched the path of a falling star. She had the strangest sensation that he was still here with her. She could almost see those haunted green eyes. And feel that explosion of anger. Could see again those lips curved into the slightest hint of a dangerous smile.

"About their finances."

Millie turned to study Byron's darkened profile. "Now, why in the world would they need help with their finances? They're already the richest family in Texas."

"I didn't say help. I said advice. Like you said, their father left a substantial estate. It's only natural that strangers would come along and try to claim a portion. Who's to say this—" his tone rang with derision "—half-breed didn't hear about Onyx Jewel's death and decide to cut himself in for a piece?"

Millie's tone sharpened. "I'll excuse that statement, since you never knew Onyx Jewel. But I did. And so did everyone in town. And I can tell you, this stranger is the image of his dead father."

"That isn't important." Byron snapped the reins and the team trotted smartly. It was a fine matched set of sleek, glossy roans, brought all the way from St. Louis, along with the brand-new carriage, to bolster his image as a successful banker. "I'm going to instruct Diamond and her sisters that unless this stranger has proof, he has no legal claim to Onyx Jewel's estate."

Her tone was incredulous. "His face isn't proof enough?"

"Not in a court of law. The law demands legal documents."

"And what about the heart?" Millie asked softly.

He turned to her and placed a hand on her arm. "I can see that you're much too tenderhearted for your own good. It's a lucky thing the citizens of Hanging Tree don't have to rely on you to make the tough decisions about loans and mortgages and foreclosures."

"Yes." She gave a sigh. "It's a good thing. Doesn't it ever bother you, Byron?"

"The first rule of banking is you can't let your heart rule your head." He glanced up as the darkened buildings of the town came into view. "I don't believe the ride from the Jewel ranch to town has ever passed so quickly before. It must have been the charming company I was with."

Beside him, Millie said nothing. But the look on her face was still tinged with anger. She was too annoyed at his earlier words to be swayed by his obvious attempt at flattery.

The carriage rolled along the empty dirt path the townspeople called the main street. At the end of town, in front of a sagging, two-story house, Byron reined in the team and the carriage came to a halt.

He helped Millie down and walked beside her up the stairs of her front porch. Before she could open the door, he put a hand on her arm to stop her.

"Thank you for accompanying me to the christening, and then to supper, Millie."

"You're welcome."

His hand tightened perceptibly on her arm. "If you don't mind, I'd like to kiss you." He bent toward her in anticipation.

Somewhere in the back of her mind, it occurred to Millie that Ruby would be thrilled at her matchmaking prowess. This was all going according to Ruby's plans. She had recently told Millie, in no uncertain terms, that she'd been alone too long. That Millie's three shy little girls, ages five, six and seven, needed a father. Only the oldest, April, could remember her father. And with every year, those fragile memories faded. As for Millie, the memories of her years with her beloved Mick would never die. But she had acquiesced to Ruby's prodding. After all, Ruby had argued, Byron Conner was a fine catch. Handsome. Proper. Churchgoing. A successful banker who was respected, if not always liked, by the townspeople.

Still, Millie couldn't put aside her annoyance at Byron's callous remarks about Onyx Jewel's son. It should have been plain to anyone with half a brain that Malachite Jewel was a tortured soul who had no interest in money. It was a father he'd come seeking, not a fortune.

She backed away to evade Byron's touch, turning her face at the last moment so that his lips merely brushed her cheek. "No, Byron. I'm sorry. It's...very late. And I'm tired."

"I see." He straightened, momentarily disappointed but far from discouraged. "Well, perhaps another time." He reached up and opened the door. "Maybe I'll stop by for supper tomorrow."

"If you'd like."

Once inside, Millie removed her shawl and hung it on a peg by the door.

She smiled, thinking about her daughters. They'd been delighted when she'd told them that Birdie Bidwell, their fifteen-year-old neighbor, would be spending the night while their mother took supper at the Jewel ranch. Her girls adored Birdie, who had been helping with the chores around the boardinghouse since she was ten. Despite a tendency toward clumsiness, she was a sweet, polite girl who had proved invaluable over the years.

As she entered the parlor, Millie's smile disappeared when she discovered that the fire had burned to embers.

With a sigh she returned to the hallway and draped her

shawl around her, then walked to the back door and let herself out.

A gust of wind sent her skirts whipping around her ankles as she walked.

A dwindling supply of logs was stacked neatly against the south wall of the shed. She bent to retrieve a log, then suddenly caught sight of something out of the corner of her eye. A menacing shadow was moving toward her.

"Oh." She straightened and grabbed up a log, swinging it like a club.

"Easy." At the sound of a man's deep voice she swung harder.

A hand closed over her wrist and the log fell harmlessly to the ground. She was caught in a vise, unable to move, while the man loomed over her.

For the space of a heartbeat she couldn't breathe. Her heart pounded so painfully she thought it might explode. Her breath came in short, shallow gasps.

Just then a beam of moonlight revealed her attacker.

"You!" Catching sight of Malachite Jewel, she tried to back away, but he was holding her fast. "I thought... You scared me half to death. What are you doing here?"

"I'm sorry. I didn't mean to frighten you." *Terrify* would have been a better word. She'd struck out blindly, as though expecting the worst. He found himself wondering who or what had brought on such fears. "I decided to take you up on your offer of a room. That is, if the offer is still good."

Unable to find her voice, she merely nodded.

"Good. I hope you don't mind that I put my horse in your shed."

"I... That's fine." Did he know what his touch was doing to her? How wildly her heart was pounding? She felt the way a deer must when it stared into the muzzle of a rifle.

Then she seemed to come to her senses. It wasn't this man

who caused such feelings. It was the fact that she'd been caught by surprise. She needed to pull herself together.

With a toss of her head she glanced down at the offending hand, and he released her.

Immediately she took a step back, feeling light-headed. "There's a livery at the other end of town. Neville Oakley will keep your horse for a dollar a week."

"I have no need. I'll only be staying the night." He could see the tension humming through her. Could hear the breathlessness in her voice. To put her at ease he said, "I see you were coming out to gather some logs. How many do you need?"

"That isn't necessary." She bent to the pile but his hand on her arm stopped her. Again she felt the strength in him.

"How many?"

She drew back, alarmed by the feelings his touch aroused. "One or two. Just enough to see us through until morning."

He bent to the pile and easily lifted an armload, then followed Millie up the steps and into the house.

He glanced around as they entered the big cheery kitchen. A scarred wooden table dominated one side of the room, surrounded by sturdy chairs. Along one wall was a huge blackened fireplace. The room smelled of bread dough rising on a warming shelf above the fireplace, and more faintly of apples and spices.

"I'll take this." She lifted a log from his arms and tossed it onto the hot coals of the kitchen fireplace. Then she placed several logs beside the hearth.

That done, she said, "The rest can go in here." She led the way to the parlor.

Beside the big stone fireplace he knelt and deposited the rest of the logs. When Millie bent to tend the fire, he stopped her with a hand to her wrist.

"There's no need. I'll do this."

He tossed a heavy log on the glowing embers. Within

minutes fire licked along the dry bark, then caught and burst into flame, illuminating the darkened room. He wiped his hands on his pants, then got to his feet and offered a hand to help her up.

"Thank you." She hated that her voice sounded so out of breath. But the truth was, the closeness of this man intimidated her.

He glanced around at the overstuffed sofa and chairs, the simple curtains at the windows, the lantern on the hearth. Though it was shabby, there was a feeling of warmth here in her home.

He turned to her, pinning her with those strange green eyes. "Where will I sleep?"

She turned away to avoid his gaze. "If you'll follow me, I'll show you to your room."

Holding a lantern aloft, she led him past the big, spacious dining room, through the kitchen, now ablaze with warmth and firelight, to a bedroom off the kitchen.

She set the lantern on a table beside the big bed, covered by a handmade quilt. "This isn't as big as the upper room. But that room is being used tonight by a neighbor girl who offered to stay with my daughters. It's the one I usually offer paying guests."

"You have daughters?" He hadn't moved. He stood framed by the doorway. It occurred to Millie that he was so tall his head nearly brushed the top of the door frame.

"I have three."

"But the banker is not your husband."

"My husband...is dead." Suddenly uncomfortable, she started toward the door and was dismayed when he made no move to step aside. She lifted her head in a challenge. "I'll say good-night now."

But still he stood, barring her exit. "You haven't asked me how I found my way to your door."

She paused. Until this moment it hadn't occurred to her to wonder. "How did you know where to find me?"

There was a subtle change in his tone. "I followed you."

His words shocked her. And yet, they shouldn't have. Hadn't she sensed his presence along the trail? It gave her the strangest feeling to know that this man had been watching her in the darkness without her knowledge. And then an alarming thought intruded. That would also mean that he'd been standing in the shadows, watching as Byron kissed her cheek. He'd not only watched but listened, as well. To everything that had been said between them.

What if she had allowed Byron…?

She glowered at him. "You had no right. No right to invade my privacy like that. No right to watch while Mr. Conner kissed me."

"I'm sorry if I've offended you. I didn't intend anything by it." His tone lightened, as though tinged by unspoken laughter. "But I must disagree with you. What you shared with your stuffy banker was hardly a kiss."

The gall of this man.

She started to push past him. "How dare—"

His hand came out, stopping her in midstride. "Maybe you've forgotten what it is to kiss a man."

He saw the look of shock and anger in her eyes. He'd intended merely to taunt her. But now, he intended more. He dragged her roughly against him. His arms came around her, pinning her to the length of him. His head lowered until his lips were brushing hers. Against her mouth he muttered, "I hope this will refresh your memory."

It happened so quickly Millie had no time to react. One moment she was angry, indignant. The next she was being manhandled by this…this savage.

All thought scattered as his lips covered hers in a scorching kiss. It wasn't just the skill with which he kissed her. That sure, easy movement of his mouth on hers. All slow heat that built and built until she could feel the fire pulsing through her veins. Or the way his hands tightened at her back, molding her to the length of him before moving slowly up and down her spine, testing, measuring. It was the hunger in it. Like a man who'd been starved. And the thoroughness. As though, while drawing out every taste, every flavor, every breath, he was laying claim to her.

He felt her breath catch, then quicken on a sigh, mingling with his as her lips parted. From beneath hooded lids he watched as her lashes fluttered, then closed, and her anger was forgotten as she lost herself in the pleasure.

His hands moved along the lush velvet of her gown, which only enhanced the soft curves and heated flesh beneath.

He hadn't intended this. Couldn't even recall how or why it had happened. One moment he was enjoying the way her eyes had darkened with anger, and the next he'd simply acted on instinct. But now that he was holding her, kissing her, there seemed no way to stop.

She smelled like her kitchen. Warm and clean, with a hint of cinnamon and other spices. But her taste was as fresh, as clear as a mountain stream.

As he took the kiss deeper, Millie struggled to hold on to some last vestige of common sense. But he was doing strange things to her mind, even as he coaxed her body to betray her. Her hands, which she'd balled into fists, were now clutching at the front of his shirt, though she couldn't recall how they got there. The sigh that escaped her lips was not a sigh of anger, but of pleasure. And the way her body was straining toward his left no doubt of the deep hunger that gnawed.

He lifted his head and stared down at her. Her mouth looked warm and moist and thoroughly kissed. Her chest was heaving on a ragged breath.

She was so desirable it took all his willpower to keep from

kissing her again. But one more kiss and he'd be lost. He knew, if he had any sense at all, he had to end this now.

"That," he whispered against her temple, "was a kiss."

Her eyes opened. She took a step back and fixed him with a hateful look.

He moved aside to allow her to leave. "Anytime you'd like another reminder, you let me know. I'll be happy to oblige."

"Why, you arrogant, pigheaded…" She was nearly choking on the anger that erupted, catching her by surprise. Nobody had ever brought out her temper like this barbarian and his bullying tactics.

For a moment she was at a loss for words. She was so furious she couldn't form a single, coherent thought. But her eyes, flashing fire, and the proud lift of her head spoke volumes.

"If you ever dare to do such a thing again, I'll…"

"I'm sure you'll fight me. Just the way you did this time."

She felt the rush of heat at his taunt. How dare he remind her that she hadn't fought him. If truth be told, she'd cooperated fully in that kiss.

Laying bare her shame was the last straw. She swung her hand in a wide arc and connected with his cheek. The impact had her palm stinging.

In silence she stalked from his room, slamming the door on the way out. In the kitchen she grasped the back of a sturdy chair and stood very still, taking in deep drafts of air to calm herself. Then, on legs that were still trembling, she made her way upstairs to her bedroom.

In his room, Malachite listened to the sound of her footsteps. When she was gone, he crossed to the window, idly rubbing his cheek while he surveyed the darkened shapes of buildings scattered around the town.

Millie Potter had come as a complete surprise. He hadn't intended this. Any of it. Not the room in her boardinghouse.

Not the kiss. And certainly not his reaction to that kiss. But, considering the chaos of these last few weeks, he shouldn't be too shocked by the fact that nothing was going as he'd planned.

He unbuckled his gun belt, placing the guns beneath the pillow. Then he shed his clothes, blew out the lantern and climbed naked into bed. With his hands under his head he stared up at the darkened ceiling and imagined Millie in her bed, one floor above.

He fell asleep smiling. Unaware that the object of his thoughts was so distraught she sat stiffly on the edge of her bed, staring at the flickering light of the lantern. Trying to calm the wild racing of her pulse. Praying to cool the heat that raged through her veins. Struggling to erase the image of that smug, arrogant man one floor below who, with a single kiss, had turned her calm, orderly world upside down.

Chapter Three

"Mama, I can't find my blue sash." Five-year-old June danced barefoot down the stairs, long red curls flying, kid boots and stockings dangling in one hand.

Millie barely glanced up from the salt pork sizzling in the pan, praying that hard work would keep her mind off the man asleep in the adjacent room. "It should be on your dresser."

"It wasn't there. I looked."

"Look again." Millie cracked eggs into a bowl. If she was careful, she'd have enough for one more day. She'd traded more than the usual number with Rufus Durfee in the past weeks to keep her family supplied with enough meat. She hoped this unexpected boarder would provide money for a few more supplies. That is, if Malachite Jewel had any money. "Have April help you."

"She won't help."

Exasperated, Millie turned. "Why?"

"She and Birdie are busy brushing out Birdie's braids."

"Now, why would Birdie do a thing like that?" Millie wrapped a towel around her hand and set aside a pan of biscuits to warm on the ledge above the fireplace. Then she started the coffee. "It took Birdie an hour to braid all that hair last night."

"But that's why she braided it," the little girl said in a

tone that suggested it made perfect sense. "So she could brush it out today. What about my sash?"

"Ask May to help you find it. But not until after you put on your boots. The floors are cold this morning."

"Yes'm." The girl flopped down in the middle of the big kitchen and struggled into coarse stockings and high-topped kid boots.

"Mama, I can't find my slate." It was six-year-old May, standing at the top of the stairs, shouting over the sound of girlish giggles that drifted from the upper rooms.

"It's probably in the parlor," Millie called. "That's where you were doing your sums last night."

"Oh. I forgot." The little girl padded down the stairs, then returned minutes later carrying her slate.

Seven-year-old April paused dramatically at the foot of the stairs and announced, "Mama. Look at Birdie."

Millie lifted a big skillet filled with browning slices of potato and onion and dutifully turned.

Looking uncomfortable, Birdie Bidwell descended the stairs, avoiding Millie's eyes. Her long braids had been brushed out, turning her pale hair into a halo of frizzy corkscrew curls.

"Oh my, Birdie, don't you look pretty."

"Really, Mrs. Potter? Do you think so? I mean..." Birdie worried the edge of her apron. "April talked me into it. But I was afraid..."

"She was afraid Gil wouldn't like it," June piped in.

"June Potter." April's voice rose in indignation. "That's the last time we'll let you share a secret."

"See if I care. Besides, if that's the way you're going to be, I'll just tell Gil what you and Birdie were whispering about last night," the five-year-old taunted.

"Oh, no." Birdie covered her face with her hands. "I'll just die if Gil knows. Please, June. You can't tell him. It's a secret. You promised."

"She isn't going to break a promise." Millie shot her youngest daughter a look that every mother mastered and was instantly recognized by every child. "Now, Birdie, I need you to run this tray over to the jail for Deputy Spitz and Beau Baskin. Then hurry back here and eat before you make everyone late for school."

"Yes'm." The girl started to fetch her wrap, when the bedroom door suddenly opened.

All four girls stared in surprise at the tall stranger standing in the doorway. He wore the garb of a cowboy. Black pants tucked into high boots. A black shirt, the sleeves rolled to his elbows. Leather holsters riding low at each hip. But his hair was the color of a raven, and he wore it longer than most men, letting it fall over the collar of his shirt. And around his throat was a strip of leather, which held a gleaming green stone that perfectly matched the green of his eyes.

Suddenly, all the childish chatter halted. There was a long, awkward silence as Millie's three daughters darted to hide behind her skirts.

"Good morning. I see I startled you." Malachite couldn't help staring at Millie. His brow furrowed into a frown.

Last night she'd worn an elegant, fashionable gown that had made her look like a queen. Today she wore a simple dress of faded blue gingham. Over that she'd tied a white apron, which only emphasized her tiny waist. Her thick mass of red hair had been tied back with a length of ribbon. Already little wisps had pried loose. In the heat of the kitchen, they curled damply around her cheeks and neck.

"Good morning." She felt a rush of heat and cursed the fact that she was blushing. But she couldn't help it. Just looking at him reminded her of that kiss. And the long, uncomfortable night she'd put in because of it.

If Malachite remembered, he was obviously not bothered by it. After studying her, he returned his glance to the children, who were staring at him.

"Who're you?" June, the youngest and boldest of Millie's daughters, took the lead, as usual.

"My name is Mal…"

It was on the tip of his tongue to say Mal Eagle. But just then Millie interrupted, "Children, this is Malachite Jewel."

"Jewel?" Birdie instantly made the connection. "Are you Miss Diamond's brother?"

To Malachite, that word still rankled. "I guess I am. And who are you?"

"I'm Birdie Bidwell. My folks live next door. I help Mrs. Potter whenever she needs me."

"Hello, Birdie." He offered his hand and she solemnly accepted.

"I've got to finish my chore." She took the linen-covered tray from Millie's hands and hurried out the door.

"And how about us?"

At June's impertinent question, Malachite turned to the three little girls, whose flaming red hair and freckled faces clearly identified them as Millie's daughters. It was a shock to realize that this was how she must have looked as a child. Like a blaze of fire. All pale porcelain skin and hair like autumn leaves.

"What are your names?" he asked.

"I'm June Potter," the youngest said bravely, though her voice quivered, betraying the underlying fear. "I'm five years old. And even though Miss Pearl—that's our teacher—says I'm too young for school, she allows me to go with my sisters. And she put me in first grade and put May in second. This is May." She touched a hand to her sister's shoulder. "She's six. And April is seven and in third grade."

"I can see that you like to talk."

"Don't you?" she asked.

"Not so much." He knelt, so that his eyes would be level with theirs, and offered a solemn handshake to each. "I guess I'd rather listen than talk."

"Like April. She doesn't talk much, either. Your hair is long. Are you an Indian?" June asked.

"My mother was Comanche." Malachite waited for a reaction.

"Our mama's..." The little girl turned to her mother. "What are you, Mama?"

"My parents came from Ireland," Millie said as she tended the stove. "But in this country we're all American."

"You've got pretty eyes," June babbled, studying the stranger. "They're as green as that stone you're wearing."

"Men can't have pretty eyes," May corrected her little sister.

"Why not?"

"Because ladies have pretty eyes. Men have..." The six-year-old considered a moment. "Men have handsome eyes."

Because she was so serious, Malachite choked back his laughter.

"Anyway," June said, "that pretty stone matches your handsome eyes."

"Thank you. The stone is called a malachite. It was a gift to my mother. That's where I got my name."

"It sounds like something out of the Bible, doesn't it, Mama?" Without waiting for a reply, June said, "We were named after the months we were born in."

Malachite couldn't help teasing, "Then I'll bet you're glad you weren't born in January, February and March."

The three girls burst into giggles. It was clear that they'd never thought of that before.

"Sit down, children," Millie called. "Your breakfast is ready." She'd had time to prepare herself to face this man without blushing. "You too, Mr. Jewel."

Mr. Jewel. The absurdity of it, and the formality, had him biting back a grin. "Where would you like me to sit?"

"Here." Millie indicated a chair at one end of the table. She poured coffee, then placed the cup beside his plate. "How would you like your eggs?"

He glanced at the girls, who continued watching him as they took their places around the table. "How are you having your eggs?" he asked them.

"Scrambled," they called in unison.

"I'll have mine scrambled, too."

Minutes later, when Birdie breezed in, they passed around platters of sizzling salt pork, scrambled eggs and fried potatoes, as well as steaming biscuits and a crock of honey. Then, at a look from Millie, they bowed their heads.

"We thank Thee for this food," little June said aloud.

"Amen," the others responded, before digging in to their meal.

"Mrs. Potter." Birdie buttered a biscuit, then popped it in her mouth. "Deputy Spitz said he thinks the only reason Beau Baskin gets drunk every week is so he can enjoy your good cooking in jail."

"Is that so? If Beau didn't spend all his money over at Buck's saloon, he could afford to buy his meals here." Millie took a seat at the opposite end of the table. But when she looked up, Malachite was staring at her in a way that had her ducking her head.

"You cook for the jail?" he asked.

She nodded. "The town pays me. I used to send over the marshal's meals, too. But now that he's married to Ruby, it isn't necessary. I just supply a meal whenever there's a prisoner, which isn't often in this town. Except for Beau Baskin, who gets drunk once or twice a week and spends the night in a cell sobering up."

Birdie said over a mouthful of biscuit, "Deputy Spitz says he asks to work whenever Beau spends the night, just so he can enjoy your good cooking, too."

Millie laughed. "Well, we won't bother to repeat that to Deputy Spitz's wife, or he may end up having to take all his meals at the jail."

"Why?" June asked innocently.

"Because," Birdie said in the tone of an older friend who is accustomed to answering youthful questions, "Mrs. Spitz would be jealous if she knew that her husband liked your mama's cooking better'n her own."

"But why?" June persisted. "Everybody knows Mama's

the best cook in Hanging Tree. Why should Mrs. Spitz mind?"

"She just would." Birdie turned to Millie. "Are you going to take us to school today, Mrs. Potter?"

Millie nodded. "I guess I have no choice. Amos Durfee sent word that he needs his boys to help in the mercantile today. And since Travis Worthing is taking his father's place on the ranch until his return from Abeline, that just leaves me. Are you sure your mama can spare you today?"

"Yes'm." Birdie glanced at the stranger, then explained. "My pa got thrown from a horse more'n two years ago. Doc Prentice fixed most of his broken bones, but there's nothing to be done for his back. Doc says he'll never walk again. So Ma has to stay close, to run and fetch for him. And I do what I can to help earn my keep. I help Mrs. Potter here, and then I help Miss Jade at the church." While she spoke she got to her feet and started to clear the table. "But mostly I help my ma."

Millie filled a basin with hot water from the stove. While April washed the dishes, May and June dried, and Birdie reached over their heads, putting the clean dishes away.

Malachite sipped a second cup of coffee and watched as Millie filled a basket with cold chicken, hard-boiled eggs, biscuits and fruit.

Then his gaze slipped to the neighbor girl, laughing and chatting, and all the while working diligently. It occurred to him that when he'd first left the village of his mother's people, he'd expected the life of the white man to be somehow easier than that of the Comanche. What he'd learned was that life everywhere was difficult and demanding. But it wasn't only the Comanche who looked out for the aged, infirm, widowed or orphaned. Despite the fact that Millie Potter was obviously struggling to raise three little girls alone, she was willing to help a neighbor, as well. He wondered just how many chores Millie Potter took on to keep her family in food and clothes. He'd spotted a cow and chickens in the shed. All the rest of their food would have to be bought or bartered. From the size of her brood, it would take some doing. The house was sturdy, but in obvious need of repair. And the furnishings, though clean and comfortable, were showing wear.

When the girls finished their chores and went off to fetch their warm wraps, Millie removed her apron and glanced around her neat kitchen.

"The charge for the room is fifty cents. You can leave the money on the kitchen table. When you're ready to leave for your father's grave, you can let yourself out and latch the back door behind you." She tossed a heavy shawl over her shoulders.

Malachite wasn't fooled by her cool, professional manner. It was plain that Millie Potter was in a hurry to get away from him. A small, perverse part of his nature made him want to see how far he could push her.

"Where is the schoolhouse?" He shoved back his chair and stood.

"On Jewel land. A couple of miles from the big ranch house. Across Poison Creek."

He took a step closer, watching the way her eyes warned of a challenge as he advanced. "Then why don't we ride there together?"

She was hugging the shawl to her, as though for protection. "There's no need..."

He reached out and caught the ends of the shawl from her hands, running the soft strands between his thumb and finger. "Do you object to my company, Mrs. Potter?"

At the intimacy of his touch, she drew herself up to her full height, bringing the top of her head nearly to his chin.

He was playing with her. Trying to push her into a corner. Well, two could play that game. She'd show him. "Why should I object? It's a long way to the Jewel ranch. I welcome someone to share the chore."

Instead of letting go of the shawl, he wrapped the ends around his finger, drawing her fractionally closer.

At once her cheeks were suffused with color.

Millie glanced up and thought, for a brief moment, that she'd detected a hint of laughter in his eyes. Did he know what his touch was doing to her? Was that why he insisted on tormenting her like this? "I'll remind you, Mr. Jewel, that if you don't unhand me this minute—" she hated the way her voice sounded, tight, breathless, but it couldn't be helped "—I will be forced to defend myself as I did last night."

His voice was warm with laughter, though he kept his features carefully schooled. "Well, we wouldn't want that, now, would we?" Very slowly he released the ends of her shawl.

As she walked away, the smile that had been playing at the corners of his lips bloomed. Millie Potter was uncomfortable in his presence. But to her credit, she didn't back away. Or give an inch.

He returned to the bedroom for his cowhide jacket and wide-brimmed hat. The day was proving to be much more satisfying than he'd anticipated.

And all because of one little fiery-haired, blue-eyed female who looked better in a housedress and apron than most women could in silks and satins.

As he made his way to the shed and began hitching the horse and wagon, he found himself wondering what Millie Potter would look like in nothing at all.

It was too bad he wouldn't be around long enough to find out.

"Do you drive the girls to school every day?" Malachite guided the horse and wagon across a rain-swollen gully. He found the press of Millie's thigh against his a pleasant distraction. Almost as pleasant as her soft, lilting voice.

"Most days one of the Durfee boys takes the children. Or Travis Worthing, a nice, sensible boy." Beside him, Millie clutched the edge of the seat to keep her balance. But even that couldn't prevent her from suddenly grabbing his arm as the wagon pitched and rolled.

Her fingers encountered rock-solid muscle. The feel of it made her throat dry. It was with a sense of relief that she was finally able to let go. "But when there's no one else available, I try to take them. The girls are so eager to learn. And I'm so grateful that they have the opportunity."

In the back of the wagon, huddled under a quilt, Birdie and the three little girls laughed and chatted as they challenged one another to spell new words or do sums in their heads.

Tied to the back was Malachite's horse, easily keeping pace with the slow, plodding movement of the wagon.

"Until Pearl came along, the children of Hanging Tree had never had a teacher or a school. I bless the day she found us."

Malachite turned to her. "What do you mean, she found you? I thought you said Pearl was Onyx Jewel's daughter."

"She is."

"Then how could she find you? Didn't she always live here on her father's ranch?"

Millie shook her head. "I guess I should explain. Diamond was the only one who grew up with her father here in Texas. The others, like you, had different mothers. When they learned about Onyx Jewel's murder…"

"Murder?" Malachite turned to her in surprise.

Millie nodded. "By a man he considered his closest friend, his banker, Chester Pierce."

Under his breath, Malachite muttered, "Bastard saved me the trouble."

Millie chose to ignore his crude remark. "It turned out that Chester had been stealing from Onyx for years, and shot him to keep from repaying his debt. When Onyx's daughters read about his death, each of them made the journey here to visit his grave. Pearl from Boston. Jade from San Francisco. And Ruby from Bayou Rouge, Louisiana."

Malachite said nothing. His eyes narrowed as his thoughts turned inward. The presence of sisters was as perplexing to him as the presence of the woman beside him.

His thoughts were interrupted as their wagon topped a rise and the Jewel ranch house and outbuildings loomed in front of them. He guided the horse and wagon around to the back porch before bringing them to a halt.

He turned to Millie. "I'll say goodbye. Thanks for the use of your room. I left the money on the table." As he handed her the reins he added, "As for the kiss, I know I ought to apologize. But it would be a lie. I'm not sorry about that."

Her cheeks flamed. "Then I can't say I'm sorry you're leaving, Mr. Jewel, because you are not a gentleman."

He tipped his hat and gave her a most undignified wink. "That's one of the few things I've never been accused of, Mrs. Potter."

He climbed down and untied his horse from the back of the rig.

"Good morning," Diamond called as the back door slammed. "How did you two happen to hook up?"

Behind her, Byron Conner stepped out onto the porch. For a moment his jaw dropped, then he caught himself.

"I decided to take Mrs. Potter up on her offer of a room in her boardinghouse."

"He slept at your place?" Byron demanded.

Before Malachite could respond, Diamond said, "I'm glad you were sensible. There's been a lot of trouble in these parts lately."

Malachite's eyes narrowed. "What kind of trouble?"

Diamond shrugged. "Cowboys found dead. Ranches failing. Like there's a black cloud hanging over our town."

"It isn't a black cloud," the banker said. "It's a black stallion."

When Malachite glanced at him, he added, "A wild mustang we call Diablo. Ever since he came to these parts, trouble started."

Diamond seemed eager to change the subject. "Well, we're all here and ready to visit Pa's grave."

"All?" Malachite asked.

The back door opened and Pearl, Jade and Ruby called

out greetings before climbing into Jade's elegant gilt-and-white carriage.

"Our menfolk are inside with the children." Diamond mounted a skittish, high-strung mare. "Carmelita's in her glory, cooking for an army."

"But what about school?" June asked in dismay from the back of the wagon. "We studied every one of our words, Miss Pearl. We were hoping to win the spelling bee."

Pearl gave her a gentle smile. "Don't worry. We'll still hold class this afternoon. I'll be back to pick you up as soon as we return. And while you children are waiting, you can join the others inside. Birdie," she called to the young girl, "I'll bet you can coax Gil to give up Amber for a few minutes if you'd like to hold her."

At the mention of Gil, Birdie's face became wreathed in smiles. Seeing it, June opened her mouth to make a teasing comment. Before she could, Millie caught the little girl's hand and muttered, "Not a word, do you hear me?"

The little girl rolled her eyes. "Yes'm."

"Thank you, Miss Pearl," Birdie called. "I'll go in and ask Gil right now." She scrambled down from the wagon and hurried inside. With any luck, Gil would notice her hair before the Potter sisters had a chance to mention it.

As an afterthought Diamond turned to Millie. "Would you like to go with us to Pa's grave?"

Millie shook her head. "I think Malachite's visit should be reserved for family. I'll stay here with the others."

She climbed down from the seat on the wagon and followed her daughters up the steps. At once Byron crossed the porch to stand beside her. She watched as the carriage with the three women moved smartly away.

Malachite pulled himself into the saddle. For long moments he studied Millie Potter, then moved his steely gaze to the man standing beside her. The look wasn't lost on Byron. With a smug smile he moved closer and dropped a hand casually on Millie's shoulder.

Without another glance Malachite tipped his hat, wheeled his mount and followed the others.

Millie sighed. "I hope the visit to his father's grave site brings Malachite Jewel some measure of peace."

"Why should you care?" Byron demanded.

"Because he's an angry, troubled man." She should be relieved that he was gone. His presence, though brief, had caused her all manner of discomfort. But the truth was, she couldn't stop thinking about the way it had felt to be crushed in his arms and kissed until she was breathless.

She waited until he disappeared over a rise. Then she turned and made her way inside the big ranch house, determined to put him out of her mind.

The grave site was on a barren, windswept hill. Hardly the spot Malachite would have chosen as the final resting place for a legend like Onyx Jewel.

"This was Pa's favorite spot." Diamond's voice lowered respectfully, as though she were in a great cathedral. "He used to say that as far as the eye could see, it was all his. The buildings, the cattle, the land. Especially the land. He loved this land."

If Malachite was surprised by Diamond's declaration, he was even more surprised by the lack of fancy markers. Just a couple of big stones marked the grave. On four surrounding mounds of earth were more stones.

"These are the graves of our mothers," Pearl explained.

"We had their remains brought here," Jade said in her musical voice, "so their spirits could be at rest with our honorable father."

"Only Diamond's mother ever lived here." Ruby's voice had a catch in it, and she had to swallow before adding, "But we were certain our mothers would wish to be united in death with the man they loved in life."

"They all loved him?"

At his look of surprise, the women smiled knowingly.

Ruby laughed softly. "*Oui*. If you had known our father, you would understand why."

He had his doubts about that. He'd come here prepared to hate Onyx Jewel. He'd learned nothing to change his mind.

But he wisely kept his thoughts to himself. "You all knew him?"

"Why, yes." Jade seemed surprised by his question. "Though we didn't get to spend as much time with him as we would have liked, we all grew to love him. I wish you could have known him, Malachite."

It was Pearl who first saw the look in his eyes and knew that he was struggling to keep his emotions in check. He seemed a man tormented, not only by the past but by what he had learned since coming here.

Motioning to her sisters, she said, "We have the opportunity to visit the grave site often. But I think we will leave you alone now to pay your respects."

The young women returned to the carriage at the foot of the hill. From a distance they watched in silence as Malachite stood over his father's grave.

"So. Here we are. At last." Malachite wasn't aware that he had spoken aloud. Or that his hands had formed fists at his sides. The women were forgotten. Everything was forgotten except the man he'd been pursuing all his life. His voice was a low rasp of repressed rage.

"I've spent a lifetime looking for you. Oh, I didn't know your name. Or what you looked like. But I looked for you in the eyes of every stranger. Listened for you in every white man's voice. Because of you I turned my back on my mother's people and traveled the length and width of the wilderness. I broke mustangs in Wyoming. Herded cows in Montana. Lived in filthy tent towns. Survived in lonely isolation. And all because of that mysterious stranger who lived inside me, driving me. Taunting me. Haunting me. And now, finally, you have a name." His tone lowered with fury. "Onyx Jewel."

At the mention of the name he experienced the usual gut-wrenching pain and rage. He'd waited so long for this moment. "I would have preferred to find you alive, so that I could tell you face-to-face about all the pain you caused a woman who loved you. So that I could strike out and hurt you, the way you hurt my mother and me. But at least I've finally found you. Even finding you dead is better than never knowing. And I had to know. Had to. It's been eating away at me for a lifetime.''

He waited, teeth clenched, eyes closed, as waves of anger washed over him, like a fire stoked by fuel and wind until it became a raging inferno. ''You had no right,'' he muttered. ''No right to take what you wanted and then leave, without ever looking back to see the ruins you left behind. Ruins of a life that once had bright promise.''

He took a deep breath, determined to fan the flames. ''Evening Star waited for you. She refused all offers of marriage. Even when her brother, the chief, ordered her to take a husband, she refused. In doing so, she brought shame to her family. Shame. Do you understand? And all for a man who didn't deserve her loyalty or her love.''

He swore, loudly, fiercely, keeping alive the fire of hatred that had burned for so long inside him. He touched a hand to the stone at his throat and felt it warm and pulsing, as though alive. In a hoarse voice he shouted aloud, ''I feel your presence here. I know you can hear me. Do you know what you did to the people who loved you, Onyx Jewel? Do you give a damn, you bastard?''

The words seemed to bounce off the rocks and echo off the walls of nearby canyons.

But the only reply was the keening of the wind.

At length he shivered, wondering how long he'd been standing there. It could have been minutes or hours.

When he turned, he realized the women were shivering, as well. Huddled together in the carriage under a thin winter sun, patiently waiting while he sought to make some sort of peace with a dead man.

But, he reminded himself as he made his way down the hill to the waiting horse, it wasn't peace he'd come here for. It was vengeance.

Chapter Four

"Where could they be? Wouldn't you think that Pearl would give a thought to her daughter?" Cal McCabe paced the floor, peering out the window every couple of minutes. At his shoulder, little Amber, who had been cooing and gooing just minutes earlier, was beginning to fuss.

"It's nothing serious. She's just hungry," Carmelita said.

"Well, sure, but none of us can do anything about that." Cal was beginning to sweat. He was new to fatherhood, and the sound of his baby's cries cut his heart to the quick.

Seeing his dilemma, Millie opened her arms. "Give her to me, Cal. Maybe I can soothe her until Pearl gets back."

She gathered the baby close and carried her to a rocking chair in the corner of the kitchen. Almost at once Amber settled down to sleep.

Millie breathed in the warm, sweet scent, so unique to a baby, and felt that familiar tug at her heartstrings. She'd loved having her babies. Loved the smell of them, the feel of them in her arms. She and Mick had talked about having a houseful of them.

Thoughts of Mick made her suddenly think about Malachite Jewel. The two men were as different as they could be. Mick had been a gentle farmer who had won her heart with his sweetness, his kindness. Malachite Jewel was seething with bitterness. There was a toughness, a hardness about him that frightened her. And an arrogance in him that just plain made her furious.

Now, what in the world had caused her to compare those two such different men? Malachite Jewel was gone by now, returning to whatever life he'd left. And Mick...Mick was gone forever. The pain was swift and unexpected. It was the thought of Mick, she told herself. Not the thought of bitter angry Malachite Jewel.

From outside, the children's voices could be heard as they engaged in a game of tag.

Cal stormed to the window for another look.

Byron Conner added to his misery by saying, "I still say one of you should have gone along with them. No telling what might have happened."

"Malachite Jewel doesn't look like the sort of man who'd let anything happen to our womenfolk." Lulled by the thought of lunch, Dan lifted his cup of coffee and inhaled the fragrance of Carmelita's venison stew.

"With all that's been going on around here, how can you say such a thing?" Byron glanced toward Cal and Adam for support. "I, for one, don't trust him. Last night he looked like he'd grow fangs and grab us by the throats if someone didn't tell him where his old man was."

Adam became thoughtful. "He looked a lot like I did when I first came to Texas. There's a whole lot of anger festering inside Malachite Jewel. It's like a boil. If a man doesn't find a way to lance it, he can go half-mad with the pain."

Millie listened in silence. Everything they were saying was true. Malachite Jewel had given them a glimpse of his hair-trigger temper and his arrogance. But she'd also sensed a deep well of pain in him. Not to mention passion.

Just the thought of it made her cheeks grow warm.

"Well. Finally, they've made it back." Byron let the edge of the curtain fall. "It's about time."

There was the sound of carriage wheels, and a moment

later the lilt of women's voices as footsteps sounded on the porch.

Cal yanked the door open and stood aside as the women entered. But when he started to close the door, he realized they'd been accompanied by Malachite.

"Took you long enough." Cal's tone was accusing.

"Sorry." Pearl kissed his cheek.

"You're cold." Contrite, he caught her hands in his and began to rub them.

"It's my fault." Malachite stepped inside and removed his wide-brimmed hat. "I didn't expect to spend so much time at the grave."

"I thought you were leaving." The words were out of Millie's mouth before she could stop them.

"I thought so, too." He turned and caught sight of her in the rocking chair, the baby snuggled to her heart. The pain was swift and shocking.

Hunger, he told himself. All that unleashed anger had given him an appetite. He glanced across the room and saw the banker watching him closely. The knowledge that his presence irritated Byron Conner gave him a sense of satisfaction. "But I've learned that the Jewel women can be pretty persuasive. They talked me into returning for a meal before I head out."

"*Bueno.* You can wash up over there." Carmelita indicated a basin and pitcher. "I have a little something you can eat."

Millie tucked little Amber into a cradle, then joined the others seated around the table. She glanced at Malachite. "What did you think of your father's grave?" she asked shyly.

It seemed an effort to pull himself back from the dark places in his mind. So many conflicting thoughts. So much to mull over. "I'd expected it to be more ornate."

"*Oui.*" Ruby nodded. "That's exactly what I said the first time I saw it."

"But it suits Pa." Diamond drizzled honey over a biscuit

and broke it into little pieces for Ony, who was snuggled on her lap. "Pa just loved this land. There's no place else he'd want to be."

The others nodded in agreement.

"And I feel him there," she added.

"*Oui.* Each time I visit, I feel his presence."

Her sisters agreed.

Millie watched the expression on Malachite's face and knew that he'd felt it, too, though he seemed reluctant to admit it.

"Did you notice Malachite's amulet?" Pearl asked.

Everyone turned to stare at the strip of leather at his throat and the gleaming jewel.

"That's very similar to the necklace each of us was given by our father on our sixteenth birthday," Pearl said. "That was Daddy's way of assuring us he'd be with us always."

Without thinking, Malachite touched a hand to the green stone. He felt a pulse of heat, as though the stone were a living, breathing thing. His mother's people believed in the spirits. And though he often tried to deny it, he believed, as well. Right now, he knew that the spirit of Onyx Jewel was present and exerting his influence on this assembly. That realization only added to his anger and resentment.

"Now that you've had a chance to visit the grave..." Cal cleared his throat and glanced around before saying, "The reason why the women persuaded you to come back here is because we had a family meeting last night, after you left. Since I'm foreman of the Jewel ranch, and the only nonfamily member to share in Onyx Jewel's estate, the women asked me to be the spokesman."

Malachite set down his cup and folded his hands in his lap. He wasn't surprised. In fact, he'd been expecting this. He'd known they would circle the wagons to protect what was theirs. That would be the reason for the banker's early morning visit. To advise his clients on the best way to shut out this interloper.

Not that he wanted any part of this. Or of Onyx Jewel's

family. He'd come here to be rid of Onyx Jewel, not to embrace him. But he wouldn't make it easy for them. Let them all squirm as they picked up their stones to toss at him. He'd take it. As he'd had to take everything else life had handed him. But in so doing, he would finally ride out of here free. Free of the burden of illegitimacy he'd carried for a lifetime. Free of all the Jewels, who wanted him to think of them as his family.

"When Onyx was murdered, Diamond here vowed to keep the ranch going just the way her pa always had. But then, when her sisters started showing up, she realized she might have to change her plans a bit. You see, we weren't…I mean, she wasn't… Oh, hell." Cal shrugged and glanced helplessly at Diamond.

Seeing his discomfort, she got to her feet and touched a hand to his arm. Relieved, he sat down.

"What Cal was trying to say is that we were all sort of caught off guard when we started learning that Pa had more than his share of secrets. I didn't behave very cordially at first. But as I came to know his other daughters, I realized that we all had a common bond. Pa. And I knew that Pa would want all his children to share the bounty of this land he loved. So I'm sorry for that cool welcome we gave you last night, Malachite. We just weren't expecting any more of Pa's surprises. I guess we figured by now all his strays had been rounded up. But if you're willing, we'd all like you to stay on and have a hand in the running of the ranch."

Diamond was grinning, proud that she'd said her piece without fumbling. The others were smiling and nodding, as well.

As always, Malachite kept his feelings carefully in check. His eyes were narrowed in thought. His jaw was clenched. But there was no denying the astonishment in his voice. "You're offering me a piece of your ranch? Without any proof of who I am? Without any questions about where I've been and what I've done with my life?"

"That's exactly what I said." At the end of the table,

Byron sulked. He'd given them every argument he could think of, but they had refused to budge on this. "But nobody would listen."

Diamond shot Malachite a quick smile. "The proof of who you are is in your face. If you aren't Pa's son, you'd have to be his ghost."

Around the table, the others laughed and nodded.

"As for where you've been and what you've done, I don't see what that has to do with now."

"He could have been in jail for all you know," Byron interjected.

"Then he and I would have something in common." Adam winked at Diamond and closed his hand over hers, then turned to Malachite. "I spent time in jail before coming to Texas. But I never thought it was anyone's business but mine."

The banker realized that Adam's words were really meant for him. It only added to his irritation.

For the space of a minute, Malachite couldn't seem to make his brain work. He'd come here expecting denial, a satisfying, cleansing battle of wills and then banishment. Even in his wildest dreams, the most he'd hoped for was a grudging acceptance of his birthright before he was turned away.

But this. This was so unexpected. So...generous. Too generous. There had to be a flaw in it.

"Sorry," he said abruptly. "I'm not a cattleman. And I have no interest in your ranch."

"I'm sorry, too." Adam spoke up before the others could interrupt. "I'm afraid we haven't told you everything. Di and I have the ranch next to this. We keep the herds separate, but during roundup and the drive to Abeline, we share wranglers. There's something else we share. Trouble. Lately we've had more than our share. First we lost a barn to fire. Now we've lost two good cowboys. They set off to capture a rogue stallion and both showed up dead along the trail. If all that isn't enough, we keep losing more and more grazing land to herds of mustangs.''

"So, what do you think is behind all this trouble?" Malachite asked.

Glances were exchanged around the table before Diamond said, "A big black stallion we call Diablo. The Devil. That mustang seems to be everywhere. That's why we could use another hand. Especially one who could be trusted.''

Malachite gave a short, bitter laugh. "What makes you think I can be trusted?"

"Your name is Jewel," Cal said.

"That wasn't my choice." Malachite's eyes narrowed.

"No one is given that choice." Adam took his son from Diamond's arms and settled him on his lap. "What we can choose is how we live our lives.''

"Like I said—" Malachite started to push away from the table "—I'm not interested in Onyx Jewel's life or his ranch.''

"If that mustang keeps on running free," Diamond complained, "we soon won't be able to hold on to this ranch. Or our land. We've already lost wranglers who are too afraid to stay. And there isn't anyone left who'll risk his life to try to catch Diablo and his harem.''

Malachite couldn't hide his sudden interest. He sank back down on his chair. "The stallion has a herd?"

Diamond nodded. "Dozens of mares. Maybe even a hundred or more. They've got the whole town spooked.''

Adam's voice dripped sarcasm. "Crops destroyed. Blame Diablo. A mare runs off. Blame Diablo. Even a sick child or a wife in difficult labor is blamed on that damned horse. And offering a bounty on him hasn't helped.''

"Are you saying you don't believe he can be captured?" Malachite asked.

Diamond shrugged. "So far, nobody's even come close to catching him." She stood and offered her hand. "I'm sorry you won't consider joining us, Malachite. It would have been real nice getting to know you. And you might have discovered that you liked us, once you got to know us."

As Malachite accepted her handshake, he cautioned himself to go slowly. He'd learned early in life that promises could be broken and that the things he most wanted in life were usually denied him. But the thought of this mustang made his heart quicken.

It would be dangerous to show them just how interested he was. "Maybe I'd consider it after all. I'd like a chance at that stallion and his harem."

"You would?" Diamond glanced around the table at her sisters, who were suddenly grinning like conspirators. "That's fine. Then we'd like to invite you to stay here in Pa's house."

They could see Malachite's enthusiasm cool by degrees. "No." He shook his head. "I told you before. I want no part of Onyx Jewel's house."

"But you're his son. We're inviting you to help with his ranch..." Adam's hand on her arm had Diamond pausing. She swallowed back the rest of what she'd been about to say. She was learning, in dealing with this large, diverse family, that she couldn't call all the shots. Sometimes she had to take a step back or risk interfering in something that wasn't her business. "Where will you stay?"

He glanced at Millie. "If Mrs. Potter doesn't object, I'd like to stay at her boardinghouse."

"No." Millie spoke quickly. Too quickly. She could feel everyone staring at her in surprise. Feeling her cheeks redden, she said, "I don't mind a boarder for a night or two. But what you're talking about is much longer. It could be..."

"Months." He pinned her with that steely gaze. "And I'd be willing to pay you generously."

For a moment Millie felt trapped. How dare he spring this surprise on her in such a public manner? Still, the thought of a paying boarder... "What do you consider generous, Mr. Jewel?"

"You charged me fifty cents for last night. I'll pay you a dollar a day. With the first month paid in advance."

"Thirty dollars..." She was mentally calculating. Oh, the food she could buy. The warm winter coats. Several cords of wood for the fireplaces.

He'd made it impossible for her to refuse. She felt the stares of the others, and the heat rose to her cheeks. Out of the corner of her eye she could see Byron's face contorted with rage.

"I'll remind you—" Byron's voice was choked with anger "—he will be spending that time hunting Diablo. Do you want the curse brought upon you and your children?"

"If anyone is to be cursed," Malachite said easily, "it should be me. Not Mrs. Potter and her family. If you believe in such things."

Both men turned to study Millie.

A part of her was angry. She'd already had a taste of Malachite's arrogance. But another part of her was secretly excited. Because of the money, she told herself firmly. Not because of the man.

She lifted her head and returned the looks of the others. This was, after all, strictly business. She had her children to think of. In the little town of Hanging Tree, there would be few paying customers over the winter months. The cowboys from the nearby ranches would spend their snowbound nights in the bunkhouse. On their occasional foray into town, they'd rather warm themselves with whiskey at Buck's saloon than settle for a hot meal at her place. This was a matter of survival.

"I'd be happy to rent you a room, Mr. Jewel."

He knew from her tone, from the challenging look in her eyes that she meant not a word of it. But he'd correctly read her need for money.

He merely nodded.

"Done." Diamond's smile was warm. "Welcome to the family business, Malachite."

As the others got to their feet to offer their congratulations,

Malachite glanced over their heads to see Millie, her cheeks flushed, her eyes bright with challenge.

For reasons he didn't want to explore too deeply, that seemed the sweetest victory of all.

"I'll accompany you back to town, Millie." Byron's unhappiness had grown in direct proportion to Malachite's happiness. He'd watched as Cal McCabe and Adam Winter had started toward the bunkhouse to give this newcomer a tour of the ranch.

Diamond had ridden off with little Ony to her own ranch. Ruby and Quent, along with Jade and Dan, had left for town as soon as they'd finished lunch. And Pearl had packed up little Amber and left for school with the children.

Byron was eager to get Millie alone. After all, it was his duty to warn her of the pitfalls of the arrangement she was contemplating.

"No thank you, Byron. There's no sense going home now." Millie began gathering up the dishes. "I'll just stay on here with Carmelita until the children return from school in a couple of hours."

"But I..." He was quickly losing his patience. He lowered his voice. "I need to talk with you."

"All right. You can talk while I wash the dishes."

"No." He caught her arm and began steering her toward the door. "I'd like to talk to you alone."

Carmelita watched without comment as they stepped out onto the porch.

"What's wrong with you today, Byron?" Millie shaded her eyes from the sun and peered at the three men heading toward one of the distant outbuildings.

"He's what's wrong with me." Byron stood beside her, glaring at the tall figure disappearing into the barn.

"I don't understand. Why should you be bothered by the sudden appearance of Onyx Jewel's son? If Diamond and the others can accept him, why can't you?"

"I'll tell you why." He gritted his teeth and struggled to

hold his temper. "He's inviting trouble to our town. And if that isn't reason enough, I don't like the way you've been behaving since he came here."

She turned to fix him with a cool look. "And how have I been behaving?"

"Carelessly. Last night, without knowing a thing about this man, you allowed him to spend the night in your home."

"I'll remind you that I run a boardinghouse, Byron. A lot of men, and families, spend the night at my place. That's how I make my living. That's how I can afford to raise my children."

"But this man...this man is different. You saw how he acted when he arrived here last night. Like a man hell-bent on destruction. You could have been putting yourself and your children in grave danger."

"I can't believe what you're saying." She started to flounce away, but before she could walk inside he caught her arm.

"You listen to me, Millie. You're an unmarried woman. If you allow this...half-wild savage to stay in your home, you won't be able to stop the gossip that will spread all over town."

She pulled her arm free and shot him an angry look. "Now it's your turn to listen, Byron Conner. The Jewels are my friends. I'd put up any one of them at my place for as long as they wanted. I'll do no less for Malachite Jewel. And if the town gossips want to chew on that, I can't stop them."

She stormed into the kitchen, allowing the door to slam behind her. Moments later she heard the sound of his fine rig rolling away.

Carmelita was busy at the sink, her hands in hot, soapy water. When Millie picked up the square of linen and began to dry, the housekeeper had to bite hard to hide the smile that played on her lips.

She'd overheard everything these two had said to each other. And she admired Millie's spunk. After all, the arrogant young banker was considered a fine catch, and everyone

knew he'd set his cap for this pretty little widow. It would
be hard for a woman with three small children to refuse what
he was offering.

And though Millie Potter might insist that she was only
taking in Malachite Jewel as a favor to friends, Carmelita
thought differently. She'd seen the way Millie watched him
when she thought no one was looking. What was more, she'd
seen the way Malachite Jewel returned the look.

Carmelita felt a quick tug of excitement. Winter here in
the hill country was usually cold and bleak. But this one
looked as if it were about to heat up considerably.

"So you think you could start working with the wranglers
tomorrow?" Cal asked as he, Adam and Malachite stomped
into the kitchen after shaking the dust from their boots.

At once Carmelita began pouring cups of strong, hot coffee. She was flattered that the men had returned to the big
house. She knew they'd stopped in the bunkhouse to intro-
duce Malachite to the wranglers. Cookie probably served
them some of that mud he called coffee. It was understood
that in the bunkhouse the men could talk openly, without
worrying about offending the women with coarse talk and
swearing.

Here in the kitchen, the talk was more subdued. Across
the room, Millie turned from the fire to watch as Malachite
rolled his sleeves and bent to the basin to wash. His shirt
strained against the ripple of muscle as he lifted a square of
linen and began to dry. For some strange reason, she felt a
tightness in her throat.

When he tossed down the towel and turned, he caught
sight of her. His frown deepened.

She returned her attention to the pots simmering over the
fire.

"I don't see why not," he said. "Might as well learn how
things are done here on Jewel land."

They looked up as a wagon rolled to a stop and the laughter of children filled the air.

As the children spilled from the wagon and danced up the steps, the conversation abruptly ended.

"Where's Pearl?" Cal called.

"Ma stayed home with Amber." Gil, nearly as tall as Cal, held the door while the younger ones slipped past him. "I told her I'd see the girls safely here."

"Mrs. Potter, look what April won." At Birdie's prodding, the shy April displayed a pretty blue ribbon. "She won a prize for knowing all her spelling words."

"Oh, honey, I'm so proud of you." Millie wiped her hands on her apron and hugged her oldest daughter.

"How about the rest of us?" Adam coaxed. "Do we get to see it, too?"

Overcome with shyness, the little girl stared at a spot on the floor.

Millie knew how difficult it was for this oldest child, who was so withdrawn and so uncomfortable around men.

"If you'll come over here," Cal coaxed, "I'll tie it around your neck."

The little girl took refuge behind her mother's back.

"Gil won a prize, too," June piped in.

"Congratulations, Gil," Millie said to the boy who towered over her.

"But he didn't keep it," June added. "He gave his to Birdie."

Everyone turned to Birdie, who blushed clear to her toes. The edges of the ribbon could be seen poking out of her pocket.

"Daniel and I stayed up late helping Ma make the prizes." Gil was gallantly trying to explain away his impulsive action. "I didn't think it'd be right for me to keep it. Besides, Birdie got every word right but one."

"That's not what you said. I heard you tell her you wanted her to have it because it was the same color as her eyes and because her hair looked so pretty." June's comment had everyone glancing from Gil to Birdie, whose cheeks were now as red as apples.

"Come, children." Millie broke the awkward silence, hoping to put an end to Birdie's discomfort. Later, when they were alone, she would have a word with her youngest daughter about repeating embarrassing secrets. "Carmelita has milk and cookies still warm from the oven."

They needed no coaxing as they gathered around the table and began to eat.

The men, free of distractions, returned to their discussion.

"I know you're not fond of the idea of working with cattle." Adam cupped his hands around the hot mug and shot the housekeeper a grateful look when she topped off his coffee. "But we're glad of the help, Malachite."

Malachite drained his cup and accepted a refill. "If you have a team of wranglers that ride the range searching for strays, I'd like to join them. I'm better suited to that than to working in the barns."

"It's hard work tracking in these hills," Cal mused.

"I'm used to hard work."

"But there'll be snow soon. Then it will be even harder."

"I could help," Gil said.

Cal nodded with pride. "Gil knows these hills better than anyone in Hanging Tree. And when he's not in school, he often goes alone to hunt."

Malachite studied the boy over the rim of his cup. "Thanks. I appreciate the offer."

The fact that this stranger accepted him man to man had Gil squaring his shoulders and standing proudly beside his father. His earlier embarrassment about Birdie was forgotten.

Cal got to his feet. "Thanks for the coffee, Carmelita. I'd better get the boys home for supper." He shook hands with Adam and Malachite.

"I'd better get going, too." Adam picked up his hat. "If I'm late, Diamond might start supper without me."

When everyone burst into laughter, Millie saw Malachite's questioning look.

"Even Diamond will tell you she's the worst cook in

Texas," she explained. "Adam prefers his own cooking to hers."

"You have my sympathy," Malachite said almost solemnly.

Adam grinned. "No need. I wouldn't trade her for a dozen cooks."

When he took his leave, Millie turned to her girls. "Time to go."

Malachite drained his coffee and got to his feet. "I'll ride with you. It'll be dark soon."

As he strode to the door, Carmelita handed him a warm, linen-wrapped package.

He shot her a puzzled look. "What's this?"

"Bread pudding."

He was thunderstruck. "I love bread pudding. But how could you possibly know that?"

She gave a delighted laugh. "I wasn't sure. But since it was Señor Jewel's favorite, I thought it might be his son's, as well. Take it and enjoy. It is my gift to you. To welcome you into the family."

The knowledge that he shared another link with Onyx Jewel had him frowning. He seemed unsure how to accept this gift. Finally, with a muttered "Thanks, Carmelita," he followed Millie and the girls out to the wagon.

Chapter Five

"What's that?" Millie glanced at the package under Malachite's arm.

"Bread pudding. Carmelita said she made it for me." He pulled himself up to the wagon seat and lifted the reins.

In the back, the girls huddled together under a quilt, whispering and giggling.

"You seem surprised." Millie took the package from his hand and placed it carefully on the seat beside her.

"Amazed. This whole day has been…" His words faded and he stared off into the distance as he flicked the reins and the wagon began to roll. He shook his head in disbelief. "I never expected any of this."

"Then you can imagine how Diamond must have felt." Millie drew her shawl tighter around her. "All her life, there'd been only Diamond and her father. And then, in the space of weeks, she had to deal with his murder and the arrival of three women all claiming to be Onyx Jewel's daughters."

"How did she take it?" Malachite asked.

"Not very well. You've seen Diamond," Millie said with a chuckle.

Malachite nodded.

"She's rough around the edges. And tough as Onyx was. But once she got to know Pearl, Jade and Ruby, she opened her heart and her ranch to them. They've become a family. And it's plain that they've invited you to become part of that family.''

His tone was rough. "I'm not interested in joining Onyx Jewel's family.''

She was surprised at the vehemence of that statement. "Then why are you staying?''

It was a question he couldn't answer. He wasn't certain himself why he had agreed to stay. He shrugged. "I guess one ranch is as good as another.''

"You've worked ranches before?''

"You could say that." He guided the horse and wagon over a flat stretch of land, then down a sloping ridge. "I told you my mother was a Comanche. When I left the People I had to find a way to survive.''

"Why do you say the People, instead of my people?''

"It is the Comanche way. We are the People. But in my case, I have no right to call them mine. I turned my back on my mother's people a long time ago.''

"Why?''

He turned to glare at her. "You ask a lot of questions, Mrs. Potter.''

Stung, she muttered, "I'm sorry. I had no right.''

There was a long, awkward pause before he said, almost reluctantly, "I left because my mother refused to tell me about my father. She wouldn't even tell me his name.''

"Then how did you...?''

"Another question?''

This time he almost smiled, and she found herself thinking how handsome he would be if he would let himself relax.

"I was summoned home when my mother was dying. She lived long enough to tell me about my father. I planned on stopping here only long enough to confront him before returning to Montana.''

"Why Montana?''

"It's deep in the wilderness. Far from civilization. Where I don't have to choose between the ways of the Comanche and the ways of the white. Where I can be left alone to be myself.''

''Then you're...not planning to stay on here forever?''

''Forever is a long time. I'll probably be ready to pull up stakes in the spring.''

Millie shivered as a cloud obscured what was left of the thin sunlight. His words echoed in her mind. *Forever is a long time.* She and Mick had pledged their love forever. But he hadn't even lived long enough to see his third child born. That was when she'd stopped believing in forever.

''Mama.'' From the back of the wagon, little June's voice roused her from her reverie. ''I'm cold.''

Millie removed her shawl and passed it back. ''Here. Wrap yourself in this. And snuggle close. We'll be home soon.''

As the four girls huddled under the extra layer of warmth, Malachite slipped off his cowhide jacket and draped it around Millie's shoulders.

''I couldn't.'' She tried to give it back to him. ''You'll be cold.''

''Either you take it,'' he said, wrapping it firmly around her, ''or we'll stop right here and have a battle to see who's stronger. I don't think you have a chance of winning that one, Mrs. Potter.''

When they pulled up to the boardinghouse, he helped her down from the wagon. For the briefest of moments he continued holding her and could feel her heart beating like a caged bird. He could feel the press of her breasts against his chest, the brush of her thighs on his and the warmth of her breath on his cheek. Then he set her on her feet and turned to lift the girls from the back of the wagon. They ran up the steps to their house, while Birdie started home.

Malachite began to lead the horse and wagon toward the shed. ''I'll unhitch the horse and bring in an armload of firewood.''

''There's no need. This isn't your job.'' She reached out to take the reins, and her hand closed over his.

For a moment they simply stared at each other.

Then he gave her a sardonic smile. "I suggest, Mrs. Potter, that you go inside with your girls. Unless you want your neighbors wondering what you're doing out here, holding hands with your new boarder."

He was aware of the wary look that came into her eyes and knew he'd hit a nerve.

Out of the corner of her eye Millie saw town gossips Lavinia Thurlong and Gladys Witherspoon just stepping out of Durfee's Mercantile. Both women stopped and stared in her direction, before beginning an animated conversation.

She turned, and without a word hurried into the house.

"I think this is enough firewood to see you through the night." Malachite deposited an armload of logs next to the big kitchen fireplace, then paused to watch as Millie rolled out dough for pies.

She worked quickly, efficiently, rolling, lifting, settling the dough over a mound of apples, then trimming the excess. When one pie was done she moved to the other, until two big apple pies were ready for baking.

Distracted, she glanced up. "Thank you, Malachite."

He studied five-year-old June, who had been given the task of snapping peas into a bowl. Her attitude was repentant after a long discussion with her mother about the value of honoring secrets. "Would you like me to set a fire in the dining room and parlor?"

"That isn't necessary," Millie said. "I'll see to it."

As he started toward the parlor, Millie called to his retreating back, "You're not supposed to be doing my work. You're a paying..."

He was gone.

With a shrug, she went back to her baking, all the while feeling slightly out of her element. After all these years of being on her own, it seemed strange having a man in the house tending to chores. Especially one so silent.

"Mama, I need help with my sums." Six-year-old May,

who had finished sweeping the front porch, stood solemnly in the doorway, her slate in her hand.

"All right, honey. We'll do them together after supper."

"But I want to do them now."

"I know you do. But if I stop now, supper won't be ready. And there's no telling how many guests might come knocking on our door. Besides, I need you to help your sister set the table."

Dejected, the little girl walked away.

With a sigh Millie made her way to the dining room. Would she always feel torn between her duties as mother and her duties as breadwinner? She hated putting the children's needs second. But without a helpmate, the most immediate need was always survival. And they simply couldn't survive unless they all pitched in and made sacrifices.

In the doorway she paused. Malachite was kneeling on the hearth, coaxing a thin flame from the pile of logs.

Muscles rippled along his arms as he carefully arranged a log, then held a flaming stick to the kindling. Soon the big room was warmed by a cheery fire.

April and May had already begun setting the table, laying out eight place settings.

Seeing this, Malachite arched a brow. "How do you know how many people to expect?"

April ducked her head, too shy to speak. It was May who said, "Mama's never sure, since this is the only boarding-house in town. So we always set out a few extra plates, just in case." The little girl's red curls bounced around an angelic face as she counted out the unmatched silverware. "Mama says most of the cowboys passing through would rather tolerate the swill that passes for stew over at Buck's saloon."

That statement had Malachite grinning. "Swill, is it? I'll bet a lot of the townspeople prefer good food to whiskey. Besides," he added, "if they stop here first, they know they'll be well fed. Then they can always spend the rest of their wages at Buck's later."

Millie found herself wondering if this man would be

among them. After all, he'd been alone a long time now, away from his childhood home, among people who weren't always friendly and accepting. He might prefer not only the whiskey but the excitement of the women at Buck's.

That thought added to her gloom. Without a word she returned to the kitchen to check on her pies.

The first dinner guest to arrive was Byron Conner. When April opened the door to admit him, he pushed past her to hang his hat on a peg in the front hall, then made his way to the dining room.

Millie was just placing a pitcher of buttermilk in the middle of the table. She forced herself out of her disturbing reverie and called out a welcome. "Hello, Byron."

He glanced around. "Where's your boarder?"

"Malachite's in his room, washing up for supper."

"His room, is it?" He frowned. Malachite Jewel was in town one day and already he'd insinuated himself into Millie Potter's home and her life. Even the fragrance of apple pies cooling by the window and the sight of freshly baked bread on a tray couldn't entirely erase Byron's dark thoughts.

He looked up as Marshal Quent Regan and his wife, Ruby, entered the room.

Millie was clearly pleased to see them. "Come right in and make yourselves comfortable," she invited.

"*Merci*." Ruby dimpled at the sight of the banker. Though happily married, she liked nothing better than to be surrounded by handsome men. "You did say I could start collecting payment for your gown, *chérie*?"

"That I did. Your meals in exchange for all the sewing you've done for me is more than fair. Make yourselves at home and I'll start serving supper in a few minutes."

"Where is Malachite?" Ruby asked.

"In his room," Byron said irritably. "Washing up."

Just then June entered, carrying a bowl of peas. "Malachite got his hands dirty carrying logs and building fires in all the rooms," she explained.

"Building fires?" Byron gave a sarcastic laugh. "Is that how he intends to pay for his room and board?"

"I thought I'd pay in the usual way. With cold, hard cash."

Millie turned to see Malachite lounging in the doorway. His thick black hair glinted with drops of water. He wore a clean white shirt and black pants tucked into black boots. Though his stance appeared casual, there was a dangerous light in his eyes. And his voice lowered to a challenge. "Now, that's something you'd know about, isn't it, Byron?"

The banker's head came up. "I pride myself on knowing a great deal about money."

"I never doubted it." Malachite deliberately turned his back on Byron while he greeted Quent and Ruby.

"I am so glad you've decided to stay." Ruby touched a hand to his sleeve.

"Why?" Malachite's brows drew together. "Why should it matter to you whether I stay or leave? Until last night, I was a stranger to you."

"*Oui.* Until last night. But Papa used to say in this world there are no strangers." Ruby's voice lowered with emotion. "There are only people we have not yet met. Today I know that you and I share something very special. The blood of Onyx Jewel."

Tight-lipped, he turned away and watched as Millie carried a platter of meat and potatoes to the table.

"Why don't you all take your places for supper," she urged.

"What about you?" Ruby asked.

Millie began to back away. With heated cheeks she said, "I thought I'd prepare a second platter. In case…" She was babbling, but she couldn't seem to stop herself. "In case anyone wants more."

"There's more than enough here, *chérie.* Sit down and join us. You've been working all day."

Before Millie could refuse, Malachite held her chair and she had no choice but to sit. When he took the seat beside her, she felt the press of his thigh against hers. Felt the brush of his sleeve along her arm.

Across the table, Byron was watching her carefully.

When the children filled their plates, Millie gave them a look. At once the three girls bowed their heads and silently mouthed a blessing before beginning to eat.

"My deputy will need a tray in the morning," Quent said as he dug into his meal. "Beau Baskin's done it again."

"Isn't it awfully early for Beau to be in jail?" Millie asked.

"Some days he gets started before noon." Quent drained his buttermilk and reached for the pitcher. "Other days he doesn't fall out of Buck's until after midnight. By the way, Millie, before he passed out he said he hoped you'd make your special cinnamon biscuits tomorrow morning. They're his favorites."

"I'll be happy to."

"I don't see why you should cater to the town drunk." Byron reached for another roll.

Millie arched a brow. "Beau Baskin may drink, but he's always been a perfect gentleman to me. Besides, I get paid to feed the prisoners. Why wouldn't I feed them what they like?"

"Because he's in jail. He's not one of your boarders, Millie." Byron's voice held a trace of impatience. "Maybe if you wouldn't make him so comfortable, he'd mend his ways."

"You're beginning to sound like Lavinia Thurlong and Gladys Witherspoon," Ruby said with a laugh. "Those two old hypocrites set themselves up as models for the whole town."

"What's wrong with that?" Byron set his fork down with a clatter. "I hope you're not going to hold out Beau Baskin as a model."

"Of course not," Ruby said patiently. "But there's room in this town for our differences. Beau has as much value as Lavinia or Gladys…or you, Byron."

Seeing that this might escalate into an argument, Millie pushed away from the table. "Excuse me. I'll see to the dessert and coffee."

Minutes later she circled the table, filling their cups, while April cut into the first apple pie and began serving it. Before the little girl could offer some to Malachite, Millie placed a bowl in front of him.

"What's that?" Byron asked.

"Bread pudding." Millie set the coffeepot in the middle of the table on a square of folded linen.

"Why does he get bread pudding while we're eating pie?" Byron demanded.

It occurred to Millie that Byron sounded exactly like a whining child. "Carmelita made it especially for Malachite. It was his father's favorite dessert."

She watched as Malachite took a bite, then closed his eyes. There was something else besides his face that he had inherited from his father. An ability to enjoy the simple pleasures of life.

Seeing everyone watching him, Malachite turned to Millie. "I hope you'll pass the rest of the pudding around. I wouldn't want to deprive anyone of this fine treat."

"Two desserts?" little May asked as her mother spooned bread pudding onto her plate. "We usually get this only at Christmas."

The others laughed as they dug in to their special treat. Millie sipped her coffee and glanced at their happy faces. For some strange reason, it had begun to feel like a special occasion.

"I'm sorry we can't stay." Quent draped his wife's shawl around her, then reached for his gun belt, hanging on a peg near the front door. "But with Beau in jail, I'll have to get back there so Deputy Spitz can go home for a couple of hours."

"Goodbye, *chérie*." Ruby kissed Millie's cheek. "It was a lovely dinner."

"I owe you a lot more," Millie said. "Come back anytime."

She turned in time to see Byron remove his hat from a peg.

"I wish I could stay. But Farley Duke is stopping by the bank to talk about another loan to expand his lumber mill." He leaned close and lowered his voice. "Maybe I could come by later and pay a visit?"

Millie shook her head. "I'm sorry, Byron. I still have to clean up and then help the girls with their schoolwork. After that, I know I'll be too tired to visit."

"Ah, yes. Your motherly duties." He glanced beyond her to the dining room, where he had left Malachite Jewel drinking a third cup of coffee. "Just remember what I said. You don't know anything about that man."

"I'll remember."

He thought about the kiss he had yet to claim. But she was already sweeping past him to open the front door. He stepped out into the cold night air.

Before he could say a word, she called a breathless, "Good night, Byron." And the door was firmly closed.

A short time later Millie wiped the table and put away the last of the dishes her daughters had washed and dried. On a warming ledge, bread dough was rising. The air was redolent with the spicy biscuits she'd prepared for baking in the morning.

She removed her soiled apron and dropped it in a basket of laundry she would tackle tomorrow. Then she made her way to the parlor. Despite her weariness, she would be unable to rest yet. She still had to help her daughters with their schoolwork.

In the doorway she stopped. A fire was ablaze, and the three little girls were gathered around the hearth with their slates.

In a corner of the room, half-hidden by shadows, sat Malachite. On the floor at his feet were his saddlebags, their contents scattered about the floor. She couldn't see what he held in his hands, but occasionally the firelight glinted off something she thought might be a knife.

At once, Byron's words of caution leaped into her mind. What did she know about this stranger?

She pushed the disquieting thoughts aside. ''All right, girls. Let's get to your schoolwork.'' Millie's voice revealed her weariness. The thought of the long hour ahead made her want to weep.

She heard April's spelling words and listened in silence while May read from her primer, helping occasionally when the little girl stumbled over a word. Then she called out a series of numbers to June and watched as her daughter dutifully finished her sums.

After checking her slate, she glanced up. ''That was very good, honey. You only had two wrong. Let's go over them so you'll know the proper way to figure the answers next time.''

All the while she worked with her children she was aware of Malachite seated in the shadows, watching and listening. She could feel his dark, penetrating stare as surely as any physical touch. She almost wished he'd stayed out at the Jewel ranch. At least then she'd have some relief from this tension. But the truth was, she desperately needed the money he would pay her.

Sensing her discomfort, Malachite returned everything to his saddlebags and tossed them over his shoulder before taking his leave. A short time later he heard footsteps on the stairs. From upstairs came giggles and whispers as the three little girls slipped into their nightclothes, then climbed into bed and mumbled their prayers.

When the house grew silent he unbuttoned his shirt and tossed it on the bed, then sat and slipped off his boots.

Barefoot, shirtless, he studied the wood carving he'd begun of a mother and her three little girls. It was crude, but already he had carved the outline of their heads. Tomorrow night, if there was time, he'd begin to refine it.

He rolled a cigarette and made his way in the darkness to

the parlor. There he held a stick to the fireplace, then lifted the flame to the tip of his cigarette and drew deeply, emitting a cloud of smoke. He tossed the stick in the fire, then crossed to the window and stared out at the darkened town.

Here and there a lantern flickered in the window of a home or business. On the hill he could make out the glint of moonlight on the church's bell.

It was a deceptively peaceful scene. But he'd had enough experience with places like this to know that beneath the calm, serene surface, there was probably plenty of trouble.

Funny. He'd sworn never to set foot in a town like this again. But here he was. And this time, he had no one to blame but himself. The choice had been his.

At the sound behind him he automatically spun around, his hand going to the gun at his waist.

Millie stood in the doorway, looking startled. "I'm sorry. I didn't mean to...I just wanted to..." She was already backing away.

"Sorry." He returned his gun to the holster. "It's just a reflex." He couldn't resist adding, to her discomfort, "Did you come downstairs to tuck me in, too?"

She stiffened her back and lifted her chin. In the darkness, he thought he detected little sparks shooting from her eyes.

The last thing she'd expected was to find him, practically naked, in her parlor. She couldn't help staring at his hair-roughened chest, at the muscles of his arms and shoulders.

To cover her embarrassment she used her most formal tone. "I just wanted to bank the fires before I go to sleep."

"I'll see to them."

"Thank you," she said stiffly.

"You're welcome." He wondered if she knew how desirable she looked in that prim, high-necked night shift. It was made of some gauzy material that clung to her body in a most provocative way, revealing the fullness of her breasts and the roundness of her hips.

What would she do if he kissed her again? The temptation

was so great he stayed where he was, afraid if he took even a single step toward her, he'd be lost.

She swallowed, and the sound seemed loud in her ears. "I'll say good-night now."

"Good night."

She turned and walked down the hall. For a moment there was no sound. Then he heard her light footfalls on the stairs.

He inhaled deeply, breathing in the scent of her that lingered in the room. Then he turned to the window and studied the sky awash with millions of stars.

This wasn't where he'd expected to be tonight. By now he'd figured to be halfway back to Montana Territory.

So why had he stayed? He knew it wasn't because of his father. Onyx Jewel's death had robbed him of any chance for vengeance. It certainly wasn't the opportunity to know his father's daughters, though there was a natural curiosity about them. As for belonging somewhere, he had his doubts. Though it had been a lifelong dream of his, he figured it was too late for that.

It was the mustangs, he knew. Nothing stirred his blood like the opportunity to be around horses. Especially a stallion that generated so much fear.

His eyes narrowed. Who was he kidding? The real reason that he was staying in this godforsaken town was the woman upstairs. The moment he'd seen Millie Potter, with that cloud of red hair and those eyes that were bluer than a Texas bluebell, he'd been lost.

He could still see her the night he'd arrived with fire in his eyes, itching for a fight. While the rest of the household had practically fainted at the sight of him, she'd stood up to him, those small hands fisted at her hips, ready to do battle.

Underneath that sweet, docile face she showed to others was grit and determination and fire.

Firewoman. That would have been her Comanche name. That was the name he would secretly carry in his heart whenever he thought about her. And it was a good bet he would do a great deal of thinking about her in the days to come.

He tossed the last of his cigarette on the flames before banking the fire. And wished he could bank the fire inside him as easily.

Chapter Six

"April," Millie called from the foot of the stairs. "Breakfast is ready. You're going to make us late. I'm driving the wagon again today."

"April didn't get out of bed," June said over a mouthful of eggs. "When I asked her why, she said she was hot."

"Why didn't you tell me sooner?" Millie set a platter of sizzling pork on the table before she made her way up the stairs.

In the room shared by the three sisters, she sat on the edge of her oldest daughter's bed. "What is it, April honey?"

"I don't feel good." The little girl's voice was muffled beneath the covers.

Millie touched a hand to her daughter's forehead. "You have a fever. Where do you hurt?"

"My tummy," the little girl said.

"Oh, you poor thing." Millie got to her feet. "You stay right there in bed. I'll fix you some broth later. Would you like anything now?"

April shook her head.

Millie brushed the damp hair from her daughter's forehead. "I'll be back in a little while. As soon as the others are through eating."

Just as she made her way downstairs, the back door was pushed open on a blast of cold air, and Birdie returned from her breakfast delivery to the marshal's office. Malachite trailed her, carrying a load of logs.

"We won't be going to school today, children," Millie called.

"Why not, Mama?" May and June looked up from the table. Their disappointment was evident. Going to school was the highlight of their days. Especially on these bleak winter mornings.

"April has a fever. I don't think it's anything serious. But she can't go to school, and I can't take you or I'd have to leave her here alone."

"But I know all my spelling words," May said with sadness.

"And I have all my sums finished," June moaned.

Malachite deposited the logs, then bent to add one to the fire. With his back to them he muttered, "I could take the girls. I'm heading out to the ranch anyway."

"You wouldn't mind?" Millie watched as he got to his feet and turned to face her. As always, she was struck by the dark, brooding look of him. He had the ability, with just one look, to reduce her to a blushing, stammering child.

"It's no trouble."

She glanced at her two daughters, who were silently pleading, and at Birdie, who was watching her expectantly. How could she deny them? "All right. If you're sure you don't mind. When their school day is over, if you're not ready to bring them home yet, they can stay with Carmelita until you finish your work at the ranch."

He nodded, while the girls broke into wide smiles.

"Mama." From upstairs came April's plaintive cry.

Millie hurried away, then returned minutes later to fill a glass with water, before climbing the stairs once more.

As she sat on the edge of her daughter's bed, a shadow fell over them and Millie turned to see Malachite standing in the doorway.

"What is it?" she asked.

"Your daughters tell me that April has suffered from these fevers for a long time."

Millie nodded.

"I brought something that might help." He held out a small packet.

Out of the corner of her eye she saw her daughter cringe. "I'm...not sure. What is it?"

He took a step closer. "Dried herbs. My mother, Evening Star, was the healer of our village."

"Herbs?"

At her hesitation he said gruffly, "A sprinkle of thistle, a handful of wormwood, a smattering of cow dung."

"Oh dear."

He opened the packet and sprinkled some in her glass of water. "I couldn't help teasing. Don't be afraid. They're simple herbs. I promise you, they'll help."

Though April lifted pleading eyes to her mother, Millie held the glass to her lips. "It won't hurt to try, honey."

When she saw that she couldn't win the argument, the little girl closed her eyes and drained the glass. When her eyes opened, there was a look of surprise in them.

"Was it awful?" Millie whispered.

"Not...not so bad," she admitted after Malachite walked away.

Minutes later the others gathered in the doorway.

"I'll take your slate to school so Miss Pearl can check your sums," May offered.

"And I'll ask Miss Pearl to write your new spelling words alongside mine on my slate." June was not about to be outdone by her older sister.

"Oh, no," April moaned. "I just remembered. I was supposed to take care of Amber today while Miss Pearl worked with June and Daniel on their new words."

"Don't worry," Birdie assured her. "Gil and I can take care of Amber." She was secretly pleased at the thought of working closely with Gil.

They fussed and fretted over April until Millie finally announced, "All right, girls. It's time to go."

They trailed her down the stairs. At the back door she kissed her daughters goodbye and watched as they climbed into the back of the wagon with Birdie. Malachite tied his horse to the back, then climbed to the driver's seat.

With a wave they were gone.

Minutes later April moaned and called for more water. As Millie hurried to her side, she found herself wondering how many trips she would make up and down these stairs before the day ended. And just what herbs were in that packet of Malachite's. Perhaps it was best if she never knew.

"Afternoon, Millie. Something smells good."

Millie, stirring a pot of soup at the fireplace, whirled around, looking slightly frazzled. "Good afternoon, Byron. You don't usually stop by for lunch."

"I rarely have the time. But I thought it would give me a chance to see you alone." He smiled and stepped closer.

Just then the back door opened and Arlo Spitz called, "Hope I'm in time for lunch."

Millie gave him a smile. "Right on time, Deputy. Come on in."

He snatched off his hat and headed toward a basin and pitcher of water on the other side of the room.

While Arlo washed, Byron frowned at this intrusion. When Arlo was done, he made his way to the dining room, leaving the two alone.

Byron studied Millie while she worked. "I'd like to talk to you now, Millie."

"All right." She lifted down bowls and began ladling soup. "Go ahead, Byron. What did you want to talk about?"

For long moments he stared at her back. Then, with a sigh of exasperation, he said, "It's about your boarder."

"What about him?" She set the bowls on a large tray, then began slicing chunks of hot, crusty bread.

"I hope you're remembering what I said…"

"Afternoon, Millie."

From the doorway came the sound of women's voices. Millie looked up to see Jade and Ruby, arm in arm, beaming at her.

"How good to see you, ladies," she called. "Make yourselves comfortable. Lunch will be on the table in minutes."

"Can we help you with anything, *chérie?*" Ruby asked.

Millie shook her head. "It's all done. Just sit yourselves down."

The two sisters walked into the dining room, where they could be overheard talking to the deputy.

Millie returned to her tray and added freshly churned butter. "You were saying, Byron?"

He couldn't hide his frustration. On a sigh of impatience he muttered, "Would you mind giving me your attention?"

Her hand paused in midair. She turned slightly.

"I think it's important that we talk about that mysterious half-breed you've allowed into your home."

Millie's eyes flashed before she turned and picked up the heavy tray. With her back to him she said, "I'll remind you that you're a guest in my home. And so is Malachite Jewel. If you ever use that term again, you will not be welcome." She turned to face him. "Is that understood?"

He flushed. "I only meant…"

"I understand exactly what you meant. And now you understand me."

She walked out of the room and into the dining room, where she began to serve her guests.

Just as she was about to take her place at the table, she heard April's voice calling "Mama."

Excusing herself, she hurried up the stairs.

"How are you feeling, honey?" She perched on the edge of the bed and touched a hand to her daughter's forehead.

"Much better. But my clothes are wet."

"That's good news. That means your fever has broken." Millie hurried away to fetch clean nightclothes and a cool, damp cloth, which she used to sponge April's face and neck.

"I made soup. Think you could try a little?"

The little girl shook her head.

"Then try to sleep awhile. I'll be back soon." Millie bent and kissed her cheek, then hurried away to see to her guests.

In the dining room she poured coffee and passed around the last slices of apple pie and bread pudding.

"Did I hear one of your daughters?" Byron didn't bother to hide his agitation. "Aren't they all at school?"

"April's not feeling well. She's upstairs in bed." Millie filled his cup before moving on to fill the others.

"Not feeling well?" Byron's brows drew together, as if he were deep in thought. Then he said, "I suppose you should have expected it."

"Expected what?"

"The curse to begin. First illness, then…"

"Not another word," Millie said sharply, cutting off what he was about to say.

"You're looking a little tired," Jade said. "Maybe we ought to send you to bed, too, Millie."

"I'm fine." Millie flushed. "I can manage."

"I'm sure you can." Jade pressed her hands to her growing middle. "I only hope I can do as well when my baby comes. Oh my, Millie. I don't believe I've ever had such an appetite. Everything you make tastes so good."

"That's because you're eating for two," Millie said with a smile.

"For three," Ruby corrected.

"That's right. Now you see why you have to eat." Millie set a second slice of pie in front of Jade. "Go ahead. It's just a tiny one."

With a delighted laugh, Jade polished off another piece of apple pie.

"Thanks for lunch, Millie." Deputy Spitz pushed away from the table. "I'd better get back to the jail."

"I have to leave, too." Ruby set down her empty cup and got to her feet. "I promised Lavinia Thurlong a new bonnet in time for Sunday's service."

"I'll walk with you." Jade got up slowly, clutching the table for support.

Millie walked them to the door, then returned to the dining room, where Byron Conner was still sitting at the table. He looked up when she entered.

"I can't believe you'd let your daughters go off to school with a stranger."

Millie began collecting the empty bowls and setting them on a serving tray. "How did you know Malachite drove the girls?"

"From the window of my office I saw them leave in your wagon. How could you do that?"

"Malachite isn't a stranger." Patiently Millie stacked the bowls, then added spoons, glasses, cups. "The Jewel family has been here in Texas longer than the town of Hanging Tree."

"But Malachite's only been here for days. And already you're treating him like one of the family."

"Byron…"

He held up a hand. "I'm only warning you for your own good, Millie. You're far too trusting. Letting him into your home is bad enough. But trusting him with your children…" He shook his head for emphasis. "The fool has stated his intention of capturing Diablo. And we all know what that means. Those little girls are far too precious to trust to any passing trail bum with a curse over his head."

"Oh, Byron. I just don't have time for…"

"Mama," came April's plaintive voice.

Millie set down the tray and started out of the room.

Behind her Byron gave a hiss of annoyance. "And I foolishly thought I'd have some time alone with you." To her retreating back he called, "I'll let myself out."

Millie made no reply. She was already halfway up the stairs.

Millie glanced out the window at the gathering shadows. The sun had long ago slipped behind Widow's Peak, casting lavender ribbons across the sky. The air had grown colder, sharper, with a bitter wind blowing in from the north.

Drawing her shawl around her, she stepped out the back door and crossed to the woodpile. It had begun to drizzle. A cold, bitter rain that chilled clear to the bone. She shivered, thinking about her children out on such a night.

Minutes later, her arms straining under the pile of logs, she scanned the horizon for any sign of the wagon.

Malachite and the girls should have been home hours ago. Where were they? What had gone wrong?

Oh, why had Byron said those awful things? Now that he had planted the idea in her mind she was being tormented with images of all manner of terrible things. Malachite, dark and dangerous, fighting to the death with Diablo, equally dark and dangerous. As the images grew, Malachite and Diablo became one wild creature, rising up, knife in hand, the hand becoming powerful, deadly hooves that were crushing her helpless daughters.

Ridiculous. She was ashamed of herself for entertaining such thoughts. She shook her head in disgust and forced herself to keep busy. There were fires to tend, a table to set, food to cook.

"Mama."

She had come to dread that sound. It seemed like a hundred times today she'd been summoned up the stairs for water, a cool cloth, a sip of broth. And as the day progressed and April's fever had abated, she had become even more demanding.

"What is it, honey?" she asked as she stepped into the bedroom.

"It's so dark in here. I can't see."

"Yes. Of course. I'm sorry, April." Dutifully Millie held a match to the wick of the lantern. Soon the bedroom was bathed in light.

"Where are May and June?" the little girl asked, as she had a dozen times.

"I don't know. They're late." Millie turned away to hide the fear she knew would be in her eyes.

"But why?"

"It's Malachite's first day at the Jewel ranch. He probably had more chores than he'd anticipated." She strove for a lightness she didn't feel. "Can I bring you up some supper?"

The little girl shook her head. "I'm not very hungry."

"All right. I'll be back soon." Millie descended the stairs and hurried to remove the apple cobbler from the hot coals. Then she busied herself in the dining room, stoking the fire, setting the table. As she arranged serving trays and filled a pitcher with milk, she found herself hoping there would be no additional guests for dinner. She didn't think she could bear making polite conversation with her neighbors. Perhaps the rain would keep them all indoors for the night.

For the hundredth time she peered into the darkness, watching for any sign of a wagon.

As she turned away, she buried her face in her hands and struggled to hold back the tears that threatened. Why, oh, why had she allowed her children to leave this morning with Malachite Jewel? What if Byron was right? Oh, sweet heaven, what was she to do? She couldn't leave her sick daughter to go out searching for the others. And she couldn't stand being here and not knowing where they were. But the curse. Oh, sweet heaven, the curse of Diablo had her terrified.

She was so distracted she didn't hear the crunch of wagon wheels or the muted sounds of voices. Suddenly the door was thrust inward on a blast of frigid air, and the children bounded in, followed by Malachite.

"Oh! Where have you been?" Millie demanded.

"We had a grand adventure, Mama." Little June danced excitedly into her mother's outstretched arms. Her hair and clothes were stiff with what appeared to be dried blood.

Blood?

"What in the world...?"

"Malachite taught us the Comanche ways," May added.

"He killed a deer with only a knife." Birdie's awe was

evident in her voice. Both she and May also bore traces of the same stiff substance. "And then he wrapped us in the wet hide so we'd stay warm and dry."

Millie couldn't help herself. As she bent and gathered the little girls into her embrace, all her fear suddenly turned to anger. Glancing over their heads, she shot Malachite a look of pure venom. "How could you keep these children away so long? You knew about the curse. You know I expected them home hours ago, and that I would be worried."

"But, Mama, we—"

As little June started to speak, Millie said sharply, "Go upstairs and change out of those clothes. When you've washed up, we'll have supper."

"But—"

"Right now. Without another word."

"Yes'm." Dejected, the two little girls turned away.

"My mama will be worried, too. Good night, ma'am. Thanks again, Malachite." Birdie excused herself and raced toward her own home.

When they were alone, Millie turned the full force of her fury on Malachite.

"Byron warned me. But I didn't want to listen. In fact, like a fool I defended you. And all the time that I was here, all alone and worried sick about my babies, you…you were so busy teaching them some foolish Comanche trick with your knife, you never even bothered to think about my feelings."

Tears welled up in her eyes and she blinked them back. She wouldn't cry. Not in front of this hateful man.

With her hands balled into fists at her sides, she faced him. "What do you have to say for yourself?"

He studied her for a long moment, noting the heaving of her chest and the tears she was determined not to shed.

In a quiet tone he said, "I'll see to the horses and wagon."

She stared in stunned disbelief as he walked out the back door, closing it firmly behind him. Leaving her no way to vent her fury.

* * *

"Supper's ready," Millie snapped. "If you can spare the time."

Malachite, returning from the shed, closed the door and dropped an armload of firewood on the hearth. Then he rolled his sleeves and washed before heading toward the dining room and taking his place at the table.

"Are we alone tonight?" May asked.

"Looks like." Millie ladled food onto their plates.

"What is this, Mama?"

May and June, sensing their mother's still-simmering temper, were unusually subdued.

"The last of the stew." Millie set a plate of biscuits on the table, along with freshly churned butter and a little bowl of fruit conserve.

"But there's no meat in mine." June lifted a spoonful and watched it drip back into the bowl.

"There are a few pieces. That's the last of the beef. Tomorrow I'll see if Rufus Durfee will trade me some meat for a few dozen eggs." As Millie filled their glasses and was about to take her place at the table, she heard April calling from upstairs.

With a weary sigh she turned away. A short time later, after two more trips up the stairs, she returned to the dining room and woodenly began to eat.

"Is April better or worse?" Malachite asked. It was the first he'd spoken since returning from the shed. His tone, Millie noted, was far from repentant.

"The fever's broken." Millie lifted her coffee to her lips and discovered that it had grown cold. She set it aside and crossed to a sideboard to retrieve the apple cobbler.

When everyone had been served, she cut a piece for herself and carried it to the table. She managed three bites before April's cries drifted down the stairs.

Gathering her dishes, she deposited them in the kitchen, then proceeded up the stairs to comfort her daughter.

When she returned she found the table cleared. In the kitchen, May was washing the dishes, and June was drying them. Malachite was reaching over their heads, placing the clean ones in a cupboard.

"That isn't necessary." Millie hated the tone of her voice. But it couldn't be helped. She'd reached the end of her patience. "As I've told you before, you're a paying boarder. There's no need to help with the chores."

He continued as though he hadn't even heard her.

Through gritted teeth she said to her daughters, "When you've finished here, go up to bed."

"What about my sums, Mama?" June asked.

"And my spelling words?" May added.

"They'll have to keep until tomorrow. Right now you're going to bed. Besides, judging by the sound of that wind and rain, it may be sleeting or snowing by morning." Millie actually hoped it would be. She'd already made up her mind that the girls would have to miss school until April's fever was gone. There was no way she would allow them to ride with Malachite Jewel again.

A few minutes later the two little girls dutifully headed toward the stairs, with Millie following. She could feel Malachite's dark gaze practically burning into her back, but she was determined to ignore him.

She was weary beyond belief. She couldn't wait for this day to end so she could fall into bed. She undressed quickly and pulled on a night shift. Unpinning her hair, she brushed it long and loose, then tossed a shawl around her shoulders and made her way to her daughters' room.

The little girls were already snuggled between the covers. Millie sat on the edge of June's bed, prepared to hear their prayers.

"Mama," June whispered. "Why are you so sad?"

"Because," she said patiently, "I was worried about you."

"But we tried to tell you what happened. Why wouldn't you let us tell you about our adventure?"

"All right." She struggled to hold herself together for one more minute. "Tell me about your...adventure. Birdie said

Malachite wanted to teach you the Comanche ways by killing a deer.''

"No, Mama. That came later," the little girl said. "First came the accident.''

"Accident?" Millie's heart nearly stopped.

"A wheel came off the wagon. The team broke loose. We nearly tipped over. In fact we would have if Malachite hadn't leaped down and righted it with his own hands. We were all crying. But Malachite shouted for us not to worry. And after he got us out of the wagon, he ran and caught the team and said he'd have to fix the wagon 'cause we were too far to walk.''

"Was anyone hurt?" Millie's pulse was racing at the image that had crept into her mind.

"No, ma'am. But then it started to rain, and there wasn't any shelter. So Malachite killed a deer and skinned it and covered us with the skin to keep us warm and dry. And then he finished fixing the wagon and brought us home. And all the way here he was worried about you.''

"About…me?"

"Yes'm. He said knowing the kind of mother you were, you'd be worried sick. But Birdie said you'd understand." Little June caught her mother's hand. "You do, don't you, Mama?''

"I…yes." She swallowed. She understood so much now. She only hoped it wasn't too late to make amends.

After tucking her daughters into their beds, she walked down the stairs, marshaling her courage for the task ahead. And prayed she'd find the words to convey her regret at her unforgivable behavior.

Finding the kitchen and dining room empty, she made her way to the parlor. It was empty, as well.

Straightening her shoulders, she walked to Malachite's bedroom and knocked. Hearing no reply, she knocked louder. The door slid open a crack.

"Malachite." She pushed the door wider and stepped inside.

The bedroom was empty. On the night table was a block of wood that had been fashioned into a carving of a woman and children. She picked it up and ran her hands over the smooth surface, shocked at the fact that, despite its lack of refinements, it already resembled her and her daughters. Feeling somehow that she had violated a privacy, she set it down quickly and glanced around. In one corner of the room was a pile of wet, discarded clothes forming a puddle on the floor. She noticed that Malachite's hat and cowhide jacket were missing from the peg on the wall.

He was gone. She gritted her teeth and swallowed a wave of bitter disappointment.

Probably gone to Buck's saloon, she thought. She couldn't blame him. At least there he wouldn't have to explain himself. At Buck's a man could find some peace. Or if he chose, he could find himself a woman who wouldn't act like a shrew. A woman who would know how to smile and make a man feel like a man.

That was something she seemed to have forgotten how to do entirely.

Chapter Seven

In the shed, Malachite rolled up his sleeves. After a long, hard day of wrangling cattle with the cowboys and then dealing with the wagon and the frightened little girls, he was weary beyond belief. But this was one more chore that couldn't be put off. He slipped the knife from his waist.

Hanging from a wooden beam was the carcass of the deer he'd killed out on the trail. With sure, even strokes he began to gut it. With each slice of the blade he thought about Millie's angry reaction.

Comanche tricks. Is that what she thought of him? A fool who would endanger innocent children, just to teach them a few tricks?

He'd expected better of Millie Potter. Somehow he'd convinced himself that she was nobler than most people. That she wouldn't judge him by his ancestry. Wouldn't care that he was the bastard son of a worse bastard, or that his mother was a member of a warrior tribe whose people had declared war on her people.

Blood drenched his hands and seeped along his arms, but he took no notice. All his thoughts centered on Millie. He shouldn't be surprised by her reaction. After all, he'd expected her to be concerned when her children hadn't arrived home by dark. It was natural for a parent to be worried, especially since she'd entrusted her children to a stranger.

And she was bound to note the dramatic change in the weather. And the truth was, he hadn't given her much reason to trust him.

But something else kept working at the edges of his mind. Now he had time to mull over what she'd first said when she'd confronted him. *Byron warned me. But I didn't want to listen. In fact, like a fool, I defended you.*

As he began carving up the meat, his eyes narrowed with sudden realization. Of course. That fool banker had been here, planting seeds of distrust. In his mind he could imagine the smug look on Byron Conner's face as he fed Millie's fears.

Millie. When she'd confronted him, she'd been fighting back tears. Tears. That bothered him more than he cared to admit. And she'd looked so exhausted. Drained. And why not? She worked from sunup to sundown without a break. She took on chores nobody else in the town would dream of in order to keep her little family together. He'd watched her. Trading eggs and butter for supplies at Durfee's Mercantile. Measuring out miserly amounts of flour and sugar for her baking. Stretching the meat to last one more meal. And on top of all that, right now she was probably more worried about little April's illness than she let on.

April. The little girl seemed more affected by the loss of her father than the other two. Probably because she could almost remember him. Almost remember a time when her mother wasn't alone and struggling to get through one day after another. Almost remember the sounds of laughter and teasing and…loving.

He continued carving up the meat, dropping the chunks and strips of bloody flesh onto the hide stretched out on the dirt floor of the shed. And with each stroke of his knife, he felt his anger dissipating.

None of this had been Millie's fault. Maybe he should have explained about the accident along the trail. Even if she wasn't in a mood to hear, maybe he should have forced her

to listen. At least then she would have known the truth.
Would have known how close they all came to disaster.

His mother had always said that one of his biggest short-
comings was his temper. That temper had caused him to flee
his village in a rage when Evening Star had refused to give
him the name of his father. That temper had caused many a
barroom brawl when some cowboy, drunk on cheap whiskey,
had slandered his heritage. And later, that temper had caused
him to flee to the wilderness after he'd been forced to pay
the highest price of all. A price that even now he couldn't
allow himself to think about without unbearable pain.

When he finished with the bloody carnage, he cleaned his
knife, then plunged his arms into a bucket of water. He
pulled on his cowhide jacket, then gathered up the hide containing the meat and made his way to the root cellar, where
he carefully stored the bounty against the coming winter.

A short time later he climbed the stairs and stepped into
the warm, fragrant kitchen.

Denied her chance to apologize, Millie had looked for
other ways to make amends. Despite the lateness of the hour,
she heated a big kettle of water, then retrieved Malachite's
wet clothes and began scrubbing. When they were clean, she
strung a line across one end of the kitchen and hung them
to dry.

That done, she set a pan of biscuits on the coals, then
rolled out fresh bread dough and began kneading. With each
slap of the heel of her hand, with each vicious punch, she
berated herself.

Malachite Jewel had kindly offered to see her children
safely to school and back. And how had she thanked him?
By attacking him the moment he walked in the door. By
suggesting that he had somehow enjoyed being caught out
on the trail, far from civilization, in freezing rain, with three
helpless little girls.

She closed her eyes a moment against the wave of shame.

How could she have behaved in such a horrible, spiteful manner?

She covered the dough with a linen square and set it aside to rise. Then she started a fresh pot of coffee. When Mick occasionally joined his friends at the saloon, he'd always been grateful for some strong black coffee on his return home. And biscuits, she thought, removing the pan from the coals and arranging several freshly baked cinnamon biscuits on a plate. Mick always claimed it took the edge off the whiskey.

Weary, she pressed a hand to the small of her back. The aroma of the coffee was too tempting. She poured herself a cup and carried it to the table. She would drink this and go to bed. Her apology would have to wait. There was no point staying up for Malachite. He might not come back until dawn. And even then, there was no telling whether or not he would be receptive to what she had to say. She wouldn't blame him if he packed up and left forever. He could always take a room above Buck's, where he'd be guaranteed plenty of high-stakes poker games and a few fancy women thrown in for good measure.

She took a sip of coffee and let it warm her. The heat of the kitchen lulled her. Resting her chin on her hands, she wondered what sort of drunk Malachite would be. She'd heard of men who couldn't handle the whiskey. Men who beat their women. Somehow she couldn't picture Malachite Jewel doing that.

Her mother claimed her father had always just tumbled into bed and snored loud enough to wake the dead. As for Mick, he'd always come home looking for loving. The thought brought a smile to her lips. The first smile she'd permitted herself in hours.

With her chin still resting on her hands, she closed her eyes. Just for a moment, she promised herself. Then she would finish her coffee and go up to bed.

It was the last coherent thought she had before she drifted to sleep.

* * *

For a moment Malachite was puzzled. In the kitchen firelight, strange shadows twisted and danced. With gun drawn, he leaned his weight against the door, shutting out the icy wind. The shadows went still. When he drew closer, he realized they were his pants and shirt, smelling of lye soap and hanging on a line.

Curious, he stepped beyond them, then stopped short.

Millie was seated at the table. Her hands were resting on the tabletop, her cheek pressed to her hands. Alongside her elbow was a cup of coffee that had grown cool.

This was a Millie he'd never seen before. Her thick red hair had been brushed long and loose and fell provocatively over one eye. Her nightgown of white muslin, with softly rounded neck and long sleeves, would have been modest except for the fact that it had slipped, revealing one pale creamy shoulder. Her shawl lay pooled at her feet on the floor.

He holstered his gun, then dropped to his knees beside her and studied her by the light of the fire. Her breathing was slow and easy. With each rise and fall of her chest, he felt his own tightening. She was so lovely. The whiteness of her skin fascinated him. As did the freckles that paraded across her nose. Such a tiny, upturned nose. He counted more freckles on her shoulder and wondered if there might be freckles on other, more intimate places. That thought brought a rush of heat.

Everything about her was small and delicate. And yet there was such strength in her. And dignity. She had carved a place for herself and her family here in this rough town. And though she worked hard and made her home a pleasant place to be, it was plain that it wasn't just her good food or her spotless housekeeping that attracted people. It was Millie herself. She was fun to be around. She genuinely liked people. And they, in turn, responded to her.

She sighed in her sleep and his gaze was drawn to her lips. They were slightly parted, perfectly sculpted. Lips made for kissing. That thought brought more heat.

He continued to kneel beside her, debating whether to leave her asleep at the table or to carry her up the stairs to her bed. If she were to stay here, she would be only a step away from his room. From his bed. Dangerous, he thought. But carrying her to her own bedroom would be equally dangerous.

The problem was solved when she stirred, then opened her eyes.

"Malachite." She lifted her head and started to rise. "I must have... How late is it?"

"Sh." He caught her hand, holding her still. "I'm sorry I caused you so much worry today."

"No. No." She touched a finger to his lips to still his words.

He struggled to show no emotion as he absorbed the sexual jolt. He could have stayed like this forever, with her touch so gentle upon him and her eyes all soft and heavy-lidded with sleep.

Very slowly he stood, drawing her up with him.

"May and June told me what happened," she whispered. "I feel so terrible about the way I behaved. If it hadn't been for you, I might have lost my daughters today. And what if April hadn't been sick this morning and I was driving the team? I shudder to think what would have happened to all of us."

The thought had already crossed his mind. "Then I'm glad it happened to me and that I was able to keep it from becoming a disaster. But I'm still sorry to have caused you such pain. I could see how concerned you were."

She lowered her head, avoiding his eyes. "I was a shrew."

He caught her chin, forcing her to look at him. "You love your children. You had a right."

"But I wouldn't let you explain."

"My fault." He stared down into her lovely face and felt his heart hitch. "I didn't try very hard to explain. I do that sometimes. Just shut down. It's the only way I can control my temper."

"I don't usually lose control of mine. I tend to get past my anger by throwing myself into my work."

He nodded. "That's what I did. Out in your shed. Worked off my temper on the deer."

She gave him an incredulous look. "You were in the shed?"

He nodded. "Carving up the deer I killed. I figured you could use the meat."

He had been out in the bitter cold, doing a kindness for her. The knowledge warmed her. And shamed her. "And here I thought…" Her mouth closed. She swallowed.

"You thought what?"

"Nothing." He hadn't gone to Buck's to cool off. That realization brought a smile to her lips. "I happened to spy your wet clothes in your room, so I washed them."

"I noticed. Why were you in my room?"

"I went looking for you. To apologize." Still feeling shaky, she said, "I made you some coffee."

"Smells good." But he didn't turn away or lower his hand. Instead, he moved his fingers slowly from her chin to her cheek. "You smell good."

She blushed. "I probably smell like soap."

"You always smell like your baking." His voice lowered, and his hand moved seductively along the smooth skin of her face. "I'll never be able to smell cinnamon and spice again without thinking of you."

His words brought a deeper flush to her cheeks. "I'll get you some—" she tried to back away, but he held her fast "—coffee and biscuits."

"It isn't food I want." He stared directly into her eyes.

She felt a jolt that had her trembling. His meaning was far too clear. "You've been out in the cold shed for hours and…"

"I know a way to get warm." His hand tightened at her shoulder, holding her close when she would have run.

He could feel her nerves jumping, could see the fear in her eyes. It only added to her charm.

"You can't, Malachite. We mustn't."

"You're telling that to the wrong person. I'm a savage, remember?" Though he tried to soften the threat with a smile, there was a dangerous glint in his eyes, leaving her in no doubt that he meant every word. "I don't have to abide by the rules of civilized society. I take what I want. Without asking permission."

"You're just saying that—" she stiffened as he lowered his mouth to hers "—to frighten me."

"Is that what I'm doing?" He brushed his lips lightly over hers and heard her moan.

It wasn't fear she was feeling; it was pleasure. The sweetest pleasure in the world. But even as she thrilled to his kiss, an alarm bell sounded in her mind.

"This is wrong." Already breathless, she reached up, intending to push him away. Instead, she found herself raking her fingers through his hair, dragging his mouth more fully to hers. Every part of her strained into the kiss.

Sweet heaven, it was even better than the first time. She thought she'd imagined it. The heat. The passion. The danger. But there it was again, building, teasing, taunting her. And she was helpless to stop it.

"It doesn't feel wrong to me." He dragged his lips from hers to roam her face. "It feels so right." He kissed the corner of her lips, the curve of her cheek, the arch of her brow. And with each press of his mouth she sighed and felt her resolve weaken.

She could feel needs beginning to surface. Needs so long denied. For the sake of survival, she'd buried them under layers of responsibility. Now they rose, stripping her of common sense. All she could think of was this man in her arms, whose kisses brought her pleasure beyond belief.

"This is madness." She struggled for some semblance of sanity. "I need time to think."

"Don't think." His clever hands moved along her sides, tracing the outline of the small, slender body beneath the filmy nightgown. When his thumbs encountered the swell of her breasts, they paused to stroke until he felt her nipples harden. Her gasp stirred his blood and tightened his loins.

"Just feel." He saw her eyes glaze before his mouth covered hers, swallowing her protest. He took the kiss deeper, feasting on her sweetness.

She tasted as cool, as clean as a mountain stream. And yet, beneath the sweetness, there was a deeper, darker flavor. A sultry hint of passion, of seduction. This was a complex woman, capable of so many emotions, which she kept carefully hidden. And he had the sudden urge to uncover all of them. And savor.

When at last his lips left hers, he moved his mouth along the smoothness of her throat.

With a little moan of pleasure she let her head fall back, giving him access.

He shoved aside the loose neckline, almost tearing the fabric in his impatience. And as his lips closed over her breast, his hands, those strong, knowing hands, explored and aroused until her breath was coming in short, ragged bursts.

His vision blurred with passion as he nibbled and suckled and drove them both higher, until, with uneven breaths and soft moans, he reclaimed her lips. But it wasn't enough. He wanted more. Wanted all. And he could have it. It was within his grasp.

As he took the kiss deeper, he sensed that the woman in his arms was beyond stopping him. He could take her here, now. That knowledge, that power sang through his veins. He felt himself standing on a precipice. One step, one move and they would both tumble into space. And they could soar.

Still, he held back. Dimly, as he lifted his head, he could hear her voice, strained, breathless, against his throat. Each word, each vibration brought him closer to the edge.

"Malachite. This isn't—I need time."

He stared down at her, eyes huge in a pale, lovely face, her heart stuttering wildly. He wanted her as he'd never wanted anyone. Wanted her warm and naked in his bed. But he'd never taken a woman against her will. Though this time he'd come dangerously close.

Did she know how close they'd both come to crossing the line?

He let out his breath on a long, slow sigh. With great care he released her and lowered his hands to his sides. "I think I'd better take that coffee now."

The heat that had enveloped her just moments ago slipped away, leaving her chilled. "I'll—I'll get it."

As she started to turn away he caught her by the upper arm. At once the heat flared between them, and he pulled his hand away as though burned.

"No. I'll get it. You go on up to bed."

"But I…"

He forced himself to take a step away, needing to put some distance between them. Even then he could feel the heat pulsing, drawing him back. She wasn't safe yet. Neither of them was. "I said go to bed, Millie. You don't want to be here now."

She heard the urgency in his tone. Recognized the danger in his eyes. Eyes that seemed to see clear through to her soul. "All right." She darted a look at him as she backed away toward the stairs. "Good night, Malachite."

He listened to the sound of her footsteps on the stairs. When she was gone, he bent and picked up her shawl, lying forgotten on the floor. He gathered the soft fabric to his face, inhaling the clean, spicy fragrance that still lingered in the folds.

What in the hell had he been thinking of? The truth was, he hadn't been thinking at all. She'd caught him in a weak moment. He'd have to be more careful in the future. If he didn't watch it, he'd be repeating the sins of his father. And that could be disastrous.

A woman like Millie Potter had no need of a man like him.

Chapter Eight

Dawn light was barely breaking over the horizon when Millie entered the shed. Her breath misted in the cold air as she hung the lantern on a hook and began gathering eggs in a basket. While she worked she thought about Malachite. He had been her last thought as she'd drifted to sleep, her first thought upon awakening.

That scene last night had convinced her that she'd made a terrible mistake. His presence was turning her neat, orderly life upside down. He was unlike any man she'd ever known. He wasn't disciplined like Marshal Regan, or methodical like Cal McCabe. He lacked the gentleness of Reverend Dan Simpson, or the smooth polish of Byron Conner. He had a way of looking at her that unnerved her. As though he knew more than he let on. And a way of smiling—suddenly, without warning—that could make her heart soar.

And when he touched her... Oh, sweet heaven, when he touched her, she lost all decency. All common sense. The man was dangerous. Hadn't he warned her he was a savage? She had no way of knowing how to deal with him.

She looked up when the door opened, then felt the heat rush to her cheeks when she spied the object of her thoughts, looking even more dangerous in the light of morning. And twice as handsome, she thought, dressed in the clothes she'd washed for him and with his hair slicked back.

"Good morning." He leaned into the door, latching it against the cold wind.

"What are you doing up so early?" To avoid looking at him she nudged the straw with her foot, uncovering another egg.

"Last night I noticed this latch was working loose. Thought I'd repair it before I go off to work at the ranch."

With his back to the door he watched her. This morning she wore a gown of faded yellow, reminding him of a buttercup. He itched to touch her. Instead, he remained where he was, his hands clenched firmly at his sides, a little frown between his brows.

"That's very kind of you, Malachite. But it isn't necessary. You've done enough." She bent to retrieve another egg, then gathered her courage and turned to face him. "I was in the cellar earlier and saw the meat. You've given me enough to feed the entire town."

"Some days I think you do feed the entire town." He retrieved some tools from his saddlebags.

When he started to work on the latch, Millie set the basket near the door. Pulling up a small stool beside the cow, she began milking. "Now that you've had a chance to see your father's ranch, what do you think of it?"

His father. The word still grated. "It's big."

"But isn't it grand? Some say it's the grandest ranch in all of Texas."

"Do they? I still say it's big."

"Do you think you'll be able to stop the mustangs from overrunning the rangelands?"

"If I ever find them."

"According to Diamond, their wranglers have tried tracking them. But they've vanished without a trace."

His eyes narrowed. "Nothing vanishes without a trace. Sooner or later I'll find them. And when I do, I'll find their leader, Diablo."

From the icy tone of his voice, Millie had no doubt of it.

She deftly changed the subject. "Where did you learn to do so many things?"

"I had no choice. Drifting around the West at an early age, I had to make myself useful if I wanted to survive." He glanced over and felt himself warmed by the sight of her, seated beside the cow, her cheek resting against its hide as she filled the bucket. "Where was your home before you came west?"

"Virginia." She knew he had smoothly turned the tables so he wouldn't have to talk about himself. But she didn't mind. "My parents came from Ireland and hired out to work on the farm owned by Mick's parents. Mick and I practically grew up together."

"What brought you to Hanging Tree?"

"Mick was seized with a desire to pull up stakes and try his luck in Texas. So we kissed our families goodbye and never looked back."

Malachite tested the latch, opening and closing the door several times until he was satisfied. "How old were you?"

"Fifteen. Mick was almost twenty."

He turned to study her. "That's young to leave home."

She flushed as she set aside the stool, then lifted the pail filled with milk. "Times were hard. I guess we had to grow up quickly. But we wanted better for our children."

"Why didn't you go back to Virginia after your husband died?"

"It was too late. Our families were all gone. Our parents were dead, the farm sold. Besides," she said, "Hanging Tree is my home now. There's no turning back."

As she crossed to the door he took the bucket from her hands. "That's too heavy for you. Here, you carry the eggs."

It was on the tip of her tongue to remind him that she carried this milk pail every day of her life. But she held her silence, enjoying his gallantry.

At the back door he set down the bucket, then turned away.

"Did you forget something?" she asked.

"I thought I'd take your wagon down to the livery. See if the blacksmith can check my repairs. I'd like to make sure it's safe before you use it again." And to see if the smith concurred with his suspicions that the wagon wheel had been deliberately tampered with.

Millie was touched by his concern. "The smith's name is Neville Oakley. Tell him I'll stop by later to pay him."

Inside, as she started breakfast, Millie found herself thinking that it had been a long time since she'd had someone to chat with while doing her early morning chores. It had been so pleasant the time had flown by.

"Mama."

She turned at the sound of May's voice.

"Why didn't you wake us for school?"

"Malachite took the wagon to Mr. Oakley's for repair. So it looks like you won't be going today."

The little girl's face fell. "I know all my spelling words."

Millie gave her a gentle smile. "That's all right, honey. You'll still know them tomorrow."

"But I—"

They both looked up at the crunch of wheels. A moment later the door was opened and Malachite strode in. As always, Millie was struck by the way his presence seemed to fill a room.

"Neville Oakley gave me the loan of a wagon while he looks over yours." He caught sight of May's happy smile and paused to tug on one of her curls. "I was going to refuse, but I thought as long as I was headed out to the ranch anyway, you and your sister might want to ride along."

"I'll wake June," the little girl shouted as she raced up the stairs.

Millie watched her daughter disappear, then began nervously wiping her hands on her apron. "Thank you. That was very kind of you, Malachite."

"Maybe I have some cold, calculated reason for doing nice things." He took a step closer and watched the way the color sprang to her cheeks. He couldn't resist touching a finger to the spot.

She forced herself not to back away. "And what would that be?"

"Maybe I'm just trying to impress you, so you'll let down your guard."

"I'd have to say your plan is working." The feel of his work-roughened finger against her flesh caused an ache deep inside. She had to resist the urge to catch his hand and hold it to her.

"I've been meaning to give this to you," he said as he reached into his pocket and handed her thirty dollars.

"You don't have to..."

"I agreed to pay you in advance." He closed her fingers around the money.

Just then the back door opened and Birdie hurried inside, her cheeks red, her breath coming in short bursts. Millie took a step back, putting some distance between herself and Malachite.

"Morning, Mrs. Potter. Sorry I'm late."

"You're just in time," Millie said as Malachite turned away and headed toward the door.

"The air's colder today," he called. "I'm going to fork some straw into the back of Neville's wagon so the girls can burrow in and stay warm."

Millie watched until the door closed behind him, then sent Birdie off to locate some warm quilts to cover the straw. For a moment she studied the crumpled bills in her hand. Since Mick's death, it was the most money she'd ever held at one time. As she shoved it into the pocket of her apron, she began mentally picking out warm winter coats for the girls. She couldn't wait to visit Durfee's Mercantile.

A few minutes later Millie was surprised to see April coming down the stairs. "Oh, honey. You shouldn't be out of bed. How are you feeling?"

"I feel better, Mama. I'd like to go to school with May and June."

Millie touched her daughter's forehead. "Your fever's gone." Maybe, she mused, there was something to Malachite's herbs. "But I really don't think you're strong enough yet to face that long ride."

"But I don't want to miss all the excitement," the little girl cried.

"What excitement?"

"May and June and Birdie told me all about their adventure. It isn't fair that I have to stay in bed while they go off and have all the fun."

Again Millie found herself marveling that Malachite had reacted so calmly to their crisis that the girls thought of it merely as an adventure, instead of the near tragedy it had been. Or had Malachite planted that thought so they wouldn't be afraid?

She drew her daughter close and pressed her lips to a tangle of red curls. "Oh, honey," she whispered. "If you had asked May and June and Birdie how exciting all this was yesterday, while they were going through it, they would have admitted that they were cold and hungry and afraid."

"Really? Do you think so, Mama?"

"I do," Millie murmured against her temple. "It's a sad fact that many of our greatest adventures in life seem more wonderful in the telling than in the living."

April shivered and Millie released her. "Why don't you run upstairs and snuggle under the blankets. Later, if you're feeling well enough, you can dress and come down and sit by the fire. And if the fever doesn't come back, I'll let you return to school tomorrow."

Satisfied, the little girl scampered away, and Millie turned. She spotted Malachite standing quietly in the doorway.

"Your breakfast will be ready in a minute," she called.

As he removed his cowhide jacket and wide-brimmed hat, he mulled over what she'd just said. Millie was right. The telling was easy. It was the living that required courage. Sometimes, more courage than any one person should need.

And sometimes a body had to dig deep to find the courage within to survive what life handed out.

"Mama, how many places should I set?" April, freshly washed and wearing a white pinafore over her gown, looked rested. She'd spent the afternoon in front of the fire, reading aloud to her mother.

"It's so blustery outside, I expect there will only be the five of us." Millie hummed a little tune while she set the rolls aside to cool.

She'd planned a special dinner for tonight. She owed it to Malachite for the meat he'd given them and the healing he'd offered her daughter. Not to mention the other kind things he'd done since his arrival.

She had taken the money to Durfee's Mercantile, where she'd bought new winter coats for her daughters, as well as sacks of flour and sugar and coffee.

She heard the crunch of wagon wheels and smoothed her damp palms down her skirt. She'd taken pains with her appearance, adding a clean apron and sweeping her hair into a neat knot.

"Mama, look." May was the first one in the door. In her hand was a pretty blue ribbon. "I won the weekly spelling bee."

"That's wonderful!" Millie kissed her cheek. "I'm proud of you, honey."

"She wouldn't have won if April had been there," June said as she hurried over to warm herself by the fire. "Everybody knows April's the best speller."

"It isn't nice to spoil your sister's moment." Millie's voice was soft, but her meaning was clear.

June hung her head and realized that she'd once again let her quick tongue get her in trouble.

Malachite entered on a gust of cold air. "What's this?" he asked. "Something smells wonderful."

"I made a special dinner."

"What's the occasion?" Malachite asked as he hung his jacket and hat on a peg by the door.

"Nothing special." Millie watched as he rolled his sleeves and began to wash. "I just thought we'd enjoy the meat you brought us."

"You can sit here, Malachite," she said, indicating the head of the table.

May chose the chair on his left, while June sat on his right. Millie sat across from him, with April beside her.

"This is nice, Mama," little June said, "having just us here tonight. Now May and I will tell you all about what we did in school today."

"That's fine, honey. I'd love to hear it. As soon as we say a blessing."

Just as they bowed their heads, there was a quick, hard knock and the front door was opened. Footsteps sounded in the hall. Before Millie could even get to her feet, several faces peered around the doorway.

"You see, Effie," came a high-pitched female voice. "We're not too late for supper."

Town gossips Lavinia Thurlong and Gladys Witherspoon stood framed in the doorway. Behind them stood Effie Spitz, wife of Deputy Arlo Spitz, who could always be counted on to furnish her two friends with news of everyone's latest transgressions.

"Oh my." Millie struggled to hide her disappointment. "I didn't expect anyone to be out on such a night." Clearly flustered, she motioned to April, who began scurrying around, setting additional places at the table. "Come right in, ladies."

"Well." Lavinia, tall and stick-thin, came to an abrupt halt at the sight of Malachite, who got to his feet.

Gladys, as round as she was tall, bumped into Lavinia and bounced backward, nearly knocking Effie into the wall.

The three women gaped until Lavinia managed to find her voice. "You'd be Onyx Jewel's son. The news is all over town. I heard you looked like your father. But I wouldn't have believed how much you look like him if I hadn't seen it with my own eyes."

Behind her, the other two women merely stared.

Remembering her manners, Millie said, "Malachite Jewel, I'd like you to meet Lavinia Thurlong, Gladys Witherspoon and Effie Spitz."

He acknowledged them with a slight nod of his head. "Ladies."

They found their places at the table, all the while studying the man who bore an eerie resemblance to one they'd known all their lives.

"How did you three happen to be out tonight?" Millie asked.

"We thought it would be neighborly to pay a call," Lavinia said as she helped herself to a thick slab of roasted venison.

Gladys nodded. "And see for ourselves if your new boarder looked like his father."

"And how did you hear about my…new boarder?" Millie gritted her teeth. As if she didn't know.

"I believe it was Effie who first mentioned it, wasn't it, Effie?"

Before the deputy's wife could say a word, Gladys went on, "And then that handsome young banker, Byron Conner, told us a bit more when we ran into him at Durfee's Mercantile."

As if on cue Byron came strolling into the dining room.

"I thought I heard your voices, ladies," Byron called. "I see I'm just in time."

The women blushed and smiled, enjoying the fact that they were in the company of the town's most eligible bachelor. While Byron offered his greeting, Millie was forced to make room for him at the table.

"Byron tells us you're working out at the Jewel ranch," Lavinia said as she slathered butter on a roll.

"That's right." Malachite noticed that the three little girls had grown silent, keeping their gazes firmly on their plates while they mechanically ate their food. Apparently they'd become accustomed to having their dinner interrupted by strangers.

"Byron also says you're interested in catching Diablo."

"Byron seems to have a lot to say about me."

Across the table, the banker flushed.

"Is it true?" Lavinia demanded.

"It might be."

The older woman glanced at her companions. "Then I think you should be warned. We have a very good reason for calling the leader of that wild herd Diablo. He is a devil. We believe that anyone who catches him will be cursed."

"So I've heard." Malachite smiled. "I don't believe in curses."

"Just so you know, Mr. Jewel. The people of Hanging Tree do believe. And we don't wish to have Diablo's curse brought upon our town and its people."

"I'll remember that as I go about my chores at the ranch, Mrs. Thurlong."

That gave Byron the perfect opportunity to goad the man he saw as his rival. As he helped himself to a scoop of potatoes, he asked, "Doesn't it bother you to take orders from Cal McCabe?"

"Why should that bother me?"

"Because his name isn't Jewel and yours is. It would seem to me, if you really are Onyx Jewel's son, you should be the one giving orders on the Jewel ranch."

Malachite could see the trap Byron was trying to set for him. He chose his words carefully. "If Cal McCabe was good enough to run the ranch when Onyx Jewel was alive, why wouldn't he be good enough to run it now?"

Annoyed that Malachite hadn't taken the bait, Byron shrugged. "I'm not saying Cal isn't up to the job. But if you're half the man they say your father was, you've got to feel hobbled. I'm told Onyx Jewel never took orders from anyone."

When Malachite held his silence, Lavinia said, in her most

sympathetic tone, "It must be difficult living up to a man like Onyx Jewel. He was a legend here in Texas, you know."

Malachite fixed her with a look. "I never knew my father. Until a short time ago, I never even knew his name."

"How terrible," she said with a sigh.

"Not at all. You see, that frees me to be myself. I don't have to imitate him. I don't have to live up to him. All I have to do is live my life, however I choose."

"And how have you lived?" Byron asked.

"Yes, Mr. Jewel." Gladys leaned forward expectantly. "Tell us about your life before you came to Hanging Tree. What was your mother like?"

"My mother was a Comanche. She was sister to the chief, Two Deer."

"A...Comanche." Gladys sat back, holding a lacy handkerchief to her mouth, as if she'd just smelled something foul. "I always knew there was something...different about Onyx Jewel."

"Different?" Malachite bit off the word.

"He didn't always conform to our ways," she said imperiously.

"Did you live in a tepee?" Lavinia asked.

"And sleep in a buffalo robe?" Effie put in.

"Don't Indians eat animal hearts?" Byron added with a smug smile.

Malachite waited a heartbeat before saying, "Yes. To all your questions." He leaned back, enjoying their shocked reactions.

"But you're...half-white," Lavinia said in hushed tones.

"Really? Which half?" Malachite picked up his cup and drank.

Across the table, Millie was amazed to see how he was handling this intrusion into his personal life. How could these people, who thought of themselves as righteous, ask such impertinent questions? As though they had the right to pry. And how could he calmly answer them?

In an attempt to stop the barrage of questions, she said, "I think it's going to snow soon. Don't you agree, Lavinia?"

"Of course it's going to snow, Millie. Winter follows autumn as surely as night follows day. Now, Mr. Jewel, about your mother…"

"Her name was Evening Star." He met Lavinia's look evenly. "And she was considered the most beautiful woman in the village."

"Well, Onyx Jewel always did have an eye for the women. Even—" she wrinkled her nose "—Comanche women, it would seem. How about you, Mr. Jewel? Have you inherited that trait from your father, as well?"

Malachite glanced at Millie and saw how distressed she was by all this.

"As I told you…" He sat back, looking completely relaxed. But Millie could tell by the dangerous softness of his voice and the glacial stare that this was all a pose. He was about as relaxed as a panther stalking its prey. "I'm free to live my life as I please. Without the influence of my father."

"Are you married, Mr. Jewel?" Lavinia asked boldly.

Very carefully he set down his cup and scraped back his chair. To Millie he said, "If you'll excuse me. I have some work to see to. Especially if I'm going to hunt a devil horse."

Before he could leave, Byron's voice stopped him. "Is that a yes or a no?"

Malachite turned to study him. The look he gave would have frightened most men.

But Byron merely gave a sly smile. "Seems like we've struck a nerve, Lavinia."

"Well." Lavinia let the word hang in the silence. Then, with a look very like a cat that had just skimmed the cream off the milk pail, she said pointedly, "As we all know, Onyx Jewel had a woman in every town. And as we have recently learned, he had children in every town, as well. Some he knew about, others who were obviously unknown to him." She glanced at her friends, then turned to Malachite. "It would seem you are a great deal like your father, Mr. Jewel. And it isn't only a matter of your looks.''

She turned a bright smile on Millie. ''This has been a lovely dinner. But I don't think I have room for dessert. How about you, Gladys? Effie?''

''Oh, no. Thank you.'' Gladys could hardly contain her excitement. She'd not only met the mysterious Malachite Jewel but seen a hint of something dark and dangerous in his eyes. That bit of gossip was enough to gain her entry into every house in Hanging Tree. And half the ranches beyond.

''What do we owe you, Millie?'' Effie asked. ''Will a dollar be enough?''

The two women followed Lavinia's lead, pushing away from the table, preparing to take their leave.

''That's…more than enough.'' Pale and ashen, Millie scraped back her chair to collect her money and see them to the door.

As they exited, Byron walked up behind her, placing a hand on her shoulder. ''I'm sorry, Millie.''

Her eyes blazed. Anger was her only defense against the tears she was struggling to hold at bay. ''Are you, Byron? Is that why you seem so pleased with yourself?''

''Millie.'' His fingers tightened at her shoulder. ''I don't like to see you hurt like this. But if the man has secrets, isn't it better that you know about them now?'' His tone was scornful. ''We all knew the man was a womanizer just like his father. Now that you know, you'll be too sensible to join the trail of brokenhearted women a man like that leaves behind.''

''Thank you for your concern, Byron. And your trust. And now if you'll excuse me…'' She held the door and waited until he stepped outside. When it looked as if he might try to linger, she slammed the door and took a deep breath, prepared to return to the dining room and face Malachite Jewel. And pretend that none of this mattered.

But the truth was, it mattered deeply. Once again the seeds of distrust had been sown.

Onyx Jewel's reputation with the women was legendary. It would seem that, despite all his protests, Malachite Jewel was indeed his father's son. What other reason would he have to refuse to answer that one important question?

Chapter Nine

Millie returned to the dining room to find her three daughters, free of their uninvited guests, awash with questions.

"Are you really going to hunt Diablo?" June asked excitedly.

Malachite nodded.

"But you heard Mrs. Thurlong," May said. "He's a devil. Anyone who catches him will be cursed."

"What's cursed?" June asked.

"It means bad luck." April's eyes were troubled. "You mean like sickness? Or even…death?"

Her older sister nodded.

"That's just a myth," Malachite said firmly.

"What's a myth?" May asked.

"A story to explain something mysterious." Malachite brooded. "The people around here have worked themselves up over a wild horse. Now they want to blame him for everything bad that happens."

"But what if Diablo really is the cause of it?" May asked.

Malachite shook his head. "He's just a mustang. He's not a devil."

"You look angry," April said.

"No. He looks sad." May glanced up from her empty plate and turned wide eyes on Malachite.

"That's because Mrs. Thurlong asked him about things he

didn't want to talk about,'' April said with all the wisdom of a seven-year-old.

"What things?" little June asked.

"If he has a wife," April said importantly. "Do you, Malachite?"

He shook his head. "No."

Millie felt giddy with relief. And angry at herself for permitting such feelings.

"Is that why you're sad?" June asked. "Because you don't have a wife?"

He said nothing. But there was a look in his eyes that kept the little girl from asking any further questions.

"We should do something nice to make you feel better," the little girl said gravely. "Like we do for Mama whenever she gets sad."

"What do you do to make her feel better?" Malachite asked.

"Sometimes we give her hugs." June started to rise.

"We can't hug Malachite." April's voice was edged with big-sister command.

Little June dropped back into her chair. "Why can't we?" she asked innocently.

"Because he's not our pa."

"Oh."

In the silence that followed, Malachite watched as both June and May remained seated and lowered their heads, digesting what their older sister had said. It was plain that April, though shy and quiet, was the acknowledged leader.

In the blink of an eye June brightened. "May we have dessert now, Mama?"

Millie walked to a sideboard, where she began to scoop bread pudding into bowls. She'd made it especially for Malachite, knowing it was his favorite. Now it suddenly seemed a foolish, frivolous thing to do. In fact, this whole celebratory dinner seemed to mock her.

She distributed the desserts, then sat down and picked up

her cold cup of coffee. She was in such a strange mood she wasn't even aware that it was cold.

"Do you want to hear about school, Mama?" June asked.

Millie forced a half smile to her lips. "I'd love to hear all about it."

"Miss Pearl wrote some new words on our slates, and Gil and Birdie knew every one. May knew three of them. And I didn't know any."

"That's all right. They were new words. You weren't expected to know them."

"That's what Miss Pearl said. And she said by next week, I'll probably know every one of them."

"You see. That's why you go to school. To learn." Millie glanced at her middle child. "And you won the spelling bee, May."

"Yes'm." May was proudly wearing her ribbon around her neck.

"I'm so glad all your studying earned you such a nice reward. What about your sums?" Millie asked. "Did Miss Pearl check your slates?"

May's eyes were bright. "I only had one wrong."

"I had three wrong," June admitted.

Millie set aside the coffee and struggled to pay attention. There was so little time to spend alone with her girls. She knew they missed these quiet times as much as she did. But the truth was, they required effort. Right now, her mind was still reeling.   "I'm sorry I had so many wrong, Mama." June looked momentarily shamed. Then she thought of something that lifted her spirits. "This afternoon Miss Pearl let me hold little Amber while she worked with Birdie and Gil on some 'rithmetic. And Miss Pearl said I was the best baby holder she'd ever seen."

It was so like Pearl to find something to praise in each of her pupils. The little girl was so proud Millie couldn't help but smile. Her heart melted as she conjured an image of her clumsy five-year-old struggling to hold a wriggling infant.

"I wish we could have a baby, Mama. One as pretty as Amber."

Millie's smile vanished. But before she could say a word, seven-year-old April said solemnly, "We can't have any more babies. Ever."

"Why not?" the little girl demanded.

"I don't know. But it has something to do with Pa being in heaven."

Millie felt the heat stain her cheeks when she glanced at Malachite. Needing something to do, she began to gather the dishes. Her three daughters followed suit, and soon the dining room table was cleared.

She looked up when Malachite walked into the kitchen and pulled on his cowhide jacket. "You're going out at this time of night?"

"I thought I'd take Neville Oakley's wagon back to him and return with yours."

She nodded. She understood his eagerness to get away. Here in the house, she and her daughters were constantly underfoot. He probably had a need to be alone with his thoughts.

While the girls washed and dried the dishes, Millie prepared her dough for the morning and set it aside to rise.

A short time later, after going over their new words and their sums, she herded her daughters up the stairs to bed.

After slipping into their nightclothes, the three little girls crawled into bed and Millie heard their prayers.

As she bent to kiss them good-night, little June muttered sleepily, "Do you think Malachite is still feeling bad about Mrs. Thurlong's questions, Mama?"

"No, honey. I'm sure by now he's forgotten all about them."

The little girl smiled. "Good. I don't want him to be sad. I like Malachite. Good night, Mama."

"'Night, honey."

As Millie made her way downstairs, she found herself thinking about what she had told her daughter. Perhaps by now Malachite had gotten over his anger at Lavinia's impertinent questions. But she hadn't. Those questions and his lack of response were burned indelibly into her mind.

She untied her apron and hung it on a peg, then made her way to the parlor, where she carefully banked the fire. Lifting the lantern, she returned to the kitchen just as the door was opened on a blast of frosty air. Malachite entered, his arms laden with firewood.

He deposited the logs on the hearth, then straightened.

"The coffee is still hot," Millie said. "And I left you the last dish of bread pudding."

As she moved past him, he reached out a hand to stop her. "I wish you'd stay a minute."

She flinched and drew away. "It's been a long day. I'm really tired."

"I'm tired, too," he said softly. "But there are some things that need saying. Stay." His tone lowered. "Please."

Reluctantly Millie perched on the edge of a kitchen chair. Malachite removed his hat and coat and hung them on a peg, then crossed to the fireplace. For long moments he stared moodily into the fire, then turned to face Millie, one hand resting atop the mantel.

"You seemed more disturbed than I was by your neighbors' questions."

"They had no right."

"That's true. But they're only asking what everyone else in town doesn't have the courage to ask."

"Or the gall," she added.

He nearly smiled. It occurred to him that she was angry for his sake.

The thought was oddly comforting. "There are some in every town. Or village."

Her head came up. "You mean your mother's people were as rude?"

Now he did smile. "People are people. Good and evil exist in all of us. Some of the Comanche were accepting of me, for my mother's sake. Others—" he shrugged "—not so accepting. I didn't expect better here. Or worse."

"You didn't have to answer a single impertinent question."

"That's true. Are you sorry I did?"

"I'm not sure how I feel. But I think it will only make them hungry for more."

"And you?" Though his tone was easy, the tension deepened. "Do you want to know more?"

"Not unless you want to tell me."

There was a long, drawn-out moment of silence. He was hardly aware of his quick intake of breath. There were so many dark places inside him. Places he'd never shared with anyone. He wasn't certain he ever could. But he sensed in Millie Potter a loyalty, a decency that were rare treasures. Perhaps...

"I may. Someday. Now I'd like to ask one more question. Do you share the town's fear of Diablo?"

She thought about it a moment before nodding. "I know in my mind that it's nothing more than a myth. But I can't make my heart believe that. Every time something goes wrong and the rest of the town blames Diablo, I find myself agreeing. What other explanation can there be for so many problems?"

"I don't know. But I intend to find out."

He wondered if she had any idea how lovely she looked in the firelight, her head bowed, her hands held tightly in her lap. Trying to rein in her agitation. Like a bird poised for flight. A beautiful, red-winged bird.

She felt her cheeks redden under the heat of his gaze. To cover her awkwardness she got slowly to her feet. "I'll say good-night now, Malachite."

"Good night. Thank you for the dinner. Even with the...unwelcome interruption, it was special."

When she climbed the stairs, he remained where he was,

staring after her. Letting old memories play through his mind.

Sleep, he knew, would not be a friend to him tonight.

Millie removed a pan of biscuits from the fire and began to scramble eggs.

Several times through the night she'd heard Malachite's faint footfalls as he prowled the rooms. She'd smelled tobacco and pictured him in her mind, sitting quietly in front of the fire or staring moodily out the windows at the darkened sky.

Her own sleep had been greatly disturbed, as well. She hadn't been completely honest with him. Though she knew Diablo was only a wild horse, she had heard the stories of his cunning, his courage and his fury at those who would capture him. Perhaps it would be best to leave well enough alone.

When she came downstairs she found all the fires started and a supply of logs on each hearth. The cow had been milked, the eggs gathered. Whatever demons Malachite had been chasing, they'd filled him with restless energy.

Now his door was closed. There was no sound from within.

Millie turned as April bounded down the stairs.

"You promised I could go to school today," the little girl called.

"That's right. As long as you're feeling up to it. Are the others awake?"

"I'll call them." April hurried back upstairs.

Millie watched her go, then returned to her cooking. A short time later Birdie Bidwell was seated at the table as April, May and June made their way downstairs.

"Are you going with us today, Mama?" June asked.

Millie shook her head. "Rufus Durfee's two sons, Amos and Damon, will pick you up and bring you home."

As she began to serve their breakfast, the door to Malachite's room opened.

Millie greeted him with a smile. "You're just in time."

"I won't be eating this morning." His eyes were dark and haunted.

Millie caught sight of the bedroll slung over his shoulder. Seeing the direction of her gaze, he said, "It's time I headed into the hills to track the mustangs."

"Where will you sleep?"

He shrugged. "Along the trail. Or maybe one of the line camps."

The little girls watched and listened in silence.

For the sake of her audience, Millie kept her voice as cool, as emotionless as his. "How long do you think you'll be gone?"

"As long as it takes."

"I'll fix you some food to take in your saddlebags."

He shook his head. "There's no need. I want to travel light. I'll catch what I need along the trail."

She refused to be deterred. Within minutes she had biscuits and thick slabs of roasted venison wrapped in a linen towel. Forsaking her shawl, she hurried out to the shed.

His horse was saddled. He finished tying his bedroll, then glanced up.

"I...couldn't let you go without something." She approached slowly and held out the packet of food.

"Thank you."

Their fingers brushed.

He turned away and made room for the food in his saddlebag.

She felt suddenly awkward and at a loss for words. She hadn't come out here just to give him the food. She'd wanted a moment alone. But now that she was here with him, she couldn't think of a thing to say. "I'm afraid for you. Afraid of the curse. Safe journey, Malachite." Her breath plumed in the frosty air.

He touched a hand to her sleeve. "The People have a saying when they are departing. May only good spirits dwell with you until we are together again."

"That's lovely. I wish the same for you." She shivered at

the warmth of his touch. "Take only good spirits along on your journey."

For the space of several seconds he stared at her, as though memorizing all her lovely features. Disconcerted, she started to turn away. He caught her by the arm and dragged her against him. She was too startled to react as his arms closed around her, pinning her roughly to the length of him. He lowered his head and kissed her with a thoroughness that left them both breathless.

Despite the chill she felt a rush of heat as she lost herself in the kiss. It spoke of hunger, of need, of deeply buried, primitive emotions. It hinted of pleasure and pain and dark, unexplored passion.

She felt the tightly coiled tension in him and was both frightened and exhilarated by it.

When at last he lifted his head and released her, she felt shaken to the core. She glanced up, wondering if he felt the same. But his eyes, dark, fathomless, gave away nothing.

He pulled himself into the saddle and, without a word, nudged his horse into a trot.

Millie raced to the open doorway of the shed to watch until horse and rider disappeared through town. Then she leaned weakly against the door, struggling to collect her thoughts.

Minutes later, shivering in the cold, she returned to the house.

Malachite woke in the predawn chill and cursed the fresh snow that had fallen here in the mountains while he slept. The trail he'd been following would be obliterated.

Frustrated, he rolled the buffalo robe and saddled his horse. Maybe, if he was lucky, he'd find some faint tracks before the snow got any deeper.

Out of the corner of his eye he caught a blur of motion. Whirling, he drew his pistol. And found himself face-to-face with young Gil, leading a spotted mare.

"Sorry to startle you, Mr. Jewel."

"You walk like a Comanche," Malachite said, holstering his gun. "What brings you up here, son?"

Recognizing the compliment, Gil flushed with pride. "I heard from the Potter girls that you were up here tracking Diablo. I wanted to help."

"I appreciate it. Looks like the snow might have killed my chances this time. But you're welcome to come along."

"Yes, sir. I'd like that." Gil dug into his pocket and removed a rolled linen cloth. He unwrapped it to reveal several biscuits filled with meat and cheese. "Help yourself. Ma sent these."

"Thanks." Malachite ate quickly then pulled himself into the saddle, regretting that there wasn't time for a cup of coffee.

As the two set off, Malachite thought about Millie and her daughters, snug and warm in their house. And then he saw again, in his mind's eye, the terror in those little girls' eyes when the wheel had come off their wagon.

What would have happened if he hadn't been there? The thought of Millie and her girls being thrown from a runaway wagon had him clenching his teeth with fury.

"Tell me something, Gil," he asked as the two of them rode side by side. "Does Mrs. Potter have any enemies?"

The lad thought a moment. "No, sir. None that I know of."

"Can you think of anybody who would benefit from the accidents that have been happening to the folks in town?"

Gil shook his head. "You don't think they're accidents?"

"That's an awful lot of clumsy cowboys. Too many, to my way of thinking."

"And the curse of Diablo? Do you believe in it?"

Malachite glanced sideways. "Do you?"

Gil chewed his lip. "I don't know what to think. But I sure would like it all to be over."

"So would I, Gil. So would I." He thought again about Millie and her daughters and the fact that they were all alone.

To keep his mind off them, he forced himself to study the

trail. He and Gil rode for hours, high in the mountains, before they were forced to admit that the mustangs were nowhere to be found.

"I think maybe it's time to head home," he said.

The two turned their horses toward the lights of town.

Millie finished pouring the last batch of candles, then glanced toward the swiftly gathering darkness outside the windows. The days had begun growing shorter. Soon she and her daughters would be confined to the house, with only an occasional brisk walk to Durfee's Mercantile to break the monotony. The long ride to school would be out of the question.

She dashed outside to gather the clothes from the line. Within minutes her fingers were stiff with cold. While she worked she found herself thinking, as she did so often, about Malachite. How was he faring in the hills that ringed the Jewel ranch? There were steep, perilous peaks and deep, ominous caverns where a body wouldn't be discovered until the snow finally melted under the prodding of spring rains.

The thought was too chilling. She refused to dwell on it.

She gathered the last sheet from the line, struggling in the bitter wind to hold on to it. It flapped and fluttered as she folded it, until it was small enough to fit on top of the other clothes. Then, lifting the basket, she turned. And nearly collided with a shadowy figure.

"Oh." She jumped back. For the space of a heartbeat she merely stared at the heavily bearded man. Then, recognizing him, she let out a cry. "Malachite. It's been nearly three weeks."

She wasn't aware that she dropped the basket. Wasn't aware that her voice was choked with emotion. She was no longer aware of the cold or the darkness. But when he opened his arms to her, she flung herself into them. And held on.

He pressed his lips to a tangle of hair at her temple and

breathed in the clean, spicy fragrance. "You're freezing," he muttered. "Come on. Let's get inside."

Keeping one arm around her shoulder, he lifted the basket. Inside he was greeted by the wonderful aroma of meat roasting and bread baking. He stood very still for a moment, as though taking it all in. The fire crackling in the fireplace. The table set for supper. The three little girls lying on the hearth, heads bent over their slates.

They looked up. Spotting him, May and June dropped their slates and hurried over to greet him.

"Malachite. You're home." Little June pointed to his bristly beard. "Look, Mama. Malachite has more hair than old Mr. Winslow."

Millie was looking. She couldn't seem to stop staring at him. Even with the beard and his long hair tied back with a strip of rawhide, he was the most handsome man she'd ever seen.

"You're just in time for supper," May added.

"I am? Now, how did I plan that?" he asked, tousling their hair.

He glanced across the room to where April still knelt, watching him over the slate she was clutching in her arms. "How are you feeling?" he asked. "Did your fever ever return?"

She solemnly shook her head.

"Good." He smiled easily and patted his bulging pocket. "I have something for the three of you. Something I found up in the hills."

May and June could hardly contain their excitement. A gift. It was so unexpected, and so rare, they began dancing around him. April merely stared in silence.

He pulled three stones from his pocket and set them on the table. Each was smooth and bright green.

"They're just like yours," little June said with a trace of awe.

He nodded. "Do you see this?" He pointed to the darker veins in the middle of each stone that were shaped like an eye. "The People believe that this is the 'third eye,' which will ward off danger. Those who wear it will be kept safe from all harm."

"Ooh."

Both May and June picked up a stone and held it in the palms of their hands. Even April's curiosity had gotten the better of her, and she ambled over to watch.

"Would you like one?" Malachite held the third stone out to her.

She backed up and hung her head.

"All right. I'll keep it for you." He dropped the stone into his pocket, then withdrew three strips of rawhide from another pocket. "After supper, if you'd like, I'll fashion them into necklaces for each of you."

"Oh, Mama. Did you hear that?" June began dancing around. "Let's hurry and eat so Malachite can make our necklaces."

"All right, now." The excitement was contagious. Millie had to fight to restore calm. "Girls, put your slates away and then wash up for supper."

"Yes'm." The little girls needed no coaxing. Even April, Millie noted, seemed to be moving at a faster pace. But she resolutely kept her eyes downcast, refusing to look at Malachite.

When they were seated around the table and had offered up a blessing, May added, "And we thank Thee for bringing Malachite home safely."

"Amen," the others intoned.

Though the moment passed quickly, Malachite found himself deeply touched.

"Did you see any bears or wildcats?" June asked as she spooned potatoes onto her plate.

"Several wildcats. Only saw one bear."

"What did you eat?" May asked.

"Rabbit. Elk. Fish from the mountain streams. But I sure did miss your mama's cooking," he said with a smile. "Especially these biscuits."

"Weren't you cold at night?" June managed to ask over a mouthful of potatoes.

He nodded. "It's bitter up in those hills. But I usually managed to find a cave or a deserted shack."

"But what did you do when you couldn't find shelter?" Millie asked in alarm.

"I curled up in a buffalo robe. I told you, Comanche are used to surviving."

"Did you find the herd of mustangs?" May asked.

He shook his head. His mood suddenly darkened.

"No tracks?" Millie, pouring milk, paused to look at him.

"There were tracks. But a fresh snowfall put an end to them. Young Gil joined me for the last day. He's a fine tracker. Maybe the best I've ever seen. But even with his help, we couldn't find the herd." He leaned back and gave a sigh of contentment, determined to keep the conversation light. "This was worth waiting for."

At his words, Millie flushed with pleasure. "There's apple cobbler."

"I'll take mine later, if you don't mind." He drank his coffee before shoving away from the table. "I left my horse and gear outside. I'd better tend to them."

Millie watched him walk away. And wondered why his return should cause such a strange sensation around her heart. How was it that this man had the power, simply by his mere presence, to make her feel almost giddy with pleasure?

She'd missed him. Terribly. And he'd only been gone a few weeks. Byron's warning rang in her ears.

How would she feel when he went away for good?

Chapter Ten

"Will you please make our necklaces now, Malachite?" June put away the last of the dishes and dried her hands.

The three girls had completed their evening chores in record time. May and June, twitching with excitement, had a race to see who could make it to the parlor first. April trailed behind, carrying her slate.

Unwilling to miss the fun, Millie picked up a basket of mending and joined them.

Malachite was seated on the sofa. On the table in front of him were the three stones, which he had been polishing to a high shine.

May and June sat on either side of him, watching with avid interest. April sprawled in front of the fire and began writing on her slate. But every so often, when she thought no one was looking, her gaze would stray to the man sandwiched between her two sisters.

Millie sat in a comfortable chair drawn up in front of the fireplace. By the light of the fire she began to sew.

"What are you doing now?" June asked.

"I'm going to drill a hole in each stone." Malachite picked up a small sharp tool and began to probe the first stone with his fingers.

Within moments he set the stone aside and reached for the second. He repeated the process until all three stones were perfectly drilled. Then he took a length of rawhide and rolled it in his fingers until the end was tightly wound. Threading it through the small hole of the first stone, he pulled it until the stone was centered. Then he did the same with the other two.

"Here are your necklaces," he said.

"Thank you, Malachite." The two little girls held them up.

"Oh, look, Mama." June moved the stone this way and that. The highly polished malachite caught and reflected the firelight, shooting prisms of color across the walls and ceiling.

Millie dropped her mending to admire the display. April's slate lay forgotten as she lifted her head to watch.

"Will you tie it around my neck, Malachite?" The little girl hurried to his side and lifted her red curls out of the way.

When June's was tied, May followed suit. Then both little girls, excitement rippling through them, paraded around, watching the way the stones picked up the light of the fire and shot it around the room.

"How about you, April? I've made you one, too." Malachite held out the third necklace to the little girl, who sat cross-legged on the hearth, watching in silence.

"Wouldn't you like to wear it, honey?" Millie asked gently.

Very slowly, April nodded.

It occurred to Malachite that she was approaching him the way a forest creature might approach a human. When she was still an arm's length away, she held out her hand. Malachite placed the necklace in her open palm.

She stared, mesmerized, at the glowing green stone that seemed alive with light.

"Thank you," she whispered shyly.

"You're welcome. Would you like me to tie it around your neck?"

"Mama will do it." She crossed the room to her mother's chair and lifted her hair as her sisters had done.

As Millie tied the rawhide, she glanced up and caught a glimpse of Malachite's eyes. For just a moment she thought she'd glimpsed a flicker of something. Pain? Sorrow? But just as quickly it was gone, and she wondered if she'd imagined it.

"There you are, honey. It's really beautiful."

The little girl closed a hand around the stone and was surprised by the heat it gave off. It seemed to pulse, as if it were a living thing.

"It's warm," she said in astonishment.

Malachite nodded. "The People believe that the stones are possessed by the spirits that dwell in the earth. These are good spirits that nurture us, feed us and keep us safe."

"I wish Pa'd had this," she said on a sigh. "Maybe he'd still be here with us."

Then she joined her two sisters, and the three little girls admired one another's necklaces.

"May we wear them to bed, Mama?" June asked.

Millie smiled. "I don't see why not."

In a burst of enthusiasm, May and June rushed to Malachite and hugged him.

"Thank you," they both said.

"You're welcome. Sleep well." He glanced over their heads to see April standing in the doorway, one hand on the warm stone at her throat, the other clutching her slate. "Good night, April."

"'Night," she said. Then she ran ahead of the others up the stairs.

Millie put aside her mending and followed. A few minutes later, after hearing their prayers and tucking them into bed, she returned to the parlor. In the doorway she hesitated.

Malachite was standing by the window, staring out at the darkness. From his profile, she couldn't tell if he was angry or sad.

As if suddenly sensing her presence, he composed his features before turning.

"You must be tired, Malachite." She crossed the room and picked up her sewing basket. "I'll say good-night."

"Don't go yet." He took several steps toward her, then seemed to catch himself. "I...just want to look at you for a moment longer."

She felt her face flame. "Don't talk like that."

He could see her embarrassment. It only added to her charm. "And why not? You're a beautiful woman."

Beautiful. She hadn't been called that in such a long time. She glanced down at her work-worn hands, the frayed cuffs of her gown. There'd been a time when she had felt beautiful. But that was before. When she'd been so young, so filled with a spirit of adventure.

For some strange reason, she wanted to weep.

He took a step closer and studied her in the light of the fire. Without thinking of the consequences, he lifted her chin. The flare of heat between them was instantaneous.

"Why can't you believe that you're beautiful?"

"It's just..." She stared up into his eyes and could see herself reflected there. "I have three children. I'm a drudge. And a workhorse. And..."

His kiss was as gentle as a snowflake. The merest brush of lips to lips. Whatever she'd been about to say was wiped from her mind.

"You have a face like an angel," he murmured against her mouth. "There's a goodness, a sweetness in you that I thought I'd never see in anyone."

His fingers combed through her hair and he gave a low growl of pleasure before his mouth devoured hers.

She was unprepared for the raw passion of his kiss. It frightened her even while it excited her. There was a barely controlled savageness in him that had her trembling.

Mick's lovemaking had always been...careful. As though he were taking great pains not to shock her delicate sensibilities. She couldn't recall a single time when he'd been so overcome with desire that he'd kissed her in this fashion.

Malachite's hands were moving over her with a possessiveness that had her breath catching in her throat. He was touching her in ways that had her sighing and molding herself to him. And all the while his mouth, that wonderful, clever mouth, was taking her higher than she'd ever been before.

"On the trail, all I thought about was you…this." When he brought his lips to her throat, a moan escaped her, and she arched herself in his arms. He ran soft, moist kisses along her skin, before burying his lips in the sensitive hollow between her neck and shoulder.

His hands moved up her sides, then paused at the swell of her breasts as his thumbs stroked her nipples. Deep inside contractions began, until her blood flowed like lava and her mind was spinning in dizzying circles.

"Malachite. Oh, Malachite." She could hardly speak over her clogged throat.

He bent his head. Through the fabric of her gown his lips closed around one erect nipple and he suckled until she thought she'd go mad from the pleasure. Exquisite pleasure that bordered on pain.

She could feel the trembling in her limbs, could feel her knees begin to buckle.

He supported her in his arms as he lowered her to the floor. And then his mouth was on hers again, and she was lost.

His lips, his tongue, his fingers were bringing such incredible pleasure. She felt as though she had just stepped off a cliff and was falling through space. Losing herself in him. Losing her senses, losing her will.

"Wait—Malachite." She put a hand to his chest and could feel the wild thundering of his heartbeat. "We…can't do this."

She sat up, her clothes in disarray, her hair tumbling about her face and shoulders. When he reached for her she drew back, avoiding contact with him. "I can't think when you touch me."

"Then don't think." His voice was rough. "Just let me hold you."

"No." Oh, did he know how desperately she longed to be held, to be loved?

Despite the trembling in her limbs she struggled to her feet. "I have to think of my reputation here in town. And that of my children. I think…" The words nearly stuck in her throat, but she forced herself to say them. "I think you should go."

For a moment there was only a shocked, terrible silence. When he spoke, his voice was a rasp of anger. "Are you suggesting I leave for good?"

She swallowed. Her heart was beating so wildly she feared it would break clean through her chest. "I think that would be best."

He walked to the fireplace, where he stared for long moments into the flames. He'd almost convinced himself that he was staying here for her sake. So that she could earn enough to take care of herself and her daughters. But maybe it was time to face the truth. And the truth was far different. Without a doubt he was a danger. To her. To her reputation.

When he turned, his eyes were cold, his voice devoid of any emotion.

"You're right, of course. It was selfish of me. And careless. I'll move out in the morning."

In the morning. She'd thought—hoped—that he would give her a good reason not to leave. His pronouncement left her stunned and reeling. Swallowing, she managed to say, "Where will you go? To your father's house?"

"No." His tone lowered dangerously. "I've told you before. I want nothing to do with anything belonging to Onyx Jewel."

"Then where will you stay?"

He shrugged. "It doesn't matter. I've been on my own for a long time now. I'll survive."

He crossed the room and brushed past her. He paused for a moment and touched a hand to her cheek.

It took all of her willpower to keep from reacting to his touch. A part of her wanted to catch his hand between hers and beg him to stay. To tell him that this had all been some horrible mistake. But another part of her argued for common sense. She had her reputation to think of. And that of her daughters.

Without a word he left the room. A moment later she heard the door to his bedroom close.

Hugging her arms to herself, she stood, listening to the sounds of silence. Since Mick's death, no man had affected her like this. No one had even tried, except Byron Conner. But Byron's prim, almost prissy ways put her off.

Malachite had the opposite effect. She was frightened of the feelings he'd unlocked in her. A hunger that could never be satisfied. A need that bordered on madness. These were feelings that had no place in the life of a respectable woman.

And now, instead of dealing with those feelings, she had foolishly, irrevocably sent him away.

In the predawn chill Millie made her way downstairs. The door to Malachite's room stood open. His bed had been carefully made. On the floor lay his bedroll, still packed. Beside it were his saddlebags, filled with more of his belongings.

With a heavy heart she noticed that the eggs had already been gathered and the milk bucket was full. When she opened the back door she found Malachite, sleeves rolled, shoulders straining, repairing the back steps.

"Malachite, why are you doing this?"

"I've noticed this since I first got here. I've been meaning to repair it."

"But you've done too much already."

"I didn't want to leave without seeing to this."

When he looked up at her she felt her heart leap to her throat. She'd hoped somehow to change his mind, to convince him that he could remain. But now, seeing the look in his eyes, she knew. He was really leaving.

How could she bear not seeing him after today?

"I'll start breakfast. You'll stay and eat with us?"

He nodded.

She hurried inside, determined that if this was all she could do for him, it would have to be enough.

By the time the girls came downstairs and Malachite entered, the kitchen smelled of coffee and biscuits and sizzling meat.

Millie paused in her work to watch Malachite washing his hands. At the ripple of muscle, the glitter of water on his dark hair, she felt a dryness in her throat and looked away.

When the back door opened on a blast of cold air, Birdie rushed in. There was a worried look on her face.

"My pa's real sick this morning, Mrs. Potter. Ma said she'll need my help, so I won't be going to school today."

"I understand." Millie placed meat, eggs and biscuits on a platter and covered it with a towel. "Take this to your mother, Birdie. I know she won't have time to cook. Tell her I hope your father is feeling better tomorrow."

Birdie took the platter. "Thanks, ma'am. I'll tell her." At the door she turned. "I almost forgot. Travis Worthing and the Durfee boys won't be going to school, either."

"Thank you, Birdie. We'll manage alone."

With a nod to Malachite and the girls, Birdie hurried out.

"Well." Millie tried to hide the ripple of excitement that shook her. She would be seeing Malachite for a little while longer. At least until they reached the Jewel ranch. "It looks like I'll be taking you to school today, girls. Come along. Breakfast is ready."

While the others ate, Millie packed a hamper with cold meat, cheese, biscuits and honey. She tucked in a canteen of water and another of milk, and for good measure added half a dozen sugar cookies.

"There's a bite to the wind today," Malachite said. "You'll want to dress warmly."

"Could we wear our new winter coats, Mama?" June asked.

"Do you think it's necessary?" Millie turned to Malachite.

He nodded. "You might want to bring along some quilts, too."

Millie went in search of them, while the girls cleared the table and washed and dried the dishes.

When all was in readiness, Malachite stepped from his bedroom with his bedroll and bulging saddlebags.

"Why are you taking those?" June asked.

"I won't be coming back here tonight."

"Are you going tracking again?" May asked.

He nodded.

The girls seemed to accept his casual response. But Millie found herself wondering what she would say when he never returned and the questions resumed.

Malachite held out a fist full of money. "I found this lying on my bedroll. I believe it belongs to you."

Millie shook her head. "You paid in advance, and that's the balance I'm returning."

He thrust the money into her hand and closed his fingers over hers. "I don't want to fight about this, Millie. It's yours. You earned it."

Before she could argue, she was interrupted by a little voice.

"Did you see the new coats Mama bought us?" Little June proudly modeled hers and was quickly joined by May.

"Well, don't you look fine." Malachite smiled.

"Mr. Durfee only had gray or black. So Mama bought us each a gray coat and said she'd make them look bright with pretty red scarves and mittens." May glanced lovingly at her mother. "But she hasn't had time to knit them yet, so we have to wear our old ones." She pulled a pair of tattered green mittens and a white scarf from a peg by the door.

"Well, even without the red scarves and mittens, I think you look as pretty as ladybugs."

"Ladybugs." Little June burst into giggles. "How come you said that, Malachite?"

He tugged on her curls. "Because ladybugs are red. And all of you have pretty red hair, just like ladybugs."

"Do you think we're as pretty as Mama?" May asked.

He glanced over her head to where her mother stood, wearing a faded black coat and a pale shawl tossed over her shoulders. "I think you are the four most beautiful ladies in Texas."

"April, Malachite called us ladies." May and her sister hooted with laughter.

But their older sister stood across the room, watching the way her mother and Malachite were looking at each other. The look that passed between them gave her a funny feeling. As if she'd seen it before. A long time ago. Maybe between her mother and father. She wasn't sure anymore. She wasn't sure of anything anymore. Not even of Pa's face. And that frightened her more than she cared to admit.

"Come on," she said, pulling on her new coat. "I want to get to school."

Outside the girls climbed into the back of the wagon and snuggled between the quilts that had been spread over a layer of straw. Feather pillows from their beds cushioned their heads. They lay snuggled together, laughing and giggling.

Malachite tied his horse to the back of the wagon, then climbed to the driver's seat. Millie sat primly beside him, wishing she could think of something pleasant to talk about. But all she could think about was the fact that this was their last hour together. They would drop the girls at school and continue on to the ranch house. He would leave. And she would go inside and be forced to make idle chatter with Carmelita while her heart slowly shattered.

"Here we are." Malachite brought the wagon to a halt and lifted the three girls to the ground, before handing the basket of food to April.

She and her sisters raced up the steps and turned to wave to their mother. Then the door was opened by Pearl. Beyond the open doorway could be seen Daniel and Gil, holding baby Amber. With a final wave the three girls disappeared inside.

Malachite flicked the reins and the horse and wagon began the trek to the distant ranch house.

"About last night," Millie began. "I've been thinking…"

"So have I." Malachite's voice sounded unusually gruff. "I had no right to put you in this position."

"But I…"

"I knew, when I forced you to take me in, that your reputation would be at risk."

"You didn't force…"

He turned to her. "I was once a Comanche warrior. I was trained to search out an opponent's weakness and then use it against him. You needed money to survive. And so I offered you enough money that you couldn't possibly refuse."

He saw her react as though she'd been slapped. Her words were clipped, betraying the hurt. "I didn't realize my lack of money was so apparent."

He pulled the wagon to a halt in front of the ranch house. Catching her chin, he forced her to look at him. "Everything about you is there, in your eyes. Your goodness, your sweetness and all the other feelings you've been experiencing since I moved in."

She pulled away and stared down at her hands. "It must have been fun watching me squirm."

"Is that what you think?" He caught her by the shoulders and held her when she tried to turn away. "Look at me, Millie." His words were low, commanding. "I said look at me."

She lifted troubled eyes to his. And saw something she hadn't seen before. Tenderness. And then, in the blink of an eye, simmering anger. "I never intended to hurt you. Not your reputation. Not your standing in the community. And certainly not your relationship with April."

"April has nothing to do with this."

"Doesn't she? Don't you see? She can't help what she is. She's your firstborn. She's been through something the other two can't remember. She lost her father. And now she fears losing her mother, as well.''

''That's sill—''

''Don't call it silly. She has every right to be worried. I won't deny that I moved into your home because I wanted you, Millie. And still do. That's why I have to leave. Because if I succeeded in my plan, your life, and hers, would be forever altered. And I won't do that to you or to her.''

''Oh, Malachite.'' She couldn't hide the tears that sprang to her eyes. She blinked furiously to keep them from streaming down her cheeks. ''I don't want you to go. But I know you can't stay, either. The people of Hanging Tree are good people. But they would soon know that you were more than my boarder. And my daughters would be the ones to pay the price for my sins.''

He smiled gently. ''How I wish you'd committed at least one sin. It would have made the leaving easier.'' He brushed his lips over hers, tasting the salt of her tears. ''Then again,'' he muttered before taking the kiss deeper, ''if you had, I'd never be able to leave.''

She clung to him, pouring all her feelings into this one last kiss.

When at last they drew apart, they stared at each other for long moments. The torment they were suffering was evident in their eyes.

He stepped down from the wagon, then held out his arms to her. He lifted her, then lowered her so slowly she could feel him with every part of her body. Her breasts tingled as they came in contact with his chest. Her lower torso felt on fire. And then he settled her on her feet and allowed his hands to linger at her waist for a moment longer. At last he walked to the back of the wagon and untied his horse.

When he had pulled himself into the saddle, he touched a hand to the brim of his hat. ''Goodbye, Millie Potter. May only good spirits be with you on your journey.''

''And you, Malachite.'' She bit hard on her lower lip to stop the quivering.

As he rode away it took all her willpower to keep from calling out to him. He crested a ridge and turned for a final wave.

Her shoulders shook as she wept silently. And wished with all her heart that she could have a second chance. But it was too late. He was leaving for good. Now only a miracle would bring him back. And she'd stopped believing in miracles the day Mick died.

Chapter Eleven

"**Y**ou are quiet today." Carmelita glanced at Millie, who had insisted on mopping the kitchen floor.

"I just don't have anything to say."

"I see." All morning the housekeeper had watched in amazement as Millie cleaned, dusted, swept and scrubbed, despite protests that she should be visiting, not working. Besides that, the house was already clean before Millie started. After all, the Jewel family only came together for an occasional supper at the big ranch house. After today it would be sparkling, with no one to admire it.

Millie had refused Carmelita's offer of coffee at mid-morning. But the housekeeper was determined to see that she stopped for lunch.

"I have made sliced beef and my special chilies." Carmelita set two plates on the table and filled two cups with coffee. "Come. You will share with me."

Millie pressed a hand to her churning stomach. "I don't think I could eat a bite, Carmelita."

"Then you will sit and watch me eat. Come. Sit." Carmelita held the chair, and Millie had no choice but to join her.

She sipped coffee while the housekeeper heaped two plates with thin slices of roast beef swimming in gravy spiced with red and green chilies.

"Was that Señor Malachite I saw driving your wagon this morning?"

"Yes." Millie clasped and unclasped her hands in her lap.

Carmelita spooned her mixture onto a tortilla and rolled it before starting to eat. "He is one handsome man."

Millie nodded.

"Eat," Carmelita commanded.

Millie took a bite, chewing woodenly.

"You two looked like you were discussing something serious." Carmelita picked up her cup and eyed Millie over the rim.

Millie forced herself to swallow.

When she said nothing, the housekeeper busied herself with a second helping. "Señor Malachite reminds me of my Rosario." She chewed, all the while watching Millie's eyes. "He is a strong man, a proud man." She saw a flicker of some emotion. "Did you know that just before we were to be married, we had a terrible fight."

"What about?" Millie pushed aside her plate. The food tasted like ashes in her mouth. She couldn't manage another bite.

"We came from very different families. Rosario's father was poor, uneducated. My father was a very wealthy man. He wanted Rosario to work a portion of his land. In return he would build us a fine house so that I could live as I always had, with my family and servants nearby."

"And Rosario wanted to be his own man." Millie reached for her coffee.

"*Sí.* What was more, he wanted me to move far away and live among the Texans."

"That must have been difficult for you."

"Not so difficult. You see, I loved him so much I would have gone anywhere with him."

"Then why did you fight?"

"He wanted to leave me, right after the wedding, and come alone to Texas to make his fortune. He promised to send for me when he had enough money to build me a finer house than my father's. He was worried that my family and friends would not approve of my choice. And he was willing to leave me rather than risk damaging my reputation.''

"How could you argue with that?"

"It was not easy to fight him when I loved him so. But I did. I told him I would go to the ends of the earth with him. But I was not willing to be parted from him for one day after he became my husband. So, unless he took me with him to Texas, the wedding would be canceled."

"Weren't you afraid he might refuse?"

Carmelita gave her a knowing smile. "It was a risk. After all, he was a proud man. He hated the idea of making me live a life he considered beneath me. And if he should refuse my terms, my reputation would be ruined. Among my people, a woman who has already pledged her love, and then is rejected, is forever tarnished. No respectable man would ask for the hand of such a woman. But I knew if Rosario loved me half as much as I loved him, he could not deny me."

"You're...very lucky, Carmelita." Millie pushed back her chair and got to her feet.

"*Sí*. A woman who has the love of a good man is the luckiest woman alive."

As Millie made her way to the other room, she mulled over what she'd just heard. All these years later, Carmelita still worked as a housekeeper. And Rosario's ranch, though it provided them with the necessities of life, was modest by Texas standards. Still, Carmelita beamed whenever she spoke her husband's name. And he did the same. The love these two people shared was rare and wonderful.

She'd had that once, briefly, with Mick. It was foolish to believe she had the right to it again. Besides, Malachite hadn't pledged his love. Or even declared it. She had been right to send him away. She had her reputation to think of. And her daughters.

When she returned to the kitchen, she found Carmelita vigorously carving a side of beef.

"Are the Jewels having a party?"

Carmelita looked up from her work. "This is for Cookie. I offered to help him prepare for a trip to the south range. He and the wranglers will be leaving within the hour."

Millie struggled to keep her tone even. "How many are going?"

Carmelita shrugged. "I don't know. But you can ask Cookie. Here he comes now."

Millie opened the door before the old man had a chance to knock. When he saw her, his face lit up with a smile. He gallantly snatched the hat from his head and removed the pipe from his mouth. "Good day, Mrs. Potter."

"Hello, Cookie." She stood aside until he entered, then closed the door against the blast of cold air.

"Señora Millie was just asking how many wranglers are going with you," the housekeeper called from across the room.

"Half the crew is already up on the north range." Cookie breathed in the fragrance of roasting meat and spices. "Everybody who's left will head on up to the south range. That's where the larger herd is wintering. We'll need all the hands we can get."

"Everybody? Including Malachite?"

"Yes, ma'am. He said he'd give us a hand with the herd while he keeps an eye out for the mustangs."

Millie was beginning to feel as if the Fates were against her. She hoped her disappointment didn't show. "How long will you be gone?"

Cookie pinched a slice of beef from the platter and chewed. "Who knows? A couple of weeks. A couple of months. As long as it takes. Onyx used to say that here on his ranch, the safety of his herd was the most important consideration. Only one thing mattered more—Texas weather."

"Speaking of weather…" Carmelita glanced out the window as the first fat snowflakes splattered on the pane. "I hope Rosario comes for me soon."

"He's already here. I saw him ride in when I left the bunkhouse. It's a regular reunion out there by the corral."

The old man frowned. "I saw Cal McCabe and Adam Winter talking to Byron Conner. Didn't look like a friendly conversation, though. So I hightailed it out of there." Cookie walked to the window and studied the gathering clouds. "I think I'd better have one of the wranglers hitch up your horse and wagon, Mrs. Potter. You'll want to be heading for home before the storm hits."

Millie nodded. "Thank you, Cookie. I'll get my things."

The old man lifted the heavy basket of meat that Carmelita had prepared and headed toward his chuck wagon, calling out orders to one of the wranglers as he walked. By the time Carmelita had banked the fires and pulled on her heavy serape, Millie joined her on the porch.

The older woman shivered. "Even after all these years, I am never prepared for these storms."

Millie nodded. "I guess I won't see you again until the snows melt."

The two women hugged. Carmelita climbed up beside her husband, who saluted Millie before flicking the reins.

"Goodbye, Carmelita, Rosario," Millie shouted into the wind before settling herself on the hard seat and picking up the reins.

As the horse and wagon moved out at a fast clip, she turned to watch the cluster of wranglers who were saddling their mounts and securing bedrolls. The tall, muscular figure she'd hoped to see wasn't among them. Perhaps he'd gone ahead to search for the mustangs. Or maybe he was just eager to be gone.

She wondered if he was thinking of her. Missing her as she was missing him. Or had he already swept her from his mind?

She guided the horse and wagon across the swollen waters of Poison Creek and fought the feelings of gloom that had settled like a dark cloud over her thoughts. What was wrong with her? After all, she'd been the one to order him to leave. And it had been the right decision. Any respectable woman would have done the same. Their situation had become impossible. They couldn't continue to live in such close quarters and be expected to deny their growing attraction.

When the wagon rolled to a stop, the schoolhouse door was flung open and her three daughters raced outside.

"Miss Pearl was hoping you'd come for us soon," April said as she helped her younger sisters into the back of the wagon. "She's worried about those storm clouds over Widow's Peak."

Millie turned to see angry black clouds churning across the sky, covering Widow's Peak like a shroud. "Snuggle under the quilts, girls." She flicked the reins. "We'll be home in time for supper."

The horse and wagon bumped across the swollen creek once more, then started up the hill at a fast clip. Soon they had left the Jewel ranch house behind as they rolled across mile after mile of rich pastureland.

Millie drew her shawl close, struggling in vain to stay warm. The snow was nearly blinding, stinging her face, freezing on her lashes. She could no longer feel her hands.

The ground was already completely covered. For as far as she could see, there was only a limitless expanse of white. The wet, heavy snow dragged down tree branches until some of them snapped, sounding like thunder in the eerie silence. And still the snow fell, blowing, freezing, until the horse had to struggle to pull its burden through the drifts.

"Mama, look," April cried. "It's Diablo."

Millie turned, following the direction in which her daughter pointed. The black stallion stood on a nearby hillside. Dusted with snow, veiled in a curtain of white, he appeared to be a ghostly specter. As she and the girls watched, he reared up, blowing and snorting.

"He's cast his evil spell on us," April shouted.

"Nonsense," Millie cried. But even as she spoke, she felt a shiver pass through her. "Huddle close together, girls. And burrow deep into the straw for warmth."

Just as Millie was turning back, she felt the wagon lurch, then begin to tilt at a crazy angle. She cried out a warning to her daughters as the wagon fell on its side and the terrified horse reared up in the traces.

The three little girls were tossed about like rag dolls before landing in the snow. Millie struggled to let go of the reins, but they were twisted about her hands and wrists. The frightened animal continued to run, dragging the damaged wagon seat, with Millie still aboard, until the harness snapped. The horse, free of its burden, raced off, sending Millie flying through the air until the leather reins were ripped from her.

"Mama! Mama!" April, May and June gathered around the still figure of their mother, who lay facedown in a snowbank.

"Don't die, Mama," April cried, shaking Millie's shoulder. "Please don't die like Pa."

"I'm...not...dead." Slowly, painfully, Millie sat up, struggling to clear the stars that were dancing before her eyes.

"Are you girls all right?" She took in the three worried faces peering down at her. "Was anyone hurt?"

"We're okay, Mama. But look at your hands."

At May's words, Millie held up her hands and was astonished to note that they were raw and bloody. But she couldn't feel any pain. In fact, her hands were so numb she couldn't feel anything at all.

Pushing herself to her knees, she shook her head, fighting a wave of nausea. Then she forced herself to stand. Thankfully, nothing seemed broken. She could support her own weight.

"Come on, Mama." April tugged on her coat. "We have to get away from Diablo before he stomps us into the snow."

"Hush, darling. That horse is the least of our worries." Millie looked around. The mustang was nowhere to be seen. "You see?"

She circled the area until she located the quilts that had fallen from the back of the wagon. Then she gathered her daughters close and wrapped them in warmth.

"My feet are cold," little June whispered.

"I know, honey. Here." Millie lifted the little girl in her arms. At once burning, searing pain shot through her hands and arms and she was forced to set her back down.

Kneeling, she said, "Climb up. I'll carry you piggyback."

The little girl wrapped her chubby arms around her mother's neck. Millie draped the quilt around her, then said, "It looks like we'll have to start walking."

"Which way?" April asked.

Darkness was already falling. And the blowing snow had obliterated familiar landmarks. Millie refused to give in to the first wave of panic. Once they reached higher ground, she vowed she would get her bearings.

"This way." She reached her hands to her daughters. With April on one side of her and May on the other, she set off.

"I have to stop, Mama." May tugged on her mother's hand.

"We can't, honey. We have to keep moving."

"I can't go another step." The little girl dropped to her knees in a snowdrift and began to cry.

Exhausted, Millie dropped down beside her and gratefully slid June from her shoulders. The little girl lay as still as death. For a moment Millie's heart stopped. Then she realized her daughter was asleep.

She started to draw the quilt tightly around the little girl, when her hand scraped something in the snow. When she lifted it up, her heart fell.

Straw. The straw that had been in the back of their wagon. They had been walking for what seemed hours. And they were right back where they'd started.

She fought to keep the tears from her voice. "Come on, girls. It's time to get started again."

"I can't, Mama." May's tears were freezing on her cheeks.

"You have to, honey." Millie lifted June to her back, wrapping the little girl's arms around her neck. Then she dragged May and April to their feet.

Holding tightly to their hands, she forced them along by her side.

In places the snowdrifts came up to their knees. Millie fell so many times she lost count. One thing kept her going. The knowledge that if she allowed them to stop, they would all die.

It was black as night now, and she peered in all directions, praying for a light to guide her. But all she saw was darkness. Even the moon and stars were obliterated by the heavy curtain of snow.

"I heard a gunshot, Mama," April said excitedly.

"It was only a limb falling from a tree."

"No. There it is again."

Millie stiffened. "Yes. I heard it." She turned. "From that direction."

They stumbled through the snow, straining for another sound. Finally there was a third gunshot. This one was much closer.

"Over here," Millie called, cupping her hands to her mouth.

"Help us," April shouted. "We're over here."

A short time later there was another gunshot. This one was very close.

"We're here," Millie shouted at the top of her lungs. "Over here."

A shadow loomed out of the darkness. As it drew close Millie saw that it was a horse and rider.

"Oh, thank heaven." She watched the rider slide from the saddle and start toward her. In that instant she recognized the silhouette.

"Malachite. Oh, Malachite." She sank to her knees, tears streaming down her face.

"Are you hurt?" There was such ferocity in his voice she actually pulled back.

"Malachite…"

He dragged her to her feet, hauling her close, his hands

biting into her shoulders. "I asked if you're hurt." His eyes blazed with barely controlled fury.

She was too overcome to speak. All she could do was shake her head.

"The girls?"

"They're just cold and frightened. How did you know we were out here? How did you find us? Oh, Malachite. I'd begun to think..." The words shuddered from trembling lips. "I'd begun to think no one would miss us. And we wouldn't be found until..."

"Sh." He gave a long, deep sigh and wrapped his arms around her. "We'll talk later. Right now, let's get you home."

"Home." At that word she found herself weeping harder. Just having his strong arms around her made her feel that she'd come home.

He lifted June from her back and placed the little girl in the snow, with the quilt wrapped firmly around her. Then he lifted Millie to the saddle of his horse. Behind her he placed May and April. He untied his bedroll and wrapped the blankets around them. Then, lifting June up to her mother's waiting arms, he caught his horse's reins and began trudging through the snow.

"Don't cry, Mama," May whispered. "Malachite's here. We're safe now."

"I know, honey." Somehow she felt comforted by those words. Despite the fact that they were miles from town, despite the fact that night had fallen and the snow was still coming down, she felt safe, secure. She knew, without any doubt, that she could entrust her life, and the lives of her daughters, to this man. As long as he was with them, they would make it.

Chapter Twelve

"Here we are." In the bitter cold and swirling snow, Malachite's calm, deep voice was reassuring as he brought the horse to a halt.

Dazed, confused, Millie peered into the darkness. "This can't be Hanging Tree. There are no lights. No buildings."

"We were too far from town. You needed shelter immediately." He helped the little girls down, then reached up for her.

She sank gratefully into his arms.

For the space of a heartbeat he held her close and pressed his lips to her hair. Then he set her on her feet and led the way through the drifts.

Millie stared in surprise. "Why, we're back where we started. This is the Jewel ranch house."

"That's right." He leaned into the door and forced it open, then reached down and picked up little June, who had dropped onto the steps, too exhausted to walk.

Inside, he gathered them around the fireplace and began to stir the dying embers. Soon, with logs and kindling, he had a roaring fire started.

"I'll find some blankets." He turned to Millie. "See that the girls strip off those wet clothes."

When he returned with the blankets, the three girls were

bundled into them and settled comfortably in front of the fire.

"You, too." With a stern look he held out a blanket to Millie.

"I'd like to fix them something to eat first."

"I'll see to it. Now strip off those wet things or I'll do it for you."

She knew, by the roughness of his tone, that he meant it. Too tired to argue, she did as she was told.

A short time later she sat huddled near the hearth, surrounded by her daughters. Even talking seemed too much effort. And so they sat, staring at the flames, allowing the warmth to slowly seep back into their bones.

The air became perfumed with the fragrance of coffee and biscuits and something wonderful bubbling over the fire.

Malachite summoned them to the table and began ladling stew into bowls. He filled two cups with coffee and sat down beside Millie.

"This is delicious," she said. "What is it?"

"Plain old rabbit stew."

Malachite glanced toward the three little girls, who were making a valiant effort to eat. But after only a few bites, weariness won out over hunger. Their little heads bobbed. They rested their cheeks on their hands and closed their eyes.

"I wonder if this says something about my cooking," he muttered.

"Poor things." Millie studied them with a look of love. "They were trying so hard to be brave."

"Like their mother." He brushed a lock of damp hair from her cheek, allowing his hand to linger a moment.

It was an achingly sweet gesture that had her wanting to clutch his hand and hold it to her. Instead she sat very still, absorbing the tenderness of the moment.

"Come on." He shoved back his chair and got to his feet. "You know this house better than I do. Show me where you'd like them to sleep and I'll carry them to bed."

He lifted little June and trailed Millie up the stairs.

"Let's put them in Diamond's old room." She opened a door and set a lantern on the dresser before crossing to the bed to fold down the covers.

She turned. It gave her a start to see Malachite carrying her daughter. It was a painful reminder of what her children were missing in their lives.

He deposited June in the big bed, then went back downstairs for May. When she was snuggled beside her sister, he returned for April.

As he started to lift her, the little girl stirred. For a moment she sighed, wrapping her arms around his neck, snuggling close. Suddenly, her eyes opened and she realized what she'd done.

"You're not my pa. Put me down," she commanded in a trembling voice.

"I was just going to take you up to join your sisters in bed."

"I can walk."

He set her down. On trembling legs she climbed the stairs and gratefully crawled in beside her sisters.

"Good night, honey," Millie whispered as she pressed a kiss to her cheek.

"'Night, Mama." April flicked a glance toward Malachite, who was standing slightly behind her mother. Without another word she closed her eyes and settled into sleep.

Millie led the way from the room, closing the door softly behind her. Downstairs she draped the children's wet clothes over the backs of the kitchen chairs, then began clearing the table.

"Leave that," Malachite said.

She shook her head. "I can't ignore this mess. Carmelita…"

He took the dishes from her hand and set them down. "I said leave it."

For the first time he caught sight of her hands. "God in heaven." He lifted them, palms up, and studied the raw, bloody flesh. "Why didn't you say something?"

"It wasn't nearly as important as the girls."

"Sit here." He pressed her into a chair by the fire and stormed outside. He returned moments later with his saddlebags flung over his shoulder. From one of the saddlebags he removed a small, slippery pouch. "Hold out your hands," he said gruffly.

Very gently he spread a thick yellow ointment over her palms. Almost at once the pain began to subside.

"What is this?" she asked.

He nearly smiled. "You don't want to know."

"Another one of your Comanche potions? What does this one contain? Bear grease?"

He met her look. There was a gleam in his eye. "The pouch is made of deer innard. The ointment is made by grinding up the heart of a buffalo, the tongue of a wild boar and the eye of a mountain cat."

She pulled back in alarm. "I wish you hadn't told me."

"You asked." Then, unable to keep a straight face, he burst into laughter. "In truth, I bought it from a soldier at a military post. It was concocted by a doctor in Boston."

"Oh, you." She lifted both hands as though threatening to smear the ointment on his shirt.

With a laugh he caught her by the wrists. "Sorry. I couldn't resist. You make it so easy to tease you."

"You can apologize by getting me a cup of coffee," she said with a laugh.

He poured a cup of hot coffee and held it to her lips while she sipped.

"Sit here quietly," he muttered, "and warm yourself."

Too weary to argue she sat back, warmed as much by his teasing as by the coffee and the fire.

"Now, tell me what happened out there on the trail." He stood by the fireplace, his arm resting along the mantel.

"I don't know. One minute we were heading home. The next April spotted Diablo. I turned to look. The wagon jolted, then tipped over. The horse broke free of the harness and ran off."

The warmth was gone from his eyes. His words were deadly calm. "You didn't pass anyone along the trail?" he asked.

She shook her head. "I didn't see anyone or anything. Just Diablo. He looked..." She swallowed and forced herself to go on. "He looked like the devil himself, watching us as we approached, then rearing up as though determined to stop us. I know you think I'm foolish but—" she shivered "—that horse is evil."

"That's nonsense."

She refused to be silent. "Oh, Malachite. Don't you see? It's as though that evil horse planned it. It was growing dark. And so cold. The worst part was knowing that no one would miss us. Folks in town would think we were still safe out here. And there was no one left here at the ranch to come looking for us."

She turned wide, questioning eyes to him. "How did you know something had happened to us?"

"I saw Diablo, too. And his herd. And while I watched, I caught a glimpse of a horse in the distance, dragging a harness. I recognized it as yours." He fisted his hand by his side, the only indication of the depth of his emotion. "I told Cookie I had to get back to the ranch."

"He didn't ask why?"

Malachite gave her a bleak smile. "When your name is Jewel, no questions are asked."

She got up and crossed to him, touching a hand to his sleeve. "I'm sorry, Malachite."

He looked up in surprise. "For what?"

"I know how you feel about being in your father's house. If it hadn't been for us, you'd be free of all this."

He lifted her hand to his lips, pressing the gentlest of kisses to her tender flesh. The anger left his eyes, to be replaced by a hint of a smile. "Uh-huh. Just think. If it weren't for you, I could be up on the south range right now, shivering in my bedroll and tending the needs of ornery cows."

She smiled. "I think my daughters are the sensible ones. If I don't soon go up to bed, I'll be too tired to climb the stairs."

Without a word he scooped her into his arms and carried her upstairs. At first she held herself stiffly. But it was impossible not to react to the press of his body to hers. She had no choice but to wrap her arms around his neck. As she did so, her lips brushed his throat and she heard his quick intake of breath.

Long before he reached the top of the stairs, she found herself wishing she could just go on like this forever. Held in his arms, feeling his strong, steady pulse against her lips.

"Which room would you like?" When he turned his head, their lips brushed and she felt a series of delicious chills along her spine.

"Any one of them is fine."

He stopped outside a closed door and pushed it open with the toe of his boot.

The bed was covered with a pale pink crocheted coverlet, decorated with deeper pink roses. On the night table was an elegant porcelain bowl and pitcher. In one corner stood a tall, oval looking glass.

"This is Pearl's old room," Millie said.

"It suits you." He continued to hold her while he glanced around.

"You can—" she swallowed "—put me down now."

He met her look evenly. "Do I have to?"

She felt the brush of his hair along the back of her hands and had to resist the urge to plunge her fingers into the tangles. "It's the only way I can go to bed."

"You're wrong. There's a better way."

"Please, Malachite. I don't have the strength to argue tonight."

"Good. That's the way I want you. Weak and easy." He saw the heat that stained her cheeks. "All right. For now we'll do it your way." He set her on her feet but kept his arms firmly around her. "Sleep now. We'll talk again in the morning."

He brushed a soft kiss over her lips and forced himself to turn away.

At the door he muttered, "But I still say my way's better."

Malachite led his horse to the barn and forked hay into the stall. He had spent the last hours out on the trail, retracing the route Millie had taken with her wagon. The heavy snowfall had obliterated their tracks, as well as the tracks of Diablo and his herd. But he had managed to find the battered remains of the wagon. And what he had found left him seething with anger.

Like before, the axle had been weakened, causing it to snap. This was no devil's curse. This was a cold, diabolical scheme. But by whom? And for what reason?

No matter what the cost, he vowed he would get to the bottom of this mystery.

Working quickly, he chopped through the layer of ice and poured water into a trough. That done, he latched the barn door and walked slowly back to the house.

His father's house. That single thought lodged like a stone in his throat.

In the kitchen he rolled a cigarette and held a flaming stick to the tip. Drawing smoke into his lungs, he tossed the stick into the fire. Then he walked to the snow-frosted window and stared out at the ghostly landscape.

The trails would be impassable. For the next few days, until the storm abated, he and Millie would be confined to this house. At least for now she and the children were safe. But would she be safe from him? With only her children for distraction? Not enough distraction, he thought grimly. He was already feeling the effects of her presence.

It would be so easy to slip into her bed. Just to hold her. The thought made him smile. Of course, holding her would probably lead to kissing her. And that could lead to a whole lot more...pleasurable things.

Enough of this, he warned himself sternly. He'd been putting off the inevitable. But at least the unpleasantness that awaited him would keep his mind off Millie and his need for her.

With an oath he crossed the room and tossed the last of his cigarette into the fire. Then, picking up a lantern, he turned and made his way up the stairs, stopping in front of a closed door.

He pushed the door inward and lifted the lantern. Though he'd never been up here until tonight, he knew this would be the bedroom of Onyx Jewel.

The four-poster bed, carved from massive timbers, dominated the room. Along one wall was a blackened stone fireplace. The other walls were hung with animal skins. Black bear. White and gray-tipped mountain cat. The pale creamy fur of a cougar. The buttery hues of an elk.

A comfortable chair was drawn up in front of the fireplace. Beside it was a table, stacked with books and ledgers. In the ashtray rested the dried, crumbling butt of a cigar.

Malachite crossed to the table and set down the lantern. Kneeling on the hearth, he piled up several logs, then added kindling. When the fire blazed, he sat down in the chair and pried off his boots, then removed his shirt.

Restless, he circled the room, stopping beside a desk to study a tintype of Onyx Jewel taken when he was young. It was a shock to see his own face on the man in the picture. And even more shocking to pick up a small, egg-shaped moonstone, which had been cut neatly in half. In the center of the lustrous, pearl-hued stone was half of a perfect star. All his life he had seen the other half, worn like an amulet around his mother's neck.

A pair of boots stood in one corner. Pausing beside them, Malachite measured his foot against them and knew, without slipping them on, that they would fit. Hanging on the wall was a wide-brimmed hat. The one he always wore was nearly identical. And the cowhide jacket he'd carelessly tossed over a chair downstairs was a match to the bloodstained one hanging here on a peg. He turned it over, studying the bullet hole in the back, made by the coward who'd shot Onyx Jewel and left him to die by the banks of Poison Creek. Malachite had heard the story in compelling detail on the day he'd visited his father's grave. Onyx Jewel's four daughters had actually wept while they'd recounted the tale. He'd seen them watching him for any sign that he had been touched by the sad story of betrayal by a man who had called himself Onyx Jewel's friend. Malachite's lack of emotion had disappointed them. For all he cared, they could have been talking about a complete stranger. In fact, that was what Onyx Jewel was to him.

Spotting the decanter of whiskey on the desk, Malachite poured himself a tumbler and tasted. It was smooth and expensive and aged. He lifted it in a salute to the tintype, muttering, "Damn you, Onyx Jewel. Damn you to hell and back. I'm not you. Not anything like you. I'm merely your seed. A seed you carelessly planted but never nurtured. Don't expect me to be your son. Don't expect me to care about this place or its people. Do you hear me?"

He downed the whiskey in one long swallow, then tossed the glass across the room and watched it shatter against the wall. With an angry oath he finished undressing and blew out the lantern before climbing into the bed. But sleep wouldn't come.

He lay in the darkness, watching the dancing firelight play across the walls and ceiling.

He hadn't wanted to be here. Had fought it, and would be fighting it still, if it hadn't been for Millie. Right now, her needs outweighed his. So he would stay in his father's house, sleep in his father's bed. But it wouldn't change anything.

The spirits haunting these rooms tonight would not touch him. He had already hardened his heart against them. And when he left this place, they would not leave with him. His heart, and his anger, would remain intact.

"Mama."

Millie dragged herself back from the edge of sleep and

struggled to sit up. In the doorway stood three little moppets, draped in blankets.

When she opened her arms, they flew into her bed, laughing and shrieking.

"June didn't know where she was when she woke up this morning," May taunted.

"Did, too," the little girl cried.

"Did not. She thought she was in heaven."

"Why did you think that?" Millie asked.

"'Cause I dreamed that Pa carried me to bed." She snuggled into her mother's arms. "And Pa's in heaven."

"That wasn't Pa. That was Malachite," April said with disdain. "He carried May to bed, too. I walked," she added proudly.

Millie winced inwardly. Had she somehow done this to her oldest daughter? Had she forced April to become so independent that the little girl had closed her heart to accepting help from anyone?

"How come we're here?" May asked.

"Because the Jewel house was close. Malachite wanted to get us someplace warm before we froze."

"I wasn't afraid," little June said. "But I was cold."

"I was cold, too." May drew the blankets up over her head. "And I was afraid. A little." She turned to her older sister. "What about you, April?"

"I was cold. And scared," she admitted. "But not because of the snow. Because of Diablo."

"I wasn't scared after Malachite found us," May said firmly.

April ducked her head, refusing to admit that Malachite's presence had made them all feel safer.

Millie gathered her daughters close and pressed kisses to their cheeks. "Well, here we are, all safe and warm, thanks to Malachite. I don't think I've slept this late in years."

She breathed in deeply. "Ooh. Smells like biscuits. I'll bet

Carmelita is making breakfast. Let's get dressed and see if we can help.''

"We don't have any clothes," April complained. "We already looked around our room." She drew the blanket close. "This is all we had."

Just then they looked up to see Malachite in the doorway.

With a smile he said, "I believe these belong to the ladies of the house." In his hands were an assortment of dresses and petticoats.

The three girls scrambled off the bed to claim their clothes.

"The pink one is mine," June said, holding out her hand.

"And the blue one is mine," May declared.

"Then I guess this pretty dress must belong to you," he said, handing the pale yellow gown to April.

She accepted it without a word.

"I'd keep this one for myself—" he held up Millie's simple white gown "—but it's too small."

May and June giggled at his joke.

"So I guess I'll let you have it." He crossed the room and dropped it on the edge of the bed.

"Thank you." Millie kept the blankets tucked modestly around her shoulders.

He wondered if she had any idea how tempting she looked, with her hair tousled and her eyes heavy-lidded from sleep.

He turned and walked to the door. Over his shoulder he called, "Breakfast is ready, so you'd better hurry."

When he left, the girls hurried to their room to dress. As soon as the door closed, Millie poured water into the basin and began to wash. She knew she was taking pains with her appearance this morning. But she refused to wallow in guilt over it. She wanted to look pretty for Malachite.

She turned and caught a glimpse of her reflection in the looking glass. Stepping closer, she examined herself, clad only in a chemise and petticoat. She found herself wishing that Malachite could have known her when she was young and pretty. There had been a time when her breasts had been high and firm, her hips softly rounded. Now her body seemed thinner, more angular. Her fair skin was tanned and freckled from years in the harsh Texas sun. She examined her hands. Already the raw, bloody flesh was beginning to heal, thanks to Malachite's ointment. But even at their best, they would never be anything but rough and callused from hard work.

She turned away, not wanting to look too closely at what she'd become. What Malachite saw, she reminded herself, was a twenty-three-year-old widow with three children.

When she was dressed, she called to the girls. They needed no coaxing. From the wonderful scents floating up the stairs, Carmelita had outdone herself.

In the kitchen they paused in the doorway and looked around. It was empty except for Malachite.

"Where's Carmelita?" Millie asked.

He looked up from the eggs he was scrambling. "Probably at her ranch. I doubt she's going anywhere until this snow melts." He nodded toward the window. "It's a good thing you're not still out there."

Millie and the girls peered out the window.

"Mama, look," April said with a trace of awe. "The snow's clear up to the top of the corral."

Millie shook her head in wonder. "I've never seen that much snow."

"I don't believe I have, either." Malachite crossed the room to join them. "I couldn't even open the back door."

"How will you feed your horse?" May asked.

He shrugged. "I may have to climb out a window and shovel a path to the barn. But there's no hurry. There's plenty of hay and oats in the stall. Come on," he called. "Let's enjoy breakfast."

Millie started to walk to the stove but Malachite turned her toward the table and held out a chair. "Just sit down. I'll do the serving."

The girls giggled as Malachite served them hot biscuits, strips of sizzling pork and scrambled eggs.

"What's so funny?" he asked.

"You're doing Mama's work," June said between giggles.

"Your mama works too hard," he said, filling three glasses with milk. "That's why I decided to make her sit here and be treated like one of her boarders."

"Are we boarders, too?" May asked.

He nodded. "But if you're really good, I may let you help me wash the dishes."

There were more giggles as they began to eat.

Millie took a tentative taste of the eggs and biscuits and arched a brow in surprise. "Why, Malachite, these are good."

He gave a nod of his head. "Thank you. You'd better be nice to me or I may open my own boardinghouse in town and run you out of business."

"Oh, I don't know." She took another bite of egg. "Somehow I can't see you exchanging recipes and gossip with Lavinia Thurlong and Gladys Witherspoon."

Now the girls were laughing harder. Even April couldn't help herself.

He leaned over and tucked a stray strand of hair behind Millie's ear. "You're just afraid they'll like my rabbit stew better than yours."

When he took his seat at the table, she picked up her coffee and leaned back, glancing around at the children's smiling faces. It had been a long time since they'd been this relaxed and happy.

Just last night she'd feared they might not live to see another day. Yet here they were, laughing and joking as though they hadn't a care in the world.

She turned to study the man who sat at the head of the table. This was all because of Malachite Jewel. Without a thought to his own safety he'd plucked them out of harm's way. He'd given them a second chance at life. And though she was very good at hiding her emotions from the others, there was no denying the truth to herself.

She loved him. Desperately.

Chapter Thirteen

"Who's going to help me with the dishes?" Malachite asked.

"I will." Little June was the first one on her feet.

"I will, too." May followed.

"All right. June, you'll wash." He poured warm water from the kettle into a pan and set it on the table. He lifted the little girl onto a stool and tied a towel around her middle. "May, you can dry." He handed her a towel. "And I'll put the dishes away."

"What about me?" Millie asked. "What am I supposed to do?"

"Nothing," Malachite said firmly. "I told you. This is your morning off. Enjoy it. It may be the only one you ever get. Why don't you take your coffee into the parlor and pretend you're a lady of leisure."

Though Millie laughingly dismissed his suggestion, she couldn't hide her pleasure.

"What about April?" Little June turned to glance at her older sister.

"I'm going with Mama," April declared.

"But that's not fair—"

Her words were cut off by Malachite, who nodded his approval. "Go ahead, April. We have enough hands here. Besides, these aren't really chores."

"They aren't?" May's eyes widened. "What are they?"

"They're fun. And when we're finished here, I have even more fun planned."

"What?" Both girls were suddenly twitching with excitement.

He merely smiled. "You'll see."

In the doorway April hesitated. Not that she cared what the fun was. But she wasn't about to allow her little sisters to have it all to themselves. "Mama, would you mind if I stayed here and helped May and June?"

Millie shook her head. "I wouldn't mind at all." She walked away chuckling. A short time later she heard squeals of laughter as the three girls bundled into their coats and mittens and followed Malachite out a window and into the snow.

"Mama, come watch us," June shouted. "We're going to shovel a path from the house to the barn."

Millie raced to the window and watched as the three little girls followed Malachite's lead and began tackling the shoulder-high drifts.

A few minutes later, unwilling to miss the excitement, she joined them.

"So." Malachite looked up with a grin. "You couldn't stand being idle any longer, could you?"

She laughed. "I just couldn't stand missing all the fun."

He tossed a shovelful of snow over his shoulder. "I didn't realize this was fun. I thought we were working."

"Looks like fun to me." Millie picked up a shovel and worked alongside him, cutting through the drifts.

It took several hours to shovel a path from the ranch house to the barn. Inside they breathed in the rich, musty scents of earth and dung that permeated the air.

While Malachite cleaned his horse's stall and added fresh water and oats, Millie milked the cows and sent her daughters searching the straw for eggs. By the time they latched the barn door hours later, the wind was hurtling in from the north, bringing even more snow.

"It's a good thing we shoveled this path," Malachite muttered. "Or by tomorrow morning we'd be trapped in the house until this latest storm blew over."

"Why do we have snow?" June's mouth was pursed in a little pout. "It isn't good for anything."

"What do you mean, not good for anything?" Malachite set down the heavy milk pail and scooped up a handful of snow. Taking aim at Millie, he said, "I'll show you what it's good for."

Millie shot him a look of mock anger. "Malachite Jewel, if you toss that I'll…"

"You'll what?" he taunted.

"I'll be forced to defend myself. And you won't like what I'll do."

"This sounds like war. All right," he called to the three girls. "Who's with me?"

"I am," little June shouted, sidling up beside him.

"Me, too," May called.

"Traitors. Wait a minute," Millie protested. "Isn't anyone on my side?"

"I am, Mama." April took a step closer to her mother.

"All right. Prepare to defend yourselves," Malachite warned. He couldn't resist tossing the first snowball. Especially since the little girls were alternately daring him to toss it, then daring their mother to do the same.

The snowball splattered against Millie's cheek and trickled down her chin. With a shout she wiped it aside and tossed one of her own, landing it squarely on the side of Malachite's head.

"You'll have to do better than that," he told her. "Well? What are you waiting for?" he called to May and June as he scooped up a handful of fresh snow.

Following his lead, the two little girls prepared their ammunition and took aim. Millie and April did the same, laughing and ducking as a volley of snowballs flew through the air. When May and June took refuge behind Malachite's back, Millie grabbed her older daughter's hand and dragged her closer. "Come on. We've got them on the run now," she shouted, scooping up more snow as she ran.

When she got close enough, she smeared the snow across Malachite's face.

"Oh, you'll pay for that, Mrs. Potter." He caught her by the shoulder and pressed a handful of snow to her face. But at the last moment she turned her head and caught the snow in her hair.

Laughing uncontrollably, they fell to their knees and began to wipe the snow from each other, while the children gathered around to watch.

"Give up?" Millie demanded.

"I guess so." Malachite shook snowflakes from the ends of her hair. "Even though we have you outnumbered, you and April seem to have the better aim."

Millie turned to her laughing daughters. "You're lucky April and I didn't want to beat you too badly."

As she started to get up, Malachite caught her by the hand and dragged her back to her knees. "Just a minute. There's one more thing," he muttered.

"What's that?"

"It's an old Comanche custom." Before Millie could guess what he was planning to do, he leaned close and brushed a kiss over her lips. "When a fight is ended, the two sides have to show that there are no hard feelings."

April gaped in astonishment. May and June, enjoying the look of surprise on their mother's face, giggled and pointed.

Millie struggled to hide the pleasure that shot through her at the touch of his mouth on hers. She braced herself against him for a moment, then allowed him to help her up. When they were standing, she said sweetly, "Now I'll show you one of our old Texas customs."

Malachite puckered his lips.

With one hand she pulled open the neck of his shirt. With the other she dropped a handful of snow down his chest. Then, before he could react, she raced toward the house.

In mock outrage Malachite called to her retreating back,

"You'd better keep looking over your shoulder, Mrs. Potter. I intend to see that you pay for this."

"I'll warn you to do the same, Mr. Jewel," she called as she ducked into the house. "Just remember. I'm a very poor loser."

The little girls were giggling so hard they dropped to their knees in the snow.

From her position at the window, Millie watched as Malachite gathered the three little girls close and joined in their laughter. At the sight of them she felt a sudden tug at her heart. And without warning, her eyes filled with tears.

"Something smells wonderful." Malachite stomped snow from his boots and dumped an armload of firewood beside the hearth.

"I figured since you fixed us such a delicious breakfast, I'd better make something special for supper to redeem myself." Millie looked up from the fire. Her cheeks were red, her hair curling damply. "I hope Carmelita won't mind that I helped myself to some of her spices."

"At the rate that snow is falling, Carmelita might not get back here until spring."

He breathed deeply. The kitchen smelled of apple and cinnamon. Mixed with the wood smoke, it gave the house a festive flavor.

"I've brought in a couple of buckets of snow," he said.

"What for?" With her back to him, Millie stirred soup in a big black kettle.

"I thought we'd melt it over the fire and use it for baths later."

Millie turned. "Oh, Malachite. What a grand idea. The girls would love warm baths before bedtime. And so would I," she admitted.

"Then we'll start heating it now, so it'll be ready after supper." He filled a round tub with snow and placed it over the fire. For the next hour, as the snow melted and heated, he gradually added more and more snow from the buckets until the tub was filled with steaming water.

Their hours in the fresh air made everyone ravenous. They needed no coaxing when Millie called them to a supper of spicy beef soup, followed by roast beef swimming in thick gravy and served with potatoes, turnips and bread still warm from the fire.

Malachite leaned back, sipping coffee. "I don't think I've ever tasted anything finer."

"I hope you left room for my apple-cinnamon biscuits," Millie said as she uncovered the basket of desserts.

"Well, maybe one bite." Malachite helped himself to one biscuit, then another. Seeing little June watching, he winked. "Can I help it if your mother's the best cook in Texas?"

She giggled. "Is she?"

He nodded. "Without a doubt. And that means trouble for me," he said, patting his stomach.

"Why?"

"Because if this storm keeps up long enough and the root cellar here at the ranch keeps yielding treasures like this, and your mama keeps putting all this tempting food in front of me, by the time the snow melts, I won't be able to see my boots."

All three girls giggled at the thought of tall, lean Malachite getting fat.

"What did you eat when you lived with the Comanche?" June asked.

"Much the same as what you eat. Deer. Rabbit. Squirrel. And for dessert, we loved dried pumpkin meat drizzled with honey and nuts."

"Mmm." May turned to her mother. "Could you make that, Mama?"

Millie nodded. "I don't see why not."

"Didn't you eat beef?" June asked.

He shook his head. "Not often. The People are nomads. We don't raise cattle. But we take great pride in our horses."

We. Millie wondered if he realized that he'd referred to

himself as one of the People. Could it be that some of the pain and bitterness was beginning to ease?

"Have you ever seen a devil horse before?" June asked.

His smile was quick and warm. "Diablo is one of the most magnificent animals I've ever seen. But he's no devil. Or evil spirit. He's just a horse. And I intend to prove it. To you and to the town."

"Nobody can catch Diablo," April said with disdain. "Marshal Regan said half the cowboys in Texas have tried. And plenty have died trying."

"I'll catch him," Malachite said softly. "And when I do, you'll realize that he's just a horse. What's more, when I bring him in, his harem will follow. And I'll have the finest breeding stock in Texas."

At the thread of excitement in his tone, Millie turned to study him. He was always so careful to mask his emotions. But this time he'd revealed a tiny glimpse of his true feelings.

"I could help you find him," June said.

He shoved back his chair and paused to tousle her hair. "And how could you help?"

She squeezed her eyes closed and thought for a moment. It was plain that Malachite had become her hero, and she would do anything to please him. "I can see for miles from my bedroom window," she said solemnly. "I could watch for him. And when I spot him, I could call you, and you could chase after him."

He was careful not to allow her to see the smile that touched his lips. "I think that's a fine idea. When will you take the first watch?"

"Tonight. Until I fall asleep."

"That's good." He began to clear the table. "You can get started right after we help your mama with the dishes."

Millie was surprised at how quickly the three girls jumped up to carry the dishes to the sideboard.

As they finished washing and drying, April asked, "What's on the fire, Mama?"

"A tub of warm water. Malachite has been melting snow

so we can enjoy a bath. If you girls will fetch your blankets, we can get started.''

The three girls raced up the stairs and returned carrying their blankets folded over their arms. Millie took the bedding and spread it out in front of the hearth to warm.

She looked up to see Malachite pulling on his cowhide jacket. "Where are you going?"

He gave her a quick grin. "I think the four of you would appreciate some privacy. I'm heading out to the barn. I'll check the horses, then bring in a supply of firewood for the night. That ought to give you an hour or two."

As soon as he was gone, the three little girls stripped off their dresses and took turns bending over the tub while Millie washed their hair. Then they climbed into the warm water and splashed and giggled. Each time the water cooled, Millie added hot water until the tub was filled to the brim.

"Look, Mama." June held up her hands. "My skin is wrinkled. What does that mean?"

"It means you're waterlogged," she said with a laugh. "I think it's time to get out."

The three little girls reluctantly climbed out of the tub and dried themselves before slipping into warm blankets.

At a discreet tap on the back door, Millie hurried over to admit Malachite, whose arms were piled high with logs. A bitter wind rushed in behind him, nearly snatching the door from her grasp.

"How was my timing?" he asked.

"Perfect. The girls are all ready for bed."

She leaned against the door and slipped the latch, then hurried over to adjust the blankets around her daughters' shoulders. "You need to get out of this draft. I think you'd better get right upstairs."

"It's going to be cold up there," April complained, following behind her mother and sisters.

"It can't be helped," Millie soothed.

When they reached their bedroom, the girls were still grumbling as they climbed into bed. Millie looked up as

Malachite paused in the doorway. In his hands was a thick layer of towels.

"Maybe this will help." He crossed the room and handed it to Millie.

"It's warm." She glanced at him in surprise. "What's in here?"

"Stones. I heated them in the fire," he explained. "Then I wrapped them in the towels. If you set this under the blankets, the bed will be warm until the girls fall asleep."

"Ooh." The little girls' complaints were forgotten as their feet rested on the warm bundle.

"Thank you, Malachite. I think I'll have to wait until tomorrow to watch for Diablo." Little June, sandwiched between her sisters, fought to keep her eyes open. But the day's activities and the warmth of the bed were too much. Against her will, her lids closed. And she drifted into sleep.

"Thank you, Malachite," May echoed before she followed suit.

"You're welcome." Malachite brushed the hair from her eyes, then took a step back.

His gaze was drawn to April. Though her eyes were heavy with sleep, she continued to stare at him.

At last she managed to whisper, "Thank you." The words were spoken so softly they could barely be heard. Then she rolled over and buried her face in the pillow.

"You're welcome." Malachite turned and walked from the room, leaving Millie alone to tuck the blankets snugly around her daughters and blow out the lantern.

Deep in thought, Millie trailed slowly down the stairs. She was feeling anxious about this time alone with Malachite. Anxious and...expectant. Anticipation hummed through her.

Being here in Onyx Jewel's big house, so far from town, wasn't the same as being in her own home. There she was surrounded by memories of Mick and their life together. There among her familiar belongings, she was master of her own fate. But here she felt completely out of her element.

This was a different world. A world of success and luxury and power. A world that could belong to Malachite, if he chose to accept it.

But it wasn't the luxurious setting or the complete isolation that concerned her. It was Malachite himself. Or, more precisely, her reaction to him. She had been barely able to resist him in her home. How would she fare in his? Especially now that she was aware of her true feelings for him?

When she entered the kitchen, she took a deep breath, then stared around in surprise. Malachite wasn't there. Nor were his cowhide jacket and wide-brimmed hat.

The tub had been emptied. Fresh water was heating over the fire. The kitchen chairs had been set up around three sides of the tub with blankets folded over them, creating an island of warmth and privacy.

She gave a little laugh of delight at his unexpected gift. Once more he had taken himself off to the barn so that she could have this time to herself.

She filled the tub with warm water, then stripped off her gown, her chemise and her petticoat. When they were carefully folded, she stepped into the warm water and began to wash herself. Unpinning her long hair, she lathered it, then ducked under the water until it was thoroughly rinsed.

Wrapping her hair in a thick towel, she leaned back and gave a sigh of pure pleasure. What did it matter that the wind howled outside the door, bringing with it sprays of snow and sleet? She and her daughters were snug and warm and safe. Thanks to Malachite.

Malachite. She felt a twinge of guilt that he had taken himself out in the cold so that she could enjoy this luxury.

She smiled. She would make it up to him tomorrow. First she would fix him a very special breakfast. The rest of the roast beef. Coddled eggs. Thick slabs of freshly baked bread smothered with Carmelita's wild-gooseberry preserves. And if she could find a pumpkin in the root cellar, she would fix him the special dessert he had described. Dried pumpkin meat drizzled with honey and nuts.

The water had begun to cool and she wished idly that she could add hot water to her bath and remain here for just a little longer. But she owed it to Malachite to dry herself and take her lantern upstairs so that he would know it was safe to return to the house.

Still she lingered, unwilling to end the moment. How long had it been since she had pampered herself with such luxury? She couldn't recall the last time she'd stolen a few moments just for herself.

She shivered and forced herself into action. Stepping from the tub, she wrapped herself in the warmth of a blanket. Pulling a chair close to the fire, she removed the towel from her head and began to brush her hair. That done, she picked up the lantern from the table and made her way upstairs.

Before she even reached the top of the stairs she heard the door open and close; heard Malachite's booted footsteps; heard the sound of a fresh log being tossed on the fire.

And as she crawled into bed, she whispered a soft sigh and listened to the erratic rhythm of her heartbeat. And knew that she'd been lying to herself. The truth was, she had been unconsciously hoping that Malachite would return while she was bathing. She had wanted him to see her. Just as she had wanted to see him. To see his face. To watch the way his eyes darkened with desire.

She brought both hands to her heated cheeks. What was happening to her? Worse, what would become of her if she allowed these fantasies to take hold and become reality?

She rolled over and squeezed her eyes tightly shut, hoping to blot out all thought. But it was impossible. Even with her eyes closed she could see Malachite Jewel. His dark eyes. His strong, powerful body. His hands, touching her, stroking her. And his mouth. That wonderful, clever mouth, claiming hers. Bringing her pleasure beyond anything she'd ever known.

Sleep, she knew, would be a long time coming this night.

On a swirl of snowflakes Malachite stepped into the kitchen and leaned his weight against the door until it was latched. He turned, breathing in the dampness of water and the fragrance of soap that lingered in the air.

He'd stood on the porch, watching through the window until Millie left the room. It had taken all his willpower to remain outside in the cold, knowing what awaited him just beyond the door.

Did she have any idea just how tempting she was, with all that pale creamy skin and fiery hair? Seeing her running a brush through her hair had been the sweetest torture. He'd wanted desperately to take the brush from her hands and see to that chore himself.

Even now, picturing her in bed had his blood pumping, his nerves jumping. It would be dangerous to go upstairs yet. The door hadn't been made that would keep him out if he wanted to give in to temptation.

Feeling nervous, edgy, he rolled a cigarette and held a flaming stick to the tip, inhaling deeply.

It wasn't just Millie's presence that was causing him such discomfort. It was the spirits he could feel here in his father's house. There had been love here. The love of a man and a woman. The love of a parent for a child.

It was almost as if Onyx Jewel were reaching out from the grave, daring him to uncover the truth after all these years. Daring him to discover the man behind the myths. The man who had boldly saved a Comanche chief's life and stolen a Comanche maiden's heart. The man who had managed to earn the love and respect of four very different daughters. The man who was revered by an entire town and honored by his countrymen from Texas to Washington.

"No," he said aloud, touching a hand to the stone at his throat. "Don't you understand? It's all too little, too late. I don't give a damn."

As if in reply the wind howled and moaned against the house, causing the windows to shudder.

Malachite felt a prickling along his scalp. Tossing his cigarette into the flames, he stalked up the stairs to face his father's room. To face another sleepless night.

Chapter Fourteen

Millie lay in her bed, listening to the sound of footsteps on the stairs. She heard them pause outside her room and her heart started racing. In the darkness she squeezed her eyes shut and prayed that Malachite would step inside.

For long moments she heard nothing, and her imagination began working overtime. The thought of Malachite storming into her room and ravishing her had her heart stopping, her breath backing up in her throat.

When the footsteps moved on, she expelled a long breath, then sat up, shoving the hair from her eyes. What in the world was happening to her? She wasn't some lovesick fool. She was a reasonable woman. A widow who owed it to her husband's memory to behave sensibly. A mother who ought to think about her children. And if that wasn't reason enough to let common sense prevail, she would do well to remember that she was a respected resident of a very small-minded community. There were a good many people in Hanging Tree who would enjoy spreading gossip about the widow Potter and the mysterious son of Onyx Jewel.

She pressed her hands to her burning cheeks. She had never before entertained such thoughts about a man. But she wanted with all her heart to be held in Malachite's arms, to be kissed. To be loved. Oh, yes. Sweet heaven. To be loved.

Too agitated to sleep, she tossed aside the covers and began to pace.

She had always thought of herself as a good person and a good mother. But what kind of mother would risk her reputation, and that of her children, for momentary pleasure? For that was all she could ever hope to have. Malachite Jewel had made it abundantly clear that he intended to return to Montana in the spring.

She ignored the little pain around her heart. It was impossible to think of spring when the land was covered with snow. Like her heart, she thought. Buried under layers of ice and snow. Until Malachite's touch had melted it and caused her heart to start beating once again.

She knew that he felt the same way about her. She'd tasted it in his kisses. Had sensed it in the effort he'd made to control his passion. Yet now, when she had finally realized that what she wanted was to share that passion, he had decided to keep his distance.

She hugged her arms around herself and turned to peer out the frosted window, all the while listening to the erratic rhythm of her pulse.

Could it be that Malachite's code of honor would not permit him to follow through on his desires? Hadn't she seen his reaction when the women from town had suggested that he was, like his father, a womanizer? Of all the insults, that had been the greatest. The one that had angered him the most. He was so determined to be his own man. Any comparison with his father brought out his temper.

She felt a tiny flutter of hope begin to take root in her soul. Perhaps, if she could make him understand that she shared his feelings, he wouldn't be so reticent. If she could make him see that this was her choice...

Without taking time to sort out her feelings, she hurried across the room and tore open her door.

Malachite pried off his boots and tossed aside his shirt before roaming restlessly around the room. He tossed a log on the fire and watched it spark and flame.

Picking up the tintype of his father, he felt again the jolt at the similarity between himself and this stranger. The same thick dark hair. The same rugged, craggy features. And the eyes. He touched a hand to the stone at his throat and felt the familiar heat. With an oath he tossed the picture aside. All his life he'd resented his father's legacy. Yet here he was, sitting at his father's desk, living in his father's house. And wishing he could, like his father, take what he wanted without regard to the consequences.

What he wanted was in the room across the hall.

Millie. God how he wanted her. If all he desired was a quick tumble, it would be a simple matter to satisfy his lust. But his feelings for her had become far too complicated. That's why he'd been making such an effort to avoid her. Ever since the accident, and coming here to his father's ranch, he'd known he was in over his head.

He rolled a cigarette, held a match to the tip and inhaled deeply. Hell, he'd known a lot sooner. Almost since the moment he met her. And certainly after he'd returned from his first foray into the wilderness. That night, watching her taking the clothes off the line, and later, seeing her in the firelight surrounded by her daughters, he'd known. Known that she embodied all he'd ever wanted in a woman. A fiery survivor, strong, independent, passionate.

Millie Potter was not the sort of woman a man could love, then leave. When he looked in her eyes and read the sweetness in her soul, he knew she was the sort who would bind a man to her forever. One taste of those lips and he'd been lost. If he allowed himself to love her completely, he would be ensnared. Trapped. In a prison of his own making.

He wasn't certain he was willing to risk it.

He snatched up the photo again, glaring at the man. "Was this your weakness, Onyx Jewel?" he asked aloud. "Did you foolishly believe that love would solve all your problems? That if a woman loved you, she would turn her back on all that mattered and be yours forever? If it's true, then I had a fool for a father.''

When his door was thrust inward, he whirled, dropping the tintype. His hand went automatically to the pistol at his waist.

For a moment Millie cringed at the sight of the gun. Then, closing the door, she leaned weakly against it. ''I thought...for a moment...I heard you talking to someone.''

''To myself. Is something wrong?''

''No. Yes. No.'' She knew her cheeks were flaming. Worse, she could feel her legs trembling and prayed her borrowed nightgown hid the evidence of her fear.

''I don't understand.'' He hesitated before holstering his gun. From the moment he'd caught sight of her, his mind had gone blank. All he knew was that everything he wanted was now here. In his room. In the flesh.

''I'm afraid I don't, either.'' She gave a shaky laugh. ''I didn't really think this through. I just decided to come here and...'' She fluttered her hands in a nervous gesture. It hadn't occurred to her that he'd be undressed. The sight of those muscled arms and shoulders, that hair-roughened chest had her breath backing up in her lungs. She was quickly losing her nerve.

''Why are you here?'' The cigarette nearly burned his fingers. With an oath he crushed it into the ashtray on his father's desk. Frustration bubbled dangerously close to the surface. Did she have any idea how she looked in that gauzy bit of fabric that revealed as much as it covered? Despite the shawl she had tossed around her shoulders, he could see clearly the outline of her breasts, the narrow waist, the slight flare of hips. He felt as jittery as that damned stallion when he got wind of a mare.

''To...'' Oh, what had she done? How could she possibly put into words what she was thinking? ''To tell you...'' This wasn't going well at all. But she didn't know how to make it right. ''To say that...''

He suddenly had it figured out. Oh, it had taken a moment

to make his brain function. And seeing her blushing and stammering caused his heart to swell until he thought it might burst clear through his chest. But now that he knew, or at least thought he knew, he wasn't going to help her through this. It was simply too wondrous. Instead, he merely stood, silent and watchful, while she struggled to find the words.

"Malachite, I don't want to..." She took a tentative step forward. "I wish you would stop looking at me like that."

"Like what?" He stayed where he was, his hands clenched firmly at his sides.

"Like a hawk watching a chick. Anyway, as I was saying, I don't want to sleep in that room."

"There's something wrong with Pearl's old room?"

"No. Of course not. It's not the room."

"The bed, then?"

She shook her head. "There's nothing wrong with the bed. Well, there is, but it isn't the bed. It's who's in it. Or maybe I should say who's not."

The corners of his lips tugged into a smile. But he stayed where he was, determined not to reach out to her first. Afraid if he did, he'd frighten her away again. And he couldn't bear that. The need for her was too great. And growing with each passing moment.

His throat felt too tight. His words sounded too gruff. "Who would you like in the bed, Millie?"

"You."

She saw the way his eyes narrowed on her. She knew by the heat on her cheeks that they were flaming.

When he didn't move, she took another step, and another, until she was standing directly in front of him. Faking a boldness that would have shocked her at any other time, she reached her hands to his bare chest. She felt him flinch. That, and the flare of his nostrils, gave her courage to behave in an even bolder fashion. She slid her hands across his shoulders and up into his hair.

This was a momentary weakness, he told himself, and

struggled to remember the rules he'd set for himself. He didn't need any traps. But the touch of her had his mind going blank again. "So you'd like me in your bed. For how long? An hour?"

She lifted herself on tiptoe to see his eyes. "Do I have a choice?"

He was fighting to keep his voice calm, while his heart was racing faster than a herd of mustangs on the run. "This is your decision, remember?"

She chuckled. A low, throaty sound that had his breath hitching. "Then I'd like you there for the whole night."

His gaze fastened on her mouth and he felt all the blood drain from his head. "One whole night. Anything else?"

She let out a long, slow sigh. "You might try making love with me while we're together."

He was losing control. And he knew, the minute he touched her, he'd be lost. He thought about backing up. Instead his hands moved up her arms, and he struggled to be gentle. But it was too late for tenderness. His big hands were rough, almost bruising as they closed over her shoulders, pinning her to the length of him. His mouth sought hers, greedy for her taste.

"One night of loving," he muttered against her lips. "I suppose I could manage."

It wasn't so much a kiss as a mating of mouth to mouth. His tongue found hers, teasing, tormenting. And all the while his hands were burning a trail of fire along her back.

She felt the heat and was all but scorched by it. Alarmed, she pulled back.

"Afraid?" he challenged against her mouth.

"Certainly not." How could she admit that she was terrified?

He gave her a dangerous smile. "Changed your mind, then?"

"No."

"Good. Because it's too late." His mouth left hers to roam her face. With unexpected tenderness he nibbled her temple and her cheek and tugged playfully at her lobe until she sighed and gave herself up to the pleasure.

But if she had expected a tender kiss, she was in for a jolt. Just as she began to relax, his tongue suddenly plundered her ear. She moaned in protest. And all the while his hands moved up her sides until they encountered the swell of her breasts and his thumbs began stroking, arousing.

She tried to pull away, but when his lips nuzzled the sensitive column of her throat, she forgot her fear. She sighed and moved in his arms, awash in feelings unlike any she'd ever known before. And when his mouth trailed lower, to fasten around one already erect nipple, she let out a gasp that could have signaled pleasure or shock.

Despite the barrier of her gown, he nibbled and suckled until she clutched at his shoulders, crying out his name. "Malachite. Wait…I…"

"Too late." He lifted his head to look at her, and she found herself mesmerized by those green eyes, now blazing with need. "I want to see you, Millie. Really see you," he whispered as he reached his hands to the neck of her gown. But instead of unbuttoning it, he simply tore it away in his haste.

The sound of fabric tearing should have stopped them cold. Instead, it seemed to prod them into an even greater frenzy. As the gown pooled at her feet, Millie felt the heat of his gaze burn over her.

"You're even lovelier than I'd dreamed," he muttered as he dragged her close and crushed her mouth under his. "And, oh, the things I've dreamed."

He couldn't get enough of the taste of her. She was a contradiction. Clean and clear as a mountain stream. Exotic and sultry as any temptress. And those hands. Those small, clever hands. The touch of them on his naked flesh had his blood heating, his pulse racing.

When she reached for the fasteners at his waist, he helped her until the last of his clothes joined hers on the floor at their feet.

He was as dark and sleek as a panther. All muscle and sinew, and so potently male he took her breath away.

"You have no idea the things I've dreamed." His eyes glinted in the lantern light. "The things I've wanted to do with you."

He watched her eyes darken with pleasure as he trailed a finger between her breasts, circling first one, then the other. "Would you like me to show you?"

She couldn't speak above the pounding of her heart. All she could do was clutch his waist as he dragged her close and ravished her mouth. And then her hands were in his hair, pulling him even closer, raining hot, hungry kisses over his face.

He couldn't get enough of her. With teeth nipping, with tongue arousing, the needs grew, tormenting them both until they dropped to their knees.

Wild, frantic, she leaned into him, sinking her teeth into his shoulder. She wanted the feel of his flesh on hers. Desperately craved it.

"Touch me, Malachite." Her voice was a raw whisper. "I want your hands on me."

He couldn't wait to oblige. The feel of his callused, work-roughened fingers against her skin was the sweetest torment. Each caress sent new shock waves through her until her body became a mass of nerve endings.

Beside them the flames leaped and danced. Inside them, the heat grew, and with it, the need.

Through a blinding mist of passion she saw him, all hard muscle and fierce green eyes, his torso sleek with sweat. She tangled herself around him, needing to feel him with every part of her being.

Millie felt as if she were drowning. Drowning in the taste, the touch, the feel of him. She breathed in the dark, musky scent of tobacco and horses and leather. Scents she had known for a lifetime. And yet with Malachite, everything was new and fresh and exciting.

He was so strong he could easily snap her in two. She

could feel the control he exerted as she was enveloped in his embrace. That only made him seem more enticing.

"Please, Malachite." She knew she was begging. Knew her voice sounded raw and wounded. It no longer mattered. Nothing mattered except the need for him. At this moment her world had been reduced to this room, this man and the pleasure his touch brought.

She arched up, her arms encircling his neck. Heat rose up between them, misting their vision, clogging their lungs. But he wasn't about to give her what she craved. What they both craved. At least not until they had feasted.

They lay, tangled in their discarded clothes. She moaned softly as his mouth left hers. The moan grew into a sob when, with lips and tongue and fingers, he took her on a wild ride that brought her to the first glorious peak.

She shuddered and cried out his name, but he gave her no time to recover as he took her even higher. Each time she thought there could be no more, he showed her more. And more.

He could feel himself losing control. And still he held back, determined to draw out every touch, every taste, every pleasure.

Nearly mad with need, he arched himself above her.

"Look at me, Millie," he growled.

His eyes were steady on hers, watching as her lids flickered and she focused on him.

"I want to see you. I want you to see me."

They were beyond thought now, beyond madness, propelled by wild, pulsing needs.

He gripped her hands, lifting them above her head, lacing his fingers with hers. His mouth covered hers, cutting off the cry that was ripped from her.

She was all he could see as he drove himself into her. With the taste of her, the scent of her filling his mind, his heart, his soul, he began to move. With incredible strength she joined him in a dance as wild, as free, as ancient as time itself.

* * *

"Are you alive?"

"Mmm? Yes. I think so."

They lay, still joined. It seemed too much effort to move. Malachite nuzzled the corner of her mouth. "Then breathe, so I'll know you're all right."

"I can't. There's something heavy on my chest."

With a chuckle he rolled to one side, drawing her into the circle of his arms. She fit perfectly, he noted. "That better?"

"Mmm-hmm."

"You're shivering."

"Probably this cold floor."

Naked, he walked to the fire and poked at the log until it erupted into flame. Millie couldn't look away. He was magnificent. But as the flames grew brighter, she caught sight of fading marks on his shoulder and was shocked at the knowledge that she had caused them. Her teeth. Her nails. Her unleashed passion.

When he knelt beside her, she looked away, feeling awkward. "I suppose I should go."

"Go where?"

"Back to my room."

He trailed a finger across her shoulder, around her throat, down her collarbone. "I thought you wanted a whole night."

"I...thought you might want me to leave now."

"Leave?" He moved his finger lower, to circle her breast. Her head came up. She saw the gleam in his eye.

"We haven't even started yet," he muttered as his lips followed the path of his finger.

She gasped and clutched his head. When she found her voice she managed to say, "Could I ask a favor?"

He lifted his head. "Mrs. Potter, at this moment you could ask me for anything."

"Could we at least use the bed this time?"

With a laugh he lifted her into his arms and carried her across the room. He lowered her to the feather mattress, then lay beside her.

"Now," he muttered, "why don't I show you a few more of the things I've been dreaming of doing with you."

"Mr. Jewel," she breathed against his mouth, "I'm beginning to like sharing your dreams."

Millie lay in the predawn darkness, listening to the silence. Always, in town, there were sounds intruding. The creak of wagon wheels, the thunder of hoofbeats, the low rumble of voices. But here at the ranch, it was so incredibly still. With the earth blanketed by snow, and the wranglers scattered with the herds, there was nothing to break the muffled stillness.

She watched Malachite while he slept, and felt again the jolt of excitement at what they had shared. All through the night they had loved. At times it had been as rough, as ferocious as any breaking storm. At other times it had been slow and achingly tender, as though they had all the time in the world.

She had never known anything like this before. She had loved Mick and he had loved her. And their lovemaking had been sweet and satisfying. But she had never tasted the dark side of passion. Had never been driven to the edge of madness and beyond. Though she ought to feel bruised and battered, all she really felt was satisfied. And pleasantly sated.

She couldn't resist brushing a lock of dark hair from Malachite's forehead. Even now, just looking at him, she wanted him. The knowledge shocked her. And tempted her to touch a finger to his parted lips.

"Careful. I may bite."

"Oh." With a little laugh she jerked her hand away.

He reached out and caught it, dragging it back to his lips, where he pressed a kiss to her palm. When he felt the wild stirring of her pulse, he shot her a dangerous smile. "Do I make you nervous?"

"Of course not."

"Liar." With all the prowess of a sleek mountain cat he

rolled over, pinning her beneath him. With one hand on her chest he whispered, "Your heart's pounding."

She pressed a hand to his chest and smiled. "So is yours. Are you afraid of me?"

"Terrified." He lowered his head until his lips were brushing hers. "There isn't much I'm afraid of, Mrs. Potter. But you scare the hell out of me."

"Good." She felt the familiar rush of heat and traced his lips with her finger. "I think I like knowing that."

"See if you like this, too." He took the kiss deeper, swallowing back the little protest she was about to make.

"Mmm, very nice." If she were a cat, she'd be purring.

"And this." He brushed kisses along her throat, then lower, to the swell of her breast.

"That's…beyond nice."

"I was hoping you'd enjoy it."

His mouth moved lower, taking her on a wild and reckless ride.

All thought was lost as they slipped into a world of soft sighs and whispered promises. A world of dark, dangerous delights. A private world, known only to lovers.

Chapter Fifteen

"What's for breakfast, Mama?" June bounded down the stairs behind her two sisters.

"Eggs, potatoes, salt pork and biscuits." Millie turned as Malachite stomped into the kitchen with an armload of firewood.

For the space of a heartbeat their gazes met and held. He shot her a smoldering look that had her bones melting. Millie felt her cheeks flush before she turned away to pour coffee.

At the table, April watched in silence. Though she didn't know why, she suddenly felt tense and irritable. "I wish we were back in town. At least there we could play with Birdie. What are we going to do way out here all day?"

At the tone of her daughter's voice Millie turned. "Don't worry your head about it. I'm sure I can find plenty to keep you occupied. Starting with your schoolwork. After breakfast I'll assign new words to each of you. And then we can do sums."

The little girls groaned.

"I might have a more appealing idea." With his back to them, Malachite fed a fresh log to the flames.

They turned to him.

"Why don't we take a day off? A day of no chores." He got to his feet, wiping his hands on his pants. "And no schoolwork."

"But what will we do?" June asked. Though she was clearly intrigued, she couldn't imagine an entire day with nothing to do.

"It will be a surprise." Malachite crossed to the table. "But first, let's eat our breakfast."

The three little girls were so excited they could barely enjoy their meal. Malachite had no such problem, however. Millie noticed that he ate more than usual, sighing over her biscuits, lingering over a second cup of coffee.

When the meal was finished, Malachite and the girls carried their dishes to the pan of water warming over the fire. With everyone pitching in, the table was cleared and the dishes washed within minutes.

The three girls turned to Malachite, who was grinning like a conspirator.

Millie was as curious as her daughters. "What do you have in mind?"

"Follow me."

He led them up the stairs and along the hallway to the far end, where a ladder leaned against the wall.

"I climbed this," he said, "and found something very interesting."

"What? What?" The three little girls danced around him, clapping their hands in agitation.

"An attic." He watched their reactions. "Filled with old trunks. I think it might be fun to go through them. What do you say?"

"Yes. Yes." June was so eager she started up the ladder, but Malachite caught her around the waist and lifted her back to the floor.

"First we'll need a lantern, peanut," he cautioned.

"Peanut." She giggled, loving her new nickname, as she went in search of a lantern.

He held a match to the wick, then climbed the ladder. When the lantern had been placed on an old table, lending its light to the entire room, he signaled for Millie and her daughters to follow.

The room was nothing more than bare floors and massive log rafters, warmed by the stone chimney that climbed one wall. Under layers of dust and cobwebs were a number of trunks and carpetbags, their contents spilling out along the floor.

"Which one will we open first?" June asked.

"How about this one?" Malachite blew the dust from a battered trunk and lifted the heavy lid. Then he stood back to allow the three little girls to examine the contents.

"Look, Mama." May held up a gossamer ball gown of shimmering white silk shot with silver threads. "I wonder who this belonged to."

"That gown is familiar," Millie said with a frown. "Now, where could I have possibly seen it?"

"In the portrait in the parlor," Malachite reminded her.

"Of course. The portrait of Diamond's mother."

"Why is her dress up here?" May asked.

Millie shrugged. "I suppose Onyx Jewel wanted to keep it as a memento of someone he loved." She saw the frown on Malachite's face and knew that he was thinking about his own mother. "Let's see what else is in here."

She helped the children remove a pair of kid slippers, an elegant satin cape and a silk dressing gown decorated with oriental symbols.

"Do you think these belonged to Miss Pearl, Miss Ruby and Miss Jade?" May asked.

"They look too old," Millie said. "But these could have belonged to their mothers."

At the bottom of the trunk lay a pair of moccasins. Though they showed wear and had probably been discarded for more than twenty years, they were as soft as the day they'd been made. Millie handed them to Malachite, who studied them for long, silent moments.

"Were those your mother's?" June asked.

He shook his head. "They're too big for a woman's foot. They must have belonged to Onyx. But they were made by my mother."

"How can you tell?" May asked.

"Because they carry her signature. See?" He pointed to the distinctive star shape etched into the side of each moccasin. "Evening Star always left her mark on each piece," he said softly. "My mother took great pride in her handiwork."

"Why don't you try them on?" June asked, wide-eyed.

He shook his head, but the others joined in the urging until he relented. Removing his heavy boots, he slipped his feet into the moccasins.

Watching him, Millie was aware of how reluctant he was to use anything that had once belonged to his father. But she could tell by the look in his eyes that he was pleased with the fit. Not to mention the comfort.

"They look good on you," she said. "It seems a shame not to wear them."

Though Malachite said nothing, she noticed that he didn't remove them.

The three little girls had already moved on to another trunk. They removed shawls, bonnets and old-fashioned gowns, which they promptly began to try on.

"Look, Mama." June draped a fringed shawl around her shoulders and paraded around the room.

The others laughed.

Following suit, May stepped into a gown, holding the flowing skirt in one hand while she waved a parasol with the other.

Even shy April got into the spirit of the occasion by lifting a wide-brimmed bonnet to her head before joining the parade.

"May we keep these, Mama, and play with them?" June asked.

"These things aren't ours, honey. When we're finished with them today, we'll have to fold them neatly and return them to the trunks."

"But nobody knows they're up here except Malachite," May protested.

"And I'd look pretty silly in these clothes," he added teasingly.

At his remark, Millie couldn't help laughing. "That's true. But they belong to your family. Maybe someday Diamond and her sisters will want to show these things to their children. I'm sure that's why Onyx Jewel had them stored up here. So that his children would know something of their heritage."

Still wearing the fringed shawl, June dragged an old carpetbag from a dusty corner of the room. The bag, worn and faded, appeared to be much older than the other things in the attic.

"I wonder what we'll find in here," she muttered as her tiny fingers struggled to pry it open.

"What's this?" April held aloft what appeared to be a handful of feathers.

For the space of several seconds Malachite merely stared. Then, taking them from her hands, he shook them until they cascaded down to the floor to reveal an ornate headdress made of intricately woven eagle feathers.

"I've never seen this," he said with a trace of awe. "But I've heard of it. Everyone in our village heard about this gift from the chief, Two Deer, to the one who saved his life."

"Who saved his life?" April asked.

"Onyx Jewel. At great peril to himself, he fought a group of buffalo hunters. It nearly cost him his life. In fact, it was my mother, Evening Star, who cared for him until his strength was restored, and he was able to return to his own people. For his courage he was given the Comanche name Warrior with Heart of Eagle. It is the highest honor a brave can achieve. Legend has it that Two Deer himself spent many hours climbing to the tops of mountains and cliffs to secure the feathers."

"You must be very proud of your father," Millie said softly.

His gaze remained riveted on the headdress. "I guess I never really thought about it. I was too busy resenting him.

But what he did was brave and completely unselfish. I see now where his daughters learned their generosity.''

"There are papers in here," June called as she reached to the very bottom of the carpetbag.

The papers had yellowed with age, their edges curled. Some were still sealed with wax, others torn and frayed. But when Malachite smoothed them out, he realized they were letters. Letters written in Onyx Jewel's bold scrawl and addressed to Evening Star at various Indian missions across Texas.

Seeing the look in his eyes, Millie herded her daughters toward the ladder. "Come, girls. I'll let you play with these clothes downstairs.''

"But there are still some trunks we haven't looked through,'' June protested.

"I think we've seen enough for one day. If you're very good you may use the looking glass in Pearl's old room.''

A full-size looking glass was a special treat indeed. All further arguments were forgotten as the girls scrambled toward the ladder.

When April, May and June had climbed down, Millie turned toward Malachite. He stood in the middle of the room, staring at the yellowed papers in his hands. He seemed completely unaware of her presence.

She followed her daughters down the ladder, leaving him alone with the ghosts of his past.

Malachite sat on the floor, his back against a trunk. Over his left shoulder spilled a shaft of yellow light from the lantern. He read each letter carefully, amazed at the depth of honesty and passion Onyx Jewel had revealed.

It was all here. A declaration of the awe and wonder of first love. An admission of guilt at having left to pursue his dreams. A pledge to keep his love for Evening Star alive forever in his heart. A letter begging her to have pity on a lonely, lovesick fool. Urging her to reconsider her decision not to live with him as his wife. There was even a letter to

Two Deer, listing his offer of the bride's price. And what a price. More than anything Malachite had ever heard offered for a bride. Two dozen of the finest mustangs. A score of cattle. Wagonloads of flour and sugar. And a pledge that he would love and cherish the chief's sister for all of her life.

When he finished the last letter, Malachite pressed his hand over his eyes in a weary gesture.

These were not the ravings of a selfish man who had stolen the love of an innocent maiden, only to leave her alone and brokenhearted. From the markings these missives bore, it was obvious that Onyx had attempted to post them. And from their condition Malachite had to conclude that they had traveled across Texas by stage and Pony Express, to no avail.

Onyx Jewel would have known the odds he was facing. The Comanche were nomads, never settling in one place for any length of time. They would never allow themselves to be seen by the very people who were invading their hunting grounds. The settlers who ran the trading posts and the riders for the Pony Express were no more trusted than any other white man. It would have been an easy matter to avoid them.

Malachite glanced down at the clutch of letters. His mother had died never knowing that the love she had kept alive in her heart had been returned with a fervor that matched her own.

His father had died thinking he had written all these letters in vain. But in truth, they had indeed touched a heart. Not the heart Onyx had intended.

Carefully, reverently, Malachite returned the letters and the eagle headdress to the carpetbag. Then, taking up the lantern, he climbed down the ladder and made his way to Onyx Jewel's bedroom.

He had a sudden need to look at the picture of his father once more. This time, he knew, he could look upon Onyx Jewel's face without anger. Without any lingering bitterness.

This time he would look through the eyes of understanding. And perhaps, in time, even love.

* * *

Millie heard the sound of Malachite's footsteps as he made his way down the hall and into his father's room. When the door closed, she returned her attention to her daughters, who were preening in front of the looking glass, wearing fancy gowns, fringed shawls and wide-brimmed bonnets.

"Do we look beautiful, Mama?" little June asked.

"Indeed you do. Why, if I didn't know better, I'd think you were princesses."

While the three girls peered at their reflections and fell into fits of giggling, Millie found herself wondering about Malachite's mood. Had the discovery of his father's letters eased some of his pain? Or had they merely opened up old wounds?

She had a sudden need to do something special for him.

As she headed for the door of the bedroom, June asked, "Where are you going, Mama?"

"Downstairs to start supper. When you're finished playing, fold the clothes neatly and leave them here on the bed. I'll put them away in the attic later."

In the kitchen she stoked the fire and set out a pan of biscuit dough. Then she made her way to the cellar and studied the contents.

"Bless you, Carmelita," she muttered as she began assembling her supplies.

By the time Malachite and the three girls came downstairs hours later, the air was perfumed with the mouthwatering aroma of roast duck glazed with cherry conserve and stuffed with bread and herbs, potatoes swimming in rich gravy and rolls sweetened with sugar and cinnamon.

Malachite stared at the table, dressed in a lace cloth, with crystal and silver shimmering in the glow of candlelight. "Is it someone's birthday?"

"Just the end of a special day." Millie had gone to all this trouble to cheer him up. She studied him, hoping to gauge his mood. But, as always, he kept his features carefully masked. "I thought it should end with a special treat."

As they gathered around the table, the girls bowed their

heads. Malachite, seated at the head of the table, surprised them by reaching out one hand to April and the other to Millie. With his head bowed he murmured aloud, "We give thanks for this food, and for those who went before us, making all this possible."

Millie felt the press of his hand and her heart soared. *Those who went before us.* With those few words Malachite had told her all she needed to know. Somehow he had found a way not only to put past hurts aside, but to use the past to build a bridge to the future.

Would his future include her?

She glanced at him from beneath lowered lashes. He returned the look. And winked.

Seeing her daughters watching her, she felt her cheeks redden. Flustered, she said, "April, you may pass the platter."

"Yes'm." The little girl handed the plate to Malachite, who gave her a grin.

She'd had no intention of smiling at him. But the effects of the day, combined with the fragrances assaulting her, weakened her resolve. Immediately she felt guilty, as though she had somehow betrayed her father.

"How did you enjoy dressing up?" Malachite carved the duck and began serving it on their plates.

"It was fun." As always, it was June who took the lead. "Mama said we looked like princesses."

"Then that must be why she made a meal fit for royalty."

"Mama's the best cook in the whole world," May announced with her mouth full.

"I agree." Malachite tasted the duck, cooked to perfection, and his smile grew. "A woman who can cook like your mother is a rare treasure."

"Is that like gold?" June asked.

"Yes. Only better. Lots of men find gold. But very few men find a woman as special as your mother."

"My pa knew Mama was special." April's tone was defiant. "That's why he married her."

"Your father was a smart man." Malachite broke open a steaming biscuit and dug into his meal.

April glanced at her mother, then at the man beside her, waiting for the familiar panicky feeling. When it didn't come, she was puzzled. Maybe it was all this good food. Maybe it had been the relaxing, playful day.

"I don't know when I've had a better meal," Malachite said as he polished off his second helping.

"It isn't over yet." Millie lifted a pan from the oven and drizzled honey over the contents. As she carried it to the table, Malachite and the children breathed in the heavenly fragrance.

"What's this?" Malachite's smile grew as he watched her spoon the mixture into bowls.

"I believe you said it was your favorite dessert. Pumpkin, nutmeats and honey, with a sprinkle of spices."

Millie watched as Malachite tasted.

"Well?" she asked. "Did I do it right?"

A slow smile of appreciation touched his lips. He caught her hands and pulled her close. And while the girls watched, he lifted her hands and pressed a kiss to each palm. "You do everything right."

April saw the flush of pleasure on her mother's cheeks and the look of love in Malachite's eyes. And though just moments ago the pumpkin mixture had tasted like heaven, it now felt like ashes in her mouth.

She pushed away from the table and fled up the stairs.

Seeing her, Millie started to follow. But Malachite caught her hand and stopped her.

"If you don't mind, I'd like to talk to her."

Millie swallowed, then nodded. She and her younger daughters watched in silence as he followed April from the room.

April threw herself across the bed and allowed the hot tears to flow. Even with her lids firmly closed she could still see the way her mother looked, her eyes crinkled with happiness, her cheeks splashed with two bright spots of color.

She ignored the knock on her door and wallowed in misery. She hated Malachite Jewel. It was all his fault that everything was changing. Everything safe and familiar seemed to be slipping away.

"April."

At the sound of Malachite's voice she turned away, curling herself into a ball. "Go away."

"I will. In a minute."

She could tell that he was crossing the room by the way his voice drew closer.

"But if you don't mind, I'd like to ask you something."

"What?" The word was out of her mouth before she could think. Not that she intended to answer his question. To prove it, she squeezed her eyes shut so she couldn't see him.

The mattress sagged, and she knew he was sitting on the edge of the bed, watching her. She wouldn't look at him. Couldn't.

She waited, wondering what he had come here to ask. Whatever it was, she wouldn't give him the satisfaction of an answer. Then maybe he'd go away and leave her alone. Leave all of them alone. Forever.

"I'd like to ask you about your father."

That wasn't what she'd been expecting. She opened her eyes long enough to glare at him. "What do you care?"

"Sometimes it helps to talk about someone you love. Someone you've lost. Someone who might be fading a bit in your memory."

She blanched, and Malachite knew he'd hit a nerve.

"Pa's not…fading. And I don't need to talk about him to remember him. Especially not to you."

"I'm sure you don't. But what about your little sisters? How can they know their father if you and your mother don't talk about him?"

"They didn't know Pa. Not the way I did."

"That's true. All the more reason why you should tell them about him."

She digested that in silence. At length she asked, "Why should that matter to you? You're not my pa. And even if you…" She nearly choked on the word but forced herself to go on. "Even if you married my mama, you'd never be my pa."

"I know that. I'd never try to replace your father. But what should I do about my feelings for your mother?"

"You shouldn't have any feelings for Mama."

"Why?"

"Because. She's…old. And plain."

"Is that what you think about her?"

April felt a twinge of shame. And guilt. But she refused to back down. "I don't care what Birdie said about Ma being young and pretty. Mamas aren't supposed to be. Especially when they're widows. I've heard Mrs. Thurlong and Mrs. Witherspoon and the other ladies in town clucking over Ma. Saying it was too bad Mick Potter died and left poor old Millie with all that work."

"Poor old Millie. Is that what you think of your mother?"

April shrugged, too embarrassed to answer.

"Do you like seeing your mother work so hard?"

"'Course not." April scrubbed her eyes. "Sometimes, when Mama doesn't know I'm watching, she gets a faraway look in her eyes. And sometimes even tears. And that makes me feel bad. But tonight…" She drew in a deep breath. "Tonight I saw something else."

"What did you see?" Malachite asked gently.

"Ever since you came to stay with us, I've seen Mama changing. Laughing and blushing for no reason. Even acting silly and flirty. Pa is lying cold in the grave, and she's forgetting all about him. And she wants me to forget about him, too."

"Your mother will never forget about your father, April. And neither will you."

"But I am." Her voice was a cry of pain. "Sometimes I can't even see him anymore when I close my eyes."

Now it was out in the open. The real reason for her pain and her fear.

He waited for the space of a heartbeat before reaching out a hand to her shoulder. When she didn't flinch or pull away he drew her closer. "It's all right if the image of your father fades in time. You don't need to see his face in your mind to keep his memory alive."

"I don't?"

He shook his head and pressed a kiss to the top of her head. "All your father wants is for you to live your life to the best of your ability. If you do that, you'll honor his memory, and keep him alive forever."

He felt her take a long, deep breath and knew that he'd said the right thing.

"Is that what you're doing?" she asked. "Honoring your pa's memory?"

He felt a knife twist inside. "I guess I haven't done much of that lately. But if it isn't too late, that's what I intend to do." He stood. "I'll leave you alone now, April."

As he opened the door she called, "Malachite."

"Yes?" He turned.

"Do you think our fathers keep on taking care of us, even though they're in heaven?"

He studied this little girl, whose eyes, though red-rimmed with tears, were wide and trusting. Though she didn't know it, she was forcing him to peer into the dark corners of his soul for the answers. He closed his eyes a moment. And what he found was a glimmer of light. A ray of hope. Not only for April, but for himself. "I think it wouldn't be heaven if fathers couldn't keep on looking out for those they love."

He closed the door and leaned against it a moment, more deeply moved by her questions than he cared to admit.

A child's heart, he realized, was an awesome treasure. One that had to be handled with great care.

Chapter Sixteen

"Malachite!" June's shout pierced the silence of the early morning. "Come quick."

"What is it? What's wrong?" The door to the bedroom was thrown open. Malachite, still fastening his pants, burst through the doorway.

Millie stumbled in behind him, clad only in her nightgown.

"It's the mustangs." The little girl's voice was shrill with excitement. "I saw them. Look."

He crossed the room to stand beside her. Peering through the window, he watched the line of horses disappearing over a rise. At the rear of the column, driving the others when they faltered, was a magnificent black stallion.

"It's Diablo, isn't it?" June turned to Malachite with a look of triumph. "Didn't I tell you I could help?"

"Yes, you did." He picked her up and gave her a fierce hug, then set her on her feet and spun away.

"Are you going after them?" she called as her two sisters watched from their bed.

He nodded. At the doorway he stopped. Millie still bore the traces of their long night of lovemaking. Lips swollen and thoroughly kissed. Eyes heavy-lidded and sultry. Bare toes peeking out from the hem of a pristine gown that had been hastily pulled on. A fiery mane of hair tumbling wildly about her shoulders.

Sweet heaven, she took his breath away.

"How long do you think you'll be gone?"

He started to touch her, then seemed to think better of it. Lowering his hand to his side, he clenched it into a fist. "As long as it takes. I intend to track Diablo until I catch him."

"But how will you make it through the heavy drifts?" she asked.

He shrugged, fighting the urge to touch her. With impatient strides he moved past her. "If that herd can make it, my horse can. Until recently he was as wild as they are."

"You'll want some food," she called to his retreating back. "I'll get it ready."

By the time he hurried down the stairs, she had prepared a breakfast of eggs and potatoes, meat and biscuits. While he ate she filled his saddlebag with enough food to see him through a week or more.

Watching her, he said with a laugh, "How many people do you expect me to feed?"

"I just don't want you to go hungry." She filled a canteen with water and tucked it into his supplies. "I believe I saw a bottle of whiskey in one of these cupboards."

As she stood on tiptoe he got to his feet and caught her by the arm, stilling her nervous movements. "All right. Slow down. Tell me what's wrong, Millie."

"There's nothing wrong." She avoided looking at him. "I just don't want to forget anything."

"Millie." He caught her chin, forcing her head up. "Something's bothering you. What is it?"

"I wish you weren't going. I've never seen a storm as bad as this one. I keep thinking, what if you don't..." She bit her lip.

"What if I don't come back?" He stared down into her eyes, seeing the worry. "It isn't the storm. It's Diablo, isn't it?"

She gave a barely perceptible nod of her head.

His big hands framed her face. His thumbs stroked her jaw. "He isn't a devil. And you needn't worry. Even wild mustangs couldn't keep me away from you." He lowered his head, brushing her lips with his.

"That's what…" She didn't finish the sentence, but they both knew what she'd been about to say. Mick hadn't come back. And his death had left his widow and children alone and afraid.

"I said I'll be back. And I will," he muttered against her mouth.

Heat flared between them and he combed his fingers through her hair before taking the kiss deeper.

He heard her moan as she clutched the front of his jacket. Out of the corner of his eye he caught sight of the three little girls descending the stairs. On a sigh of frustration he lifted his head and took a step back.

"Remember where we were," he muttered. "We'll finish this when I get back."

He picked up his saddlebags and tossed them over his shoulder.

"Malachite." June's voice stopped him.

"Yes?" He turned.

She stood on the bottom step, looking very small and very solemn. "I want you to come back. But April said, if you bring back Diablo, you'll bring bad luck on all of us."

He winked and shot her a reckless smile. "I'll be back. With Diablo." He glanced beyond her to the middle of the stairway, where April stood alone, watching him in silence. "And I'll prove he's just a horse."

When he opened the door, a gust of wind rushed in, causing the sparks in the fireplace to leap and dance.

With a tip of his hat, he stepped through the doorway, pulling the door shut behind him.

Millie and the girls rushed to the window to see him trudge through the snow to the barn. A short time later they watched as horse and rider picked through the heavy drifts, following the trail of the mustangs.

* * *

Malachite crept to the top of a snow-covered hill and watched the herd below. For four days he had trailed them as they'd crisscrossed the territory, pausing only long enough to snatch a few hours of rest. Hunger drove them ever southward in an attempt to outrace the snow. But they'd been thwarted in their efforts. Instead of abating, the storm had continued, sweeping across Texas with surprising ferocity.

Malachite smiled as he watched the stallion work the herd. The name given him by the townspeople was apt. He was a demanding devil, nipping a mare that lagged behind, boldly plunging through belly-high drifts to break a fresh trail when the herd balked.

The stallion led them unerringly toward the protection of a box canyon. The steep walls offered shelter from the storm. Here and there were grassy patches that would provide much needed food. As they approached the narrow opening, Diablo stood back, sniffing the air, studying the surrounding hills for any sign of predators. Seeing none, he allowed the others to file past. Soon, while the stallion stood guard, the herd began foraging.

Malachite crept back to where he'd tethered his horse and helped himself to cold meat and biscuits. He couldn't risk a fire. Not that he had need of one. The thrill of the hunt had the blood pumping hotly in his veins.

When he'd eaten his fill, he slipped the rope over the end of a fallen tree and tied the other end around the pommel of the saddle. He'd known, if he was patient and persistent, he'd find his moment.

For the sake of the herd, the stallion had just made a critical mistake. Though there was ample food and shelter in the canyon, there was but one way to exit. And Malachite was about to see to it that the escape route was cut off.

A slow smile spread across his face. "I've got you now, you magnificent devil."

Millie stirred the pot of stew and watched as fresh snowflakes floated past the window. The days had seemed so long since Malachite left. She'd struggled to fill her days with work, to keep her mind off him and the dangers he faced. While she swept and scrubbed and busied herself with all manner of chores, it was almost possible. But the nights were another matter. Visions of him crept into her dreams. Dreams tormented with images of a devil horse, eyes glittering, hooves flashing, rearing high and crushing his stalker with powerful blows. She'd been awake since dawn, struggling to banish the image of Malachite, bloody and beaten, lying helpless in the snow, waiting for death to claim him.

She wasn't the only one who'd been troubled. Her three daughters, suffering from the long days of confinement, had become tense and irritable.

"April hogged the covers again last night," May complained.

"Did not."

"Did, too. And you deliberately rolled yourself up so I couldn't get them back."

"I rolled up so June couldn't put her cold feet on my back."

"I don't do that," the little girl protested.

"Do, too."

"All right, girls. That's enough." Millie rapped the wooden spoon against the rim of the pot with such force the three little girls fell silent. Taking a deep breath, she prayed for patience. "There must be a solution to this problem."

"There is," April said, pouting. "Let me sleep by myself. I'm tired of sleeping with my little sisters."

Millie arched a brow. Why hadn't she thought of it herself? "I think you have a very good point, April." She saw her daughter's eyes widen. "All right. Unlike our house in town, we don't need to save the extra rooms for boarders. There are enough rooms here that each of you may choose one for yourself. Now, where would you like to sleep?"

For the space of a minute the little girl was speechless. She'd never been given such a choice before. Always she'd had to share. Now, suddenly, the choices seemed endless.

"Do we have to choose now?"

Millie shook her head. "Why don't the three of you look around and decide. Supper will be ready in an hour or so. By that time, I'll expect each of you to choose which bedroom you'd like."

Their bickering was forgotten. The three little girls raced up the stairs, each one eager to choose the perfect bedroom.

Millie smiled as she went about setting the table. The children's voices drifted down. Peals of laughter. Squeals of excitement. Endless chatter. Doors were opened and closed. Footsteps sounded overhead. Finally the three girls trooped down the stairs, looking very pleased with themselves.

"Well?" Millie lifted a pan of biscuits from the fire.

"I've chosen Jade's room," April said. "'Cause I like the big soft bed and those mysterious oriental scrolls on the bed linens."

"A very good choice." Millie fought to remain as serious as her daughters. "What about you, May?"

"I decided on Ruby's room. She left bits of pretty ribbons and lace everywhere."

That would appeal to her prissy, romantic middle daughter, Millie thought. "All right. And you, June?"

"I want to stay where I am," the little girl said solemnly.

"Diamond's room suits you, then? Is it because it's simple and rugged?"

The little girl shook her head. "It's...the window."

"The window?"

"She spends half the night staring out that window," April said with a note of disdain, "watching for Malachite."

Millie felt her heart contract. Didn't she do the same? "It's settled, then." She turned away and began to ladle soup into bowls. "After supper you can move your things into your new rooms."

"We already did," April announced.

Millie bit back her smile. They were taking no chances that she might change her mind. "All right, then. Let's call this supper a celebration of your new freedom."

The three little girls dug into their meals. All their earlier squabbles were forgotten as they slathered butter on freshly baked bread and discussed the merits of privacy.

"I can curl up into a ball and have all the blankets to myself," April said with a sigh of contentment.

"And I can kick out my legs without being told to lie still," May added.

"When I want to look out the window I can climb out of bed without having to crawl over anybody," June said with obvious delight.

Millie walked to the fire and poured herself a cup of coffee. What they were saying was all true. Yet it had taken her years to learn to sleep alone. And now, after just two nights with Malachite, her big bed felt cold and empty.

She started back to the table when a sudden glance out the window revealed a dark form against the snow.

"Malachite. Malachite." His name was torn from Millie's lips. Coffee sloshed over the rim of her cup. She took no notice.

She flew to the door, her daughters behind her. They watched as Malachite closed the door to the barn and started toward them.

In the corral the dark forms of the skittish, nervous mustangs milled about. And coming from the barn were the bellows of rage from their leader, the black stallion, Diablo.

"Where did you sleep?"

"Most of the time I slept out in the open. Wrapped in a buffalo robe."

"Were you cold?"

"Sometimes."

"Weren't you afraid?" This from April. It was the first time she'd spoken since Malachite returned. As always, fear was uppermost in her mind. Especially fear of the danger that was rumored to accompany Diablo.

Malachite shook his head. "Being alone in the night

doesn't scare me half as much as being alone in a saloon with a roomful of drunken cowboys."

"Why?" June asked.

He winked. "I'll tell you some other time."

"Tell us about Diablo. How did you catch him?"

Millie and the girls gathered around the table while Malachite ate. So far he had finished two bowls of hot soup, several slices of roast venison, four rolls smothered with blueberry conserve and two cups of steaming coffee. Now he leaned back, draining his cup before biting the end of a cigar.

"I cut off his escape from a canyon, then went in and lassoed him."

"Didn't he break the rope?" June was hanging on his every word. "Everybody in town says there isn't a lasso that can hold Diablo."

"He is strong. And I think he'd have broken free if I'd used a single rope." Malachite pushed away from the table and lifted a flaming stick from the fire, holding it to the tip of his cigar. "But as soon as he was caught, I added a second, then a third lasso, just in case."

"Did he fight you?"

"He's not fond of ropes." As always, the things he left unsaid spoke volumes.

"How did you get the others to follow?" May asked.

"That part was easy." Malachite exhaled a cloud of rich smoke. "Once I had their leader, I figured they'd trail along. They depend on Diablo. Trust him. But they've learned not to trust man. A few of the bolder mares followed closely. The rest are still out there, too afraid to come in. But in the next few days they won't be able to resist the lure of food and shelter. This storm was a blessing in disguise. With so much snow covering the grass, they're practically starving."

"Why did you put Diablo in the barn?" Millie asked.

"In the mood he's in, no corral would hold him." His tone was filled with admiration. "He's the strongest mustang I've ever encountered."

"If that's the case, aren't you afraid he'll kick down the stalls and break loose anyway?"

Malachite shook his head. "There are three ropes holding him. But if he gets too crazy through the night, I'll hobble him for his own protection."

"Through the night?" Millie glanced at him in alarm. "Do you intend to watch him all night?"

"I have no choice." Malachite kept his tone even to hide the emotions churning inside him. The sight of Millie had his palms sweating and his throat dry. He'd love nothing more than to lie with her in the big feather bed upstairs. But the situation right now was impossible. He cautioned himself to keep his wits about him. "For the next couple of days I can't let Diablo out of my sight."

"Because he's a devil," April said solemnly.

"No. Because he's a wild horse who wants to escape back to the wilderness."

Millie wasn't even listening to the sparring between her daughter and Malachite. All she'd heard was the words Malachite had spoken. The next couple of days. Millie gathered up the dishes and turned away to hide her disappointment. For the next couple of days, she and Malachite would have to remain apart.

But at least, she reminded herself, he was back home with them. Safe and sound after his adventure. And he had returned bearing the prize he had sought. She would take comfort in that and bide her time until he could enfold her in his arms again.

As if reading her mind, Malachite tossed his cigar into the fire and crossed to her. Rubbing his knuckles over her cheek, he muttered, "I missed you."

"I missed you, too." She wanted desperately to put her arms around his waist and rest her head on his shoulder, just for a moment. Instead she stood very straight, avoiding his eyes. "And I'm so glad you've come home."

He was aware of the control she was exerting. He wouldn't

add to her discomfort, though it took all his willpower to keep from dragging her against him and ravishing her mouth.

He turned away and pulled on his heavy cowhide parka. As he let himself out into the frigid darkness, her words played through his mind. *So glad you've come home.*

Home. Did she have any idea what she had just said? All his life he had longed to hear those words. Yet he had spent a lifetime feeling adrift. A man between two cultures. Believing that he had no real home.

As he strode toward the barn he turned and glanced through the window, which was illuminated by firelight. It framed such an ordinary picture. A mother and her three children clearing the table, then washing and drying the dishes. But to him it was the most extraordinary scene.

And all because he had somehow begun to believe that he could put himself in the middle of it. And belong.

Chapter Seventeen

"Good morning, Malachite." Millie closed the barn door on a swirl of snowflakes. "I brought you some…"

When she turned, the words died on her lips. She caught her breath at the sight that greeted her.

The townspeople had been right. This creature, rearing and pawing the air, was watching Malachite with a look of pure hatred. He looked like the devil himself. As did the man who faced him.

"Not now, Millie." Malachite's voice was deadly calm.

"But you haven't eaten since…"

He flicked her a glance, then returned his attention to the mustang. "Go back to the house. It isn't safe for you to be here."

"But the girls…"

"Keep the girls away from the barn today." Despite the softness of his tone, there was a thread of steel to it.

She studied Malachite. A heavy dark beard covered his cheeks and chin. His eyes were red from lack of sleep. But there was a look in them as wild, as determined as that of the stallion.

She hadn't really come to bring him the food on the tray. That had just been an excuse to satisfy the need to see him. But seeing him made her realize the futility of her actions.

He had gone to a place she couldn't follow. A place as dark, as daunting as the creature facing him.

"I...yes. Of course." She set the tray down in the straw.

She needed no coaxing as the mustang reared again, bringing his deadly hooves crashing into the boards of his stall. As she pulled the door shut behind her, she could hear the sound of wood splintering.

Perhaps, she thought, Diablo really was a devil. He was certainly the strongest, most defiant mustang she'd ever seen.

But if she were a betting woman, she'd put her money on Malachite.

Millie and the girls watched as Malachite led Diablo out of the barn, keeping a firm grip on the lead rope.

In the past week he and the stallion had not been apart. Malachite had slept in the barn, washed in the barn, taken his meals in the barn. And though Diablo still resented him, the animal had been driven by hunger to accept food from this man's hands.

Each time Malachite entered the stall, the stallion flew into a rage. But slowly, inch by painful inch, the rages had lessened, until this morning the horse had stood, silent and quivering, as Malachite slipped the lead rope over his head.

Now, as they passed the corral filled with Diablo's harem, the horse lifted his head, filling himself with the scent of the mares, which carried on the air. The herd reacted restlessly, moving in slow circles, keeping their leader in sight.

Malachite led the horse to an empty corral and turned him loose. At once the stallion charged the enclosure, bucking and rearing, battering the prison with his hooves.

And all the while Malachite stood just outside the corral, watching, waiting.

When Diablo grew weary of the fight, Malachite opened the gate and walked toward the horse, holding out his hand. In it was a carrot, dug from the dirt of the root cellar.

"I think you'll like this," he muttered as he offered the treat.

Diablo snorted and pawed the ground. When that threat didn't work, the stallion backed away. But when Malachite continued coming toward him, the animal sniffed, then accepted the carrot.

"A wise choice." Malachite smiled. "But then I never doubted that you were a very smart horse."

Diablo pricked up his ears, listening to the familiar sound of Malachite's voice. It had become a constant in his life. Soothing. Murmuring. As had this man's hands. Gentle. Easy.

"Before this day's over, you're going to trust me enough to accept something more from me." Malachite uncoiled the leather draped around his shoulder. When he held out the bridle, the stallion sidestepped away. Unconcerned, Malachite kept coming toward him until the horse relented enough to sniff the leather.

"Take a good smell," Malachite whispered. "It's going to become a part of you. Very soon now, you won't even notice it."

As he spoke he lifted the bridle over the horse's head, brushing its mane, its ears, until the ripples of tension ended and Diablo stood perfectly still. Then, moving slowly and deliberately, Malachite adjusted the bit and draped the ends of the reins over the horse's neck.

All the while Millie watched with growing fascination. The relationship between man and animal was as complex as a courtship ritual. She felt her cheeks begin to burn. Had Malachite played her as patiently? Doing everything he could to gain her trust, before leading her to the next level? Dear heaven. She lifted her hands to her face and turned away.

"Where are you going, Mama?" April stood a little apart from the others, watching every movement with a kind of horrified fascination, convinced that this would be a duel to the death.

"Inside, honey. I thought I'd start supper."

"But Malachite is getting ready to saddle Diablo," June cried. "Can we stay and watch?"

Millie nodded. "Go ahead. I'll call you when supper is ready."

"Don't you know anything?" April chided her youngest sister. "Diablo will never let Malachite ride him."

At her oldest daughter's somber tone, Millie shivered. Before making her way inside, she turned for one last glimpse of man and horse. They were, she had to admit, evenly matched. Each was fiercely independent. Truly magnificent. And each was determined to win.

"Mama. Come quick."

June's shouts had Millie racing toward the porch. What she saw took her breath away.

Malachite was in the saddle. But at first glance, it wasn't clear who was in control. The stallion took off at a dead run, racing across the corral, heading directly toward the fence. When he reached it, he reared up, frantically pawing the air. When that failed to dislodge the weight on his back, he circled the corral, bucking and twisting. Several times he threw himself sideways against the railing, hoping to crush the legs of his opponent. With incredible speed, Malachite was able to fling himself from one side of the horse to the other, deftly gripping the pommel for support.

As each of his attempts was thwarted, the stallion seemed to be losing speed. Though he continued circling the enclosure, his rage gradually dissipated. And without realizing it, the horse began responding to the gentle direction of the man in the saddle. With soft words of encouragement, with a nudge of his knee or slight tug on the reins, Malachite was able to take the animal through a series of commands.

Finally, as proof of his success, Malachite slid from the saddle and ordered the horse to stay. Walking from one side of the corral to the other, he never once turned to look at the horse.

"He's going to be trampled," April predicted. "Diablo has been waiting for this chance."

Millie found herself holding her breath.

Malachite paused at the gate, turned and reached out a hand. When he gave a whistle, the stallion came trotting to his side. At once Malachite patted Diablo's head and dug a carrot from his pocket as a reward for a job well done.

The horse nuzzled his hand before chewing contentedly.

"See." Little June couldn't resist taunting her older sister. "You were wrong, April. Malachite wasn't trampled. In fact, Diablo likes him."

"He only pretends to like Malachite. Mrs. Thurlong said we should never trust the devil."

"Malachite says Diablo isn't the devil. He's just a horse."

Instead of being persuaded of the horse's innocence, April seemed even more determined to believe the myth. "If bad things aren't happening to Malachite, maybe they're going to happen to one of us instead. Mrs. Thurlong says…"

Millie had heard enough. "All right, girls. I think it's time to go inside and wash up for supper."

As the three little girls made their way inside, Millie remained where she was, watching Malachite put Diablo through his paces. There was no reason to believe Lavinia Thurlong's nonsense. But April's words disturbed her more than she cared to admit. A tiny chill coursed along her spine. She trusted Malachite completely. After all, he truly believed that the stallion was nothing more than a clever, beautiful mustang who had managed to elude capture through sheer luck. But it was hard to discount the fact that this animal had roamed freely for more than a year, despite the fact that dozens of cowboys had hunted him. And it was impossible to deny that everywhere Diablo went, death and destruction seemed to follow.

The house was quiet. April, May and June had long ago gone to their beds. Millie banked the fire in the kitchen and poured the last cup of coffee. Sipping, she stared out the window at the darkened outline of the barn, wondering if Malachite was already asleep. It wouldn't be surprising, considering the bone-jarring hours he'd put in today.

She understood Malachite's need to be close to the mustang. Yet she missed him. Desperately.

Was it selfish to want him here with her, holding her,
comforting her? She couldn't help it. The ache around her
heart seemed to grow with each day. Sometimes she found
herself wishing Malachite had never heard of the defiant
black stallion or the legend that surrounded him. Still, if he
hadn't been challenged to hunt the mustang, he would have
stuck to his original plan to return immediately to Montana.
They would have never had the chance to know each other.
To fall in love.

Love. It was so wonderful. And so terrible.

She loved Malachite. Loved him desperately. And that fact
was definitely complicating her life. She knew her feelings
for him were damaging her relationship with her firstborn.
And if April's distrust wasn't bad enough, there was her
reputation with the people of Hanging Tree.

Oh, why couldn't life ever be simple?

She pressed a hand to her mouth. With a sigh of frustration
she turned away and nearly collided with the man who had
been occupying all of her thoughts.

"Malachite. I didn't hear you come in."

His hands closed over her shoulders. "That's obvious."

"Would you like to share my coffee?" She offered him
the cup and he drained it.

"I could make you some more."

She started to turn away but he held her still.

"I didn't come here for coffee."

"Food, then."

"You know what I'm hungry for, Millie." His fingers
reached for the top button of her gown.

She went very still, feeling a rush of heat that left her
weak. "What about Diablo?"

The smile he gave her was wicked. "He and I have been
sharing a lot lately. But he'll have to learn that I don't share
my woman."

My woman. The sound of it sent a little thrill racing along her spine.

He watched her eyes go soft and cloudy as he undid the second button.

She brushed her lips across his cheek. "Your hands are cold."

"Sorry. It's freezing out in that barn."

"I'm not complaining. It's just that I'm so impatient to have them on me," she whispered against his lips.

The urgency of her words had him fumbling with the next button. "For nights I've been thinking of you, upstairs in that big feather bed. The pictures in my mind almost drove me mad."

"The bed's still there," she murmured as he gathered her close. "Just waiting for us."

"I don't think I can wait that long." He brushed his lips across her cheek. "I need to taste you. Right now."

The kiss was long and slow and deep. And when it ended, he continued holding her, raining kisses across her nose, her cheek, her temple. And all the while his hands caressed her as though he were holding a fragile doll.

The tenderness was so unexpected she released a sigh, whispered like a prayer.

He responded to the change in her. In himself. He had come here in a rush, hungry for the taste of her, the touch of her. But now, he realized, there was no need to rush. Now there was time to feast, to savor.

He loved the sweetness of her, the clean, unexpected freshness. She offered herself like an unexplored treasure.

He lifted his hands to the pins in her hair, tossing them aside as his fingers combed through the strands. He loved the silky texture of her hair. He buried his face in it, delighted at the faint fragrance of sugar and flour and vanilla that clung to it, enticing him, making him hungry for more.

This was a rare pleasure. One he'd wanted to savor for such a long, long time. Here, with Millie in his arms, he could put aside the cares of the day and lose himself in long, slow kisses and whispered promises.

His hands were careful now as he slid the gown from her shoulders.

"Your skin is so pale." He brushed a kiss, as gentle as a snowflake, over the soft, sensitive curve of her neck and felt her tremble.

She reached a hand to the buttons of his shirt and he stood very still, watching her as she undressed him. When his clothes joined hers at their feet, he drew her close, needing the feel of her flesh against his.

"I love these freckles." His lips burned a trail of kisses down the slope of her shoulder.

She smiled at the unexpected tenderness. "I always hated my freckles."

"I love them. Every one of them." He drew out the flavor of her warm flesh as he counted them with the tip of his tongue.

She brought her hands to his waist and lifted herself on tiptoe to nip at his throat. At the brush of her flesh against his, he gave a quiet moan and drew her down to the floor, cushioning her body with his own.

She lay on top of him, her hair falling around them like a fiery curtain. And still his kisses were light, feathery whispers over her face, her throat. When his lips moved lower, he began to feast on her breast.

Even now, with the fire slowly building between them, their movements were slow, unhurried. As though they had all the time in the world.

She floated on a cloud of contentment. This was what she'd been craving. The demands of the day behind them, a log blazing on the hearth and Malachite's hard, firm body beneath her.

She loved the feel of his hands on her, stroking, soothing. And his clever mouth, teasing, arousing.

"I've missed you so much." She brushed soft kisses down

his throat, across his shoulder. Her hair swirled forward, tickling his chest. "Missed this."

"Not as much as I missed you." He drew her face to his for another long, leisurely kiss. "Knowing you were here, just a few steps away, is what kept me warm out in the barn. What kept me sane."

He'd come here in a fever, needing desperately to satisfy the hunger for her. But now, lying with her, holding her, he felt all the tensions draining away. In their place was a calming, soothing feeling, seeping into every pore.

He needed this more than she would ever know. Needed tenderness after the raw, uncontained violence he'd experienced in the past. Needed to prove, not only to her, but to himself, that he wasn't as wild, as primitive as the creature he'd captured. And so he stroked and soothed and pleasured her. And himself.

Millie felt his heartbeat begin to accelerate as she brushed kisses across his chest. Could feel the control he exerted over his muscles as they bunched and tensed.

When he rolled her over she wrapped herself around him like velvet, her movements fluid, languid. And as their arousal grew, he took her on a slow journey of pleasure.

The sky outside the window was thick with clouds and black as midnight. A cold north wind gusted, flinging snow like pebbles against the house. In the corral a mare whinnied, and there was an answering call from the barn. But inside the ranch house they were aware of none of these things. Here, there was only a man and a woman and a love so deep, so compelling they were lost in it.

Her body seemed boneless, soft and pliant and as fragile as silk. When at last the need became so great they could no longer wait, he took her with a slow, measured rhythm that had her gasping his name. She opened for him, then drew him close and began to move with him.

She whispered his name as she arched, tensed, then slipped over the edge.

Overwhelmed by the sweetness, the tenderness, the simplicity of what they had shared, he followed.

"Cold?"

"No. Not with your arms around me."

Neither of them had moved. Neither was willing to shatter the fragile mood that still enveloped them.

"Can you stay the night?" She traced a finger around his lips. Such strong, firm lips. She'd waited such a long time to taste them. "Or do you have to go back and tend your horse?"

"Diablo's fine in the barn." He pressed his mouth to a tangle of hair at her temple. "The worst is over. I think I've earned the right to sleep in a bed tonight."

"Have you missed it so much?"

"Not the bed. I've missed the woman who shares it."

"Anyone I know?"

He chuckled. "You wouldn't recognize her. By day, she's a sweet, simple boardinghouse owner. By night, she's a temptress."

"Sounds dangerous. You'd better be careful."

He framed her face with his hands and bent to taste her lips. "It's too late. I'm already in over my head."

He kissed her. Long and slow and deep. She wrapped her arms around his waist and returned the kiss.

Suddenly he was on his feet and she was in his arms as he strode across the room.

"Now what?" she asked.

"I've had enough of cold, hard floors. It's time to try that big feather bed upstairs." He smiled down at her. "Mind waiting a minute for another kiss?"

"I guess I can wait. But I'll expect you to make it up to me."

He gathered her close and started up the stairs. "You can count on it."

Chapter Eighteen

The storm had blown over. The Texas sun, free of storm clouds, began to work its magic on the drifts of snow. Water dripped from the roof, running in little rivers down the icicles hanging over the porch.

With the bitter wind retreating and a gentler breeze warming the air, Malachite recruited the three girls to help in the barn.

"What do you want us to do first?" After the days of confinement, five-year-old June, dressed in her warm coat, scarf and mittens, couldn't wait to get started. She was eager to explore ranch life, which was far different from her life in town.

"You can let the chickens out and scatter some grain in the yard for them. They've been cooped up in here too long."

Malachite turned to May. "You can search the straw for eggs and take them to the house for your ma." He winked. "Maybe she'll make us one of those fancy custards for supper."

The two little girls raced off to complete their chores. When Malachite turned to April, she visibly tensed. He could tell she wasn't happy about being here. But curiosity, and perhaps boredom, had won out.

"I thought maybe you could muck the stalls," he said casually.

She shrugged. "I figured I'd get the dirty work." She picked up a pitchfork and headed toward the first stall. "What are you going to do?"

"I'll give you a hand."

She wasn't happy about having to work alongside him, but at least she wouldn't be doing the chore all alone. "What about Diablo's stall?"

"Leave that for me."

Malachite set to work, pitching the manure and matted straw into a cart. Beside him, April worked in silence. When the first stall was empty, they moved on to the next. Soon, all the stalls had been cleaned except Diablo's.

Malachite led the stallion to an empty stall before tackling the job of cleaning this last one. While he worked, April climbed to the top of the railing and watched.

"Will you turn Diablo over to the town now that you've caught him?"

Malachite peeled off his cowhide jacket and bent to his task. "Why would I do that?"

"Because there's a bounty on him. Mrs. Thurlong said the town was offering a reward to any cowboy who caught him."

He lifted a forkful of manure. "What do you suppose the townspeople will do after they pay the reward?"

She shrugged. "Shoot him, I guess."

He turned to glance at her. "Why would they destroy such a fine piece of horseflesh?"

"So the devil in him can't get loose to cause any more trouble."

Malachite shoved the pitchfork into a pile of straw and rested his hands on the handle while he studied her. "You don't really believe that silliness, do you, April?"

"I don't know what to believe." She looked away, unable to meet his eyes. "Folks said he'd never be caught. And that if he was, he'd never allow himself to be saddled and ridden."

"Looks like folks were wrong. Now what?" Malachite persisted. "Should he be killed even though they made a mistake?"

She shrugged. "I don't know."

Malachite went back to his task until the cart was loaded. Then he pushed it outside. After that he began to fork fresh straw into each stall.

April climbed down from her perch and began to work alongside him. "If you're not going to give Diablo to the town, what will you do with him?"

"I thought I'd keep him. He'll make a fine ranch horse. He's the smartest animal I've ever worked with."

"Aren't you afraid of what will happen to you if you keep him?"

Malachite shot her a sideways glance. "You mean you still think a horse can cause terrible things to happen?"

"Not if he's just a horse. But if he's a devil..."

"That does it." He set down his pitchfork and caught her by the hand. "Come on."

"Where are we going?"

He led her to the stall where Diablo stood watching. At the sight of the stranger, he snorted and backed away.

"Stand right here," Malachite commanded as he entered the stall.

April stood at the entrance, ready to bolt if the horse made a move toward her.

Malachite approached slowly, his voice soothing, and allowed the mustang to take his scent before getting closer. When he had hold of the lead rope, he beckoned April to approach.

"Don't make any sudden moves," he commanded.

Her hand went to her throat. Without realizing it, she closed her fingers around the smooth, round stone of her necklace. Malachite had once told her it would protect her and give her courage.

"All right," Malachite said softly. "Come here."

Though April was frightened, she did as she was told. When she stepped closer, the stallion lowered his head and nuzzled her hand.

"He wants you to pet him," Malachite said.

She brushed her hand over his nose. When Diablo didn't move away, she boldly moved her hand up along his neck.

"I...think he likes me." Her voice was filled with awe.

"Of course he does. I told you he's the smartest horse I've ever known."

"Do you think I could...ever ride him?"

"I don't see why not. But we'll wait until he becomes accustomed to the saddle." He pulled a carrot from his back pocket. "He likes his treats. Would you like to be the one to give it to him?"

She held out the carrot and watched in fascination as the stallion took it from her and began to chew contentedly.

"Look, Malachite. He let me feed him. Did you see?"

He nodded. He had "seen" something else. Something far more important. A light in a little girl's eyes, where before there had only been doubt and unhappiness. And had heard something as well. An inflection in her voice that signaled excitement.

"Can I go tell May and June?"

"Of course you can."

"I'll be right back," she promised. "I don't want you to think I'd leave without finishing my chores."

Malachite stood absently petting the stallion while he watched her dance out of the barn as though she had wings on her feet.

"You may not be a devil," he muttered, "but you've definitely just worked a miracle."

"What have you done to April? I haven't seen her this happy in years."

Millie and Malachite were lying in the big bed in his father's room. The only light came from the glow of hot coals in the fireplace.

This was their refuge from the day's chores. At night, after the girls went to sleep, they would steal away to this room, eager to hold each other, to whisper. To love.

They both looked forward to this special time, when they could forget about everything except each other.

"I didn't do a thing." He nuzzled her neck. "It was Diablo."

She pushed a little away to stare at him. "Aren't you the one who told me he was just a horse, without any special powers?"

"Did I say that?" He drew her back down into his arms and pressed a kiss to her temple. "Maybe I was wrong. All that mustang had to do was let April pet him, and she walked around all day with the biggest smile on her face."

Millie pushed away again, this time sitting bolt upright. "She touched that horse? And you didn't stop her?"

"I was the one who encouraged her."

"You risked my daughter's life with that—that creature?"

She was halfway out of bed before he caught her and dragged her back. Holding her firmly against him, he wrapped his arms around her waist and muttered fiercely, "Do you honestly believe I'd risk harming any one of the girls?"

Millie held herself stiffly in his arms. But his words were already softening her resolve. "Of course I don't." She turned, touching a hand to his face. "But Diablo's a wild thing. You said yourself you didn't want the girls going near him."

"When I'm not around. But when I'm with them, there's nothing to fear. Pretty soon he'll become so accustomed to people, he'll be as gentle as an old barn cat."

She opened her mouth. But before she could issue a protest he kissed her, hard and quick. "Diablo's not a killer. Or a mystical creature. He's just a wily, beautiful mustang that needs a little time to adjust to people. And you said yourself he made your daughter happy.''

She relaxed and melted against him. ''I think you've just convinced me.''

''Good.'' He pressed a kiss to the corner of her mouth. ''Now, Mrs. Potter, maybe I can convince you that you'd be more comfortable without that nightgown.''

''I think, Mr. Jewel, you've already won all the arguments you can hope for tonight.'' She laughed, a clear tinkling sound that wrapped itself around his heart.

He lowered her to the pillow and covered her mouth with a hot, hungry kiss. And found himself praying that it would always be this easy to bring the lilt of laughter to her lips.

Something dragged Malachite up from the depths of sleep. He stirred briefly, then began to slip back. Then he heard it again. A shattering, heart-wrenching sound. A moan. A sob. A cry. He felt movement beside him, and the shifting of the mattress.

At once he sat up. As his eyes adjusted to the darkness, he could make out Millie's figure across the room, standing by the window.

''What is it? What's wrong?''

She didn't speak. But he could see the way her shoulders shook as she continued crying silently.

Tossing aside the covers, he went to her, wrapping his arms around her. She didn't return the embrace. She continued to stand, rigid, unyielding, swallowing back hot, scalding tears.

''Tell me what's happened, Millie. Was it a dream?''

''I...yes.'' Her voice was muffled against his chest.

The very thought of anything hurting her, even a dream, had him feeling fiercely protective. ''Have you had the dream before?''

She let out a sigh. ''Too many times to count.'' She touched him then. Just a hand to his cheek. It was cold as ice.

"Come back to bed, Millie. You're freezing."

"I'm afraid to go back to sleep."

Without even knowing what the dream was about, he hated it. "We don't have to sleep. We'll talk."

She started to shake her head.

"We don't even have to talk, then. We'll just warm each other."

At that she allowed him to lead her back to bed. When he plumped the pillows, she leaned against them, drawing the blankets up to her chin.

He lay, one arm under his head, the other clasping her hand. By the faint light of the embers he could see the tears still wet on her lashes.

"The dream was about your husband, wasn't it?"

She nodded.

"About the way he died?" When she didn't respond he said softly, "It might help if you talk about it."

She looked at him, then away. "I've never talked about it. Not to anyone."

"Why?"

"Because there wasn't anyone to tell. The townspeople all knew. When word came in that Mick had been found thrown from his horse, they had plenty to say among themselves."

Thrown from his horse. No wonder she had seemed so tense and edgy when he'd gone after Diablo. But she hadn't said a word. She'd let him go, even though she must have been terrified.

She continued in that soft, breathless tone. "No one really talked to me about Mick's death. April and May were too young to understand. All they knew was that their father was never coming home again. And all I knew was that I had to find a way to take care of myself and my two children and the baby that would soon be born. There was no time to grieve. The same day I buried Mick, I took in my first boarder. And I've been working ever since."

She fell silent for a few moments before saying softly,

"I've always thought that if I had been with Mick, tending him after the fall, he wouldn't have died."

"It wouldn't have made any difference." His tone was flat, lifeless.

"How can you say that with such certainty?" She was suddenly angry, restless. For the first time she looked at him. And saw a look in his eyes that mirrored her own pain.

"Answer me," she said. "How can you know Mick wouldn't have died if I'd been there with him?"

Instead of speaking, he slipped out of bed and crossed the room. When he located his tobacco, he rolled a cigarette, held a match to the tip and inhaled deeply.

Millie watched as he walked to the window to stare out at the blackness.

When he finally spoke, the words seemed pulled from somewhere deep inside him. "I was with my wife and child when they died in Montana. But I couldn't save them."

Wife and child. She felt as if she'd been slapped. All this time they had spent together, he had never mentioned them. This was the first that she'd heard of their existence.

"What…" Her throat was dry as dust, the words bitter on her tongue. "What was her name?"

He continued to stare out the window. His tone was flat, emotionless. "Her name was Anna. Her father was a rancher. A very powerful, very wealthy rancher. He had forbidden us to marry, but we were young and headstrong. She said she didn't care that I was a Comanche. But her father cared. He sent a sheriff to arrest me. I spent six months in jail until a federal judge came to town for the trial. He ordered the sheriff to turn me loose. Said I hadn't committed a crime. And despite threats from her father, Anna left her ranch and came back to live with me."

"And your…child?"

"A son. Barely two months old when he contracted the fever. I used all of my medicines, but he only got worse."

Millie thought about the concern he had shown when April had her fever.

"Then my wife grew ill. Each day was worse than the day before."

"Were there no doctors in Montana?"

He did look at her then. The look in his eyes was so bleak she felt a knife twist in her heart.

"There was a doctor. In the town where we lived. But he refused to treat the wife of a Comanche. He called our union unholy. The work of the devil."

Millie felt all the breath leave her lungs. "Couldn't her father persuade the doctor to see her?"

"Her father said his daughter was already dead to him. He actually said she would be better off dead than married to an Indian."

Millie's hand flew to her mouth to hold back the gasp of outrage. "But the baby was an innocent party to all this. That baby was his grandson."

Malachite shook his head. "The hatred had choked his heart and soul. He no longer acknowledged his daughter. Or his grandson. When they died, I buried them alone. And then I turned my back on the town that had turned its back on them. I moved up into the hills, away from people. Away from their hatred."

He turned and flicked the cigarette into the coals. "But I didn't really leave the hatred, the bitterness behind. I carried it with me. And allowed it to fester in my heart like a poison. It wasn't until I came here, and met you, that it started to drain away. With you, I dared to hope again. To believe there could be a life without hatred."

As he had done with her, Millie crossed the room and wrapped her arms around him, hoping to comfort him. "I'm so sorry, Malachite."

"I'm sorry, too." He crushed her against him. "It seems we all have a private hell we have to visit from time to time."

It was true. But her hell contained only sudden death. His contained enough bitterness, enough cruelty to choke most men.

She led him back to bed and drew him down with her. And as they kissed away each other's pain, they sought to comfort in the only way they knew.

Hours later, as they lay in each other's arms, Millie whispered, "I hope in time I can erase all the unhappy memories."

"You already have," he murmured against her lips.

But later, when she slept, he again paced the room. And slipped back to that dark, painful place deep inside him. A place he had never revealed to anyone. Until tonight.

Chapter Nineteen

"I hope you made lots of food, Mama." May proudly set an overflowing basket of eggs on the kitchen table.

"I guess that means you're starving."

"Yes'm. Morning chores sure do make me hungry."

While May and June hung their coats on pegs, April and Malachite nudged off their dung-covered boots before heading toward the basin and pitcher. The two rolled their sleeves and began to wash. When they were through, they took their places at the table.

As soon as Millie could even set down the platters, they were hurriedly passed around. "Have you forgotten something?" she asked.

At once they joined hands and bowed their heads.

"We give thanks," April intoned, "for this food and for each other."

Millie smiled. "Now you may eat."

They needed no coaxing as they savored biscuits, coddled eggs and thick slices of roast beef.

"Mmm," April mumbled between bites. "Everything tastes better after the chores are done."

Malachite winked at Millie across the table. "Well then, if you'd like to enjoy your supper as much as you're enjoying breakfast, I could find enough chores to keep you busy for the rest of the day."

Instead of the expected moans and groans, the girls surprised him with eager questions.

"Could we maybe stop by the bunkhouse on the way to the barn?" June asked.

"I suppose so. But it's just an empty building until the wranglers return from the range."

"Could we visit them when they return?"

"Only if Cookie says so. Cookie's in charge of the bunkhouse. Nothing goes on out there without his approval."

"I'd like to see the herds," May said. "And maybe help with the calving and the branding the way Miss Diamond does."

Millie's mouth opened at such an admission from her thoroughly feminine middle child.

"I'd like to work with the horses," April announced.

Millie's coffee cup halted midway to her mouth. "When did you decide you liked horses?"

"When I started working in the barn with Malachite. There's something about the smell of new straw."

Little June made a face. "And manure."

April ignored her little sister. "And the feel of their noses when they let me pet them. And the feeling of being high in the air when I ride them."

"You...ride them?" Millie glanced beyond her daughter to the man seated beside her. He seemed to be very absorbed in spreading fruit conserve on a biscuit.

"Don't look so afraid, Mama. Malachite said it was all right."

"How long has this been going on?" Millie demanded.

"All week," her daughter said proudly. "He's even been letting me ride Diablo."

Before Millie could say a word, Malachite said dryly, "I think Diablo is the one who's allowing you to ride. If that stallion didn't like you, he'd let you know it, and nothing I could say would change it."

"But aren't you afraid of what might happen?" Millie asked.

"Not anymore," April said, touching a hand to the stone at her throat. "I have my necklace for courage."

"Remember what I told you." Malachite gave her a long, steady look. "Your courage doesn't come from a necklace. You have to find your courage inside yourself."

"But how come I never found it until after you gave me this stone?"

"It was there all along," he said. "All you had to do was give yourself a chance."

She turned eagerly to her mother. "Malachite said I have a natural way with horses. He said if I set my mind to it, I could probably be as good as him."

"I have a way with chickens." June swallowed a mouthful of egg. "Don't I, Malachite?"

"Indeed you do." He shot her a wicked grin. "You're probably the best chicken feeder I've ever seen."

The little girl beamed with pride.

"And I'm the best egg gatherer, huh, Malachite?"

He ruffled May's hair. "The best."

Millie cleared her throat. She couldn't recall when she'd seen her daughters looking so proud and happy. She got up from the table and took her time wrapping a towel around her hand before lifting the coffeepot from the fire. She used the extra time to blink away the tears that were threatening. Her shy little flowers were beginning to bloom. The knowledge made her at once sad and happy.

Oh, if only they could stay here in this little slice of paradise, isolated from the world for a lifetime.

"I believe I'll use some of those eggs to bake a cake," she said as she began to refill Malachite's cup.

"I was hoping you'd say that."

They all looked up at the sound of approaching wagon wheels. The girls raced to the window, then shouted, "It's Miss Pearl and her family. And look. There's Miss Diamond and Adam and little Onyx. Oh, and that looks like Miss Jade's fancy carriage. And Miss Ruby. And…"

Millie would have dropped the coffeepot if Malachite

hadn't steadied her hand. When she set it on the table, he pressed her suddenly cold hands between his.

"Looks like the snow's melted enough—" his gaze held hers "—that the trails are passable again."

After these weeks of isolation, she should be happy for the company. But the truth was, she knew the arrival of the others meant the end of their privacy. The end of their happy idyll.

She walked with Malachite to the door. But as she pulled it open to admit their guests, she noticed that he stood discreetly to one side, taking care not to touch her or even look at her. As if he had built a wall between them. She had a sudden urge to weep.

"Millie. Malachite." Pearl, carrying baby Amber, rushed up the steps, followed by her husband and sons. Behind them came a stream of family members. Diamond and Adam and baby Onyx. Jade, swollen with child and walking very slowly on the arm of Reverend Simpson, and behind them, Ruby and Marshal Regan. Byron Conner stepped out of his rig and helped Lavinia Thurlong and Gladys Witherspoon to alight. Behind them were Deputy Arlo Spitz and his wife, Effie.

At the sight of them, Millie had to stifle a groan.

"We saw the smoke and didn't know what to make of it," Pearl called.

"Sorry." Malachite could see that Millie needed a moment to compose herself. "Mrs. Potter and her girls got caught in the storm. This was the closest place to seek shelter."

"Sorry? What in the world are you apologizing for?" Diamond asked. "This is your home as much as ours, Malachite." She turned to Millie. "I'm just glad you were able to weather the storm without too much trouble." She glanced around. "Carmelita isn't here?"

"She's at her ranch." Malachite shook hands with Cal and Adam, Dan and Quent and the deputy. "She left before the storm hit."

"So you and Millie and the girls have been here alone for the past couple of weeks?" Byron Conner shot a glance at Millie's pink cheeks, then at Malachite's stern profile.

Behind him, shoving each other to be first through the doorway, were Lavinia and Gladys. At his words, they both stopped, stared, then wiggled inside.

Ruby clucked in sympathy. "Everyone in town knew you hadn't made it home, *chérie*. We were all praying that you had found safety somewhere."

Millie knew she was blushing. That only made her blush more. Especially with everyone staring at her. "Thank you for your concern. I hope Carmelita won't mind that we've used up quite a bit of her food."

"We'll see that Carmelita gets fresh supplies as soon as Rufus Durfee can deliver them." Diamond's eyes narrowed on her brother. But before she could ask any questions, little Ony toddled toward the table and reached for a cup. Diamond managed to catch it a second before it shattered. She swung the toddler to her hip, then said, "Maybe we should send the children into the parlor to play."

"I've got a better idea," April announced. "If you'd like, we could go to the barn and I'll show you our surprise."

"Surprise?" Diamond asked above the din of little Onyx crying and baby Amber cooing and the children all chattering.

With as much drama as she could muster, April announced, "Malachite caught Diablo."

Everyone stopped talking. The room was so silent that each drop of water falling from the roof could be heard on the porch.

"You don't mean it." Adam slapped Malachite on the back.

"I'll be..." Cal crossed the room to shake his hand.

"You caught the devil?" Gladys Witherspoon's voice rang with fury. "And you didn't kill him?"

Malachite's eyes narrowed. "You know better than that. That horse is no devil."

"There's a bounty on his head," Lavinia declared with the voice of authority. "The town wants him dead."

"That isn't so." Reverend Dan Simpson helped his wife to a chair. "The town just wanted him caught. What Malachite does with him is his business."

"Is it?" Lavinia pulled herself up to her full height. "And will it be his business when he brings disaster down on all of us?"

"Now, now, Lavinia." Marshal Regan removed his hat and wiped a sleeve across his brow. The presence of these busybodies always made him sweat.

"That horse has left a path of death and destruction in its wake," Lavinia declared.

Gladys nodded her support.

Malachite's voice was dangerously soft. "You can't really believe that."

"We've seen the proof." Lavinia's voice rose several notches. "Our town has seen a few dozen cowboys go chasing that mustang and never come back. There are ranchers who were once prosperous and are now failing. And now we've had a snowstorm that's trapped thousands of cattle out on the range, without food or shelter. I don't see how you can argue with the facts."

Before Malachite could offer a word, Byron interjected, "Seems to me Malachite Jewel's denying his own culture."

Malachite rounded on the banker. "What would you know about my culture?"

"I've been talking to some folks who know about your kind. The Comanche believe that an evil spirit can take over a man or an animal. And they believe that death is the only way to end the evil spirit's power."

Malachite's eyes were smoldering. But his voice remained dangerously soft. "You've forgotten something, Conner. My mother may have been Comanche. But my father was a clear-headed Texan who believed that the animals should be put to good use. I've already trained Diablo to the saddle. Furthermore, I intend to use him to breed better, stronger, faster horses. And this ranch, and this land, will be better because of him.''

Byron had no chance to respond. At Malachite's words, Diamond demanded, "How did you know what Pa believed?"

"I found some of his letters in the attic. I discovered a lot about Onyx Jewel I never knew. I guess...I'm learning to understand my father."

Diamond's eyes glittered with unshed tears. She surprised everyone by flinging herself into his arms and hugging him fiercely. "Oh, Malachite. When you were talking, I swear I heard Pa's voice coming out of your mouth."

"*Oui, chérie*. It was the same for me," Ruby muttered as she pressed a kiss to his cheek.

His sisters gathered around him, smiling, hugging, all talking at once.

Embarrassed, he tried to pull free.

Across the room, Millie couldn't hold back the smile that tugged on her lips.

Seeing it, Malachite turned away and said gruffly, "Well, how about that visit to the barn now? Anybody care to see our dangerous mustang?"

Husbands and wives collected their children and followed Malachite out the door. Lavinia, Gladys and Effie strode after them, looking for all the world as though they were about to face the devil himself.

April and her sisters, eager to show off, danced ahead.

Byron Conner turned back when he noticed that Millie had remained behind.

"Aren't you coming?" he asked.

She shook her head and turned away, setting the kettle over the fire. "I'll stay here and make some coffee. You go ahead."

"What's the matter?" he challenged. "Afraid?"

She blanched, and he knew he'd hit a nerve.

"Of course not. But somebody has to fix a meal for company. With Carmelita gone, it's up to me."

He turned away with a knowing smile. So. For all her brave talk, she was afraid of the mustang.

Millie had just shown him a way to salvage his relationship with her and drive a wedge between her and the half-breed at the same time. Now he would wait and watch for the perfect opportunity.

"I'd rather you not go too close to his stall." Malachite halted just inside the barn, and the others followed suit. "I think the sight of all these strangers might spook him."

Across the length of the barn, Diablo stood in his stall, silent and watchful.

"Oh my." Pearl touched a hand to her throat. "He's...frightening. Frightening and beautiful."

"That he is, *chérie.*" Ruby sighed. "I have heard some of the talk about him, but I never expected him to be so...splendid."

"I may not be the best judge of horseflesh," Diamond said with a trace of awe, "but that stallion is magnificent."

Malachite nodded. "Despite a lifetime in the wild, his coat is glossy, his eyes so clear you'd think he could see through you. He's the finest horse I've ever handled. It would be a waste to kill an animal like him."

"I don't see why you should have to destroy him," Marshal Regan said, "as long as you're certain he's really tame."

"He is. I give you my word."

They all watched as the stallion tossed his head and whinnied.

"He scares me," little Daniel whispered.

Beside him, his older brother, Gil, stared transfixed. "I've spotted him dozens of times up in the hills leading his herd. But up close, he's..." He shook his head in wonder. "He's like a king."

Seeing all their attention riveted on the mustang, April couldn't resist revealing her newly-discovered courage.

"Malachite lets me ride him."

There was a collective gasp from the others.

"Considering what happened to your father, I can't believe you would be so reckless." Lavinia's voice rang with disapproval.

"I'm always careful," the little girl said softly. "Besides, Malachite says I have a real gift with horses." She turned to Malachite. "Could I feed him a carrot?"

"I don't think so, honey."

"I'd like to see that." Byron turned to the others. "Wouldn't you?"

Malachite shook his head. "There are too many people around. Even though he's learned to trust us, Diablo's still a wild creature."

"Please," April pleaded. "You can go in first, Malachite. I'll do everything you tell me."

The others looked at her in disbelief, fascinated that anyone would want to go near such a creature.

Malachite thought back to his first introduction to the shy little girl. She had come so far. It would be a shame to stifle her first attempt at a public display of bravery.

He nodded and reached for the carrot in his back pocket. "Come on."

The others crowded around as Malachite and April approached the mustang's stall. While April waited outside the stall, Malachite entered, speaking softly. Diablo sidestepped and shifted.

When the horse settled down, Malachite signaled April to enter. He handed her the carrot, and she, in turn, offered it to Diablo.

"Take it, Diablo," she murmured. "You're going to like your treat."

The crowd let out a collective sigh when the horse lowered his head and took the carrot from her hand.

While he chewed, she patted his head. "Good boy. Good Diablo."

Moments later, as she and Malachite emerged from the

stall, the little girl was caught up in hugs and embraces from everybody.

"That was so brave," Daniel said.

"Oh, I wish I could do that," Gil admitted.

Even her sisters, usually so quick to tease, were filled with admiration for what she had done.

"Well, I, for one, do not like this." Lavinia pressed her lips together in a look of distaste. "You are inviting evil on this child."

"And on this ranch," Gladys said.

Without a word in his own defense, Malachite started to lead their party from the barn. But Byron's next words had him stopping in his tracks.

"Maybe there's a reason why Malachite Jewel was able to capture Diablo when no other cowboy could."

Everybody halted.

Malachite shot him a dark, challenging look. "And what would that be, Conner?"

"I told you I've made a study of the Comanche culture. Your people believe that an evil spirit can be transferred from man to animal and back again."

"What are you suggesting?" Lavinia asked.

Byron gave a knowing smile. "Maybe Malachite Jewel is as much a devil as that mustang. Maybe this town will only be free of evil when both of them are gone."

It took all of Malachite's willpower to keep his hands clenched at his sides. The years had taught him the futility of striking out at such fools.

Instead he said softly, "I guess only time will tell whether or not you're right."

He turned and stalked back to the house.

Behind him, the crowd followed in silence. But several were mulling over Byron's words. And wondering if they were indeed in the presence of evil.

Chapter Twenty

As they entered the kitchen, they were greeted by the wonderful fragrance of fried onions and potatoes wafting on the air. Thick slabs of roast beef simmered in gravy. And fresh biscuits were browning on the fire.

"Mmm. Something smells wonderful." Diamond breathed deeply.

Her husband pressed a kiss to her cheek. "Smells a whole lot better than the lunch I'd planned. Cold beans and biscuits along the trail."

"When are you going to learn to cook, Diamond?" Lavinia's tone was tinged with condemnation. "It isn't fitting that a man should be cooking for his wife and baby."

"You're right," Diamond remarked with a perfectly straight face. "I've been thinking of bribing Carmelita to come work for us. That way Adam and I can spend even more time with the herd. And I'd know that little Onyx would be looked after the same way I was when I was little."

"I'm shocked and appalled." Lavinia's tone was tinged with self-righteousness. "That you would even consider having someone else cook and look after your child when you're perfectly able to do it yourself."

Everyone could see Diamond's temper beginning to climb. She'd had little tolerance through the years for Lavinia and her sidekicks, Gladys and Effie.

"It was different for your father," Lavinia continued. "After all, he didn't have a wife to look after his motherless child. But you have no such excuse."

"I don't need an excuse. I'll do as I damned well—"

"Why, I think it's a wonderful idea, Diamond." Millie stepped between the two women. "Carmelita is feeling lonely and unnecessary now that you've all left home. I think she would love to be included in your life again."

Diamond's scowl turned into a smile. "You really think so?"

"Yes, I do." Millie indicated the table in the dining room, set with the Jewel family's crystal and silver. "I hope you've all brought your appetites."

"Millie, you've been reading my mind. I was just thinking it would be nice to eat before we started on our way." Diamond took her son from Adam's arms and led the way, with the others following.

When they were alone in the kitchen, Malachite caught Millie by the arm as she started to pick up a platter.

"Leave that a minute."

She glanced up at him in surprise. "What's wrong?"

"Nothing. I just need to hold you."

She sighed and leaned into him, taking comfort from his warmth, his quiet strength. He, in turn, felt his anger begin to dissipate. How could he harbor anger when he held this angel in his arms?

"I suppose they'll expect me to go back to town with them," she whispered.

"I suppose." He pressed his lips to her hair.

"I don't see how I can refuse. I mean, I have no reason to stay now that the trails are open." Her heart was silently pleading with him to say something—anything—that would prevent her from leaving.

"The gossips would tear you and your daughters to shreds if you didn't go home now that the storm has passed. As it is, they'll probably make your lives miserable for a while."

"I don't care about my reputation. Oh, Malachite. I don't want…"

They stepped apart as the door opened.

Diamond's eyes widened at the sight that greeted her. "I wonder if I could have some milk for little Onyx."

"Yes. Of course." Millie bumped against the table, turned and picked up a pitcher.

Diamond took it from her hands and returned to the dining room. But as she went through the motions of pouring the milk, one thought remained uppermost in her mind. There was no denying what she had just seen. Though they had tried to look innocent, she had seen the flush on Millie's cheeks. And the little frown line between Malachite's brows had told her he was less than pleased at the unexpected interruption. She couldn't wait to tell her sisters that Millie and Malachite had been embracing.

Maybe there was hope that he'd stay at the ranch after all. And the Jewel name would continue on in the little town of Hanging Tree.

A few minutes later Malachite, still scowling, made his way to the table. Millie followed, carrying a tray of biscuits. She seemed nervous and flustered.

"That was quite a show your daughter put on for us in the barn." Byron Conner's glance flicked over Millie, then back to Malachite.

"Show?"

"With Diablo. Feeding him a carrot from her hand." He smiled at her sudden pallor. "I suppose that's not nearly as dangerous as some of the things she's been doing these past weeks. But that's understandable. Even the most civilized creatures become wild," he added meaningfully, "if they're left too long without the rules of society."

Lavinia, Gladys and Effie were watching and listening with glittering eyes.

"Now that the trails are open, I'm sure you're eager to get back to town." Lavinia was enjoying the scowl on Malachite's face.

"Yes. Of course." Millie couldn't bear to look at Malachite. "But I can't leave until I've cleaned everything and changed all the bed linens. It may be hours before I'm ready to go."

"Leave it for Carmelita," Byron said with disdain. "That's her job."

"I couldn't possibly. The responsibility is mine. I'll see to it."

"Then I'll wait." He crossed his arms. "Those who rode here with me can ride back with the marshal."

Quent Regan flinched, knowing he'd be subjected to endless miles of Lavinia's gossip.

His wife, Ruby, seemed unaware of his discomfort. "*Oui.* Of course they can ride with us."

Byron surprised everyone by saying, "I think Malachite should come with us. And," he added, "I think he should ride Diablo. Everyone in town will want to see the devil stallion and the man who captured him."

Malachite shook his head. "I don't think we're ready for that."

"What's the matter?" Byron taunted. "I thought you said you had saddle-trained him? Are you afraid to let us see your skill? Or are you just afraid the devil will show himself for what he is?"

Malachite knew he was being manipulated. But his temper was on a short fuse. "Sure. Why not? It's time the townspeople learned they have nothing to fear."

Byron lowered his head to hide his gleam of triumph.

"We'll all go with you," Diamond said. Now that she had seen her brother and Millie embracing, she was determined to keep throwing them together. Though the role of matchmaker was new to her, she discovered that she liked it.

Across the table, Millie moved her food around the plate, unaware of the flow of conversation around her. The only thing she knew was that she was returning to the house Mick had built for her. And unless she could persuade Malachite to change his plans, he would soon be leaving Hanging Tree for good and returning to Montana.

Everything would be as it had been before. And yet nothing would be the same. It had all changed. And all because she had lost her heart to this man.

"What do you think, *chérie?*"

Millie's head came up. She realized they were all looking at her. "I'm sorry. What did you say?"

"I said we'll all help you clean. That way, you'll be done in half the time and home before supper."

"There's no need."

"We insist," Ruby said firmly. "Pearl and I will tackle the bed linens, and you and Diamond can clean the kitchen. Jade will sit here and hold little Amber. The men can take the children outside," she added pointedly, "so they aren't underfoot."

"She means it." Quent Regan shoved back his chair and got to his feet. "You'd better follow me. You don't want to be around when the womenfolk make up their minds to start cleaning."

With so many willing hands it took no time at all to have the house sparkling. A short time later, their chores completed, the women pulled on coats and shawls and made their way to the porch, where the men and children awaited them in the wagons.

It was a strange caravan that made its way over hills and across gulches swollen with water from the melting snows. Reverend Dan Simpson and his wife, Jade, took the lead in Jade's elegant white-and-gilt carriage. Having taken pity on Marshal Regan, they had offered to take Lavinia and Gladys with them. Despite the presence of the preacher, the two women hadn't stopped talking since the journey began.

Ruby and the marshal shared a wagon with the deputy and Effie. Without her two friends, the deputy's wife had fallen silent, storing up all the gossip she could for the coming weeks. The fact that the widow Potter had spent weeks alone with Malachite Jewel would give her an entry into everyone's kitchen.

Pearl and Cal and their family followed behind, with the boys seated in the back and baby Amber between them.

Diamond and Adam were astride their mounts, with little Onyx held firmly in Adam's arms. Millie and her daughters rode in Byron's fine carriage. A skittish Diablo, with Malachite in the saddle, took up the rear.

Halfway to town they spotted two horsemen. As they drew near, they recognized Rufus Durfee's two sons, Damon and Amos. When the boys caught sight of Malachite astride the black stallion, their mouths dropped open in astonishment.

"It's the devil," Damon shouted. "Wait'll we tell everybody in town."

"Wait," Malachite called as they wheeled their mounts. But they were too excited to heed his voice as they took off in a swirl of snow and mud.

An hour later, as their procession started through town, they could see the effect of the boys' news. Crowds of people lined the street, from Neville Oakley's stable, past Durfee's Mercantile and all the way to the far end of town where the Golden Rule stood with its bell tower gleaming in the late afternoon sunshine. And all straining for a glimpse of the devil horse and the man who had captured him.

As Byron's carriage rolled past, Millie could hear the ripple of excitement from the crowd.

"There he is."

"My God. It's Onyx Jewel's ghost."

"No wonder he captured the devil. It takes one to know one."

Some women in the crowd crossed themselves as Malachite and Diablo passed by. Others turned their children aside so they wouldn't look directly at the source of all their troubles.

One man shouted, "Now you've done it. We'll probably all lose our ranches."

But a few, caught up in the excitement, cheered and applauded as Malachite rode past.

"He certainly has a strange effect on people." Byron turned to glance pointedly at Millie, seated beside him. She had been subdued throughout the entire journey. "They either love him or hate him."

Hearing the venom in his tone, she lifted her head and met his look. "You've made it clear how you feel about him. What I don't understand is why?"

Byron shrugged. "I don't consider him a worthy heir. The Jewel empire is worth a great deal of money. What does a man like Malachite Jewel care about that? By the time he's through charming those silly women—" he indicated the four sisters, who, along with their husbands and the others, had pulled up in front of Millie's house "—it'll be worthless. And he'll be back in Montana breeding his string of useless mustangs," he said wrinkling his nose in distaste.

"It's more than that," Millie said softly. "You don't hate a man over money."

"Spoken like a woman who has never had any. If you knew how long it took to amass a fortune, you wouldn't be so quick to see it squandered." He flicked the reins. "But I suppose you're right. It is more than that. Since Malachite Jewel's arrival in our town, I've been worried about you."

She drew her shawl tighter around her shoulders, as if to shut out his words. "You needn't worry about me, Byron."

He touched a hand to her arm. "But I do worry. If you aren't careful, Millie, you'll have people talking. And it wouldn't do for a woman alone to have any…unpleasant rumors about her past. Especially if she hopes to one day become the wife of the town's most respected banker."

"Why, you arrogant—!" She bit off the rest of the distinctly unladylike words she'd been about to hurl. "Do you really think I would marry you?"

He pulled up in front of her boardinghouse and brought the team to an abrupt halt. Turning to her, he said softly, "By the time the town gossips get through with you, you'll be lucky to attract a trail bum with less than a dollar in his pocket. But I'm willing to forgive and forget. Just as I'm willing to forgive and forget the fact that you spent the past weeks alone with a man who was once in jail.''

He'd hoped to shock her. And he wasn't disappointed. The look on her face was one of stunned surprise.

"How did you know that?"

"That Malachite Jewel was in jail? I checked with the authorities in Montana. They told me all I needed to know. But I am surprised that you knew it, as well.''

"Malachite told me."

"Ah. How convenient." Byron climbed down, then held out a hand to help her from the carriage. "I suppose he gave you some sad story about the unfortunate circumstances that brought him so low.''

"I will not discuss this with you," she said stiffly.

"It's just as well. I doubt you'd care to hear the whole sordid story of Malachite Jewel's tawdry past.''

Stung, she helped her daughters down, then turned her back on Byron and hurried to join the others, who stood watching as Malachite and Diablo made their way through the throngs.

Several boys raced alongside the horse and rider, dazzled by the unexpected excitement of the day. Even during the town's festival, they had never seen such a crush of people.

As Malachite drew the stallion to a halt in front of Millie's boardinghouse, the crowd surged forward, forming a ring around them. Diablo's eyes widened, and he sidestepped neatly before rearing.

The crowd, hushed and afraid, fell back.

"Onyx," an old man shouted. "I knew someday you'd come back to Hanging Tree and rescue us from that devil.''

"My name isn't Onyx." Malachite slid from the saddle, keeping a firm grasp on the reins. Addressing the people, he said, "For those of you who don't know, my name is Malachite Jewel. Onyx Jewel was my father.''

At his pronouncement, his four sisters clasped hands and

nearly wept, aware that it was the first time he'd shown any pride in his name.

"As for Diablo," he went on, "he's no devil. I came here to prove that to you. He's just a horse."

"Then how do you explain all the bad things that have happened since he showed up around here?" an old man taunted.

"I can't explain them. I only know they weren't caused by this mustang."

"Why should we believe you?" a woman called.

"I don't know." Malachite shook his head sadly. "You have no more reason to believe me than you have to believe that this horse caused all your misfortunes. I can only hope in time you'll see that a horse can't cause a blizzard or cause a ranch to fail or cause a man to die."

"Where are you planning to keep that stallion?" Rufus Durfee asked.

"For now, I'll keep him out at the Jewel ranch. Why?"

"Well, I figure if the Jewel ranch starts to fail, we'll know who to blame."

"Fair enough," Malachite said with an easy smile. "And if the ranch continues to prosper, will you admit that Diablo is nothing more than a fine stallion?"

Rufus scratched his head, mulling over the question. Slowly he nodded. "Sounds about right to me."

"How about the rest of you?" Malachite turned to study the crowd, which had grown strangely quiet.

The widow Purdy stepped forward, leaning on her daughter's arm. "I knew your father, young man. Onyx Jewel was a sensible, honorable man. Looks to me like there's a lot of him in you. What you're saying makes sense." She turned to the others. "I say we give Malachite Jewel and his horse a chance to prove themselves."

A murmur of approval rippled through the crowd. Heads began to nod, and voices could be heard murmuring their agreement.

"Well now," Marshal Regan called. "Since that's decided, I say you should all return to your own business and let Mr. Jewel get on with his."

Millie gave a deep sigh of relief. Seeing Byron's look of rage, she turned to Malachite. "Please stay for supper."

He winked. "I was hoping you'd ask."

"Can I take Diablo to the shed?" April asked. "I'll be real careful. I promise."

Malachite handed her the reins, and she proudly led the stallion away, much to the amazement of those still watching. But as she reached the door of the shed, the horse suddenly pulled free and began rearing and snorting.

April let out a bloodcurdling scream and fell to the ground. As the crowd watched in shock, the horse reared again and again, its hooves battering the snow-covered ground with such fury blood actually flew through the air.

"God in heaven—no!" Malachite reacted instinctively, drawing his gun while racing forward. And all the while his mind recoiled from the thought that he had caused harm, and possible death, to innocent little April.

Chapter Twenty-One

Marshal Regan cradled his rifle and followed Malachite at a run.

The rest of the crowd took off in hot pursuit, some crying, some shouting, many swearing. All were afraid of what they would see, yet drawn with horrified fascination to witness yet another proof of Diablo's curse.

Malachite dropped to one knee and took aim. From somewhere beside him he could hear Byron Conner's voice urging him to shoot. Sweat trickled into his eyes, blurring his vision. He wiped it away with his sleeve. What he was about to do required perfect aim.

Just as he was about to squeeze off a shot, April flung herself into his arms with such force she knocked him backward.

"No, Malachite! What are you doing?" she screamed.

"I thought…" He sat up, holding her a little away to make certain she was really unharmed. Even then he was afraid to believe his eyes. But the proof was here in his arms. She didn't have a single scratch or cut. There was no trace of blood on her. And still he could hear Byron's high-pitched voice, ordering him to shoot the stallion. "I thought Diablo had gone mad and was attacking you."

"Not me, Malachite," she said between labored breaths. "See." She pointed.

It was then that he noticed the bloodied remains of several snakes lying mangled in the crimson-spattered snow.

"Wait," he hollered before Marshal Regan could fire off a shot. "Don't shoot."

Stunned, Quent lowered his rifle. With the toe of his boot he kicked at the snow. "There must have been a nest of rattlers," he said with a trace of awe. "Most horses would run a mile in the other direction to avoid them."

"But Diablo loves me," April said. "He'd never let anything happen to me. Would he, Malachite?"

"No, honey. I guess he wouldn't."

"Diablo saved my life," she said.

Malachite got to his feet, still holding the little girl in his arms. He was trembling, he realized. For the first time in his life he'd been absolutely terrified.

He looked at the stallion, standing quietly, eyes wide and knowing, fixed on the little girl.

"You were going to kill Diablo, weren't you, Malachite?" April asked in a small voice.

He nodded, feeling a tightness in his chest. "Of course I was. I'd never let anything hurt you, April."

"Oh, Malachite. You love me even more than Diablo." At the realization she buried her face against his neck and began to sob.

At the sight of them Millie stood very still, tears streaming down her face, clinging tightly to her other two daughters.

Behind them, the crowd watched in silence. But many wiped away tears of their own.

"I think maybe we've just seen a sign," the widow Purdy called out.

When the others turned to her, she explained, "What we just witnessed was certainly not the work of any devil. I'd say this proves, once and for all, that the dark cloud that's been hanging over our town has been lifted. Thanks to Onyx Jewel's son."

Leaning heavily on the arm of her daughter, she walked away. Slowly, one after another, the rest of the crowd fell back, leaving Malachite and Millie and their families alone. To weep. To embrace. And finally to rejoice at their good fortune.

"Congratulations, Millie." Byron Conner pushed his way through the crowd until he was beside her. While she held her arms stiffly at her sides, he gathered her against his chest and brushed a hand along her back. "You must live under a lucky star. If that stallion had been after April, there would have been no way to save her. Unfortunately, I didn't have a gun with me. Otherwise, I'm sure I would have been quicker than Jewel or the marshal."

At the moment, Millie's heart was too filled with love and gratitude to harbor any ill will. With quiet dignity she pushed free of his arms and made her way to where Malachite was still standing, holding April in his arms.

"I'll never forget this." She wrapped her arms around both of them and pressed a kiss to her daughter's cheek.

"I think this calls for a celebration," Byron announced loudly.

"Would you like that, April?" Millie asked.

The little girl nodded.

"Then I'll make a special supper in your honor." She caught hands with May and June and led the way into her house, with Malachite and April following. Byron and the entire Jewel family trailed behind. And as fires were stoked and a hearty meal prepared, the big old house was once again filled with the sounds of happy conversation and the trill of childish laughter.

"Oh, Millie, I don't know when I've had such a fine supper." Pearl sat back, cuddling little Amber, who had fallen asleep.

Adam polished off a second helping of custard. "It was a meal worthy of a holiday."

"This day feels like a holiday," Millie said as she circled

the table and topped off their coffee cups. "I thought, for a few terrible moments, I'd lost my daughter." She paused to drop a kiss on April's head. "But she's safe and sound, thanks to Malachite."

"I didn't save her. Diablo did."

She met Malachite's gaze across the table. "But he's your horse. And you trusted him, even though I didn't."

"You had every right not to trust him."

"Will you let me ride him again soon, Malachite?" April asked.

At Millie's gasp he muttered, "I don't think you ought to press your luck."

"But you will, won't you?"

"When your mother says you can."

He gave her a wink, and her smile bloomed. If anyone could persuade her mother it was Malachite.

At the end of the table, Birdie, who had been pressed into service for this unexpected celebration with the Jewel family, sat next to Gil. Whenever they thought no one was looking, they exchanged long, silent glances.

"Gil, maybe this is a good time to tell everyone about your surprise," Pearl prompted.

Gil looked suddenly uncomfortable.

"What surprise?" Birdie asked.

"I've known for some time that Gil's clever mind has moved beyond my small classroom." Pearl's pride in her adopted son was evident in her voice. "So I sent some of his papers to an eastern university, and they've accepted him for a course of study."

"You're…going east?" Birdie's smile faltered.

He shook his head. "Ma wanted me to. She's told me all about her childhood in Boston. And I guess it'd be nice, having lots of people and houses and streets and such. But I can't leave Hanging Tree. I just wouldn't want to live if I couldn't saddle up a horse and go out into the hills by myself sometimes."

"The university enrolled Gil in a course of home study.

And the dean remarked that Gil had written some of the finest papers and completed the toughest mathematical equations he'd ever witnessed in a student.'' Pearl exchanged a proud smile with her husband. "Can you imagine? Our Gil has been singled out by one of the finest universities in the country?''

Uncomfortable with all the praise, Gil suddenly stood and began collecting dishes. "Come on, Birdie. I'll help you clear the table.''

The two young people escaped to the kitchen, where their voices could be heard in muted conversation.

"I'm afraid I'll have to leave this fine company.'' Byron pushed away from the table. "I'm meeting with Frank Cooper tonight about his mortgage.''

Diamond swore. "You're not going to foreclose?''

Byron gave a negligent shrug of his shoulders. "I'm not free to discuss Frank's business. But he's an old man. I think everyone in town has known for some time that his herds are dwindling. The last straw was when his barn burned.''

"But where will he go?'' Diamond pounded a fist on the table. "Damn it. He's lived his whole life in Hanging Tree. He was one of Pa's oldest friends.''

"I believe he and Nellie have relatives in St. Louis. Life will be simpler there.'' Byron started across the room.

"You know what folks around here will say.'' Diamond glanced at her husband, then at Malachite. "It's Diablo's fault.''

Byron smiled as he took his leave.

For long minutes after he left, no one spoke. The news of another failed ranch had shattered the festive mood.

"Come on,'' Adam said, "I've got some good cigars. Why don't we go out back and smoke while the women finish up in here?''

"It's too cold outside.'' Millie pointed to the parlor. "Go in there and enjoy your cigars. And if you'd like, I'll bring you some elderberry wine.''

The men gave her no argument as they exited the dining

room. A short time later, as she approached with a tray containing a decanter and glasses, she heard the low rumble of masculine voices.

"What'll you do with the rest of those mustangs, Malachite?"

"As soon as I can saddle-train them, I'll take them up to Fort Denver. The soldiers there pay top dollar for good saddle horses."

Millie shivered. Fort Denver was halfway to Montana. Malachite had said he'd be returning to Montana by springtime.

"What about Diablo?"

"I'm going to use him to found a dynasty. I've already spotted two mares with the same fine bloodlines. If they successfully breed, I'll know I'm on the right track."

"So you won't follow your pa into the cattle business?"

"I've got nothing against cattle. And I think my father made a wise choice, settling here. But I think one day this land will be worth more than those cows."

The men, being cattlemen, couldn't resist scoffing.

"But I'm a horseman," Malachite went on. "That's what I love. And a man has to follow his heart."

The voices abruptly stopped when Millie entered.

"Here you are, gentlemen." The air was sweet with the rich aroma of tobacco. A fire blazed on the hearth. Millie filled the glasses, then passed them around. "Do you need anything else?"

"Not a thing." Malachite walked her to the door, allowing himself the pleasure of touching her cheek before she hurried away.

He closed the door and turned back to the others. "As I was saying, a man has to follow his heart. And if a man has spent a lifetime loving his ranch, it seems to me he'd find a way to keep it from failing."

"Every rancher knows it's a gamble." Cal McCabe watched smoke curl over his head. "Hell, your daddy nearly went busted half a dozen times. Things got so bad once, I was the only wrangler left. Onyx and I did everything ourselves. The calvings, the brandings, the roundups and the drive to Abeline.''

''But he made it work. He didn't fold. And he didn't quit.'' One more mark in his father's favor. ''Cal, I wonder if you might ask that smart son of yours to do something.'' Malachite studied the gleaming tip of his cigar for a minute.

''Sure thing. But what's this all about?'' Cal asked.

''There's been something nagging at me all evening.''

The men waited.

Malachite drained his glass in one long swallow. Then, in low tones, he told them of his concerns. And laid before them his plan.

Overnight the winds had shifted from northeast to southwest, chasing the bite from the air.

Millie felt an unreasonable need to clean her house from top to bottom. After sitting unused for several weeks, the rugs and linens definitely needed an airing. The clothesline bloomed with patched sheets and threadbare blankets.

The kitchen was steamy from the pans of water heating over the stove. She laid out her assortment of mismatched dishes and began to wash and dry. When they had all been put away, she tackled cobwebs and dust and dirt, sweeping, scrubbing, until the entire house gleamed.

When the last load of laundry had been folded and put away, she made herself a cup of tea and sat wearily at her table.

She stared around at the peeling walls, the faded rugs, the shabby furniture. It hadn't helped. All the scouring, all the backbreaking work had been in vain. She hadn't been able to block out the thought of Malachite and what she'd overheard in the parlor.

Already he was hard at work at the ranch, saddle-training the mustangs. This morning, when she'd driven the wagonload of children to school, she had detoured past the Jewel ranch on her way home. Malachite was out in the corral,

working with a skittish mare. There had been time for only
a quick embrace and one mind-numbing kiss before he'd
returned to his work.

She wasn't sure she could go on like this, with so many
miles between them. Malachite refused to stay alone in his
father's home, preferring instead to sleep in the bunkhouse.
And he adamantly refused to return to her boardinghouse,
saying the gossip would destroy her daughters' reputations.

She should be grateful for his thoughtfulness. Most men
would take what they wanted without a second thought to
what others said. But he'd had firsthand experience in such
matters. She thought about what had been done to him in
Montana. That he had survived was a miracle. But he'd been
forced to pay too dear a price while enduring the cruelty of
others.

She drained her cup and stirred the pot of stew simmering
over the fire. Then she drew on her shawl and made her way
to the wagon. She was grateful that Gil had offered to drive
the girls over to the Jewel ranch after school let out. That
would give her a chance to see Malachite, at least for a few
minutes, before returning home.

Millie flicked the reins as the horse and cart crested a hill.
The scene below stirred her heart. The hillside teemed with
lowing cattle. To one side of the barn, several new corrals
had been built. Each enclosure held several dozen mustangs.
Malachite could be seen moving among them, culling those
that would be trained to saddle.

As she drew near, she saw the great black stallion saddled,
standing outside the corral. While she watched, April
emerged from the ranch house and raced toward the big
horse, vaulting into the saddle. And while Millie's heart
stopped, the mustang took off at a trot. It was several minutes
before Millie could breathe again. And when she did, she
realized that her daughter was handling the big horse with
all the skill of a cowboy.

"Look, Mama," April shouted as Millie's wagon came to

a stop. "I've been practicing all afternoon so I could surprise you."

"You certainly did that." Millie touched a hand to her heart. "I thought for a minute I was seeing things."

Malachite made his way to the wagon, and Millie's heart did another flip. Would it always be this way? she wondered. Would her heart always react in this crazy way whenever he was near?

"I've been wondering when you would get here." He lifted her down, brushing his lips over her face as he did. Then, keeping his arm around her waist, he led her toward the corral. "April wants to show off what she's learned."

They stood together, watching as horse and rider made figure eights around the ring.

"She's turning into a fine horsewoman."

At the trace of pride in Malachite's voice, Millie turned to glance at him. "She has a fine teacher."

"Not to mention an excellent bloodline."

Millie laughed. "Must you always think about horses?"

"Who said anything about horses?" The look he gave her had her pulse racing.

Just then a horse and cart came from the direction of the bunkhouse. Inside were May and June, seated on either side of Cookie, who held a pipe clenched tightly between his teeth.

"Afternoon, Mrs. Potter," he called. "Malachite, I thought May was ready to handle the reins."

Malachite nodded. "Whatever you say, Cookie."

As they rode past, Malachite glanced up at the sky. "Not a cloud to be found."

"Now, why would you want clouds on such a perfect day?"

He leaned close, pressing his lips to her temple. "I want a storm. Right now. So you'd have to spend the night."

"Oh." She looped her arm through his as the horse and cart rounded the barn. "You could always spend the night at my place in town."

"Don't tempt me, woman." He turned to watch April bring Diablo to a halt and slide easily from the saddle.

"Looks like I have to get back to work. If all goes according to plan, these mustangs should be ready for Fort Denver in another day or two."

"A day or two?" Her fingers closed over his arm. "You'll be leaving…so soon?"

"The army's in a hurry for their horses. And I'm eager to see what price they'll bring." Seeing the stricken look in her eyes, he caught her hand in his. "What's wrong, Millie? You knew that's what I'd planned."

"Yes. Of course." She hoped he didn't hear the pleading in her tone as she said, "Come to town tonight. At least for supper."

"I wish I could." He brushed a kiss over her cheek. "But I have a meeting tonight."

"A meeting?"

"With Cal and Gil and a few others."

She tried to hide her disappointment. "I understand."

Malachite felt a sudden wave of frustration. She didn't understand. And he couldn't explain. "I'll try to stop by afterward. I can't make any promises, but I'll do my best."

Millie watched him walk away. The day had suddenly turned cold. Or was it just the chill around her heart?

"When I grow up I'm going to train horses with Malachite." April twirled around the cramped bedroom she shared with her sisters, too excited to settle into bed.

May, tired from her afternoon in the pony cart, yawned. "Is that what Malachite said?"

"No, silly. He doesn't know. But I'll tell him soon." April danced over to the bed, where her mother sat tucking the blankets around little June, who was already sound asleep. "Malachite said I'm good with horses, Mama. Really good."

"I know, honey."

"When are we going to marry Malachite?" May asked.

"What?" Millie's head snapped around.

"We can't marry Malachite." April used her big-sister tone of voice. "Only grown-ups can get married."

"Mama's a grown-up. Can she marry Malachite?"

"Uh-huh. And Birdie said she'd better."

"Now, why would Birdie say a thing like that?" Millie demanded.

"'Cause Mrs. Thurlong and Mrs. Witherspoon and Mrs. Spitz told everybody that no unmarried lady could spend all that time under the same roof with a man like Malachite without doing something." The little girl stifled a giggle. "I think they're talking about kissing, aren't they, Mama?"

"Yes, honey. I guess they are." She lifted the covers and waited for her oldest to climb in. Then she pressed a kiss to her cheek and whispered, "Don't forget your prayers."

"'Night, Mama."

"Good night, honey."

Deep in thought, Millie descended the stairs. In the kitchen she began to pace.

Though Malachite's attitude toward his father had softened, his pride would never permit him to accept anything from Onyx Jewel's estate. How, then, could she convince him to take on the added burden of a woman with three children?

Suddenly she was reminded of the story Carmelita had told her. Hadn't she taken a desperate gamble to win the man she loved? And hadn't she proved that a man, even a poor man, had a right to his pride?

She was as desperate as Carmelita had been. And as hopelessly in love.

Without giving herself time to think through her plan, she hurried next door and asked if Birdie could stay the night.

She had some very serious business to attend to.

Chapter Twenty-Two

Malachite sat with Cal McCabe and his son around a cozy fire in the newly renovated parlor of Onyx Jewel's first home in the Texas wilderness.

The timbers used to build the original structure would have taken a team of mules to haul. Yet rumor had it that Onyx Jewel had done the work completely alone, his only tool an ax and two strong arms, one more reason for Malachite to admire his father's tenacity.

"You're sure, Gil?"

The young man nodded. "Yes, sir. I went over everything you asked for. The numbers don't lie. I'm sure of my figures."

"And the wire from St. Louis?"

"It came today. It confirms what you suspected."

Malachite glanced at Cal. "You know what this means?"

Cal's eyes narrowed. "I know." He shook his head. "It's like we've come full circle. First your father. And now you." He shot Malachite a warning look. "Don't make the mistake your pa made. Take this to the marshal. Let him handle it."

"I intend to." Malachite got to his feet. "And then I have some other…business to attend to."

He shook hands with Gil and Cal before heading for town.

* * *

"It was kind of you to see me tonight, Byron." Millie perched uncomfortably on the edge of the chair he had offered her. She'd never been in his office before. It was intimidating, with its mahogany desk and shelves of ledgers.

His very businesslike jacket had been hung carefully over the back of a chair. His sleeves had been rolled above the elbows. Beside his hand was a glass of whiskey. The decanter next to it was half-empty.

"I always have time for business, Millie. You did say this was business, didn't you?"

"Yes." She swallowed. "I...have need of some money."

"And you thought I'd just loan you some?"

"That's what bankers do, isn't it?"

"Sometimes." He folded his hands. "What would you offer in exchange?"

"I thought I could..." Dear heaven. Was she really going to say it? Mick's house? No, she corrected. Her house. Her legacy. To use as she saw fit. "I thought I could mortgage the house."

"For what purpose?"

"To...make some repairs." She felt her face flame. She'd never been good at lying.

"A wise choice. That shabby place could use some repairs."

It was the way he said it that had her stiffening her spine.

"But there's no need to mortgage your house." He steepled his fingers and studied her. "There's a simple way to get the money you need."

She arched a brow.

He studied her as though gauging her reaction. "Marry me."

"You can't be serious."

He waved aside her protest. "I'm a wealthy man, Millie. I could have Farley Duke and his crew from the sawmill over to your house within the month, turning it into the finest house in town."

"Byron, you know I don't love you. Why would you want to marry me?"

He took a sip of the whiskey, enjoying the smooth, aged texture, the quick flash of heat. "I'm tired of living alone. There isn't much stimulation in a town like Hanging Tree. I want a pretty wife. One who can cook and entertain. One who is well liked by the people here. You are all those things, Millie. And in return, I would improve your lot financially. I could show you things, buy you things you've never seen before. Once or twice a year I have to go to St. Louis on business. Naturally you would go along. There would be fine dinners and the theater and shopping."

She didn't know whether to laugh or weep. What he was offering was cold and empty and meaningless. "And what about my children?"

He gave a little sigh of impatience. "They would be well taken care of. They'll soon be old enough to go away to school."

"Away? Byron, they're practically babies. They're only five, six and seven."

"You're far too protective. I suppose it's because you were widowed so young. Naturally the children could spend their summers here with us."

Their summers. "Do you feel any…affection for them at all, Byron?"

He set the tumbler very carefully on the desk blotter, aware that it would leave a ring on the wood. "Of course. They're…nice little girls. A bit shy for my taste. But they'll get a fine education. And I'll see to it that they all make good matches in time."

Millie clenched her hands tightly together. "Did you know, until this moment I hadn't realized that I've never heard you speak to them?"

"Don't be silly."

"No. It's the truth. For all the times you've been in my house, sat at my table, enjoyed my food and my company, you've never said a single word to my daughters."

"You said yourself, they're only five, six and seven. Why would I waste my time talking to them?"

"Waste!"

"Are you here to talk about my relationship with your daughters or my relationship with you?"

"We have no relationship. And this discussion is over. I'm afraid I've made a terrible mistake." She stood.

Before she could cross the room he came around his desk and caught her by the arm. "What you're saying is I'm not good enough for you, but my money is. That is why you came here, isn't it? To beg?"

She itched to slap his face. Instead she wrapped herself in dignity and said, "I came thinking I could arrange a business deal—to mortgage my house for some much needed money. I never thought of it as begging. And I place too high a value on my daughters and myself to even consider your ridiculous suggestion."

He drew her close. His voice was an angry hiss. "Your miserable little house isn't worth the matches it would take to burn it to the ground. The only thing you have of value is yourself. The sooner you accept that, the easier your life will be."

"Take your hands off me."

With an abruptness that shocked her, his voice, his demeanor changed from cool to crude. "I'll bet you didn't say that to the half-breed, did you?"

She looked into his hard, cold eyes and wondered why she had ever thought to come here. "I didn't realize until now that you have no feelings for anything except your precious money."

She tried to pull free, but he tightened his grip until she cried out in pain.

"You're hurting—"

Her words were cut off by his mouth, crushing hers. She broke free but he shoved her hard against the wall and closed a fist in her hair, yanking her head back before pressing himself against her. She could taste the whiskey on his breath, and with it the stench of bitterness. Gone was the smooth veneer of polish he showed to the town. Now there was only cruelty and anger and a driving desire to dominate.

Using all her strength, she managed to push him back.

He reached into his breast pocket. And when he withdrew his hand, he had the satisfaction of hearing her little gasp of shock as she caught sight of the glint of light reflecting off the object he held.

It was a very small, very deadly gun.

Malachite was still feeling grim after his meeting with Marshal Regan. He had laid out the facts that Gil had uncovered. And the lawman had agreed with his conclusions. There had been a devil in this town, all right. But it hadn't been a horse. It had been a mean-spirited, moneygrubbing banker, bleeding helpless ranchers dry and playing fast and loose with money that wasn't his. Malachite wondered how many accounts they'd find in Byron Conner's name when the audits were complete.

He wondered, too, about the accidents that had been attributed to Diablo. Had Conner somehow been responsible for them, as well? Marshal Regan wasn't too hopeful about getting a confession. After all, there was a big difference in punishment between bank fraud and murder. And unless the banker was caught red-handed, no jury would believe him capable of such violent acts.

Malachite's spirits lifted as he neared the boardinghouse. He hoped it wasn't too late. He didn't want to have to wake Millie. He wanted her awake and alert to hear what he had to say.

A smile touched his lips. If all went according to plan, she'd soon be in her bed anyway. But he doubted either of them would get much sleep tonight.

He was relieved when he saw the faint flicker of a lantern. With a light heart he knocked on the back door. After several minutes the door was opened. Birdie poked her head out.

"Evening, Birdie. I'm looking for Millie."

"She isn't here, Mr. Jewel."

He grinned. "Something going on at church tonight?"

"No, sir. She said she was meeting Mr. Conner at the bank."

Malachite's smile was wiped from his face. His blood froze. Without a word he spun away and began to run. With every step, he prayed that he wasn't too late.

Millie's breath was coming hard and fast as she struggled to hold Byron at bay. But he was strong. And seething with fury.

"You think you're too good for me?" He had a hand on her throat and began to squeeze until she could feel herself fading. "When I'm through with you, even the half-breed won't want you."

She managed to free one hand and raked it across his cheek.

With a hiss of pain he slapped her so hard her head snapped to one side. But just as he grasped her by the throat again, the door to his office was shoved open.

"Working late, I see." Malachite's voice was deadly calm. Only the muscle in his jaw gave any evidence of the depth of his fury.

He'd come here with no plan except to save Millie. Now, seeing the gun in Byron's hand, he knew he would have to move carefully. He couldn't do anything that would put her at risk.

He closed the door and leaned against it in a careless pose, one foot crossed over the other, his arms folded over his chest. "Is this the only way you can get a woman?"

Byron locked an arm around Millie's throat and pressed the gun to her temple. "She thinks she's your woman. She's wrong. Now, drop your gun, Jewel, and kick it over here. Or I'll blow her pretty face off."

Malachite tried not to look at Millie as he tossed his pistol aside. It hurt too much to see the bruise on the side of her temple and the pain in her eyes. Her hair, her beautiful, fiery hair, now fell in tangles around her cheeks. Cheeks wet with tears.

"Is this any way for a banker to treat his clients? How the hell do you expect to get away with it?" His voice was still soft, though the anger was beginning to seep through. "Do you think you can abuse her and then just let her go? Do you think Millie is the kind of woman who will keep her mouth shut about something like this?"

"If she wants her precious daughters to live, she'll have no choice."

He heard Millie's gasp of pain and decided to change tactics. He couldn't bear to hurt her any more than she was already hurt.

"Everything's changed now, Byron. I'm here. And you'll have to kill me to shut me up, won't you?"

"It won't be as much pleasure as I'd planned for Millie. But I can handle it."

"I'll bet you can. You've killed before, haven't you, Conner?"

"What are you saying?" Millie asked.

"Tell her," Malachite said. "Tell her about all those cowboys who died mysteriously while hunting Diablo."

"Are you suggesting that I'd know something about them?" Byron's lips peeled back in a sneer. "How could I have managed that?"

"By trailing them until they were far enough from town so nobody could hear a gunshot. It was a simple enough matter to leave their bodies where they'd be disposed of by wolves or other scavengers."

Byron's eyes glittered, and for a moment it seemed he would admit his crimes. But then he seemed to think better of it. "Maybe you think I caused the blizzard, too?"

"I'll allow the blizzard," Malachite said. "Even you don't have that kind of power. But let's talk about the times Millie's wagon was tampered with and her daughters were nearly killed."

"I'm sure I can find folks in this town who will swear I was here at the bank when it happened."

"Of course you can. But when I took the wagon to Neville Oakley for repair, he confirmed what I suspected. The axle on Millie's wagon had been deliberately cut in such a way that the accident would occur out on the trail."

He saw the startled look in Millie's eyes.

Byron gave a chilling smile. "And you think I did it?"

"You could have gone into Millie's shed without notice."

"So could half the town."

"That's true. But I began to wonder what the purpose of that accident had been. Was it merely to get rid of me? A gunshot along the trail would have been simpler and cleaner. But maybe there was something more to it."

"Like what?" Byron demanded.

"Like the need to keep the fear alive. Nothing like an accident to have the whole town buzzing." His eyes narrowed. "And one thing more. Three little girls would be a distraction to a man who wanted their mother all to himself."

The look on Millie's face had changed from pain to shock to outrage.

"That's an interesting theory, Jewel. Do you have any others?"

"As a matter of fact I do." Malachite unfolded his arms and took a step closer, pausing only when Byron drew back the hammer and cocked the pistol at Millie's temple.

"A lot of ranches have failed in the past year. More than at any time since the town first started."

"Are you suggesting that I had a hand in that, as well?"

"You hold the mortgages on every ranch that failed."

"That may be. But I also happen to be the only banker in the territory."

"Exactly. That gives you a great deal of power." Malachite turned his back on Byron and walked to a shelf containing an assortment of ledgers like the one on his desk. And all the while his mind was working, looking for a way to get Millie free of this monster's grasp. "If I were to go through all these ledgers, I wonder what I'd find."

"I don't think you have the mentality to understand complicated bookkeeping."

"Probably not. But I'll bet I could find someone who did."

"I'm not about to permit anyone else to look over my work."

Malachite's tone was measured. "Someone already has."

Byron's eyes narrowed. "What do you mean?"

"I mean I asked young Gil to do a survey of the ranches around here. What their value is, how much money is owed, who holds the mortgages. And guess what he came up with?"

For the first time Byron showed a flash of fear. "He can't prove a thing."

"Maybe. Maybe not. But it's a start. When Gil takes his findings to the marshal and the marshal takes them to a federal judge, you're going to have a lot of explaining to do. Especially when the judge finds out who your uncle was."

Byron blanched. "How did you find out?"

"Who—" Millie's throat was so painful, every word was an effort. She swallowed and tried again. "Who is his uncle?"

"Was," Malachite said through clenched teeth. "His uncle was Chester Pierce."

She sucked in a long, painful breath. "The man who killed your father?"

"The same. I've heard the whole sordid story from my sisters. It seemed the greedy bastard wasn't content to earn a fortune off my father's money. He wanted it all. And was willing to kill a man who had been his lifelong friend to have it. But greedy men always make mistakes. That's what stopped Byron's uncle." He pinned the banker with a chilling look. "That's why I finally caught on to what you were doing."

"There have been no mistakes." Byron's voice rose

slightly and his hand, holding the gun, trembled. "I vowed I would never make the mistakes my uncle made. I've been very thorough."

"Not quite thorough enough. You made one mistake." Malachite was already calculating the odds of wresting the gun from Byron's hand without harming Millie. "The rattlesnakes."

Byron frowned. "I don't understand."

"You overplayed your hand, Conner. Rattlesnakes don't like snow. There's no way they'd have crawled out of a warm, cozy nest. And if they had, and if they'd been there for long, they'd be too frozen to be a threat to anybody. So I knew they'd been tossed there just minutes before Diablo attacked."

Byron's eyes flashed. "There wasn't time for anything more elaborate. But it doesn't matter. A thing like that would never hold up in court."

Malachite's tone lowered to a dangerous whisper. "Now, I could understand if the attack had been against me. But you knew April was handling Diablo. And she was your intended victim. You wanted her hurt. Or worse." Malachite's eyes smoldered with carefully banked fury. "You stood in the crowd and watched and waited for a little girl to be attacked. And you felt nothing."

"Oh, dear God." At the sudden realization, Millie went limp.

It was the opportunity Malachite had been waiting for. While Byron was forced to support her weight, Malachite leaped forward, pushing Millie aside as he went for Byron's throat.

"Now you're going to pay, Conner." Malachite's fist smashed into Byron's nose, causing a geyser of blood. "For the innocent cowboys who died at your hand. Admit you killed them."

"Never."

The next blow landed on Byron's jaw, snapping back his head. "This is for the ranchers who lost heart and gave up on their land." He buried his fist in the banker's midsection. "But especially for what you did to Millie and her daughters." It was a solid blow to the head that had Byron's knees buckling.

The two men reeled, bumping against the desk, toppling to the floor as they grappled and struggled for control.

Millie shook her head, fighting a wave of nausea. When she looked up, she realized that Byron still had hold of the gun, and it was now pointed directly at Malachite's chest.

"Go ahead," Malachite taunted. "Let's see if you're man enough to kill a man face-to-face. Or would you prefer I turned my back?"

With a look of triumph the banker said, "Oh, I'll enjoy killing you. More than any of those cowboys I shot. This will give me a whole lot more satisfaction than juggling the books and helping myself to failing ranches." His evil smile grew. "And before you die, you ought to know that I intend to own the Jewel ranch, as well. By the time I'm through with those sisters of yours, I'll have them buried so deeply in debt they'll never be able to get out. And when I foreclose, they'll thank me for not taking the clothes off their backs, as well. You see, my Uncle Chet taught me very well. And this time, there will be no mistakes."

As his finger closed around the trigger, Millie lifted a ledger from the desk and brought it against his head with all the force she could manage. A volley of gunfire exploded in the room.

At the sound of it, Millie burst into tears. "Oh, no. Oh, Malachite. What have I done?"

Marshal Quent Regan strode across the room and caught Byron by the hair, tossing him against the wall, where he crumpled to the floor.

At once Millie fell on Malachite, sobbing hysterically. "Where are you shot? Oh, Malachite. Please don't die. I'm so sorry. I just wanted to help. Oh, please, Malachite, don't die."

"All right." His arms came around her in a fierce bear hug that had her gasping.

"No. Stop that. Where are you hurt?" She pushed far enough away that she could look him over.

There was no sign of blood.

"I heard a gunshot," she said in wonder. "How could he have missed you at such close range?"

"It was my gun that fired," Marshal Regan said. "Our slimy banker was so busy boasting, he never even heard me coming in."

"Oh. Thank heaven." Millie burst into fresh tears and fell into Malachite's arms.

With aching tenderness he cradled her against him, while he pressed soft kisses to the bruise at her temple. When he thought about what had nearly happened, he was still terrified.

He looked up as a crowd began to swarm into the office. Diamond was there with Adam. Pearl and Cal stood beside the desk with their son Gil, who was already beginning to collect the ledgers. Ruby crowded through the doorway, along with Reverend Dan Simpson.

"What in hell are you all doing here?" Malachite demanded.

Cal gave a sheepish grin. "After you left the cabin, I had to confide in Pearl. After all, we share everything."

"And I insisted that if you were anything like Daddy, you'd go straight to town and try to handle this yourself."

"So Pearl and Cal came and got Adam and me." Diamond was still aiming her gun at Byron, even though it was plain from his battered demeanor that he wasn't going anywhere. "And I said I wasn't about to let you have all the fun."

"*Oui*," Ruby added. "Though I would not call this fun. But we are family now. And family sticks together."

"My sentiments exactly," Marshal Regan said with a grin. "I was just reassuring everybody that you were going to let me handle this. The next thing I knew, Birdie came running to my office to say you looked mad enough to kill." He glanced at the others. "We all knew where you were headed."

"I guess," Malachite said as he got to his feet and helped Millie to stand, "there aren't too many secrets in a family like this."

"None at all." Diamond shoved her gun into its holster as the marshal tied up the banker and herded him toward the door. She turned to Malachite and Millie with a knowing smile. "So if you two are planning to sneak off and do anything without us, you'd better think again."

Before either of them could offer a denial, Birdie came rushing through the door. She came to a screeching halt when she caught sight of Byron Conner's bound hands.

"Birdie, you're supposed to be with my girls," Millie said sharply. "What are you doing here?"

"Sorry, Mrs. Potter. But the girls aren't alone. Reverend Simpson," she said, turning to Dan. "You'd better come quick." Her voice came in short bursts, and it was clear she'd run the whole way. "Doc Prentice is over at Mrs. Potter's."

"Doc Prentice?" Dan's skin turned a sickly shade of green.

"Yes, sir. And he said to fetch you quick 'cause Miss Jade is about to make you a daddy."

While the marshal hauled his prisoner off to jail, a strange procession made its way through the darkened town. And though Millie insisted that she was strong enough to walk, Malachite carried her the whole way in his arms.

"I've learned my lesson," he muttered against her temple. "Until you're safely home, I'm not letting you out of my sight."

Chapter Twenty-Three

"Miss Ruby." Birdie poked her head in the parlor of Millie's boardinghouse. "Some ladies from your dress shop are at the front door asking for news of Miss Jade."

"Thank you, Birdie. I'll see to them." Ruby swept by, looking slightly frazzled. It didn't do to have her customers seeing her in yesterday's wrinkled gown. But it simply couldn't be helped. The night had been one of chaos, beginning with a near tragedy pitting Malachite against Byron Conner, and ending with the most joyous of blessings. The birth of nephews, she decided, smoothing her skirts, was far more important than the way she looked.

"Miss Diamond? Miss Pearl?" Birdie again poked her head in the parlor.

Diamond, with little Onyx at her hip, turned from the fireplace.

Pearl, cradling baby Amber, looked up from the horsehair sofa. "Yes, Birdie?"

"Mrs. Thurlong and Mrs. Witherspoon are at the back door, trying to get in through the kitchen. They said they won't leave until someone lets them see the new twins."

"Oh dear." Pearl looked as if she couldn't possibly cope with the town gossips at a time like this.

Diamond gritted her teeth. "Don't you worry about a thing. I'll handle those two."

Birdie followed along, eager to watch the fireworks. But before she got two steps, she heard Jade calling her from the dining room, which had been turned into a temporary dispensary and nursery.

Inside, the new mother was comfortably ensconced in a makeshift bed of quilts and pillows. In her arms was a tiny bundle. Dan, usually so calm and self-assured, was standing by the window with a dazed look in his eyes. In his arms was an identically wrapped bundle.

Doc Prentice was giving his final instructions as he replaced his instruments in his black bag. "I want you to stay put for at least two weeks. I'll come by every other day to check on you."

"But we can't possibly impose on Millie for two weeks," Jade said in her softly accented voice.

"You heard me. Two weeks. No climbing. Nothing more strenuous than walking to the kitchen and back."

Jade shot him an incredulous look. "My grandmother traveled to the home of the emperor just days after my mother was born. And my mother claimed she returned to the operation of her pleasure palace, the Golden Dragon, within hours of my birth. I don't see why I can't go home tomorrow."

"Because I said so." Doc turned to Dan. "Your wife has just given birth to twins. If you have to sit on her, I want her here until I say otherwise."

Dan nodded. "Okay, Doc. But if I were you, I'd send her home within the week or you'll have a little wildcat for a patient."

"I'll think about it. In the meantime, you two relax and enjoy your blessings. You have two fine, healthy boys."

When he left, Jade smiled at Birdie. "I'm afraid I'm going to need some help for a while. Would you be willing to come and work for me, Birdie?"

Birdie's eyes lit up. The thought of helping with two little angels had her heart dancing. "Yes'm. I'll go ask Mrs. Potter right now."

"There's no need. Dan and I already asked Millie if she could spare you." She couldn't help adding, "We agreed it might be nice if you had some experience. Who knows? You might soon be taking care of a baby of your own."

Birdie's cheeks turned a becoming shade of pink. She'd been thinking that very thing. Every time she looked at Gil McCabe.

But she merely lowered her eyes and said softly, "Yes'm." Hearing a commotion outside the door, she turned away. "But right now I'd better take April, May and June up to Durfee's Mercantile. I promised Mrs. Potter I'd keep them busy for a few hours."

"That's a fine idea," Jade said. "I'm sure this has been far too much excitement for them. You might want to see if Daniel and Gil would like to go along."

Gil? Birdie's flush deepened and she ran a hand over her hair before opening the door.

In the kitchen Adam, Cal and the marshal juggled cups of coffee while helping themselves to Millie's biscuits.

"Hurry, girls," Millie called. Throughout the night she had remained a sea of calm despite the chaos swirling around her. "Birdie's ready to take you to Durfee's."

She handed each of her daughters a precious penny and another to Birdie. "You may buy a peppermint stick. But remember, when Mr. Durfee offers you the candy jar, don't touch the candies until you've made your choice. Mr. Durfee doesn't like sticky fingers."

"Yes'm," they called as they bounded away.

A few minutes later Gil and Daniel, pockets jingling with coins, joined them.

When they were gone, Millie picked up her empty laundry basket and headed outside, where sheets and colorful towels flapped in the breeze. She had managed to do an amazing amount of work, considering all the interruptions. But she pushed herself to do even more in order to keep her mind occupied.

Malachite, who stood brooding by the window, watched her with a frown.

"You ought to try these biscuits." Adam held out the plate. "They're just about the best I've ever tasted. I don't know how Millie does it."

Malachite shook his head. "I'm not hungry."

"The coffee might do you some good," Cal suggested.

Malachite didn't respond. Instead he strode across the room and let himself out.

"What's eating him?" Adam asked.

"You mean you've already forgotten what it was like to be miserable and in love?" Quent Regan chuckled. "I saw that look in your eyes every time Diamond got within a mile of you. And I felt the same way the first time I laid eyes on Ruby," he muttered. "Like I'd been run over by a team of mules. And every time I'd get to my feet, she'd smile at me and I'd be run over again."

The three men shared a laugh. Love, they agreed, could be the most wonderful feeling in the world. And the most horrible.

"I wonder what he's going to do about it?" Cal mused.

"Do?" The marshal laughed again. "He's going to do what we all did. Chase that little woman until she catches him."

Millie gathered the sheet off the line, folding and folding until it was a smooth, perfect square. Then she set it in the basket and reached for another.

From behind a strong hand closed over her wrist.

She whirled. "Malachite. You startled me. What are you—"

"Not a word, do you hear, Millie? Just come with me."

He hauled her along until they reached the shed. Inside, Diablo lifted his head as they entered, then returned to his oats.

Malachite released her, then latched the door and leaned against it.

"What is this all about?" Millie demanded.

"I need to talk to you. And I sure as hell can't do it in there." He indicated the house.

"It is a bit hectic. But it will pass." She studied him, so tense and edgy, and felt a quick slice of uneasiness. "You seem angry about something."

"Should I be?"

She shrugged and started to turn away.

"Why were you at Byron's office?" His words had her stopping.

"I...don't see that's any of your business."

"I'm making it my business. Now tell me why you were there."

"I...needed money. I thought I could get a loan from the bank by mortgaging the house."

"Why do you need money?"

"Malachite, this isn't your concern."

"Tell me, Millie. Why did you want the money?"

"I can't tell you that."

He folded his arms over his chest. "We're not leaving here until you do."

Her eyes filled with tears and she quickly blinked them away, mortified that her emotions were so close to the surface. "It doesn't matter anymore. I can't get the money now. And if I told you why I wanted it, you'd only hate me."

He closed the space between them and his hand snaked out, catching her before she could move away. He held her hand between both of his, idly smoothing his thumbs over her pale skin. "Believe me, Millie. I could never hate you. But you're going to tell me."

She swallowed. "First you have to promise not to interrupt. And promise you won't get angry."

He nodded.

"All right." She stared down at their linked hands, avoiding his eyes. "It would be a lie if I said I was only doing this for my daughters. Because the feelings I have for you aren't like anything I've ever known before. The way I feel…'' She shook her head. ''It frightens me. But I know that even if you didn't feel the same way, I could go on living. I've learned that life doesn't end when your heart is broken.'' She took a deep breath. ''I wouldn't have done it except that I was desperate. You see, April, May and June—'' she struggled to find the words ''—you've made such a difference in their lives. Before you came here, they were so shy and so wounded. It broke my heart to see them struggling to find a way to fit in with all the others in this town…all the others who were part of a family. And then you came along and changed everything. You talked to them. You listened. And you liked them even when they weren't very likable.''

He started to speak but she went on quickly. ''It wasn't just the fact that you helped them find their courage. It was so much more. You taught them to trust again. And to love again.'' Millie tried to smile but her lips trembled, and the sight of it nearly broke his heart. ''And I knew if you went away and left them, they would be shattered. And I couldn't allow that.''

''What does this have to do with—''

She held up a hand. ''You told me that you were leaving soon for Fort Denver.''

He nodded. ''To deliver the mustangs.''

''Yes. And after you deliver them, you'll continue on to Montana.''

''I never—''

''Malachite, I know that a woman with three children can be a tremendous burden to a man. Especially a man used to being on his own. And I know what a proud man you are. You would never ask help from anyone.''

''Help? Millie, I—''

She put a finger to his lips to silence his protest. ''You promised.''

She took a step back to break contact. She needed to stand alone if she wanted to get through this. It was so difficult. She took another breath. ''There wasn't enough time to sell the house. But I thought if I could borrow against it, that would give us enough money to see us through the first year. I figured we could survive in a cabin in the wilderness.''

"A cabin—"

"Or even a tepee, if that's what you wanted. Just so you'd allow us to be with you. I'd do whatever I could to help. And then, with both of us doing all we could, maybe we'd save enough to pay back the loan. Then we could sell the house, and there would be even more money to live on. Just so we could all be together. Like a family."

"Is that what you want?"

She swallowed and looked away. She had her own pride. But she was beyond that now. Beyond shame, as well. "More than anything."

"What do you think I want, Millie? Why do you think I stayed?"

"You stayed to capture Diablo. So you could add to your herd of mustangs. You said yourself you intended to return to Montana and be with your horses."

"That may be what I planned. But plans have a funny way of changing. Especially when you lose your heart to someone."

Her head came up. She stared at him as if she couldn't believe what he had just said. "But yesterday you told me you were leaving."

"To deliver the mustangs."

"But you said in the spring..."

"I guess I did. But that was before I fell in love."

"You...love me?"

"Hopelessly. Desperately. And now, after hearing all this, I think I love you even more." He took a step toward her, watching her eyes. "Millie, there are things you don't know about me. Things I wish now I'd told you. It would have saved you so much pain and heartache."

"It doesn't matter, Malachite. I don't care about your past. Nothing you say will make any difference."

"Good. Then I think you should allow me my turn."

When she opened her mouth, he pressed a finger to her lips. "Remember when I told you about turning my back on the town and going off to the wilderness?"

She nodded.

"Have you ever heard of Grasshopper Creek?"

She shook her head.

He smiled. "I guess folks in Texas don't care about what goes on beyond their own borders. Anyway, I fled to a place in Montana called Grasshopper Creek to hide away and lick my wounds. And while I was there, I discovered something that brought thousands of prospectors swarming over the hills."

He was making no sense. "Prospectors?"

"Gold, Millie."

"You found…gold?"

He nodded. "So much, in fact, that I guess I'm one of the richest men in Montana. Maybe even the whole west."

"Rich? You're a rich man?"

"But you see it didn't matter. I still lived in my little cabin, raising my horses. And if I hadn't been summoned to my mother's deathbed, if I hadn't come here seeking revenge on my father, I'd still be there, living like the poorest man in the world." His voice lowered with feeling. "Because I was the poorest man in the world, Millie. I was living without love. Without anyone to share my life. All I had was gold. You and your daughters made the difference. Now my life feels so full. So rich."

She shook her head, trying to take it all in. "And here I was worried about asking you to take on four more mouths to feed. And about offending your pride."

"What you did…" He tipped up her face. "What you did was so generous, so brave. And so damnably foolish." He took a deep breath. "I was here in town last night to tell the marshal what I'd learned about Byron. Then I came here to ask you to marry me. When I heard that you were at the bank, in the company of a man I'd just learned was a killer, I think I went a little crazy." He framed her face with his hands and stared down into her eyes. "If I lost you, Millie, I wouldn't survive it. I love you so much."

"And I love you, Malachite. More than I ever thought possible."

"Oh God, I never thought I could be so lucky. Will you marry me, Millie?"

"Oh, yes. Yes." She offered her lips for a long, lingering kiss and felt the familiar thread of excitement curl along her spine. "Oh, Malachite. I can't believe our good fortune. That you should love me the way I love you. That you want to marry me and stay here in Hanging Tree. Oh, let's go tell the others. The girls will be so—"

He caught her hand and pulled her back into his arms. And kissed her until she was breathless.

"We'll tell them later."

"But—"

"Millie, you know I love your daughters. And I'm learning to love those sisters of mine. And their husbands and babies. But all this family togetherness is driving me crazy. For now, for a little while at least, I want you all to myself."

Her smile grew. With a look of love that was so dazzling it nearly blinded him, she wrapped her arms around his waist and lifted herself on tiptoe to kiss him.

"You're right. They can wait. They can all wait. For now, for a little while longer, it will be our secret. Now, tell me again how much you love me."

"Sh." He lowered her to the straw.

And decided to tell her without words.

Epilogue

"I've never seen Cookie looking so happy." Marshal Regan pointed to where the old man was carving thick slices of roast beef and stacking them on a huge platter under the careful direction of Carmelita.

A table, groaning under the weight of enough food to feed the entire town, extended the length of the front porch.

The last of the snow had melted. A gentle breeze was perfumed with the first hint of spring flowers. It was a perfect day for a wedding.

A steady stream of wagons and carriages rolled over the hills. The house and yard were abloom with families from town and the surrounding ranches. Many of them had never been to the Jewel ranch before and were eager to see how the family, considered Texas royalty, lived.

"Why shouldn't Cookie be happy?" Malachite muttered. "He doesn't have to wear a new suit and make a fool of himself in front of the entire town."

"Ah. Prewedding jitters. I'm glad to see you're human, just like the rest of us," the marshal said with a grin.

"You mean you were all this nervous when you married my sisters?"

If the others noticed how easily the word *sisters* slipped from his tongue, they chose not to mention it. There was a time they had thought this mysterious, angry man would rather die than acknowledge his family. Now he was building a bond that grew stronger with each passing day.

Cal slapped him on the back. "Hell, I felt like heading for the hills. But it was the price I was willing to pay to spend the rest of my life with Pearl."

Quent nodded. "Adam here was the only one whose wedding was simple. But that was because Diamond wanted it that way. In case you hadn't noticed, Di doesn't care much for pomp and ceremony. And she certainly doesn't want the whole town knowing her business."

"Lucky man," Malachite muttered.

"I'd say you're one lucky man yourself." Adam nodded toward the group of wranglers heading behind the barn with a jug. "Need a little courage?"

Malachite shook his head. "What I need is to see Millie."

"Not a chance." Cal chuckled. "The women consider it bad luck to see the bride before the wedding."

"Here." Dan passed around the expensive cigars he'd ordered for the birth of his twin sons. "Let's have a smoke."

They were silent for a few minutes as they struck matches and puffed, watching wreaths of smoke curl above their heads and dissipate into the air.

"I saw you riding out earlier," Adam said. "For a minute I thought you might be hightailing it out of here."

Malachite grinned. "I just wanted to ride to the grave site. Had a few things I wanted to talk over with my father."

"He'd be proud of you," Cal said.

Malachite touched a hand to the green stone at his throat and felt the pulse of heat. "Not as proud as I am of him. I made him a promise. That I'd have my mother's remains brought here to rest beside him."

"That'll make your sisters happy. Say," Cal added with a burst of pride, "did I tell you that the bank examiners were so impressed with Gil's research, they've offered him the job of running the bank?"

The others slapped him on the back and offered their congratulations.

"Of course, they'll expect him to complete his courses from the university," Cal cautioned. "And someone from St. Louis will be looking over his shoulder. But they said since their biggest investor recommended Gil for the job, they wanted to keep him happy." He stared pointedly at Malachite and offered his hand. "Thanks for speaking up on his behalf."

Malachite accepted his handshake. "No need to thank me. Gil's the smartest and most honest young man I've ever met. He's the logical choice to run the bank and regain the trust of the townspeople."

"Maybe he and Birdie Bidwell will be the next ones walking down the aisle," the marshal said.

That had Cal grinning. "I wouldn't be surprised."

"While we're offering thanks, Malachite, I'd like to add mine—" the marshal offered his handshake to Malachite "—for persuading Millie to let us buy her house."

"Thanks aren't necessary." Malachite squeezed his hand. "Millie's really happy to know the house will stay in the family."

"I bet you'll be happy to move out of the rooms above the dress shop, with all those feminine frills and gewgaws," Dan said.

Quent nodded, then lowered his voice. "But there's another reason. Ruby's saving the announcement until after the wedding so she won't steal Millie's thunder on her big day. But the reason we need the house is that we're...expanding."

"A baby?" Adam thumped him on the back. "When?"

Quent shrugged. "Late summer, I expect."

The others clapped his shoulder and offered handshakes.

Quent turned to Malachite. "I suppose you'll be making an announcement like this sometime next year."

To hide the quick flash of emotion, Malachite took a moment to study the ash at the end of his cigar.

Abruptly he muttered, "I don't care what you say, I need to see Millie. Now."

As he ambled off, the three men chuckled.

Adam dug into his pocket. "Five dollars says he doesn't get past the pack of hens guarding the blushing bride."

"You're on," Cal said, matching his bet. "I'm putting my money on Malachite. How about you, Quent?"

The marshal took the money from both men. "I'll hold your bets. But being a lawman, I won't take sides. Dan?"

Dan shook his head. "It wouldn't do for the town preacher to gamble. But my money's on Malachite." As he turned away, he called, "Let me know who wins. I'd better get on up to the house and get ready for the ceremony."

Malachite made his way through the throngs of guests, being forced to stop every couple of steps to accept a handshake and a word of congratulations.

Once inside it was even harder to move. There were people everywhere. They explored the big, rustic kitchen. They toured the cavernous dining room with a table large enough to seat twenty or more guests. They milled about the formal parlor, furnished with ornately carved high-back chairs from Mexico, which were paired with elegantly embroidered footstools from Europe. A Turkish rug covered the floor and Irish linen curtains graced the windows.

Already rumors abounded about the mysterious Malachite Jewel, who had captured and tamed a mythical mustang. The millionaire who had discovered gold in the wilderness. Whose mother was sister to a powerful Comanche chief and whose father was a legend in Texas.

"Here he is now."

A ripple of excitement went through the crowd.

"I hear all he has to do is look at a wild horse and it's tame."

"Got those three shy little girls eating out of his hand, doesn't he?"

"I was told he walked clear across Montana until he spotted gold nuggets just sitting there waiting for him."

"He'll probably discover gold on the Jewel property, too."

"Hell, he already discovered gold. Not too many women can cook and keep a house like Millie Potter. Man would be a fool not to keep her."

"Malachite Jewel's no fool. No sir."

The man they were whispering about accepted a hundred handshakes and words of congratulation before he finally managed to make it to the stairs.

In his haste he took them three at a time.

"Hurry up." Impatient, Diamond shouted for the third time, "Ruby, I swear, if you don't send Millie out here soon, I'm going to come back there and rip down that screen."

"Very well, *chérie*. But let me smooth down the skirts first."

Jade, seated on the sofa, held little Jasper, who was sound asleep, while Birdie, seated beside her, held a wiggling, cooing Jet.

Diamond was pacing, balancing little Onyx at her hip. Pearl was bouncing Amber on her knee.

Ruby had already dressed April, May and June in their frilly gowns of palest green, with matching ribbons to tie back their long red curls. At their throats were the necklaces Malachite had made for them. They had insisted upon wearing them, over Ruby's vigorous disapproval.

"It simply isn't done," she had argued. "Strips of leather. Primitive stones." She had wrinkled her pretty little nose.

But they had refused to budge.

"Malachite made them just for us. Because he loved us." April's voice vibrated with such pride Ruby had been forced to back down. After all, hadn't her own father given each of his daughters a necklace as a sign he would always be with them? Malachite was definitely his father's son.

Now, as they waited, the three little girls were making a valiant effort to sit still.

Moments later Ruby folded back the ornamental screen

she had set up for privacy. There was a collective gasp when they had their first glimpse of Millie in the gown Ruby had made.

"Oh my." Pearl blinked and dabbed at her eyes.

"You have outdone yourself," Jade said as she took in the softly rounded neckline, the long, tapered sleeves, the full skirt, gathered here and there with white satin bows. On Millie's feet were white satin slippers. Her hair was soft and loose. Tucked here and there among the curls were sprigs of ivy and wildflowers.

"I asked Ruby to keep it simple." Millie turned to Diamond, who could always be counted on to tell the unvarnished truth. "What do you think?"

"I think..." Diamond circled her, nodding, smiling. "I think you look so good, Malachite may forget his manners."

That brought a flush to Millie's cheeks and a chorus of laughter from the others.

They looked up at a loud knock on the door.

From outside came Gil's muffled voice. "Reverend Dan's ready to start the service."

The women got to their feet, carrying their babies. As they opened the door, they found Malachite just about to knock.

"You mustn't see your bride yet," Jade said. "You have to wait until she comes downstairs."

"I've waited all I can." His presence filled the doorway.

At the sound of his voice, the three little girls jumped up and ran to him. At once he got down on his knees and gathered them close. After a quick, hard embrace, he held them a little away. "Oh, look at you."

"Do you think we look pretty?" June asked.

"You're the prettiest girls I've ever seen."

"We're wearing your necklaces," May said.

"I see. That makes me very proud."

Ruby stood in front of Millie, vainly trying to block Malachite's view. "You must leave," she commanded. "It isn't right to see her yet."

Instead of arguing, he got to his feet and took a menacing

step forward. That had Ruby backing up, until she bumped into the bride.

"Millie. I have to see you," he bellowed. "Now."

Millie touched a hand to Ruby's arm. "It's all right," she whispered. "You go now and join Quent. Tell Dan we'll be downstairs in a few minutes."

When she and the others were gone, Millie looked up to find Malachite staring at her so intensely she felt her heart leap to her throat.

"Have you changed your mind?" she asked.

"About you?" He shook his head. "Never." He caught her hands in his. "But I'd rather face a dozen Diablos than have to face that crowd downstairs."

"It will all be over in a little while. And then there will be just us."

"Us." He spoke the word like a prayer. "I honestly thought I'd spend the rest of my life alone. Just me. But now, in a few minutes, I'll have a wife and three beautiful daughters."

He removed the leather strip from around his neck. "I'd be honored if you'd wear this."

Millie turned to allow him to tie it. Then she touched a hand to the shimmering green stone that seemed to pulse with heat and life. "I'll wear it with pride. Always."

"Always." He drew her close for a long, slow kiss.

A moment later they stepped apart when little June tugged at their sleeves.

"Malachite?"

He knelt down so that his eyes were even with hers. "Yes?"

"After you and Mama are married, is it all right if I call you Pa?"

He had to swallow twice to get rid of the lump in his throat. But he managed to say, "That'd be fine. But you don't have to." He turned to include April and May. "I understand that you already have a father."

"That's right. April said we're the luckiest girls in the

world." June's little hand found its way into his big one. "'Cause now we have two daddies. One in heaven and one here with us."

He couldn't help himself. With a sigh he gathered the three girls close and crushed them to him, burying his face in their hair, brushing his lips over their soft cheeks.

"And both of your fathers will always look out for you," he managed to whisper.

They looked up as a shadow fell across the doorway. "I was sent up here to tell you folks to get a move on," Cookie said around the stump of a pipe in his teeth. "You got a lot of family and friends downstairs waiting for you."

Family and friends. Those words brought a smile to Malachite's lips.

He straightened, still holding little June in his arms. Then, with April clutching his hand and May clutching her mother's, they started down the stairs.

"I don't think this is the way it's supposed to be done," Millie whispered. "I think it's supposed to be just the bride, not all of us together."

"It's always going to be all of us together." He paused to press a kiss to her lips. At once he felt the rush of heat. Whatever frustration he'd been feeling, it was gone now. And in its place was the most amazing feeling of peace.

He'd come to Hanging Tree, Texas, at war with himself, seeking vengeance. What he'd found was the most astonishing legacy. A history he hadn't known. A history of fierce independence, of diversity and, most of all, love. He'd found an abundance of strange women who were slowly becoming sisters. And best of all, a woman and her daughters who charmed him, who delighted him, who filled up all the empty places in his life. Who loved him without question. Who allowed him to love in return.

Love. That was the legacy of Onyx Jewel. He was a man who'd loved often. And well.

As Malachite, son of Onyx Jewel, took the last stair and began the walk toward the preacher, still holding on to Millie and her daughters, he felt suddenly overwhelmed by all the love.

"Thank you," he whispered to the father he'd once rejected, "for leading me here to the greatest treasure of all."

* * * * *

Dear Reader,

I hope you enjoyed reading THE JEWELS OF TEXAS series for Harlequin Historicals as much as I enjoyed writing it.

Malachite is the fifth and last in the series. It was my intention with this book to bring the story full circle, discovering Onyx Jewel through the eyes of his son, seeing the growth of his very large, very diverse family.

I used the stallion Diablo as a metaphor for Malachite, and he, in turn, for his father and the founder of the dynasty, Onyx, who are all wild creatures, strong, independent, wary of people, but capable of great loyalty and trust once they have formed a loving bond. The Jewels personify the men and women who stir my imagination. They are legends who forge their own trails through a primitive wilderness. And along the way they manage to find friendship, laughter and the most precious treasure of all—true and lasting love.

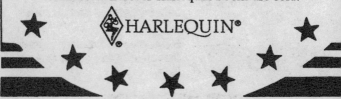

Presents Extravaganza

25 YEARS!

It's our birthday and we're celebrating....

Twenty-five years of romance fiction
featuring men of the world and captivating women—
Seduction and passion guaranteed!

Not only are we promising you three months of terrific
books, authors and romance, but as an added **bonus**
with the retail purchase of two Presents® titles,
you can receive a special one-of-a-kind keepsake.
It's our gift to you!

Look in the back pages of any Harlequin Presents® title,
from May to July 1998, for more details.

Available wherever Harlequin books are sold.

HARLEQUIN®

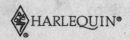
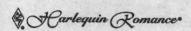

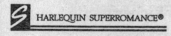

Welcome to *Love Inspired*™

A brand-new series of contemporary inspirational love stories.

Join men and women as they learn valuable lessons about facing the challenges of today's world and about life, love and faith.

**Look for the following April 1998
Love Inspired™ titles:**

DECIDEDLY MARRIED
by Carole Gift Page

A HOPEFUL HEART
by Lois Richer

HOMECOMING
by Carolyne Aarsen

Available in retail outlets in March 1998.

LIFT YOUR SPIRITS AND GLADDEN YOUR HEART
with *Love Inspired!*™

Steeple
Hill™

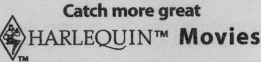

 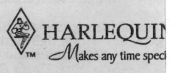